the Turncoat

RENEGADES OF THE REVOLUTION

DONNA THORLAND

NAL NEW AMERICAN LIBRARY

New American Library
Published by New American Library, a division of
Penguin Group (USA) Inc., 375 Hudson Street,
New York, New York 10014, USA
Penguin Group (Canada), 90 Eglinton Avenue East, Suite 700, Toronto,
Ontario M4P 2Y3, Canada (a division of Pearson Penguin Canada Inc.)
Penguin Books Ltd., 80 Strand, London WC2R 0RL, England
Penguin Ireland, 25 St. Stephen's Green, Dublin 2,
Ireland (a division of Penguin Books Ltd)
Penguin Group (Australia), 707 Collins Street, Melbourne, Victoria 3008,
Australia (a division of Pearson Australia Group Pty. Ltd.)
Penguin Books India Pvt. Ltd., 11 Community Centre, Panchsheel Park,
New Delhi–110 017, India
Penguin Group (NZ), 67 Apollo Drive, Rosedale, Auckland 0632,
New Zealand (a division of Pearson New Zealand Ltd.)
Penguin Books (South Africa), Rosebank Office Park, 181 Jan Smuts Avenue,
Parktown North 2193, South Africa
Penguin China, B7 Jiaming Center, 27 East Third Ring Road North,
Chaoyang District, Beijing 100020, China

Penguin Books Ltd., Registered Offices:
80 Strand, London WC2R 0RL, England

First published by New American Library,
a division of Penguin Group (USA) Inc.

First Printing, March 2013
10 9 8 7 6 5 4 3 2 1

N
A REGISTERED TRADEMARK—MARCA REGISTRADA
L

LIBRARY OF CONGRESS CATALOGING-IN-PUBLICATION DATA
Thorland, Donna.
The turncoat: renegades of the revolution / Donna Thorland.
p. cm.
ISBN 978-0-451-41539-4
1. Philadelphia (Pa.)—History—Revolution, 1775–1783—Fiction. I. Title.
PS3620.H766T87 2013
813'.6—dc23

Set in Janson Text
Designed by Spring Hoteling

Printed in the United States of America

PUBLISHER'S NOTE
This is a work of fiction. Names, characters, places, and incidents either are the
product of the author's imagination or are used fictitiously, and any resemblance
to actual persons, living or dead, business establishments, events, or locales is
entirely coincidental.
    The publisher does not have any control over and does not assume any
responsibility for author or third-party Web sites or their content.

For my husband, Charles. *Contra mundum.*

the Turncoat

One

The Jerseys, August 1777

Kate didn't like Mrs. Ferrers. Something about the beautiful young widow was off. To exclude the newcomer on account of such vague feelings, however, would not be Quakerly, so Angela Ferrers, along with every other woman in Orchard Valley, was at Grey Farm that sweltering morning, packing supplies for the Continental Army.

"Yet Colonel Donop still refused to divulge the lady's name at his court-martial," Mrs. Ferrers said to her spellbound audience. "For all the good it did him. When the disgraced Hessian returned to find his lover—seeking vengeance, explanations, or further dalliance, who can say?—I'm told he discovered nothing but a cold hearth and an empty house." The Widow folded back her fine cotton sleeve and reached for the pickle jar.

"Mrs. Ferrers, please don't." Kate tried for a note of polite deference and decided that polite frustration would have to do. "If you put your fingers in the jar, the brine will spoil."

They were gathered in the kitchen, painted terracotta pink by Kate's classically minded grandmother, around the pine worktable where she had learned to roll piecrust, pluck fowl, hull beans, and keep careful record of household stores.

Kate handed Mrs. Ferrers a ladle. The Widow cradled it like a royal scepter and went on with her story, the pickle jar entirely forgotten.

"But tell us, Mrs. Ferrers, about your late husband." Mrs. Ashcroft was a dour Quaker matron of the old school, but today she sounded like a five-year-old asking for a bedtime story.

"Peter was a born Friend, like myself, and after our marriage we farmed his father's land in Rhode Island," Mrs. Ferrers began, "where we had, two years ago in the spring, the most extraordinary incident with a cow . . ."

The woman was an expert tale spinner, but she talked more than she worked.

Kate tried to be fair-minded. It was Mrs. Ferrers, rising from her bench beneath a rather convenient ray of sunlight during the Sunday meeting, who had convinced the congregation that Arthur Grey's proposal to offer supplies did not contradict their Quaker pacifism. It was Mrs. Ferrers who argued that their goods would not prolong an already bloody war, but would save the lives of the men and boys starving in the Continental Army. Aiding the Rebels was an errand of mercy. The town drove cattle all the way to Boston when the British blockaded that city. They could certainly spare a few wagonloads of grain for men starving almost on their doorstep.

Angela Ferrers' Quaker demeanor was pitch-perfect. She thee'd and thou'd when appropriate. She conformed to the Society of Friends' preference for plain dress. She wore no lace, no gaudy colors, no frills, yet she stood out among the other ladies.

Her skirts were hemmed to show a tasteful, but well-turned, hint of ankle. Her bodice was expertly tailored. The beige cotton of her ensemble set off her hair and eyes. Peeking out from her collar, cuffs, and lacings were a chemise and stays of the most impeccable white. Even her teeth gleamed.

She fooled the other ladies because they wanted to be fooled, because they saw in her an ideal reflection of themselves. But she did not fool Kate.

The pickle jar was just the latest of her mistakes. Earlier that day she had stepped into the fireplace in the summer kitchen without hitching her skirts high enough. Only timely intervention from Kate had prevented the Widow's skirts catching fire. Her pockets, though, clinched it. She didn't have any: not a single one in her fitted skirts, jacket, or stays. The impracticality of it was astounding.

Kate left the women packing salt pork into the last of the barrels and debating the merits of linen versus cotton baby swaddling, and went to find her father at his secretary in the back parlor. It was dark and cool there, and she welcomed the relief from the sticky heat of the kitchen. She shut the door behind her.

It was her favorite room in the house, where she played the harpsichord in the evening and indulged her father's un-Quakerly taste for ballads. Floored with Brussels carpet, painted in hues of sea blue and wheat gold, hung with classical scenes and furnished with a set of horsehair lolling chairs that bristled like angry porcupines, it served both as the Greys' private sanctuary and their preferred place to entertain guests.

At sixty, Arthur Grey was still a vigorous man. The years had softened his hawklike features, but his eyes burned bright and his frame was lean.

"Are the wagons packed?" he asked.

"Almost. What will you do when Reverend Matthis discovers the contents of the last wagon?"

"What kind of an unmannerly oaf do you take me for, young woman? I will offer him one of your excellent pies, of course."

"I meant the contents *under* the pies," Kate persisted.

"That would be blueberries?" He turned from his secretary to cast a merry eye on his daughter.

"That would be rifles, sixty, with shot."

"You disapprove."

"I'm afraid for you."

"Be afraid for the Regulars. I'm still a damned good shot."

"You mean to stay with Washington, then." She tried to hide her disappointment. Her father had been an officer in the French and Indian War; a man, at one time, of violence; and a close friend of the Virginian who now commanded the Continentals.

"These may be the times that try men's souls, but our masters in London have tried my patience. I didn't fight in the last war to put up with a standing army on my doorstep." He pressed his seal into the wax pooled on the envelope. It bore no address.

"It's your soul that Reverend Matthis will think the worse for wear. He'll read you out of the meeting."

"Would that be so terrible, Kate? I wasn't born a Friend. I was convinced. Largely by your mother. She was a damned sight better-looking than Matthis, in any case."

Kate laughed out loud. "I give up. Go and frustrate King George . . . How long will you be gone?"

He rose without answering and slid his hand along the mantelpiece, fingertips flying over courses of dentils, acanthus, frieze, and metope, to rest upon the stalk of an exquisitely carved pineapple. A tiny door swung open, revealing a cubby. He held up the letter. "For our friends in Philadelphia, by the next courier," he said, and slipped the missive into its hiding place. When he closed the panel, between the acanthus-twined pilasters, the joint was invisible.

"Before you began writing treasonous letters to Rebels, what did you use that hidey-hole for?" Kate asked.

"Tobacco. Your mother hated me to smoke in the house. And it's a Committee of Correspondence with like-minded gentlemen, not treason. Still, it wouldn't do us any good to let the Regulars get hold of any of my letters, particularly that one. It's important. I'm informing Congress that I will accept their commission and have tendered my advice on whom they might consider sending to Paris."

"Mrs. Ferrers says that Howe has landed at Head

of Elk and will begin arresting Rebels." Everyone feared they would soon march on Philadelphia, de facto seat of the rebellion since the first Continental Congress had convened there three years ago.

"Then you'll be safer with me away." He handed her a heavy purse of golden guineas.

"What is this for?" she asked.

"Uncertainties."

A suspicion formed in the pit of her stomach. "How long will you be gone?"

"That's one of the uncertainties. I'm sorry, Kate." He capped the inkpot, closed the doors of the secretary, and put his arm around his daughter.

"I'll be lonely without you."

"Then marry, Kate."

"Never. 'For I've been warned, and I've decided, to sleep alone, all of my life.'"

"Don't put your faith in maudlin ballads. I seem to remember that one containing a philandering father."

"A handsome devil of a philandering father."

Arthur Grey grunted. "Well, they got that half right." He paused, and something in his manner made Kate recall the time when she was a little girl and contracted a hoarse, bellowing cough. She had rebelled against taking the ichorous green tonic prescribed by the doctor, but every morning Arthur Grey had talked her into swallowing the draught.

"What?" she asked.

"I've asked Mrs. Ferrers to stay with you until Howe goes to ground for the winter."

"No! I'm fine by myself. The Regulars know that Quakers are pacifists."

"Tired, hungry soldiers don't always trouble to pay for food, or firewood, or to discuss politics with the people they rob. Regulars or Continentals, for that matter. Mrs. Ferrers is staying."

"She'll drive me mad."

"She is a sensible lady of great experience. Provided she doesn't set herself on fire, you should have a quiet few weeks, and she'll be gone by the first snow."

By late afternoon, Kate was longing for snow.

The wagons departed in good order, though Silas Talbert, their neighbor to the south, returned an hour later when his horse went lame. This was generally perceived as the signal for the ladies to depart, though Kate found herself wishing that they had stayed later, both to occupy the chatty Mrs. Ferrers and to put the house to rights.

Kate spent the early afternoon scrubbing tables, sweeping floors, and taking count of their provisions. During these activities, Mrs. Ferrers was, not surprisingly, nowhere in sight.

They had sent away more than half their stores with the men. It would be a lean winter for Kate, Mrs. Ferrers, and Margaret and Sara, the two young girls who helped with the house and lived in the room above the winter kitchen.

Kate was in the cold room counting apples when the rider broke through the line of trees at the end of the barley field. She could see him from the second-story window, crossing straight over the meadow.

It was Silas Talbert again, but this time his horse

was very definitely not lame. He was shouting. Kate lifted the sash and leaned out the window, wishing for a breeze to break this dizzying heat, and finally his words reached her.

"Regulars. Cavalry. Heading north. They'll be on the house any minute."

Kate stepped back from the window. Below she could hear Talbert riding away, his message delivered, his own family and farm to think of.

Her father's words came back to her: it wouldn't do the Greys any good if his letters fell into British hands. And no matter how he made light of them, those letters were treason.

Kate wasn't certain if the distant thunder she heard was horsemen or the blood pounding in her ears. Hungry soldiers, who wouldn't stop to ask their allegiance or talk politics. The thunder grew louder, and Kate looked back out the window. The road was hidden by a long stand of elms, but the sound of hooves carried over the field, and the branches shook with their passing.

She ran down the stairs and into the back parlor.

Kate expected an empty room and a cold grate. Instead, a woman stood at the fire, her back to the door, negligently feeding the contents of the secretary to the flames.

"Mrs. Ferrers?"

The woman turned. Gone was the plain young Quaker widow of the morning. In her place stood a powdered, perfumed, bewigged lady in silks and satins. Her dress was closely fitted, and the oyster pink satin shimmered in the firelight. Her wig was tinted the same soft pink, pale curls piled high on her head. She wore a diamond around her neck on a silky ribbon, and rings on her manicured hands.

Her cheeks were rouged, her skin powdered porcelain white, her eyes rimmed with kohl. The entire effect was stunning, particularly to a girl like Kate, raised in a community that eschewed such finery.

At a loss, she said, "There are men on the road. Cavalry. Regulars."

"Yes. I know. A day earlier than I expected. Thirty men, I should say, in scarlet with buff facings, two pistols each, a carbine, and a saber. The man who leads them is tall, has fair hair that he does not allow to grow past his shoulders, blue eyes, and rather full lips."

Stunned, Kate stepped farther into the room. "How do you know all this? They haven't even reached the drive."

As she spoke, the jingle of spurs came distantly from the road.

"Because," said Mrs. Ferrers, closing the secretary and smoothing her spotless pink satin, "I've been waiting for him. Colonel Sir Bayard Caide commands a battalion of His Majesty's horse in these, his Colonies, and has systemically murdered, robbed, and raped civilians in the execution of his duties. I have come, my dear child, to destroy him.

"Now," Mrs. Ferrers went on coolly, "you are my niece. I am your dear aunt Angela from Philadelphia, staying with my dull Quaker cousins in the country. I will dazzle the colonel and persuade him to spend the night. You will see that a fit dinner is laid on for him and his officers. Is that clear?"

Kate found her voice with difficulty. "I'm not going to help you a kill a man. It's not our way." It sounded prim even to her own ears.

Mrs. Ferrers laughed, deep and throaty, a genuine sound, quite different from the hollow simper she had used in front of the ladies that morning. "My dear girl, I'm going to destroy him. You don't have to kill a man to do that. Caide is a sybarite, a sadist, and above all things, a soldier. The cavalry is perhaps the only place where men like him can exist within the confines of the law. He thrives on violence with a bit of style. And what, after all, is an army in the field? I don't need to kill him. I need only ruin him."

She paused, abandoned her pose of elegant bravado, and spoke with chilling seriousness. "General Howe has landed at Head of Elk with *eighteen thousand* Regulars and Hessian mercenaries. He means to march on Philadelphia and take Congress and the capital. There will be arrests, hangings. Caide carries the plans for this attack, the routes, troop placements, and supply lists, from Howe to his subordinate General Clinton in New York. If I can relieve Caide of these dispatches, the colonel will be disgraced. At the very least, he'll lose his commission. And in one move we can disarm a man who has caused us no end of trouble and gain an advantage over our enemy on the march—perhaps even have a chance to stop the British before they reach Philadelphia."

"I can't help you. I've sworn not to intervene in the conflict. We all have. You too . . ." Kate trailed off. "You're not really a Quaker, are you?"

Mrs. Ferrers shook her head. "I'm sorry, Kate, but it was safer, until now, to keep this from you. I have known your father since the last war. I came here to convince him to join Washington. And I have remained to lie in wait for Bayard Caide."

"But how did you know this . . . this . . . Caide man would come here?"

"Your house is the biggest estate in the county. It's on the main road north. He was bound to stop here, but he's too close on the heels of your father and the other gentlemen. Kate, you must help me. Your father will be traveling slowly. The wagons are heavy. If Caide doesn't stop here tonight, he will overtake your father. Caide would give no quarter to Rebels carrying supplies for the Continentals."

Kate could hear the men in the yard. Thirty mounted soldiers made a good deal of noise. She must think. She must decide. She must go out and speak to these men, and, it was becoming all too clear, she must lie.

"Kate." Mrs. Ferrers spoke urgently now. "Are there any other papers in the house that could incriminate your father? You must show me."

She remembered the letter in the mantel. "No." The panel was well hidden, the letter safe, and Mrs. Ferrers was clearly not to be trusted.

"Good. Now." She took Kate's hand in her own and led her to the front of the house. "We go to meet the enemy."

The two women emerged into the afternoon sunlight and Kate was blinded by the glitter of polished spurs and weaponry. The man who slipped lightly from his horse and took the steps two at a time to bow deeply before Mrs. Ferrers was tall and broad-shouldered. Kate found herself watching the play of muscles beneath his closely fitted cavalry breeches. Slim, erect, he did indeed have blue eyes, and was most certainly an officer, but his lips were thin, and his hair was neither fair nor short, but long and black, and encased in a tightly wrapped silk queue. He was not, in short, Bayard Caide.

Two

Peter Tremayne was saddlesore, hungry, and acutely aware of the picture he must present to the locals. There was a reason why the British Regulars were so easily caricatured: the stereotype was often true. They were rough men, badly supplied, and far from home. His own mother wouldn't have let them past the door in their faded regimentals, and yet the colonists were required to quarter soldiers in their homes.

Today Tremayne carried General Howe's plans for the campaign against the Rebel capital, Philadelphia, in his dispatch case. He had hoped to join John Burgoyne on the expedition north but instead had endured a month at sea with hesitating Howe and his fractious military family, a tedious, hot journey plagued by bad winds all the way from New York. These prolonged a ten-day cruise into a one-month ordeal. Galloway and the other Philadelphia Tories had seduced the general south with promises of a country teeming with Loyalists, but Tremayne failed to see how a territory such as the Jerseys, so hostile that the British could not march their army through it and were forced to approach by sea, would yield up a groundswell of support for the Crown. His horse had died on board ship, and the heat and the unfamiliar mount were adding to his bad temper.

He very much wanted a hot bath, a soft bed, and gentle company, but he was resigned to accept a cold basin, clean straw, and the grateful affection of his horse, if any of these things were to be had. His troop had been sniped at all the way from Head of Elk. The grannies of Pennsylvania were disturbingly good shots, and they seemed to spend more time loading rifles than embroidering cushions. America was the stuff of a career soldier's nightmare, a morass becoming deeper by the day.

The neighborhood they were passing through promised somewhat more hospitality. He had met Quakers in England and America and found them kind and generous, if naive and somewhat dour folk, and they were largely if not Loyalists, then at least pacifists.

Despite the rigors of travel, he was glad to be out of the city. He had been raised in the country, and on long rides he found he rather liked the American landscape. He could forget, for a time, the halfhearted manner in which his superiors were prosecuting this conflict, the lives and fortunes being poured into this pointless war.

The manor house was well sited, built in the classical style, and if its proportions and ornament were fifty years out of date in England, its scale promised some modicum of wealth and comfort. Five windows across and two stories high beneath a graceful dormered roof,

with granite stairs rising to a pillared porch, and red brick on a foundation of local stone. Charming.

The lady who greeted him at the top of the stairs was certainly the most *decorative* Quaker he had ever seen, resplendent in up-to-the-minute shell pink satin. She would put half the women of King George's court to shame. He bowed, kissed her hand, and said something polite in passing to the niece, who looked as plain a piece of country business as he'd ever set eyes on.

The lady, Mrs. Ferrers, immediately put the girl to heating water for a bath. The size of the house promised beds, for himself and his officers, and something about the lady's too-familiar gaze told him that gentle company might be his for the asking.

"When will General Howe invest Philadelphia with his troops, Major? We hear the army has disembarked at Head of Elk. A glorious victory, to win back the Rebel capital, surely," Mrs. Ferrers flattered.

Kate tried to hide her amusement by taking a sip of watered rum. The glass sweated in the August heat and dripped onto her apron. She should have taken it off, as a mark of respect for their visitors, but she found she had precious little respect to spare for Redcoats.

They were seated in the back parlor, along with a young man introduced to Kate as Lieutenant Phillip Lytton. He divided his time between shifting uncomfortably on the frayed horsehair chair and glancing surreptitiously at Kate.

Her seat in the corner of the room, wedged between the harpsichord and the sewing table, allowed her the luxury of studying the major. Peter Tremayne, Viscount Sancreed, had at least one quality that Kate approved: he was immune to the charms of Mrs. Ferrers. He must, she decided, be a few years past thirty. Tall, lean, correct but not ostentatious in his tunic, he had wiped his boots carefully outside and wisely chosen the lolling chair with a slipcover.

"It will be a victory by default, and hardly glorious," he replied. "Philadelphia is open on all sides. It has no defenses. Congress will flee, along with most of the Rebel population."

"Then you must be looking forward to winter quarters in the city. I hear that General Howe keeps merry company." Mrs. Ferrers, Kate was realizing, had taken the wrong tack with Peter Tremayne. Prepared to dazzle quite another man, one amenable to flattery and enamored of high living, she had no notion how to seduce a sober, tired aristocrat with a long road in front of him.

Tremayne didn't answer, only smiled thinly and sipped his rum.

Phillip Lytton, looking painfully young and decidedly uncomfortable, rushed to fill the silence. "Yes, it will be very gay. Captain André—he is on the general's staff and much admired—has already planned a masque for next week. I hope we'll be back in time to take part."

"What you hope for, Lytton, is a swift end to this pointless conflict." Tremayne put his empty glass down. "Howe has the advantage. He should press it, and take Washington while he can. Any general but Howe would have beaten Washington by this time."

Lytton began to stammer his apologies.

Kate, used to discoursing on matters political with her father, spoke before thinking. "And any general but Washington would have beaten Howe, I believe is the opinion of the *London Times*. But you and they are wrong."

Lytton stopped fidgeting. Mrs. Ferrers closed her fan. And Peter Tremayne, for the first time all afternoon, looked less than bored. He sat up in his chair.

Mrs. Ferrers, desperate to break the tension, moved to fill Tremayne's empty glass. He laid his hand over the cut crystal without looking up at her.

He fixed his cold blue eyes on Kate. "Miss Grey, do you mean to tell me that you have discerned a strategy in Washington's tactics?" Tremayne's voice dripped with sarcasm. "I can think of no successful general in history to equal him for retreat and failure."

"My niece means no such thing. She's just going to check on dinner."

Kate ignored Mrs. Ferrers. Like her father, she enjoyed few things more than getting to grips with a noble argument. "I hesitate to correct you, Lord Sancreed, but I can. Fabius Maximus, sometimes called Cunctator—the Delayer. He hindered and harassed an enemy superior in numbers until that enemy's strength was eroded. His tactics during the Second Punic War helped Rome defeat Carthage."

Peter Tremayne smiled, an openmouthed, crooked expression of genuine delight that made Kate flush. Lytton and Mrs. Ferrers were quite forgotten. "You know your military history. But Fabian tactics won't answer here. Rome had a trained army of veterans.

Men sworn to twenty years' service. Washington has only poorly armed militia, whose enlistments are about to expire."

"Yes," Kate said, undeterred, "he has something remarkable indeed. A volunteer army."

Mrs. Ferrers stood up. "Mr. Lytton, will you help me bring up a butt of wine?"

Kate barely noticed their departure. Tremayne abandoned the lolling chair to perch on the harpsichord bench beside her. She was scarcely conscious of his proximity, so determined was she to hear what he might say next.

"Volunteer or no, Miss Grey, you are dependent on Britain for manufactured goods. Where the might of armies may be insufficient, simple economics will prevail."

"We rely upon you for goods, Lord Sancreed, because you legislate that we must do so."

"Granted. You might build your own industries. But where will you turn in the short run for powder and shot, ordnance, and the machinery of war?"

Kate opened her mouth, but realized she couldn't speak the word that rose naturally to her lips. There was only one answer to Tremayne's question: to France, of course. Up to this point, they had been talking tactics. To answer his question would be to talk treason.

Kate, used to plain-speaking farm people, realized that she had been skillfully led into betraying herself. Her lips remained open, and her tongue felt strangely dry, as she experienced a tiny epiphany: the world beyond Orchard Valley was very complicated indeed.

She became aware of his physical closeness and stifled an urge to shrink back. She could not stop herself from looking at the secret panel on the mantel, just behind Tremayne.

Treason. To speak the name of France, where no doubt Congress was already begging powder, shot, and ordnance, was to speak treason. And behind a slender walnut panel, folded, signed, and sealed, was also treason.

She willed herself to look away and to answer the man looming over her. "Quakers are pacifists, Major. I've no notion where to acquire such things."

A quarter of an hour of Mrs. Ferrers' company in the parlor convinced Peter Tremayne that he would be better off with the affections of his horse. Her manner was polished and charming. She laughed prettily at his jokes. She paid him deft compliments and asked a steady stream of flattering questions. She would have been at home in any London drawing room, and like most of the English ladies of her class, she ventured no opinions, offered no counterarguments, tendered no opposition to anything he said.

So when the country niece, whom he had barely noticed, betrayed an argumentative nature and a curiously martial education, he was intrigued.

She had made no impression on him outside the house, and later had contrived to hide behind the harpsichord in the parlor. The girl was a baffling contradiction. Her plain clothes, long, undressed hair, and unmarried status marked her as an innocent, but she had the frank and aggressive manner of an experienced woman.

He moved closer and noted her wide, expressive eyes and fine skin. Of her body beneath the shapeless jacket he could tell nothing. Her skirts were wrinkled and appeared damp and charred at the hem, and he suspected that the granules clinging to her hair were bits of piecrust. He was, against all reason, enchanted.

The aunt had panicked when the girl started talking politics. The widow was clearly a Tory, anxious to preserve her property and favored status during the occupation. Kate was something different.

Quaker women, he knew, were encouraged to be freethinkers, and had even been known to preach at their meetings. Whatever Kate was, though, she was guileless. He had baited her easily and noted her sudden flush when she realized what he had done.

Her eyes had betrayed her. There was something hidden in the fireplace behind him. He was uninterested in her secrets. Quakers weren't inclined toward intrigue. But his thoughts were turning inevitably to seduction, and this just might prove an opening gambit.

"Quakers are pacifists, Major. I've no notion where to acquire such things."

"France," he supplied. "The Rebels will seek aid from France. The Old Enemy."

"But surely that would bring the French into open war with Britain."

"Yes. And for that reason, France won't risk such aid unless the Rebels win a significant victory. Trenton, no matter how many Hessians were captured, was a skirmish, not a battle." Without taking his eyes off Kate, he ran his hand along the mantel behind him, felt the spring, and pressed.

He didn't turn to look. The expression on the girl's

face, her dark eyes wide, told him he'd found what he was looking for. The sound of surprise she made was curiously erotic to him.

He turned to the opening he had discovered and fished out a sealed letter. He turned it over in his hands. No address. "How charming. A secret letter. Miss Grey, whomever can you be writing to?"

*K*ate had been reluctant to trust Mrs. Ferrers. Now she wished fervently that the missive had been fed to the fire.

Peter Tremayne turned the letter over in his long, slender fingers. "No address. Now that is mysterious."

Kate realized that Peter Tremayne was playing a game unfamiliar to her.

"Perhaps we should open it to determine its direction?" He fingered the seal on the letter.

She held out her hand and spoke as she would to an errant child. "It isn't addressed to *you*. That much is clear."

He looked at her open palm curiously and appeared to consider it a moment. He held the letter out to her, but before she could grasp it he snatched it back and trapped her extended hand in his empty one.

His thumb slid over her palm, invading, intimate, alarming.

Kate was a stranger to seduction. Youthful crushes had come and gone without the heady sensation his touch was eliciting, which she dimly recognized as lust.

An excellent word choice, as lust was inappropriate desire, and nothing could be more inappropriate than a Quaker coupling with a soldier, a man of violence, a killer. All of this passed through her mind in an instant. She called upon common sense to extricate her from Tremayne's grasp but discovered instead a latent talent for banter.

"Now you possess my hand and my letter. That leaves you no hands free."

He slipped the letter into the breast of his tunic. "Now my left hand is free. What do you suggest I do with it?"

She willed herself to look away from his long, elegant fingers and instead found her eyes trapped by his pale blue gaze. Her voice sounded tiny and far away when she spoke. "The Latin word for left was *sinistra*. Sinister. The Romans mistrusted the left hand."

His voice was very soft now. "So should you."

Her whole body was tensed, waiting for his touch, but it didn't come.

Instead he continued to caress her trapped hand, circling his thumb intimately in the center of her palm.

He released her and stepped back just as the door opened behind them. He must have heard Mrs. Ferrers and Lytton in the passage. Kate had been deaf to the world.

Mrs. Ferrers didn't so much as glance at the open panel in the mantel. She breezed in on a raft of chatter, followed by a bright-eyed Lytton. "You'll find a tub laid on in Mr. Grey's room, top of the stairs. Dinner is being brought out to the barn for your men. We can dine after you've had your bath."

"We'll pay for the foodstuffs we consume, of course." Peter Tremayne kissed Mrs. Ferrers' hand on his way out, taking Lytton with him. He sketched a polite bow in Kate's direction, betraying none of what had just taken place.

Mrs. Ferrers shut the door behind the men, and stood silent and still until the stairs stopped creaking and the door to the best bedroom closed above. She crossed the room, pressed the secret panel shut, and rounded on Kate.

"You're either a very stupid or a very clever young woman. I can't decide which."

Kate felt very stupid indeed, but she met Mrs. Ferrers' gaze steadily. The older woman scrutinized her. Kate couldn't stop herself from pushing back her hair, and was distressed when pie crumbs fell out.

Mrs. Ferrers laughed. "We'll just have to see, won't we?" She swanned out of the room on a tide of rustling silk, leaving the scent of gardenias behind her.

Kate smoothed her apron and shook her plain skirts out. She was not clever, but she was sensible. Peter Tremayne had her father's letter, and somehow she must get it back.

The heat broke in the evening.

Sara and Margaret were unused to serving dinner, and it showed. Flustered from their dealings with the soldiers in the barn, suspicious of Mrs. Ferrers, and terrified of Tremayne, they broke glasses, spilled wine, and, Kate suspected, finding what looked like a bit of quill caught between her teeth, had neglected to thoroughly pluck the chicken.

Tremayne sat in her father's chair at dinner and noticed none of this. Mrs. Ferrers sat opposite. In between,

Kate, Phillip Lytton, and two of Tremayne's junior officers made up the dinner party.

Kate had contrived to seat herself beside the major. Mrs. Ferrers appeared to have abandoned her efforts to engage him, and turned her attention to dazzling the junior officers, who were now enjoying one of her anecdotes. The complete tale of Colonel Donop, Kate noted in passing, was far saltier than the version offered to the Quaker matrons of the morning.

Phillip Lytton had progressed beyond casting surreptitious glances at Kate and moved on to enthusing about the London stage.

"I saw *The Rivals* just before I left London. It's a marvelous play. You would like it. The heroine's name is Lydia—"

Tremayne was in good humor. "I don't think Miss Grey's people approve of the theater, Lytton."

Lytton was mortified. "I'm sorry, Miss Grey. I'm afraid I know very little about Quakers."

"Don't be, Mr. Lytton. I've never been to a play myself, but the major is wrong. My people quite like the theater."

Tremayne raised an eyebrow. "Oh, yes?"

"Yes. General Washington's favorite play is *Cato*."

Lytton was baffled. "Is General Washington a Quaker?"

"No, Lytton. Miss Grey is a Rebel."

"Are you really, Miss Grey? I've yet to meet a Rebel."

"We prefer the term 'American.' And I suspect you meet them all the time, Mr. Lytton, but they are too sensible to declare themselves to you." Unlike me, Kate added to herself.

Tremayne was obviously enjoying himself. "Yes, we do meet them all the time, Miss Grey, but the trouble is they're too busy running away to chat with us. I believe I've just bitten into the chicken's beak."

"I wouldn't be surprised. You've frightened the maids out of their minds. I expect you'll find they've sweetened the mustard and put salt in the pudding." Kate had addressed herself to their end of the table, but Tremayne pitched his answer to her alone.

"Really? I quite enjoy finding the sweet and the savory in the same dish."

"Then you'll be well satisfied with dinner tonight." Kate pushed another mysteriously tough bit of chicken to the side of her plate.

"I wasn't speaking of dinner."

Lytton had stopped eating, uncertain where the conversation was leading. Tremayne ignored him. "That reminds me. Would you like your letter back?"

The other end of the table erupted in raucous laughter, and one of Tremayne's officers began to perform a trick with a spoon, a pickle, and a saltcellar that promised to stain the tablecloth.

Kate proceeded like a child shod in pattens on a slick of ice: cautiously. "Yes. I would like it back."

"Then leave your bedroom door unlocked."

"You are embarrassing Mr. Lytton," Kate said, blindsided by the directness of his response. She had expected clever baiting, and had his demand been different, she would have welcomed this plain speaking.

Lytton stood up, his chair screeching over the floorcloth, unheard beneath the drunken laughter at the other end of the table. "Sir. I protest—"

"Sit down, Mr. Lytton. Miss Grey is quite capable

of defending herself. And locking her door if she chooses."

Lytton looked uncertainly at Kate, who decided that the situation, and the fate of the letter, was getting out of hand. "Yes, please, Mr. Lytton, do sit down and finish your dinner. The major is only joking. Isn't he?"

Tremayne rolled his eyes. "Yes, Lytton, I'm having a bit of fun."

Kate smiled reassuringly at Lytton, and he sat back down. "Tell me more about the play, Mr. Lytton."

He spoke at length about Sheridan, and blushed when he described the leading actress in the play. Kate listened attentively, and Tremayne made no further mention of the letter, but when the puddings were served, Kate looked up to discover the major studying her with more than casual interest. What she failed to observe was that Mrs. Ferrers, entertaining her guests effortlessly at the other end of the table and directing with rather less success the efforts of Margaret and Sara, was studying Lord Sancreed with equal, but far less benign interest.

*V*iscount Sancreed was not a bad officer. In an era of purchased commissions and only intermittently competent soldiering, Peter Tremayne was a professional. Born to wealth and privilege, but unsuited to politics, he'd entered the cavalry young and grown into leadership. The command of a troop of horse—a small thing in the grand scheme—suited him admirably.

He had probably once been quite like Lytton, though the army tended to attract fewer prudes in his day. He regretted teasing the boy, and knew Lytton bore watching. He was chivalrous and prickly and, without some good advice, would most likely end up gutted in some pointless duel.

But Lytton was for tomorrow and the long road to New York. Tonight Peter Tremayne had other quarry.

Kate Grey's mysterious letter, most likely to some unsuitable lover, lay snug in his tunic. The lady herself had retired, and the state of the lock on her door remained an open question. The household was still awake, the maids banking fires and extinguishing lamps. When quiet settled over Grey House, Tremayne would try her door.

He had considered a more forceful approach. The aunt was careless and left the girl alone with him after dinner once more, but Tremayne didn't touch her. He was wholly smitten, but still uncertain. If she was worldly, and inclined to arranging such matters for herself, she could leave her chamber unbarred. If she was inexperienced, she had only to throw the bolt.

He knew she was attracted to him. And the proximity of Grey Farm to Philadelphia was improving his attitude toward winter quarters in the City of Brotherly Love. Even if he was unsuccessful with her tonight, future visits might prove more rewarding. It occurred to him that his mind was turning to seducing a farm girl with pie crumbs in her hair, and he laughed out loud at himself.

His cousin, Bayard, had mocked him for choosing this duty, for retracing by land the miserable journey they had just undertaken by sea, for being Howe's errand boy. Carrying Howe's dispatches to Clinton in New York was hardly glorious soldiering. But it was preferable in Peter Tremayne's mind to the other less palatable missions he knew Howe had ordered that night. He had no desire to kidnap private citizens, no matter what their politics, and thought that abducting Rebels from their homes smacked of Tudor intrigue. If the parties sent forth from Head of Elk with orders to drive deep into Rebel territory and capture members of Congress were not instructed to throw such men in the Tower, it was only because Philadelphia offered nearer prisons.

Mrs. Ferrers had served rum in the parlor, an expensive luxury since molasses had stopped reaching the blockaded American harbors. Tremayne sought, and found, a bottle of local whisky in the kitchen and poured himself a glass. He returned briefly to the parlor, where he opened the secretary and helped himself to pen, paper, and wax.

The rooms were creaky, hot, and old, but the mattresses were fresh and the bed curtains free of dust. Returning to his room, he arranged his kit for the morning, listened with satisfaction to the house retiring for the night, slipped out into the corridor, and closed his door behind him.

Kate's room lay at the end of the long hall, past the stairs. The scuffed boards groaned beneath his boots and he wondered to himself if the aunt was deaf or just unusually broad-minded. Another, less charitable thought occurred to him: that there were Tories aplenty who would pimp their wives, daughters, or nieces to British officers in exchange for trading concessions and protection. Howe had been accompanied on the journey from Boston not only by his charming mistress,

Mrs. Loring, but by her husband as well, who profited handsomely from the arrangement.

When the door to his right opened, Tremayne was prepared for a woman's tirade, but not for drawn steel. Lytton emerged, flourishing his saber, already realizing that it was a poor weapon in the confined space of the hall.

"Trouble sleeping, Lytton?"

"You weren't joking about Miss Grey."

Tremayne sighed. This was a lecture best delivered under other circumstances, but here and now would have to do. "Phillip, this is the way men and women arrange things."

"She's only a girl."

"She's older than you are, and quite capable of locking her door. Go back to bed. The whole house will hear me if I break her door down, and you can hack me to pieces then, if you don't bury your saber in the doorjamb first."

Lytton had no facility for clever words. Wounded pride was writ large on his face, and wounded pride was a dangerous thing in a young man with a sword. He stepped in front of Kate's door, barring Tremayne's way. "Put the saber down, Phillip. Someone is going to get hurt, and I assure you it will not be me."

"I won't let you pass, Lord Sancreed."

Lytton failed to anticipate the short, sharp move with which Tremayne disarmed him, and the blow that knocked him to his knees. From his place on the floor he hissed, "You are a scoundrel and a rake, sir."

"And you are young and foolish, and infatuated. Examine your own motives before you adopt a pose of chivalry, Phillip. You aren't interested in preserving the lady from my advances. You are frustrated that your own weren't more successful. *The Rivals* indeed."

Tremayne stepped over and past the wheezing boy and laid his hand lightly on the latch to Kate's door. He would look an utter fool if it were locked.

He pressed, and the door swung open.

*K*ate had heard the two men arguing in the hall. Peter Tremayne seemed to do rather a lot of arguing. Then again, so did she.

She supposed Angela Ferrers would have laid a scene for seduction, but Kate had no intention of seducing, or being seduced for that matter. Quakers were good at convincing people. Her mother had convinced her father after all. She must simply convince Peter Tremayne to return the letter.

She heard a scuffle, the sound of metal clattering to the floor, and her door swung open.

She realized a moment too late that she was standing in front of the bed, and that that wouldn't do. She stepped away, which brought her, in the confines of the small room, closer to the door. And to Tremayne.

He stood on the threshold, one hand tucked casually into the pocket of his tunic. "Mr. Lytton has had an accident. He tripped on the carpet."

"There isn't any carpet in the hall," Kate answered.

"Yes, well. He is extremely clumsy. May I come in?"

She wanted to say, "Yes, please." His pale blue eyes and crooked smile made her smile involuntarily in turn. Tonight his long hair was tied loosely at the back of his neck and snaked inky black over the gold braid on his shoulder. Instead, she observed, "The door was unlocked."

"Yes. Is that an invitation? Only, you see, I should like Mr. Lytton to hear you consent to my presence in your bedroom."

"Another few hours in your presence, Major, and I will know when I am about to be maneuvered into a corner."

"I was hoping for something rather softer. The bed, for instance."

"Give me back my letter, and I will consent to your presence in my room." She held out her hand.

He produced the envelope from his tunic, and this time laid it on her open palm. Her fingers closed around the letter, and Tremayne stepped over the threshold, kicking the door neatly shut behind him. "Now I have both hands free and at your disposal, Miss Grey."

He took another step and closed the distance between them. She backed toward the bed, then realizing it, stopped herself. "What a puzzle you are, Miss Grey," he said and, without touching her, bent his head to brush his lips lightly against hers. She opened her mouth to speak and his tongue darted inside. The sensation shocked her, and she opened her lips farther. He pressed his advantage, running the tip of his tongue lightly over the surface of Kate's.

She felt his hands, still tentative, on the small of her back and at the nape of her neck. She might, she realized, easily break his grasp, if she had the will to do so, but the heat of his body as he stepped closer eroded her resolve.

Uncertain of what to do with her hands, she slid them under his tunic, over the fine lawn of his shirt and the hard muscles of his chest. Her heart was pounding, her breath becoming short. She felt an unfamiliar heaviness at the apex of her thighs and found it thrilling and terrifying all at once.

Tremayne lifted his head and drew back to look down at her, tipping her chin up with one hand and caressing her neck with the other. "Say yes, Kate. Or say no, and I'll leave." He dropped his hands and stepped back from her, withdrawing his warmth with his touch.

He never heard her answer. The battering of the front door below drowned out her words, and the clatter of weaponry and opening of doors throughout the house signaled an end to their privacy.

Tremayne heard Lytton hammering on Kate's bedroom door. He reached out and pulled sharply on the ribbon that bound her shapeless jacket closed. The amateur embroidery came away in his hand. It seemed all the more intimate because the handiwork, though clumsy, was her own. He pressed it to his lips, sketched a small bow, and slipped from her room, before his presence there could cause her any embarrassment.

Lytton, standing just outside her door, would not meet his eyes.

Tremayne collected his kit and found the rider below in the kitchen. The man was lean, old, and wiry, dressed in fine but plainly cut brown cloth. "Rebels. A raiding party. They're pillaging a farm on the West Road. They mean to burn it."

The man was obviously local and known to the Greys.

"How many?" Tremayne asked sharply.

"Forty. Maybe more."

"On foot?"

The man shook his head. "Mounted. Well armed. Organized."

"Damn. Right. Lytton. Mount up. This is what we're paid for."

Mrs. Ferrers arrived in the kitchen in a far more attractive, if less artless, state of dishevelment than the one in which he had left Kate. He wondered briefly what the girl would look like with a touch of her aunt's polish and élan, and dismissed the thought just as quickly. Kate had her own charm, which needed no ornament.

"What's happening, Mr. Talbert?" the widow asked.

The old man took his hat off. "Mrs. Ferrers. Ma'am. Rebels, attacking the farm to the west."

"Thank you for your hospitality, Mrs. Ferrers." Tremayne followed Lytton out into the hall and was about to dart up the stairs when he saw Kate, clutching her jacket closed, standing in the door to the parlor.

Her ribbon was still in his hand. "Your Rebel friends are attacking a farm to the west," he said to her.

"Yes," Kate said.

"I must go. Protecting His Majesty's loyal subjects and such."

"Yes," she said again. He could see her chest heave and fall in the confines of her sensible cotton stays.

"Miss Grey?" He cocked his head, realization dawning on him. "Is that your answer?"

"Yes."

She bit her lip, and he could tell she wished to say more. He waited.

"That is, you must understand, I have never said

yes before. To anyone." Then she laughed. "Not that anyone asked. But you are quite outside my experience, Major, in every way."

"I rather thought so. And I'm glad of it." He stepped close to her but could not touch her here in view of so many. He spoke quietly, for her alone. "I won't take the responsibility lightly. Wait for me."

The daunting prospect of an enemy engagement at night against men who knew the territory better than he dwindled to a minor impediment. He slipped her ribbon through the button loop on his sleeve and tied it, then bowed and was gone.

*T*he Miller house was already burning when thirty-odd mounted men thundered to a halt outside the place. There were no Rebels to be seen. The house was old, at least a hundred years, and flames had already engulfed the steep gables and melted the lead from the casements.

"Waste. A vast, natural paradise. More land than anyone can settle. And this." Tremayne spoke more to himself than to anyone else, but Silas Talbert, mounted on the horse that had earlier that day made a remarkable recovery, answered him.

"It's a rare man on either side of this war whose reach is equal to his grasp."

They watched the house burn. There was little to save, and no point in pursuit.

On the cold ride back after Talbert left them, Tremayne's thoughts turned to Kate, and he fingered the ribbon at his cuff. A showy flourish, a bit of schoolboy romance, plucking the lace from her jacket, but well worth the result.

He recognized infatuation, though he'd not felt it in a long time. Affairs, some of them long and satisfying, he had pursued since his late teens when he had left home for the army. He had enjoyed briefer encounters as well, none more debauched than in the company of his cousin and brother officer, Bayard Caide. It occurred to him that there were elements of his past—and regrettably, with this late war, of his present—that made him an unfit companion for a Quaker girl.

Those considerations were for tomorrow, though. Today, she waited for him.

The house looked different in the cold blue light of dawn. The windows that yesterday had glowed softly with welcome now stared like empty sockets.

He'd hoped to wake only the servants by knocking quietly, but no one came. Lytton joined him on the porch. "There's no smoke in any of the chimneys, sir."

"What?" Fear stole over him. The viciousness that would cause a man to burn his neighbor's house led to worse things in a conflict like this. England's own Civil War had been rife with atrocity, and the Colonists seemed determined to replay that internecine struggle. He pounded hard on the door.

It swung away from his hand.

They searched the hall, parlors, and bedrooms, and finally the attics and cellars, calling out for the women; but of the servants, Mrs. Ferrers, and Kate Grey, they found no trace.

Recalling with sickening apprehension and the first cold sparks of anger Mrs. Ferrers' anecdote about the cruelly deceived Hessian colonel, he reached for the oilskin packet in his bag, and the papers entrusted to him by General Howe.

The envelope was still there, but when he examined the pages in the cold morning light, they were utterly blank.

Three

After Tremayne had gone, Kate had remained in the parlor listening to the clatter of spurs and hooves on the paving. There was little talk. She was not surprised. She'd seen it before. Her father was one of the men their community called upon when Indian raids threatened, and she knew from experience that men who had been wakened in the middle of the night for skirmishing were rarely garrulous.

She slipped her hand into her pocket and was reassured to find her father's letter there. Absently, she attempted to tie her jacket shut, and blushed when she realized that a man was now riding into the dark with her ribbon around his cuff. She subsided into the lolling chair where he had sat that afternoon and tried to get her mind around what she had just done.

Kate had always been the gray mouse of Grey Farm. Most of her friends were married or courting by now. She knew that some of them enjoyed an advantage of appearance and, most saliently, of disposition. Few farmers wanted a tart-tongued girl for a wife.

Marriage, of course, was not what Peter Tremayne was offering. Untempted by matrimony, Kate had never considered that she might discover needs not easily satisfied outside the bounds of wedlock. Or a man who brought out those needs.

Perhaps, had she not met Peter Tremayne, the matter would never have arisen.

She shut her eyes and replayed their encounter abovestairs, imagining what they might have done next had Silas Talbert not intervened.

It was then that it occurred to her that Silas Talbert had been rather too conveniently alert today. He had spotted the British on the road, when but for the lameness of his horse, he should have been miles away with Kate's father. And he had spotted the Continentals tonight, at the unnamed farm to the west. Kate tried to remember which of their neighbors lived due west of them. Only the Millers, outspoken Tories, she realized, who had abandoned their property several weeks ago to seek the protection of the British.

She was still sitting in the lolling chair when Mrs. Ferrers found her. The Widow was no longer dressed in the brocade robe she had worn earlier that night, nor her shell pink satin, nor her sensible Quaker ensemble. Now she was dressed for riding in dark gray wool. Only her cloak, edged with costly furs, hinted at her earlier élan. "We haven't much time. I hope you can saddle your own horse."

"Yes, of course," Kate said, and sat up. "But why?"

"You can't be here when they come back. Tremayne

will realize that these"—Mrs. Ferrers flourished a sheaf of closely written pages—"are gone."

"You stole Howe's letters," Kate said hollowly. "How?"

"It was simple. I waited for Tremayne to visit you in your bedroom. It was clear this afternoon that you had the best chance of distracting him. You've done well, but I can't leave you here. Is there someone in the neighborhood who can take you in until Howe goes to ground in Philadelphia?"

She could go to her friend Milly's, of course. Milly's mother-in-law, Mrs. Ashcroft, had been among the matrons fawning over Angela Ferrers that morning. Milly herself, six months gone with child and unable to travel, had stayed home. Kate considered what it would be like to shelter under her roof. To be the unwanted spinster guest, secretly pitied but welcomed as a pair of extra hands, though Milly would never treat her like that. Openly. But it would be true, all the same. Kate felt angry, manipulated. She had asked very little of life so far, and tonight she realized she had gotten even less.

"I'm not leaving. Major Tremayne is coming back," she said, but even as the words left her mouth she recalled Mrs. Ferrers' story of Donop the Hessian colonel, tricked by the beautiful rebel spy.

"Yes," Mrs. Ferrers agreed. "He's coming back. And not to steal ribbons from your jacket. Do you know what happens to spies, Kate?"

"They hang." She recalled the boy from Connecticut caught behind British lines. Hale. His name had been Hale.

"No. They hang men. Women disappear. It's only glamorous in novels, Kate. If we are successful, we can't boast. Spying is a dishonorable trade for women, for precisely the reason you despised me this afternoon, and you despise yourself now. We exchange our virtue for their secrets. If we fail, we don't have the privilege of a public trial and famous last words. Our reward for failure is an unmarked grave."

"What will happen to him?"

"Tonight? Very little. They'll find the Miller farm burning, much as the Millers deserve. Tomorrow, when he reaches New York without the packet, court-martial and a swift return to England, I should think."

"I think I'm going to be sick."

"Then do so quickly. I must reach Washington's camp before Major Tremayne realizes we are gone." Mrs. Ferrers turned to go, then paused in the door and betrayed, for the first time that day, a hint of unfiltered emotion. Kate realized it was pity. "I wouldn't feel too sorry for him, Kate. He has money, power, and privilege at home. Even if he is just a decent man caught in circumstances beyond his control, he's better off out of it."

Kate paid Margaret and Sara two weeks' wages each and sent the girls home across the tall rye fields. She watched their lantern bobbing in the darkness, until the waving grain swallowed the light. Then she saddled her horse.

She had no desire for Angela Ferrers' company on the road to Milly's, and nothing further to say to her. The spy's knowing manner and sudden, belated sympathy were an affront to Kate's pride. But Mrs. Ferrers wouldn't go away. She insisted on seeing Kate safely beyond the reach of Peter Tremayne before she continued on to the Continental lines.

Kate knew the Widow was not motivated by motherly concern for her safety. The truth was that Kate knew too much. If she was arrested, she could betray the woman, and worse, if Tremayne discovered who Kate was, she might be used as a bargaining chip against her father.

When Kate thought of Peter Tremayne, she recalled with shocking vividness the warm scents of leather and wool and whisky, the fine weave of his linen shirt beneath her fingertips, and the soft wool of his tunic. The memory brought a flush to her cheeks. She turned to find Angela Ferrers, on her horse, trotting alongside her with the negligent grace of a cavalier and watching her with unconcealed amusement. Kate spurred her mount to escape the woman, but she kept pace.

They were within sight of the Ashcrofts' rambling hilltop farmhouse, their journey together nearly at an end, when the Widow took Kate's reins and drew both horses to a stop. Angela Ferrers surveyed the silent orchards rolling away in all directions, and the empty road behind them. When she was quite satisfied they were alone, she spoke. "We probably won't meet again, Kate. You're angry, because I've used you, but I hope you'll see past that and accept a word of advice. What Tremayne was offering, you can have from any man you like, if you take the proper precautions."

Kate hated how the woman seemed to read her mind. She had no privacy in her own thoughts. "That is not all that I wanted from him."

"Yes, but that is all he was offering. I'm sorry if this hurts your feelings. You did me a great service this evening. I'm trying to return the favor. You might know your way around a kitchen better than I do, but you don't understand the first thing about the world outside Grey Farm." Then, with an odd smile and an appraising glance, she added, "Though you're a quick study, I'll grant you."

Kate wrenched her reins away from the spy. "You've drawn my father into the war, embroiled me in treason, and driven me from my home. I don't want any more of your favors. I'm going to spend the next two weeks with Milly and then go home to harvest our rye. Fornication does not figure in my plans."

"Only because you are infatuated with Peter Tremayne," said the Widow coolly. "You'll feel the same way about the next handsome man who falls into your orbit. You're too passionate for spinsterhood and too independent for marriage. Your father's been selfish, keeping you to himself. He should have found you a husband before you became so set in your ways, or taken you to town, where you might have found other outlets for your intellect. But there are alternatives to marriage and spinsterhood."

"Don't talk about my father—"

"Quiet!" she hissed, and turned to look back down the road.

Kate froze. She heard distant thunder. No, not thunder. Not quite. A bass rumble vibrating up through her mount. It was a familiar tune played with a missing note. And then she knew where she had heard it before: at Grey Farm, this morning, when Tremayne's troop had descended on the house.

"Tremayne." Kate turned to look at the empty road behind them.

Angela Ferrers pursed her lips. "I think not." For the first time that night, she looked uncertain.

Ever since the Widow had donned her shell pink satin and begun feeding Arthur Grey's letters to the fire, Kate had been caught up in events beyond her control. Throughout, Angela Ferrers had been confident and decisive. A few moments ago, Kate had hated her for it. Now its absence chilled her. "Who then?" Kate asked.

"These men are riding with muffled spurs. That's not Sancreed's style at all."

The Widow reached for the pistol fixed to Kate's saddle. She'd taken it as a precaution against bears. Kate gripped it hard and backed her horse away.

The spy's voice was icy. "We don't have time for your Quaker scruples. Does your friend's husband have any reason to fear the Redcoats?"

Kate's stomach lurched. "He was with Congress, but he's home now. Milly's having a hard time carrying."

Mrs. Ferrers cursed. "They're coming to arrest him. You can't stay here. We have to ride for it."

The Widow spurred her mount and cantered hard up the hill. Kate followed. They drew level with the house, but Angela Ferrers didn't slow.

Kate turned to look at the sleeping gables, where Milly lay heavy with child, then back down the still-empty road. There was enough time, just. "I'm sorry," she said. "I have to warn them." She plunged down the gravel-strewn drive toward the house.

A lamp flared in an upstairs window as Kate reached

the garden gate. The casements were open to the warm night air, and Milly's long red tresses blew like pennants in the breeze.

"Is that you, Kate? What's that noise? What's happening?" Milly's pale skin was luminous in the moonlight, her freckles like fairy dust over her nose and cheekbones. Kate wasn't surprised to see her up and restless in the middle of the night. For the first three months of her pregnancy, Milly had slept all the time. Now, three months further on, she seemed to sleep not at all.

"Yes, it's me, Milly. The Redcoats are coming for Andrew. He has to leave."

Kate was dimly aware of the spy reining up behind her.

"Kate," the Widow said urgently, "we can't be found here."

The plans. Angela Ferrers and those damnable stolen plans. She and Angela would hang as traitors if they were taken with those papers. And Milly's husband would be implicated. Kate had only brought them greater danger by stopping here.

The muffled clatter of hooves was unmistakable. Now Milly heard it too.

"What should I do?" Milly asked, bewildered.

Angela Ferrers looked up at the girl in the window, whose hands were clutched over her round belly. For a fleeting second, the Widow appeared stricken; then she shook her head and said, "I'm sorry," and led Kate, unresisting, into the woods.

The farmhouse and barn were built on a hilltop, and the thickly forested ground fell away sharply behind it. It was a steep drop, and Kate was forced to crouch in her saddle, digging her fingers into her horse's mane, to keep her seat.

Angela Ferrers took the hill like a steeplechase on home ground. At the bottom was a cider house. The spy tied their horses up behind it and pressed her lips to Kate's ear. "They will loot the house. We can't risk attracting their attention by making for the road now. We must stay hidden until they leave."

From their hiding place Kate could see only the shadows beneath the eaves of the old house. The night was warm, but the cider-tinged air tasted like autumn and the press smelled sharp and metallic: sour apples and damp stone.

Kate listened to the thunder above grow to a crescendo, then die away as the soldiers reached the hilltop. She heard the butt of a pistol hammering on the thick oak door. Then, faster than anyone could have answered, wood splintered, boots pounded over floorboards, glass broke.

This was not supposed to happen here. The Ashcrofts were Quakers. Andrew was dangerously close to being read out of the meeting for his involvement with Congress, but that was just words, men talking in rooms. Peaceful men. Kate's father had taken up arms both for and against the Crown, but Andrew Ashcroft had never raised a hand against man or beast in his life. Soldiers were supposed to protect people like them, not batter down their door in the middle of the night.

Milly screamed.

Kate was moving before she realized it, climbing the hill blindly, scrambling over rotting apples and dead leaves.

It was hard, rocky, useless ground, churned with

twisted roots and steeper here than where she'd descended on horseback, but it didn't matter. She must reach the top. Her hands scrabbled at last over level ground, and she craned her neck to see over the crest of the hill, then froze.

Kate had expected destruction, broken windows and burst cushions, but not this. Milly's husband lay on the ground, bleeding. He was unconscious, and the deep gash across his forehead ran red over his face and nightshirt. His mother, who had listened to Angela Ferrers with girlish delight only that morning, knelt sobbing on the ground beside him.

And Milly was being dragged toward the barn. Her hair was the color of her husband's blood in the torchlight. Her swollen frame was awkward beneath her thin lawn shift. She struggled, impotent as a kitten, against five dragoons in tall bearskin hats. They paid her no heed. She dug her heels into the ground, and they lifted her over their heads and carried her.

Kate opened her mouth to scream, but a hand clapped over it, and a heavy weight landed on her back, pressing her down into the carpet of dead leaves. Then Angela Ferrers rolled them down the hill and out of sight.

They came to a stop in the hollow of a broken tree. The Widow's voice was an icy whisper. "There are a dozen dragoons up there. Trained soldiers. We are two women, with only one weapon between us. Even if you overcame your pacifism, we could not prevail by force of arms. There are other ways to fight, but here and now, you cannot stop what is happening to her. Rape is not fatal. There is no such thing as a fate worse than death. If they found us here with these papers, Milly and her husband would hang with us."

The door closed on Milly, and the screams turned to sobbing. Kate shut out the other sounds, guttural and grotesque. It went on for longer than she thought possible. Then the barn door sighed open on its Quakerly, well-oiled hinges. There was more shouting, and the sound of men mounting up, hooves plowing the earth and fading into the distance, and finally silence.

Kate waited in the quiet dark until Angela Ferrers released her. She climbed to the top of the hill once more and looked out. The garden was trampled and littered with broken crockery and glass. They'd tossed furniture through the upstairs windows, chairs and books and Milly's sewing table and the cradle Andrew had carved and painted just that summer. There was no sign of Milly, or her mother-in-law, or Andrew Ashcroft.

"They'll take him to jail in Philadelphia," Angela Ferrers said. "His mother was wise to go with them. She can petition Howe for his release."

"And Milly?" Kate asked, though she did not want to hear the answer.

"Will serve them on the road until they tire of her."

Kate wanted to be sick, but her stomach was empty and would not oblige her. The barn doors gaped open, so she crossed the moonlit hilltop and pushed one, then the other closed.

There was a carbine leaning against the wall of the barn. It had been hidden behind the open door, the leather straps of the powder horn and the cartridge box looped around the barrel. One of the dragoons must have left it there while he took his turn in the barn. Kate could imagine him, hulking in his bearskin hat and scarlet coat, too busy plundering to realize he'd forgotten his gun. He would be back for it.

She turned to see the Widow staring also. They heard the hoofbeats at the same time, and turned together toward the road. Two dragoons crested the hill and stopped, as surprised to see Kate and Angela Ferrers as the women were to see them. For a moment, no one moved. Then one of the dragoons laughed and the other said something crude, and they spurred their horses and rode hard toward Kate and the Widow.

"Run," Angela Ferrers said quietly.

Kate didn't hesitate. She plunged into the trees behind her and ran tumbling and sliding down the hill. She could hear the dragoons, crashing through the trees, and turned for an instant to look. All she could see were flashes of red and sharp metal glinting in the moonlight. A hand gripped her sleeve and pulled hard and Angela Ferrers said, "Never look back."

They reached the horses, and Kate flew into the saddle. She dug her heels into her beast's flanks. Branches whipped her face, tore at her clothes. She crouched low over her mount as she jumped a broken tree stump and skidded downhill to emerge, after what seemed like an eternity, on the road below the house.

Angela Ferrers was beside her. She flashed Kate a quick, pleased smile, which faded when the dragoons broke through the trees.

"Whatever happens, whatever you hear, *just keep going.*" The Widow spurred her horse to a gallop. Kate followed. She had never ridden so fast. She'd always been a poor horsewoman, but desperation freed a certain

grace. They were swallowing the road in great plunging strides, but still the dragoons came on. And they were closing on them.

She'd been told to ride, but she didn't know how they could possibly outpace professional soldiers on first-class mounts. Or what they would do when the men overtook them. The men who had taken Milly to the barn.

Kate risked a quick glance, and discovered the Widow now had possession of her pistol. Before Kate's amazed eyes, the woman loaded, primed, and cocked the gun in a series of deft, purposeful movements. Difficult to do in the dark. Trickier mounted. Almost impossible on a galloping horse at night. And done in the twinkling of an eye.

Then Angela Ferrers fell back, twisted gracefully in the saddle, and fired.

The first dragoon jerked like a marionette. His gun flew up in the air, spun, and fell to the ground. His horse slowed, and his body, caught fast in the stirrups, bobbed along with it, a cork on the seas.

The second dragoon pulled back on his reins, checking his mount. He was unarmed. The man who'd left his carbine leaning against the barn. His wide eyes followed the ghastly progress of his dying comrade's horse, moved to where Mrs. Ferrers now stood her own mount to reload, flicked over his shoulder to check the route back through the woods.

There was a moment, as the Widow tamped and primed the pistol, when Kate realized she ought to object.

Then the Widow fired. The second dragoon tumbled from his horse to land with a sickening crack on the packed-dirt road.

Then Angela Ferrers was beside her again, galloping into the dark night with the pistol tucked into her saddle. She met Kate's heartsick stare with a level gaze and said, "I told you not to look back."

After that they left the road and cut across country.

Dawn was close when they reached Wilmington. Dead horses were the first indicators of the Continental presence. The smell was the second. Thousands of unwashed men were camped in sorry disarray around the small Dutch-roofed house. Here and there were pockets of order—small, disciplined bands led by commanders with some training or aptitude—but mostly it was chaos, and the contempt in which Peter Tremayne held the American militia appeared well earned.

They were challenged twice. The first sentry had no shoes, the second no shirt. Both times Mrs. Ferrers spoke a password, and they were allowed to continue.

The farmhouse was ancient; men, trestles, maps, and chairs were crowded to the walls of the structure by the massive central chimney. Clerks sat two to a stair on the narrow flight that buttressed the door, hunched over ledgers balanced on their knees. The east side of the house was serving simultaneously as a hospital and a common room, with instruments and bandages heaped together with cooking utensils. Kate stifled her impulse to tidy it.

Mrs. Ferrers kept her hood on, and drew Kate to a corner of the parlor to wait.

A meeting was breaking up in the room next door. Kate studied the men as they filed out. The officers of the Continental Army looked like farmers, merchants, shopkeepers, artisans, and trappers, because that was what they were. Kate recognized the quiet desperation of men who have gone too far down a dangerous path to turn back. If the war went badly, these men would all hang. And so would her father.

The house emptied, became quiet. Then they were summoned.

Sitting before a trestle covered with maps was a man Kate recognized from her father's description, some twenty years out of date. Even seated, he towered over the other man in the room. Washington wore a dark blue velvet suit, well cut but bald at the cuffs and collar. Beside him, a slender, fair-haired youth sat copying orders.

Both men rose when the women entered. Mrs. Ferrers, as Kate was learning, had a theatrical turn of mind. She threw back her hood and laid the packet on the table before the general with a flourish.

The young man closed his book and prepared to leave, but Washington put a hand on his shoulder. "Stay." He nodded to Mrs. Ferrers. "You were successful?" he asked, opening the packet. He scanned each page and passed it to the young man. "Have a look at this, Mr. Hamilton. You were quite right."

"Only partially," Mrs. Ferrers admitted, drawing up a stool and seating herself. Kate followed her example. "Caide didn't come. Peter Tremayne was the courier."

The young man blanched. "Caide is still at large?"

"I'm afraid so, Alex. And there is worse. Howe is arresting members of Congress in secret. We encountered a party of dragoons riding with muffled spurs in the Jerseys, and I am sorry to report that they did not observe the niceties of war."

Kate fought nausea once more as she remembered the sounds coming from the barn. *The niceties of war.*

Washington set the final page down and addressed Mrs. Ferrers. "Have you read this, Angela?"

"Yes. Howe means to invest Philadelphia for the winter. He thinks he can end the war by taking the capital and holding it."

"He has the men to do it, too."

Washington's secretary spoke. "Let the British have Philadelphia. Howe has mistaken a symbolic target for a strategic one. It's not worth risking the army in an open battle."

Washington smiled thinly. "Congress will expect us to make a stand for Philadelphia."

"Then it's a pity they haven't given us the money or the men to do it," replied Hamilton.

"It is a fight we must make all the same." Washington spread a map on the table. Running across the bottom was an engraving of the city as seen from the Jersey side of the river, a forest of steeples, masts, and brick. "Philadelphia lies in the fork of the Delaware and Schuylkill rivers. She is approachable by land only from the north. If we can hold the rivers and the roads to the north, we can cut off Howe's supplies. With no food and no fuel he must surrender his army or march it through the Jerseys, where he has made no friends this past year."

"Philadelphia is not Boston," Hamilton insisted. "There is no high ground on which to mount cannon. We cannot hold the river indefinitely. We don't have the men to defend the forts. Mercer was built for a garrison of more than a thousand, and Mifflin is nearly as large."

Their argument reminded Kate of her own debates with her father. It obviously pained Hamilton to disagree with Washington, but he did it anyway.

"You don't need to hold the river indefinitely," Kate interjected. "Only until it freezes."

"This is Miss Kate Grey, Arthur's daughter," supplied Mrs. Ferrers.

If Washington was surprised by her presence, or her ready grasp of tactics, he didn't show it. "You are correct, Miss Grey."

"Howe will understand the danger. He will do everything in his power to take the river," Hamilton insisted.

"Yes," the general agreed. "That is why we must keep one step ahead of him."

"What of our agent in Boston?" Hamilton asked.

"Still with Howe, but trapped like a fly in amber," Angela Ferrers said. "And I can't get near Howe. His intelligence officer, John André, knows me by sight."

"*Cinaedus*," Hamilton said under his breath. A lover of men, Kate knew, though her knowledge was gleaned from an unusually thorough classical education, and not from hearing the insult hurled. Quakers were not inclined toward oaths or epithets.

Angela Ferrers shrugged. "Whatever else Captain André is, he is a shrewd spymaster. He will be alert to espionage. And unfortunately for us, most of our allies will flee with Congress. Philadelphia will be entirely in the hands of Quakers and Loyalists."

A chair screeched over the floorboards. Kate

realized belatedly that it was hers. "I will go," she said. She said it without thinking, only dimly aware that she had stood up, moved by the same spirit that had called her, only very occasionally in her life, to speak at the meeting.

Washington looked at her closely. "I'm sorry? You will go where, Miss Grey?"

The Widow and Hamilton were watching her as well. Kate wished the spirit had more staying power. She sat back down and turned to Angela Ferrers. "You told me there are other ways to fight, without killing. You said Philadelphia is full of Quakers. I'm a Quaker. I can go to Philadelphia and watch General Howe."

"The Quakers of Philadelphia are not like the country Friends you grew up with," Washington said gently. "Howe's circle is dissolute. His officers drink, gamble, and chase women. Such a task is not something I would ask of any gently raised woman. Mrs. Ferrers is . . . unusual."

"You don't need to ask me. I'm volunteering. Manners and fashion can be learned, like Latin or Greek. No one is born like that. It's all artifice: beauty, and grooming, and fine clothes. I can learn to be like Mrs. Ferrers."

Mrs. Ferrers' flash of annoyance was quickly replaced by amusement. "Yes, I rather think you could," she agreed. "But your father would never consent."

"He thinks I'm at home." It was the truth, but it would lead to a lie, which Reverend Matthis said tarnished the soul. But silver also tarnished from disuse, and after what she had seen tonight, Kate did not think she could keep her soul clean in a cupboard. "My father does not know I am here. Since we arrived in camp, Mrs. Ferrers has not spoken my name outside this room. And if I leave for Philadelphia tonight, my father need never know I was here."

Washington and the Widow exchanged glances. "If you go to Philadelphia and spy on Howe, you will be in constant danger," he warned. "Mrs. Ferrers knows and can tell you that the British will not trouble themselves to try a woman caught spying. They fear losing what popular support they have." Washington looked uncomfortable. "There are other dangers for a woman, as well. You would do well to consider your future, and how it might be altered, your prospects changed by this undertaking."

Kate didn't need to consider. Her mind was made up. Tonight she had glimpsed something of the life she might have led as the lover of a man with a lively intellect and a passionate nature. Circumstances had closed the door on such a connection, almost as soon as it had opened. Tremayne was her enemy, and after what she had seen his countrymen do, she could not think of him otherwise.

"By prospects, you mean marriage. I have none to alter. As for the other dangers you speak of"—she took a deep breath and tried to banish Milly and the dragoons from her mind—"they are as likely to befall me in my home as in Philadelphia. In which case, I would rather meet my enemy by day than find my door battered down in the middle of the night."

"Miss Grey," said Washington, with something approaching amusement, "you have had the great good fortune to inherit all of your father's character, and none of his looks. I am only sorry we have not met before."

"It was an unlikely circumstance while my mother was alive," Kate answered honestly, aware that Washington had come north on business in the past, and her father had been forced to meet him in a tavern. "She would not abide slaveholders in the house."

Angela Ferrers raised her manicured eyebrows. Hamilton looked discreetly away. And Washington stood and bowed. "Fortunately for me, Congress has not the principles of your late good mother. Godspeed you to Philadelphia, Miss Grey." He passed Howe's plans to his secretary. "Copy these and add them to the packet for Congress. It would be a great favor to me if you carried the papers yourself."

"Of course, General," said Hamilton.

She was going. It took a moment to sink in. She would not sleep in her own bed tonight, might not return home for several weeks. She remembered her father's letter, safe now in her pocket. "Will you take this, too, Mr. Hamilton? It's from my father, to Congress."

"Of course." Washington's secretary favored her with a courtly bow and an appraising look. He must think her an unlikely spy, Kate realized.

She drew the letter from her pocket. Dawn light was filtering into the room, and though the paper looked right, the seal was wrong. It was not her father's signet.

She took the letter to the window and broke the seal.

Washington addressed Mrs. Ferrers. "Madame, is there anything you require for your journey?"

"Fresh horses would speed us on our way."

Kate unfolded the single sheet of paper in the envelope. The couplet was Latin, clever and lewd. She laughed out loud at the effrontery of it.

It was signed simply, *Tremayne*.

Four

The Germantown Road, October 8, 1777

Another man would have gone home. Another man, disgraced, demoted, stripped of command and given the choice to rebuild his career from the ground up or retire quietly into private life, would have chosen retirement.

Viscount Sancreed escaped court-martial in New York with his life, but he lost his command and his standing. Caught in a judicial limbo, Peter Tremayne lingered in the city, writing letters of apology to General Howe for losing the man's dispatches, and requests for aid to friends and superiors, in particular Bayard Caide. Caide was one of Howe's favorites, part of the select company who danced, diced, and drank with the general well into the night.

In the end it was Caide who secured his return, intervening with Howe and arranging for Tremayne to become an officer on the general's staff. Tremayne's official duties would consist of discouraging looting in occupied Philadelphia. He had lost his troop, but a staff office was better than languishing in New York.

It was also better than the long trip home to England, which would be full of self-recrimination. He had weighed carefully the alternatives, and it was the prospect of that journey, the long weeks in his cabin, meals in the company of naval officers, noses a-twitch with the scent of scandal, that convinced him to remain and redeem himself if he could.

All this he had considered in New York. Now, six weeks later, in the saddle beside Bayard Caide, patrolling the farms north of Philadelphia, he was beginning to regret his choice. Tremayne had arrived to take up his staff post only last night, and Bay had instantly swept him out for this foraging party in the morning.

Bay, his kinsman, whom he had grown up alongside in Somerset, had been a wild youth. As teens and fellow cavalry officers they had gambled, drunk, and whored their way through London until the army sent Bay to India and Peter to Ireland.

India had done nothing to curb Bay's wildness. He returned from ten years' service under hotter suns with new vices and a high-handed arrogance, tolerated because the Subcontinent had forged him into an officer of extraordinary skill and charisma. Bay insulted his fellow officers, seduced their wives, beat his servants, and was throughout it all utterly and devastatingly charming. His peers envied him. His men loved him, albeit with an affection tempered by fear.

They reined up outside a pretty clapboard farmhouse surrounded by rolling fields of winter wheat and barley. A faint aroma of malt indicated a brewery somewhere on the premises.

"Dyson, find the beer, and some wagons to carry it." Bayard Caide's voice was controlled arrogance, almost musical—that of a man who expected to be heard and obeyed. He slid from his horse with the natural grace he had possessed since boyhood. The wind ruffled his wheat-colored hair, which curled around the collar of his jacket. His eyes, Peter had first noted as a child, were the same pale blue as his own.

He looked up at Tremayne. "Don't go offering to pay for the beer, Peter. Or anything else, for that matter. The brewer is a Rebel, and as such, his property is forfeit."

"How do you tell the Rebels from the Tories, Bay?"

"The Rebel women are prettier." He slapped Tremayne on the back and led him into the stone-walled kitchen.

It was a well-scrubbed and busy room, with an ancient sideboard groaning under the weight of mismatched pottery. The two women standing behind the pitted trestle table were indeed unusually pretty. The older was no more than thirty, and her sleeves dripped with muslin frills and Mechlin lace. The mistress of the house, no doubt. The younger was barely out of her teens, and from her dated skirts and cheap leather stays, she must be the maid.

Caide bowed politely to the lady. "Ma'am."

He reached for her hand, but she stepped back. Her black brows knitted, and an angry flush crept over her fair skin. "What do you want?" she asked.

The maid, more attuned to Bay's mood than her mistress was, sidled toward the low door. Lieutenant

Dyson, a hulking brute from some northern factory town, and just the sort to toady to Bay, appeared in the doorway, cutting off her escape and blocking the light. He advanced, not on the girl but on the kegs racked against the wall.

"Beer, to start with," said Caide, but he wasn't looking at the beer.

The keg nearest the door was already tapped. Dyson turned the handle, and the beer pattered onto the floor and spread over the stone tiles.

"You're no better than thieves," the lady said.

Bay fingered the cord hanging from the clock jack on the mantel, and pulled a sprig of sage out of one of the bundles drying overhead. "Cooperation, second," he said, inhaling the pungent herb, "or perhaps you would rather watch your livelihood run out over the floor?"

Dyson took another tap from a set hanging on the wall, and hammered it into the next keg. The lady flinched at each blow, and the maid began sobbing.

"What will it be?" asked Bayard Caide.

Tremayne barely heard him. The structure possessed none of the classical elegance of Grey House. The woman behind the trestle was not poised or quick-witted, nor did she have pie crumbs in her hair, but the situation reminded him all too much of a Quaker girl he couldn't get out of his head. The room seemed suddenly overpoweringly hot and close.

Caide advanced on the women. "If you are loyal subjects, you will of course want to help His Majesty's trusty servants in any way they might require."

Tremayne knew this preamble all too well. Once, he would have shared in it.

"Excuse me. I think I'll go see to the wagons."

Bay turned, the women forgotten for the moment. "Come on, Peter. It will be just like old times." He scooped a tankard from the sideboard and held it under the spluttering tap, then offered Tremayne the beaker. "And there's beer."

"I find I'm not thirsty." He was parched, but he knew he would choke on that beer, and what would come after it.

Caide shrugged and downed the beaker. "Suit yourself. Dyson, watch the door."

Out in the crisp air, Bay's men were loading wagons with sacks of barley. From inside the farmhouse, Tremayne heard a loud crash. The trestle table, overturned. Then the musical note of a single, fine piece of china dashed against a wall, followed by the deeper chord of a shelf full of earthenware swept to the ground. The curtains rustled, and Tremayne knew that Bay's ugly little drama had reached its climax.

It would have been easier to bear if he had not been guilty of similar indulgences. Certainly, as a young officer he had used his authority to commandeer supplies and other less tangible benefits. He knew all too well how it was done. You put the men to some heavy-lifting task, set a lackey to guard the door, demanded goods or information the locals were unlikely to have, then bargained, and finally threatened, until the line between coercion and force became indistinct.

Before Kate, before Grey Farm, he might have done the same. Hell, *at* Grey Farm, truth be told, he had almost done so. Now, with little sound coming from the ravaged kitchen, all Tremayne could picture was Kate, plain, disheveled, disarmingly clever Kate, at

the mercy of someone like Caide, at the mercy of someone like himself. He felt sick.

He must have looked it, too. Caide emerged some
time later, stooping from the low batten door, and
rolled his eyes at Tremayne. "Developing a conscience,
Peter? It won't do you any good in this war. Dyson,"
Bay called to the lieutenant idling beside the door.
"Your turn." Dyson smiled his vicious, heavy-lidded
smile and ducked into the kitchen. There was no noise
this time.

"These people," Caide said, turning his attention
back to Tremayne, "won't give up until they've been
taught a lesson. You've said so yourself."

"Yes," Tremayne said, placing his foot in his stir-
rup. "Only I'm not so certain of the pedagogy anymore." Mounted on his horse, he continued. "Anyway,
I thought you recently became engaged to some gilded
Tory heiress. What do you need farmers' wives for?"

"Ah, well, that's just the thing. I need farmers'
wives because I am engaged to the most dazzling creature in Philadelphia. And once married, I swear to you,
I shall cleave to her bosom and forsake all others. But
until then all she does is tease and leave me with an itch
that needs scratching."

"Clearly your reputation has been slow to reach
Philadelphia. I can't think of a respectable matron in
London who would allow you to marry her daughter."

"Well, fortunately, Lydia's mother is *respectably*
dead. And her father's at sea. Sumatra way. Making a
fortune in pepper or some such thing."

"You'd be wise to marry her before the blockade
is lifted and her father gets a look at you," Tremayne
advised.

"The thing is all sewn up. Aunt and uncle wrote to her father for consent. We're to be married in the spring. Only waiting for her father's return. Howe's brother will issue a pass so he can land."

"With his fortune in pepper."

"I'd take her with two pecks of pepper. She's magnificent. Chestnut hair like silk. Eyes so dark they're almost black. Skin like new snow."

"If the thing is all sewn up," Tremayne reasoned, "then there should be nothing to stop you from scratching your itch with her."

"No. I'd like to, and I daresay she'd let me, but no. In this, if in nothing else in my life, I'm determined to do the thing properly. I won't bring my bride to the altar in an embarrassing condition, or my children into the world with questionable legitimacy."

Tremayne couldn't argue with that. "What if she's frigid?" he prompted.

Caide cast a sly glance at Tremayne. "I said I haven't bedded her. I didn't say I haven't sampled the vintage. In company, she's a picture of grace and manners. In private, she's got a wild streak a mile wide. She's *perfect*."

"For you, certainly," Tremayne replied. "I wouldn't wish an innocent girl tied to you for life."

"That makes two of us, cousin."

They reached Germantown at dusk, where Howe was still encamped with the bulk of the army. "I'm for a glass of whisky and bed," Tremayne said. He was staying with Caide until he could find his own lodgings in the city. He hoped that Philadelphia would prove more welcoming. Whatever the feelings of the people of Germantown had been before their home became a battlefield, they wanted the British gone now. The pretty stone houses that had once lined Main Street were shot to pieces. Blood spatters stained the remnants of the whitewashed fences and window shutters, and yards were littered with blood-caked doors, called into service as makeshift operating tables after the carnage, and abandoned, indelible with gore, in the aftermath.

"No. You're for a game of cards with Black Billy. He wants to see you."

Tremayne dreaded meeting Howe. "Liar. He didn't answer any of my letters. He's only put me on his staff to keep you happy."

"Not so. He has a job for you."

"Mucking out his stable, most likely."

Caide laughed. "Whatever task he appoints you, you'll do it and like it, or you'll never see a command again."

Whatever penance Howe had in mind was likely to be far nastier than cleaning stables. The worst part was that Caide was right. Tremayne would never see command again in this theater if he failed to please Howe.

Which was why he found himself, boots polished, braid glimmering, hair tied neatly at the back of his neck, at the doors of the elegant little manse Howe had appropriated for himself. Light blazed from every bullet-riddled window, and the thick, waxy smell of expensive candles and pricier scent met him in a wave of heat at the door.

Bayard Caide was in his element here among the crowded tables of cardplayers, the impromptu boxing matches, the dicing, and, in the shadowy corners, the illicit couplings with Philadelphia's Tory daughters.

Or wives, in the case of General Howe. Tremayne found him holding court at a table littered with punch glasses, broken pipes, and discarded dice. Mrs. Loring, his mistress, resplendent in teal silk, sat beside him, her husband nowhere in evidence.

"The prodigal returns, Major Tremayne." Howe rose from the table to clap Tremayne heartily on the back. "You'll have to be on your guard here. Philadelphia has no shortage of beautiful American women." A young girl at Howe's table, too young, probably, to be out with this company, blushed prettily. "And I'm certain at least half of them are spies." He turned to his mistress. "Viscount Sancreed here was beguiled by the Merry Widow."

Mrs. Loring pursed her lips in distaste. "Really, Major. I would have thought that woman was growing too long in the tooth to beguile any man."

"The Merry Widow?" Tremayne inquired politely, feeling for the letter in his breast pocket, folded beside the ribbon.

Howe smiled sourly. "Your mystery lady, Major, is a notorious agent. The French used to pay her to stir up trouble in Ireland. I believe she was calling herself Ferrers when you met her."

Tremayne had heard all of this before in New York, and wished desperately to change the subject, but Mrs. Loring was enjoying herself. "Hessians, of course, prefer their women coarse."

"Yes," he confirmed. "Mrs. Ferrers is how she styled herself. A Quaker lady." During his court-martial, he had omitted entirely the presence of a young woman in the house, and had never once uttered the name Kate Grey. The letter in his breast pocket revealed her to be a Rebel. She was a traitor, and a spy, and she had destroyed his career. And against all reason, he still wanted her.

"Come now, Peter," the general said, and led him out of the room and into a spacious parlor where the carpets were rolled back and a boxing match was taking place. "I have a job for you."

The combatants fought barefoot, their breeches rolled up, shirts discarded. Whatever business Howe wished to transact was clearly secondary to laying his bet. "Three crowns on André," he said, placing his wager and nodding at the swarthy black-haired man, whose footwork was better than his punches. He was fighting a larger, slower man, but they were well matched. André was faster, more agile, but the bigger man was more powerful.

"What sort of job, sir?" Tremayne asked, attempting to recapture Howe's attention.

"Two jobs, in fact."

The bigger man landed a blow, and André went down, but only for a moment. He rose back up like a buoy, with a wicked smile and a glint in his eye. He would have a black eye in the morning.

Something told Tremayne that André did not take kindly to being bested. In his next move, he proved Tremayne right. With speed and grace, he executed a series of dirty maneuvers just clean enough to be allowable, but ungentlemanly all the same, bringing his opponent down in a bloody heap on the boards. It was, reflected Tremayne, exactly what he would have done.

André collected a tidy pile of winnings, and a simpering blonde slipped his shirt over his shoulders.

"Good man," Howe opined, collecting his own

winnings, Tremayne, and André, and heading out onto the terrace and into the cool night air. Steam rose off André's glistening chest. "Captain André here has need of you, Peter."

Dirtier than cleaning the stables. On the surface, Captain André was a staff officer and charming dilettante, his name already connected with several of the town's Tory daughters, most often with the notorious Peggies: Shippen and Chew, though Shippen was said to be the odds-on favorite. No doubt they were charmed by the ambitious Huguenot's gallant manner and exotic good looks; his coal black hair and gold-flecked hazel eyes. His dress and manner, no doubt learned during his education in Geneva, were altogether impeccable. Few would guess he was the son of a middling Huguenot merchant.

But his brother officers knew André as a hardened veteran of the siege of Fort St. John. He'd spent nearly a year in captivity after the garrison surrendered, and came away from the experience with a bitter dislike of Americans. Those within Howe's close circle knew him better as a calculating and ambitious spymaster who would stop at nothing to further himself.

"You can identify the Merry Widow," Howe explained to Tremayne.

Tremayne didn't like where this was going, and fought against the urge to touch the letter and the ribbon concealed in his breast pocket.

André drained the glass of punch he was holding and fixed his remarkable gold-flecked eyes on Tremayne. "Mrs. Ferrers won't come near us, Lord Sancreed, because I can identify her. She's working through someone else. We need a name."

Kate. Her name was Kate. And she was false, ruinously false, duplicitous and beguiling. "I'm not certain I can help you. I wouldn't know the first thing about ferreting out a spy."

"That is unfortunate." General Howe sounded disappointed. "Do you know what chevaux-de-frise are, Major?"

"Frisian horses. Some kind of river fortification," Tremayne ventured. He was a soldier, not a sailor.

"An incredibly nasty bit of business," Howe replied. "Pine boxes thirty feet square and weighted with stone, topped with iron pikes. Float 'em downriver, sink 'em, and no ship can pass without exact knowledge of their locations."

"*Our* ships cannot pass," supplied André. "Philadelphia is a trap fast closing around us. The Rebels control the roads to the north. We are surrounded by water on the south, east, and west. We must have the Schuylkill and the Delaware or we cannot supply the city. Washington hopes to starve us out of Philadelphia and force a winter march on us."

Howe downed his beaker of punch in a single draught. "The chevaux-de-frise protect the approaches to Rebel forts Mercer and Mifflin—if we attempt to bring our ships with their naval cannon into range of the forts, they will be holed and sunk. And if we attempt to move the chevaux-de-frise, our craft will be blown to flinders by the long gun batteries in the forts. My brother, the admiral, has four frigates loaded with supplies sitting idle in the Delaware. He cannot reach us." Almost as an afterthought, Howe added, "Colonel Donop has offered to lead a land assault on Mercer."

Donop. The Hessian colonel beguiled and disgraced by the Merry Widow—Mrs. Ferrers—at Mount Holly. The man had lingered there for three days, enjoying the lady's favors, when he might have brought his men to reinforce Trenton. The dalliance let Washington slip across the Delaware on Christmas and take the town. The capture of Trenton and of Colonel Rall's garrison of a thousand Hessians and their field artillery had been disastrous, and had all but destroyed Donop's reputation.

"Well, he would, wouldn't he?" André said, hardly troubling to disguise his contempt.

"I won't allow it until there is no other recourse," Howe barked. "It's throwing away lives to attack by land if we can't bring our ships to bear on the fort at the same time."

"Hessian lives," added André, as though these were of less consequence.

"How can I be of help?" Tremayne asked. "I'm no sailor, and I'm no engineer."

"Washington has anticipated our every move against his river fortifications, rushing reinforcements to our exact points of attack. Mrs. Ferrers is here, supplying him with information. I require you to find her, and deal with her."

"Quietly," added André.

"I see." Tremayne bristled. "You wish me to be an assassin?"

"Not at all. We wish you"—André began to tie his cravat—"to discover Mrs. Ferrers and her agents. When you do so, you will be returned to command. I will do the rest."

"It's a generous offer," Tremayne conceded. "May I think about it?"

"No." Howe had lost all trace of avuncular jollity. "We are a month away from being starved out of the city, Major. Do you know what would happen to this army if we had to march twenty thousand men and another five thousand loyal civilians through Rebel territory to New York? It would be a slaughter. Mrs. Ferrers is in Philadelphia. It is your duty to find her and lead us to her. The woman almost ruined you. You need have no gentlemanly scruples in this matter. Her capture and . . . removal . . . are of the utmost importance to me. Is that clear?"

It was. All too clear. "Yes, sir. Thank you, sir."

"Good!" Howe seemed his merry self again. He led Tremayne back into the house, where the petite blonde reappeared and attached herself to Captain André like a limpet. "Now, for the other matter I spoke of. You and Bayard Caide are cousins, I believe."

Tremayne made no effort to clarify the relationship. They were, in the eyes of the law, cousins. What else they might be was a source of speculation and gossip for London society. Viewed from a certain angle, the two men looked more alike than cousins.

"Yes. We grew up together."

"He's always been wild," Howe added, as the man they were discussing came into view, wrestling with a fellow officer on the cold marble floor of the carved and painted foyer, beneath the wide and elegant curved staircase.

"Yes," Tremayne agreed.

"Wild is to be expected. Milkmaids don't win

battles. But cruel we cannot tolerate. We are losing the people." Howe gestured at the crowd with his wineglass. "Don't be fooled by the fops who have attached themselves to the army. This is a country of dour Quakers and Puritan farmers. His ruthlessness has come in handy at times, but he's a blunt instrument. His raids are stirring up sentiment against us, and we have precious little goodwill here. If we do have to evacuate the city, you can be sure the locals will not forgive us your cousin's actions."

"What would you like me to do?" Tremayne thought back on all the years of his childhood spent covering for Bay. For the girls he ruined, the fights he got into, the servants he beat. And his mind turned inevitably to the farmhouse today . . .

"I like Caide. I don't want to come down hard on him. Just get him to the altar as fast as you can. His fiancée's a lovely little thing. Maybe marriage will tame him."

Not, reflected Tremayne, if the girl was as described—a nascent sybarite with a wild streak to match Caide's own.

"Ah!" Howe exclaimed, looking up at the head of the stairs. "Here she is now."

The girl descending the stairs was everything Tremayne had expected. Her hair was elaborately curled and piled high on her head. Her brows were artfully plucked and tinted to set off dark, painted eyes. She wore no powder, because her skin was as white as milk already. She wore a diamond on a velvet ribbon around her neck, dyed to match the pale blue of her gown, which plunged to a perilously low square neckline. Her skirts were hemmed to show a daring amount of ankle, and from her wrist dangled a painted fan. An artful, useless creature, of the sort Tremayne found most distasteful: powdered, plucked, and primped, and choked and cuffed with pearls like pigeon's eggs. Everything from her brocade pumps to her plunging neckline spoke of citified sophistication and coquetry.

Worst of all, the girl was Kate.

Five

The girl who had accompanied Angela Ferrers to Washington's headquarters six weeks ago would have stopped dead in her tracks at the sight of Peter Tremayne. The coquette who emerged from Mrs. Ferrers' crucible of artifice and subterfuge might only have dropped her fan, and recovered nicely by the time her silk-shod feet touched the marble floor.

The woman who had survived a month in the decadent salons of occupied Philadelphia, and captured the affections of its most louche scion, betrayed her surprise to only two men in the room, and Peter Tremayne alone had the knowledge to interpret the flash of panic in her kohl-rimmed eyes.

Caide broke off from his match to down a beaker of punch and sweep the girl into his sweaty arms. She forestalled his too-intimate embrace, turning lithely to offer Peter Tremayne her hand. "Who is this, Bay?" she asked, as though she had never set eyes on Tremayne before.

Caide released her and bowed. "Peter, may I present my fiancée, Miss Dare."

"Lydia," Kate supplied, looking him steadily in the eye and challenging him to say different.

He took the hand offered, which for six tortured weeks he had desperately wished to possess again, as Caide completed their introduction. "Lydia, my heart, my love, my joy, may I present my cousin, Major Peter Tremayne, Viscount Sancreed."

Tremayne planted his kiss lightly on her stiff fingers and released her arm to fall like an unstrung marionette at her side. Caide was too drunk and excited to notice.

"Don't you know, Bay? We've met before," Tremayne said.

Again the flicker behind her eyes, which only he could read.

"Where was that, Major?" She covered her fear with a flourish of her gilded fan.

"Boston, I believe," he said, careful to choose a city Bay had never visited.

Caide, now deep in his cups, was oblivious to the charged environment. "Never been there. Full of filthy Rebels." He slipped his arms around Kate from behind and drew her back flush against him, burying his face in her elegantly mounded hair.

It was a gesture Tremayne had seen before. When they were boys, Bay was fiercely attached to his mother. He would flee to her for protection from their outraged tutor, or Tremayne's father, whichever one had caught them at their latest exploit. Bay would wrap his arms around her, nestle his cheek against her shoulder in the curls of her wheat-colored hair, and beg her to intercede for them.

But the hands now clasped around Kate's waist were the same hands that had held the farmer's wife down that morning, in the pretty clapboard house with the stone-walled kitchen.

"Bay," she murmured in his ear, "I'm tired. I want to find Peggy's mother and go home."

"No, you mustn't go." He released her and swung her round him like a child. "Peter's only just arrived. And I've promised Robert a rematch."

"There will be other nights."

"I'll take her to find her chaperone," Tremayne offered. "I've had enough carousing myself."

Caide rolled his eyes at his cousin, as he had done since they were twelve and he first began cajoling Tremayne into wilder and wilder adventures. "My cousin, the Puritan." Bayard pulled Kate to him and kissed her possessively, then turned to Tremayne. "Off you go, then. Take her and join the other women."

Kate faced a dilemma. To remain was to risk exposure: public, devastating, deadly. To be left alone with Tremayne put her at equal risk. She had ruined his life. He might do anything.

When in doubt, Kate reflected, go on the offensive. "I believe the last time we met I asked you to deliver a letter for me, Major Tremayne."

"Yes. I'm sorry. I still have it." He touched the breast of his tunic, indicating the presence of the letter. "I'm afraid I was forced to open it, when I couldn't determine its direction." His manner was genial, courteous.

This time she used her fan to hide her face from him, flicking the rice paper and rosewood open with a practiced gesture. "It's nothing but old news now, I expect. I shall take it back." She struggled to sound as languidly disinterested as he did, and dared to hope for a moment that he might indeed return her father's letter.

"On the contrary. I found it very illuminating." He offered her his arm instead, and Kate took it. She had learned from Mrs. Ferrers to distrust the timbre of a man's voice, the set of his shoulders, how he used his hands. All these could be schooled, controlled, practiced. The eyes, though, rarely lied.

Peter Tremayne had mastery over his voice. His posture was relaxed, his hands moth-light upon her arm. But his eyes were cold.

"Really? Did others find it so?" Kate risked a quick glance at her fiancé, already to grips with his opponent, a circle of gamblers surrounding the match, as Tremayne led her from the room.

"Let's find your chaperone, shall we?" His grip was light but firm. She had no choice but to follow.

She paid little attention to the direction he took until a short, sharp tug pulled her out of the crowded hall and into a darkened room. The chamber was tiny, barely big enough for the two of them. Tremayne threw back the shutters, flooding the room with moonlight.

"Hello, Kate," he said, his bitterness unmasked. "Or is it Lydia? I should have guessed. The heroine in Lytton's awful play."

"Lydia is my middle name. I'm Katherine Lydia—"

"Grey." He cut her off. "Yes. I know. I read your

father's letter to Congress. You are the daughter of Arthur Grey. The Grey Fox. An old friend of Washington's, and now one of his most trusted commanders."

"I thought I would never see you again." She attempted to keep all emotion out of her voice.

"You certainly saw to it that my return to Philadelphia was unlikely."

"I thought you would be court-martialed," she explained.

"I was, thank you. My cousin interceded for me. Damn it, Kate. Who the hell are you? The farm girl, or this . . . bird of paradise . . . who would marry a man like Bayard Caide?"

"He's your cousin."

"Yes, and I probably know him better than any living man. I can tell you that he is no fit husband for a woman like Kate Grey. But for this creature I see before me, he may be very fit indeed."

He was angry, as Kate had never seen a man angry. Mrs. Ferrers had been right to bring her away that night.

"Will you expose me?"

"We had a bargain." He spat the words. "The letter in exchange for your company."

"You never gave me the letter."

"You and your aunt laid a trap for me."

"Not for *you*." It came out before she could stop herself. She could no longer control her emotions, so she turned away from him. The room was so small and he was so close that when he spoke, she could feel his breath on the back of her neck.

"No. Not for me. For Bay. You wanted Bay. And now you have him." His disgust was palpable. He grasped her shoulders and turned her roughly around. "You claim to be a Quaker, a pacifist."

"I am."

"The intelligence you are feeding to Washington will starve this city and compel twenty thousand men and God knows how many women and children on a forced march through hostile territory."

"Yes. A forced march. Not a pitched battle. An evacuation, not a bloodbath."

"You're deluding yourself if you think there won't be blood on your hands. Do you have any idea what it would be like to march this army and its followers through the Jerseys in winter? Thousands will die. Civilians first, make no mistake. Women and children certainly. But armies don't lie down and die on the road. They'll cut a bloody swath through your blueberry and rye fields and make no distinction between Rebels and Tories before the end. And still, they will die."

She shut the images out of her mind. "No. It won't be like that. Howe won't leave it too late. If he goes before the ground freezes, he can make it to New York. There doesn't have to be any killing."

"Good God, you really believe that, don't you?"

"Yes."

He laughed then, but there was no humor in it, and she realized his patience had snapped. He advanced on her, backing her against the wall. "Howe offered me my troop, my career, my honor back if I brought him the spy in his midst. If I brought him you."

She was trapped. Her heart pounded. "What are you going to do?"

"That depends on you."

"I'm not a whore."

"You're a spy. In a woman, they are one and the same. My cousin pays you, unwittingly, in secrets. I'll pay you in silence."

And he kissed her. Openmouthed, aggressive, demanding. So different from his coaxing kiss at Grey Farm. But still him. And still her. So she met the challenges he made with his tongue, his lips, his teeth, and returned the startled look in his eyes when he lifted his head and showed himself to be as much affected as she was.

But bitter. "Very nice. What else has Bay taught you?" He reached for her skirts and gathered the silk in greedy handfuls.

She wrenched it back and glared at him. "If you intended some sordid coupling in this closet, I'm sorry to disappoint you."

"You, madame," he replied, taking a deep breath and composing himself, "are a lying bitch. You want me as much as I want you."

"I want independence more."

"You are a fanatic."

"No doubt fanatical whores are a new experience for you."

"Yes, the common ones lack all conviction. Speaking of which, where is your dear aunt?"

"New York, I think."

"A pity. Because I must deliver up a spy to Howe, and Aunt Angela would have done nicely."

She tried to get past him. He put his arm out, barring her way.

"The price of my silence is not negotiable."

"The letter. Give me the letter as a token of good faith, and I shall consider your demand."

He reached inside his jacket, but he did not produce her letter. Instead, he drew forth a shabby filament of embroidered silk. It was the ribbon he had torn from her bodice at Grey Farm.

"You may think me cruel, Kate, but the man on your trail is crueler. André knows Mrs. Ferrers is in the city. He is, at the moment, unaware of your existence."

She stared at the tattered ribbon in Tremayne's fingers. "You didn't tell them about me? At the court-martial?"

His lips twisted into a smirk. "Neither then in New York, nor just now with the general."

But he had not been the only witness to her actions at Grey Farm. "What of Lytton and your other officers?" she asked.

"They were not required to testify. I took full responsibility for the loss of the dispatches. Do not mistake self-interest for chivalry. It is one thing to be tricked by a notorious temptress and spy. It's quite another to be duped by a farm girl. Give me Mrs. Ferrers, and I will protect you."

"But you *were* duped by the farm girl, and you *did* want her."

He tucked the ribbon back into the breast of his tunic and turned to go, then paused on the threshold. "I still want her, Kate, but I can make do with the whore instead."

Six

He left, slamming the door behind him. Kate found
her own way to the stables, and called for her own carriage, pausing only to dispatch a message for her chaperone pleading sudden illness. She was stopped, twice,
by acquaintances attempting to cajole her into staying,
but she put them off deftly. From the time she left
the room to the moment the carriage door closed, her
public mask never once slipped.

Kate had arrived in Philadelphia at the end of
August, shortly before Howe's army, her fictitious
identity already carefully established by Mrs. Ferrers'
agents. She posed as the cherished niece of a childless
merchant couple. The couple, selected by Mrs. Ferrers,
was real enough. The Valbys dealt in lumber. They'd
kept their politics to themselves in the early days of the
war, and had provided a steady stream of useful, albeit
low-level, intelligence to the Rebels since the capture
of the city. Since they were too old and too staid to run

with Howe's fast set, their respectability established Kate's own.

Kate was not wholly unsuited to the role of heiress. Though rural Quakers, her parents had shared an inquisitive turn of mind and desired Kate to have all the advantages of both a practical and a feminine education. From her mother she had learned Latin, French, and Greek, and from her father, geometry and history, and his own passion, tactics. For the feminine accomplishments, the Greys had employed, briefly, a drawing master, a needlewoman, and a music teacher. Drawing and needlework were unmitigated disasters. Music was Kate's only success.

To this pedagogy Mrs. Ferrers had added tutelage in subterfuge and espionage, for which Kate displayed an affinity and talent. She taught Kate how to encipher messages, apply paper masques, and mix invisible inks; to conceal scraps of paper inside a button; and to lie with a honeyed tongue.

These were the arts of the spy, whom the Ancients considered the most despicable of men, the snake in the grass. In this case, Kate reflected, the snake came in chintz, voile, and silk. Her entire wardrobe had previously consisted of two sets of practical stays in cotton canvas and her mother's sturdy hand-me-downs. Now she possessed two painted chests filled with gowns selected and fitted by the Widow. For a Quaker girl raised to "keep out of the vain fashions of the world," it was like donning the costume of an exotic nation: Kate Grey, Princess of Abyssinia.

"You have good eyes, good bones, but your neck is too long for your height, your shoulders over-broad, your waist too low," Mrs. Ferrers dictated, as Kate stood stiffly before the dressmaker's mirror, pins like porcupine quills bristling over the unfinished gown. "The Greeks understood proportion. They sculpted ideals." She gestured as she spoke. "The shoulders so far apart, the waist, so high, the neck so long.

"So we bring the waist up here, the shoulders in here, and"—the seamstress pinned furiously to carry out Mrs. Ferrers' bidding—"the cuffs up here . . . and we use color, shape, and light to fool the eye."

The final result, Kate was forced to admit, was striking.

Bayard Caide had agreed.

She had not set out to snare Caide. Before Cornwallis invested the city with his advance guard of three thousand men on September 26, her goal had been to cultivate the Tory daughters of the town. It was they, Mrs. Ferrers advised her, who would have access to the most freely spoken military gossip. It was they who would flirt daily with Howe's officers in the salons, parlors, and coffeehouses. Her goal must be to become one of the decorative, simpering girls privy to the military gossip bandied so casually about by the general's men: to become invisible.

Befriending the ubiquitous Peggy Shippen was not difficult. Kate had encountered door latches with more personality, broader interests, and deeper discernment. It was easy to practice Mrs. Ferrers' tactics on the seventeen-year-old girl: to listen more than speak, to ask flattering questions, to feign excited interest. It had not worked on Peter Tremayne, but it was balm to the spirit of a spoiled creature like the Shippen girl.

Once established as Peggy's boon companion, Kate

went everywhere: to the lunches, whose groaning boards turned her stomach when she thought of Washington's starving army; to the violent games and races designed to keep the soldiery out of trouble; to the genteel concerts hosted in the assembly houses.

Respectable girls like Peggy and Kate, however, were not invited to the private parties Howe threw with the pretty but married Mrs. Loring by his side. Only girls engaged or married to officers attended such events.

At first, Kate's presence went unremarked. Her fictitious wealth and very real allure were not extraordinary among the loyalist families who had sought refuge in Philadelphia. She was, as she had hoped, invisible. Until she opened her mouth.

It was the chessboard that attracted her attention, on that gray and rainy afternoon. Peggy Shippen was prattling on about the handsome, but to Kate's mind dangerous, Captain André, as the girls moved through the crowded rooms of the fashionable City Tavern. Half the high command had drifted to the elegant redbrick building to play cards, drink tea, and fight boredom.

She noticed the board, and the fatal move that would follow, before she noticed the sandy-haired man playing opposite André. Her dislike of the remarkably handsome captain with his coal black hair and gold-flecked eyes, instant and irrational, had been formed the day before, when she'd seen him manipulate Peggy Shippen as skillfully as she herself did. Maybe more so.

Malice got the better of Kate, and she came to the aid of André's opponent. "If you move your rook, you'll be in check in two," she said.

The man's hand had been hovering over the piece. Without turning, he spoke. "I had been attempting to advance my pawn to the end of the board, to make it my queen."

He turned. She noted the full lips, the eyes of star-tling, cold, familiar blue, and the pointed, almost feral jaw. "But now"—he stood up and took Kate's hand—"I have eyes for no other woman."

Kate did not blush. For a fleeting moment, she looked into this man's eyes, and her mind was filled with Peter Tremayne. Then the illusion passed. The two men could not be more different. Except for their eyes. "Perhaps that's why you play so badly. You don't spend enough time looking at the board."

André snickered, but his fair-haired opponent only cocked his head at Kate.

"American women defeat me utterly," he said. "Pray God the Rebels never throw any of their ladies against us, or the Colonies are lost."

"If your brother officers are as charming, all they need do is coax the women from the field," Kate said, and meant it. There was something about the man's swagger, his unassailable confidence, the fact that he had turned to his advantage a barb that might other-wise have humiliated him in front of another man, that intrigued Kate. Until André spoke.

"Leave off, Bay. Miss Dare isn't commanding an army at the moment. Make your move."

Bay. Bayard Caide. She felt suddenly light-headed. Caide touched her hand to his lips. "I will see you in the field, Miss Dare."

Kate, aware that this was as close to fainting as she had ever been in her life, took Peggy Shippen's arm in what appeared to be a display of sisterly affection. Peggy giggled and led her from the room. Kate could barely hear her.

"Rich. Richer than either of us. I've heard he amassed a fortune in India. I think he's a baronet. That would make you a lady. They say he's slept with half the women in London, sometimes with more than one at a time, though I'm not sure how that would work. He's almost as good-looking as André."

"Peggy, let's have a cup of tea."

"Tea. Yes, tea. Mrs. Curran says there'll be no more by the end of winter, that we're already really drinking the powder out of the soldiers' pockets. Then we'll all have to drink chocolate, like the Rebels."

The next day Kate took her easel, her paints, and her appalling lack of artistic talent to the square in front of the old Third Street Barracks where the Regulars drilled. Peggy Shippen accompanied her, complaining ceaselessly about the cold.

Shortly after noon, Caide appeared, in company again with Captain André. "The result might be somewhat improved if you spent more time looking at the canvas," Bayard Caide opined, standing over Kate's easel with a critical eye.

She stepped back from her work. "It looks better from a distance."

"Really?" Caide asked, taking another step back. "How far do you suggest? Boston?"

"I suppose you can do better?"

"It's really a subject for charcoal, anyway." Caide

picked up the sketchbook lying on the grass, selected a crayon, and sat cross-legged on the ground.

Kate settled opposite him with the drilling soldiery at her back. Watching him, she couldn't help but think of Peter Tremayne, of the intensity of his gaze that night in her bedroom, and later, when he plucked the ribbon from her bodice. Bayard Caide brought that same focus to the blank page.

He handed the tablet back to her.

Bayard Caide had drawn her. Not as she sat, swaddled in a heavy wool cape with her back to the marching men in red, but in the guise of a classical goddess. One of the more carnally minded ones. Beneath the few strokes delineating, for decency's sake, wisps of drapery, were the contours of her body as it rested on the sloping ground. But her attitude was subtly altered, more languid and sensual. This was in keeping with the company surrounding her on the page: satyrs and nymphs drilled in formation in the background.

Kate blushed. "Howe's men," she punned, "have never looked so Martial."

"My goodness, Miss Dare, did your tutor forget to lock away the dirtier epigrams?"

"My mother, actually. She had a great affection for the lustier Roman poets. May I keep this?"

"Of course. Although I would hesitate to display it in gentle company," Caide said, riffling through her paint box. "Would you like me to color it in for you?"

"I'm not certain I've brought enough pink for all the nipples."

He laughed out loud. "You might show it to your friend Peggy. She seems like the sort who might benefit from a diagram." He pitched his voice only to Kate, but there was no need. Peggy and André were strolling the other side of the square, Peggy's shrill laughter the only noise capable of carrying so far. "And André is no schoolmaster," he added.

"No, he's not," agreed Kate.

"I'm partial to oil myself, but pastels will do," he said, rummaging through her supplies. "Good paint is damned hard to come by in this Puritan backwater, mind you. Don't you like André?"

"No. I don't like him."

"Good God. A gently bred lady with an opinion. You're not supposed to have them, or didn't anyone tell you?" Caide selected several colors, including pink, and set to tinting the sketch.

"I thought we were allowed opinions on bonnets, ribbons, and bows."

"Well, do you like *them*?"

"I've developed a recent affection for them. André manipulates Peggy. He's not in love with her," Kate observed, watching Caide's hands move over the drawing.

"How can you tell, Miss Dare, when a man is in love?" He used the pads of his fingers to blend the colors.

"I think," said Kate, remembering evenings in Grey House when her mother was alive, "that when two people are in love, they pay each other the compliment of honesty. Like my parents. I never once heard my father enthuse about my mother's eyelashes, but they shared everything with each other. My father would relate some story he read in the *Gazette*, and my mother would tell him some goings-on among the neighbors and then one of them would connect it to a story from scripture or a tale among the Ancients and before you knew it they'd spun some theory out of whole cloth that explained the weather, the new taxes, and the fall of the Roman Empire all in one."

"So I mustn't speak of eyelashes if I'm to win your affection?" Caide teased.

"I really wish you wouldn't."

"Win your affection or speak of eyelashes?"

It was the first of many meetings. And like all Kate's activities in the City of Brotherly Love, it fed the river of information that flowed through her to Washington. She might be appallingly bad at sketching, but she was exceedingly good at counting. She committed to memory the number and types of soldiers drilling in the yard, both Hessians and Regulars, and noted the sizes and positions of their guns.

She did not meet more than once a week with the Widow and could not, of course, record such matters in straightforward letters to Hamilton. Howe was no fool. All of the post leaving the city was monitored. And even the best cipher, if used too frequently, could be broken. So she followed the protocol that she and Hamilton had established between them for their clandestine correspondence. She drafted a letter to "cousin Sally" in the country. She used a paper mask, a stencil of a bird in flight, laid atop the smooth cream bond. Hamilton possessed its twin. Inside the lines she wrote her true message. She thought of these words as the underpinnings, the petticoat and stays of her report. Then she removed the stencil and dressed the words in a frothy nonsense about balls and recitals and engagements. Hamilton had only to place his mask over the missive to read between the lines and the message would be clear.

Kate returned the next day to discover Bayard Caide and his easel occupying what she thought of as her spot. "You can't paint worth a damn," he told her when she pointed out that he had usurped her, "but you've got an excellent eye for composition. And light. This spot is perfect."

"Yes, but it's *my* spot," Kate insisted.

"There's plenty of room," he drawled. "You can set up next to me."

"I can't. People will say you are courting me."

"Am I?"

"Are you what, Colonel?"

"Courting you?"

"I suppose that depends on whether you come back tomorrow."

He did. And the day after.

He made an ill-starred attempt to tutor her on the finer points of painting, and learned what better-paid pedagogues had discovered before him: she was hopeless.

"I've seen better efforts from twelve-year-olds," he critiqued, as she attempted to draw the church steeple—and several of Howe's gun placements that happened to be in the foreground.

"I won't inquire as to circumstances. In any case, I'm doing my best," she said, knowing that her best was awful.

"Here," he said, and came to stand behind her, close enough that she could feel his breath on the back of her neck. He took her right hand in his. "Take your thumb and forefinger, like so, and look through them. Now raise your hand until the steeple is between them. Do you see?"

"Yes, I see."

He leaned close, his lips almost touching her ear, and said patiently, "Pretend the steeple is a tiny model, and you can grasp it between your thumb and forefinger. Do you have it now?"

His breath was warm against her neck. What she had was an overwhelming urge to press her body back against his. "Yes, I think so."

He drew her hand down to the page, his arm brushing against her breast. "There. That is the size of the steeple in your picture. Like so." He guided her fingers, and she drew two parallel lines. "Now the roof. Take your pencil"—he lifted her hand again—"and line it up with the angle of the roof. Now lower it," he said, and this time, his left arm snaked around her waist and drew her back against his hard body.

He held her there, perfectly still. She realized that her body had stiffened and that she was breathing in short, shallow gasps. She felt as if she were teetering on the edge of an abyss with this man, and there was a voice inside her head urging her to jump.

She found her own voice, but it sounded tiny and far away. "I think I understand, Colonel."

He let her go and stepped away abruptly. "I rather think not," he said. "You are a lovely girl and I've enjoyed these meetings, but I won't be here tomorrow," he told her, folding his easel and wiping his hands on the grass.

"Because I'm unteachable?" she asked, blindsided by his sudden retreat.

His manner changed abruptly. He struggled to hide it, but regret crept into his voice. "Because I could teach you altogether too much, Miss Dare." He did not step closer, but only reached out and took her hand, holding it well away from his body. "I am not a good man, not a nice man. I don't have any of the virtues your provincial parents would desire in a suitor. And you are, despite your tart tongue, an innocent." He bent his head, brushed his lips over her outstretched fingers, and said simply, "Good-bye."

He turned his back on her and strode toward the barracks.

"Will I see you at the City Tavern?" she called after him, wondering what had gone wrong.

"Probably not. I'll be away for several days. And His Majesty, or at least his agent here in Philadelphia, has other work for me. Foraging. Visiting some Rebels in the countryside who have been reluctant to sell us stores. Farewell, Miss Dare."

Kate felt the chill of the day strike through her fur-lined cloak. She knew the tactics Bayard Caide employed while "foraging." She had forgotten, briefly, who and what he was.

Her interest in Caide ought to be entirely professional. He was close to General Howe, and could be a source of high-level intelligence. But in the days that followed, Kate realized that she missed their meetings for entirely different reasons. When she was growing up, men treated her as the woman her father raised her to be: an equal. There was no subterfuge, no artifice, no flirtation. She was a simple girl, and she thought those arts beyond her reach.

Mrs. Ferrers had admitted her to the mystery: that nothing was beyond the grasp of an intelligent woman. Not even conquering a man like Bayard Caide. And there was a thrill to matching wits with a man—however abhorrent—who was her equal. It was a thrill she had first tasted with Peter Tremayne.

She reminded herself that Caide was a monster, away on monstrous business, that he was an enemy, and that he was not Peter Tremayne. None of that stopped her from listening intently for news of him.

At the end of the week she learned that he was back in the city, but he did not return to the square, and Kate abandoned her artistic efforts altogether. It was getting too cold for painting outdoors anyway. Neither did he appear at Mrs. Curran's, or at the Thursday-night dance at Smith's City Tavern, where respectable girls went to meet British officers.

Kate lingered long into the night at Smith's, and only gave up and called for her carriage when Peggy's complaints became too much. Kate was late meeting Mrs. Ferrers in the Valbys' darkened kitchen. The Merry Widow took great care not to be seen going into or out of their home. She never visited by day, only after dark, and then quite briefly. Kate had no knowledge of the means she used to smuggle information out of the city and to Washington's camp. It was safer that way, but Kate was acutely aware of how fragile her connection to home and safety had become.

"Tell me about Bayard Caide," she said to Mrs. Ferrers. Glamorous Aunt Angela had disappeared, and in her place had materialized, depending on the night, a plain, middle-aged maid, or a taciturn, lean, and wiry groom. Tonight she wore men's clothes, and drank whisky, neat, from one of Mrs. Valby's fine cut glasses. She poured Kate a dram and pushed it across the table.

"He is the man I came to Grey Farm to destroy," she said, and waited.

Kate had shed her shimmering silk day dress, brushed the tinted powder from her hair and now sat in a voluminous damask robe at the simple wooden table. The grandeur of the Valby home, and of the elaborate mansions and meeting rooms of the city, had filled her senses when she first came to town, but there was a comforting familiarity in the Valby kitchen, with its well-worn, sturdy pine surfaces, and the faint but lingering scent of warm bread from the slowly cooling bake ovens, which plinked reassuringly as their brick expanded in the chill night air.

"Yes. He was as you described," Kate said. To herself alone she added: Except for his eyes. You didn't tell me he had eyes like Peter, pale blue, cold and mischievous by turns. "Tell me more."

"Bayard Caide is not a simpleton like Peggy Shippen, or a romantic like Peter Tremayne. You cannot play him as you have them. He is far too steeped in corruption and far too intelligent for that."

"You want to know Howe's next move. No one is closer to him than Caide."

"And no one is more dangerously mercurial. Would you like to know why he was posted, so young, to India?"

Mrs. Ferrers narrated the story with dispassionate candor: how Caide had whored and drunk his way through London as a young officer; how he had a proclivity for dueling, and had killed three men in that way; how he might have gone on in that manner had he not beaten a young subaltern almost to death; how his cousin, and best friend, had taken the blame, and been posted to Ireland, before the whole sordid tale came out.

Caide had escaped the incident with a reprimand

and a punitive posting to Bombay, where his behavior
didn't alter, but was channeled into the violent business
of Empire. There he acquired a taste for opiates and
hashish, which he continued to indulge when he returned to England. He rose swiftly in rank, while his
cousin, Tremayne, attainted by scandal and hampered
by scruples, stalled in his career.

The tactics of fear and intimidation that Caide had
learned on the Subcontinent were proving unpopular,
but effective, in the Pennsylvania countryside. "His
men are not quartered in the city. Howe won't have
them here. He launches his raids from a rural camp
which we have failed to locate. I could bring you men
he has tortured, women he has abused." Angela Ferrers
spoke with distaste. "Some women are drawn to a man
like that. You may be tempted, because of your upbringing, to despise and punish yourself for what you
have become. Do not use Bayard Caide for that purpose. No man or woman deserves that." And with that,
she drained her second glass of whisky and left.

*I*t had been more than a week since Kate had
last encountered Bayard Caide, and Peggy
Shippen was examining a miniature landscape in a
gold frame at George Haughton's Tuesday auction.
The London Coffee House on Front Street, hard by
the docks, was not suffering as other businesses during the occupation were. Though the Rebels still controlled the Delaware, and no merchandise had reached
the city for weeks, the vendue masters continued to
hold regular auctions, their inventory swelled by the
estates of those who had fled the city, and replenished

by the Regulars and Hessians who looted, in their spare time, what was left. From his headquarters in Germantown Howe had attempted to stem the tide of looting and rape in Philadelphia with threats and proclamations, but court-martials remained a near daily occurrence. Desperate to protect the inhabitants from his own men, Howe had begun hanging convicted offenders.

"It will look lovely over my dressing table," Peggy opined.

"Very handsome," Kate agreed. Her eye was drawn to the paint box—Chinese, lacquered, with a scene of the Pearl River Delta, Macao most likely—that lay unregarded in a heap of knife boxes and snuff cases. She didn't care to think of how it had arrived there.

The top and sides of the box were largely intact, but the bottom was disfigured with chisel marks. Kate suspected it had been pried off a lacquered stand. Her father had bought her a similar painting table when she embarked on her short artistic career. Inside, the pigments were largely in good condition, and barely used. Brush marks feathered the surface of most of the colors, but only lightly, and none was dried or cracked.

"I thought you gave up painting," Peggy said over her shoulder.

"Colonel Caide has had a difficult time finding paint in the city. I thought I might purchase this and offer it to him next time we meet."

"You're just lucky that your father's away at sea. My family let me know they won't abide Caide, no matter how much money he has. He has a terrible reputation, unlike André," Peggy said, trying on a Chinese shawl.

"I suppose it hasn't occurred to them"—or you, Kate added silently to herself while dabbing her finger in the paint box—"that André might simply have a better reputation because he's better at hiding his sins?"

"You're quite set on snaring Caide, aren't you?" Peggy observed, in a rare moment of lucid interest in something besides herself.

"As set as you are on André," Kate replied. Although for entirely different reasons.

Peggy's eyes sparkled with what Kate realized was as close to cunning as the girl would ever come. "Then buy your paint box. Because I know where the colonel has been spending his days."

Kate did not have sisters growing up, and by the time she would have confided in siblings about her daydreams and infatuations, her mother, to whom she would naturally have turned, was gone. She recognized wistfully the steady stream of speculation that poured from Peggy, as they navigated the maze of warehouses near the dock, as the heady effluvia of puppy love. She wondered aloud about André's parents, his childhood, his education, his plans for family and children.

And Kate allowed her to ramble on, because even if she were willing to crush Peggy's dreams, the sort of insight she possessed about André was entirely outside the purview of her assumed identity. She had recognized in him the same calculated approach to human interaction that Mrs. Ferrers preached and practiced. When he thought no one was looking, André examined Peggy as he might a horse, to see how far and fast she would run. He was always assessing, adjusting, manipulating. To what purpose, Kate was uncertain, but she knew it could be nothing good.

Her own mind did not run in a romantic direction with Bayard Caide. She could not imagine what circumstances had produced such a paradoxical man, at once violent and artistic. When she did daydream about houses and children, about what it would be like to present a man to her father and profess her intention to marry, it was Peter Tremayne who inhabited her fantasies. But he was an ocean away because of her, and if circumstances ever conspired to reunite them, she would hang. The empty warehouses they passed, still redolent with the mingled scents of departed tea, nutmeg, and pepper, were silent testimony to the effectiveness of her espionage. It was because of spies like her that the Americans still held the river, still held a hope of retaking Philadelphia. And for that, if the British caught her, she would die.

Kate recognized immediately the building to which Peggy led her: the Southwark Theater. She had never been there herself, but knew it from an engraving that had appeared in the *Gazette* when it was built a decade ago. The theater had a spotty history, closing and reopening as Puritanical fervor waxed and waned. Congress had closed it down during their session in the Quaker city, and the resident players decamped for Jamaica. Most recently it had served as a hospital for the British wounded at Germantown.

The back door was open, and Peggy and Kate climbed a set of dirty wooden steps to a narrow hall. There were two doors at the top, but Kate had no doubt which led to Bayard Caide. The door on the left was painted in a masterly trompe l'oeil, with the door-jamb done as a stone portal and the door itself a fiery abyss. In the foreground, a three-headed black dog barked, all mouths open, on a chain.

"What an ugly dog!" Peggy said, scrutinizing the figure.

"It's Cerberus," Kate supplied. "Guard dog of the Underworld."

The door opened.

"Be careful," drawled Bayard Caide. "He's carnivorous. And hungry, like his master."

Peggy took a step back, revealing Kate to the slightly dilated eyes of Bayard Caide.

Kate stood her ground. "You're drunk. We'll come back later."

Caide moved quickly and unexpectedly. He grabbed Kate round the waist and whisked her inside, kicking the door shut on a shocked Peggy Shippen. He threw the bolt and caged Kate, her back to the door, in the prison of his arms.

She smelled no alcohol on his breath, only a curious smoky spice that she did not recognize. But his eyes betrayed his altered state of mind, even as they raked her from head to toe at close range. She found them mesmerizing. Neither spoke a word. Only the head-splitting sound of Peggy pounding on the door interrupted the silence.

"Let me in!" Peggy screamed. "Or let her out!"

"Go away, Miss Shippen," Bay said firmly, his eyes challenging Kate to object.

"I'll bring back the law," threatened Peggy.

The Crown, of course, was the law in Philadelphia

at the moment. And the Crown's representative was General Howe, who doted on Caide like a wayward son.

"You can go, Peggy," added Kate. "I'm fine." *I hope*, she added to herself.

Kate was uncertain if she heard Peggy sniff on the other side of the door, or if she merely imagined it. She certainly heard Peggy's slippers scuffing the stairs as the girl departed, but her eyes never broke from Bayard Caide's.

She opened her mouth to speak at last and he silenced her with his own. He had barely touched her in any other way and he made no effort to close the distance between them now; only persisted skillfully in an oral communion that sapped the strength from Kate's limbs.

He tasted like nutmeg and pepper, his tongue gliding over hers, insistently sharing the ghost of whatever strange narcotic he had consumed.

He broke away and stepped back. "Your plumage is brighter than that of all the other birds but you're nothing like those fluttering magpies."

"I try not to flutter. It's uncomfortable in tight stays."

Caide laughed. With his body no longer blocking her view, Kate took in the room. Or theater, as she realized. They were standing on the stage.

It was a disaster. Its recent use as a hospital had left it wrecked. A pile of burnt chairs indicated where the seating had gone. Most of the paneling had been ripped from the walls and presumably burned as well. The windows were filthy, and the curtains had been torn from their rails for God knew what purpose. Shredded green baize dripped from the dented brass fittings.

But the light was dazzling. Unshadowed by taller buildings, facing the water, with all its glorious reflections, the stage was bathed in sun from the Palladian window at the back of the hall. Light played over the unfinished canvas that stretched from one end of the boards to the other: a meandering brook beneath a shade tree, with the Delaware River Valley in the background.

"What are you doing here, Miss Dare?"

She wondered for a moment if he had an inkling of her purpose, some preternatural ability to see past her assumed identity. She conquered her moment of panic and said, "I thought you could use the paints."

"No politely reared young girl would visit a man like me on her own."

"I wasn't on my own. I came with Peggy."

"But she's gone now, and you aren't."

"Are you asking me to leave?"

"No," he said, taking care to keep well away from her. "I'm asking if you know what you are doing. I'm not nice. I'm not safe. I want you. Howe takes a dim view of his officers debauching the locals, so I stopped coming to the square in order to put temptation out of my way. But now you are here, alone with me. Temptation indeed."

"Do you want the paints or not?" Kate said, her voice unnaturally loud from nerves.

He seized the box, took it to a chaise placed in the center of the stage, stretched his lanky form across the tattered upholstery and began examining the contents. "Why ever not? These are quite good. Too good to waste on André's daub." He indicated the scenic painting with a nod of his head. "Where did you get them?"

For the moment, she realized, she was safe from further seduction. The paints held all his attention. She wasn't quite sure how she felt about that. Relieved, certainly, but disappointed as well. His mercurial temper was well known, but this erratic, keyed-up state was a product of something else.

"At George Haughton's vendue sale at the Coffee House. I should go. Peggy Shippen is a notorious gossip and will ruin my reputation if I let her."

"I thought she was your friend."

"She is. But she subscribes to a variety of feminine friendship that prizes novelty over loyalty."

"Most women do. But not you."

And she was once again the focus of his intense gaze.

"No. Not me. But I must go."

"Don't."

"People will talk. I'll hurt my chances of finding a husband."

"You mean you'll hurt your chances of shackling yourself to a boring milksop. Stay. I'll teach you to paint properly."

"You say paint, but I think you mean something quite different." She edged toward the door, watching for the move he would make to stop her.

"I won't do anything you don't want me to."

She laughed nervously. "That is exactly what I'm afraid of. It's a rather sentimental landscape," she said of the monumental canvas.

He took the change of subject with good grace. "André's work. Not mine. I'm painting it in for him. In exchange for the use of the theater."

She noticed his easel then, dwarfed by the giant

backdrop. She crossed to the painting, and examined it critically. It was Icarus, naked, silhouetted by a blazing sun, dripping wax and blood. The carmine had run down the canvas, pooling on the lip of the easel. Kate felt an overwhelming desire to dip her finger in it.

"Most people think the Greeks were the great artists," he said.

"They understood proportion. They sculpted ideals," she replied.

"They understood nothing. They created soulless mannequins. The Romans were the true artists. They believed in gravitas. They saw the beauty in every line on a senator's face. They were unafraid of experience, unafraid to paint the truth."

"But you never paint what you see in front of you."

"I paint the truth. The truth and what I see in front of me are two different things."

"What kind of drug have you been taking? You're not drunk. Or belligerent."

"Opium. Would you like to try it?"

"No, thank you. One form of ruin is all I can tolerate in a single day."

She was reaching out, unconsciously, to touch the pooled vermilion. He caught her hand. Their eyes met, and he studied her face with an artist's discernment. "Does that mean you consent to the more conventional kind of ruin? I can't decide if you're endearingly trusting, or just deliciously reckless." He led her by the hand to the chaise he had only recently vacated.

Her heart pounded and her breath grew short but she had determined before coming not to flinch beneath his touch. "A little of both, I should expect."

His arm circled her waist, and he lifted her and set her to lie lightly on the frayed damask.

It still held his warmth, and with it, the promise of intimacy. Desire slid through her, fast and sweet, like sap down a maple, but her courage failed her. "Colonel, please don't."

"Don't what? And you may call me Bay." He hadn't touched her since setting her down, but his posture on the edge of the chaise foretold mischief. Now he traced the line of her cheek, her jaw, her neck, with his delicate artist's hands.

His finger outlined her mouth and she parted her lips, tasted his fingertip with her tongue. His other hand traveled south to draw lazy patterns over her décolletage. His touch was intoxicating. When he slung a leg on the chaise to part hers, her hips rose to meet him.

"Good girl," he coaxed. "Do you trust me?"

"No," she said, but made no move to stop him.

"That's because you aren't stupid." His lips nudged hers apart, his tongue darted in to lick hers, and the teasing hand at her breast slipped beneath the fabric of her gown, her stays, and her chemise. She groaned into his mouth when his thumb circled her stiff nipple.

He lifted his head. "Look at me, Lydia," he commanded, in the voice that she dimly recognized he must use with his men.

Her eyes snapped open. He was smirking in satisfaction. "You're like me, Lydia," he said, releasing her breast to pull her skirts up around her waist. He drew her knees up until her heels were flat on the chaise. "There's something broken in you. Something that doesn't care what Peggy Shippen and the wagging tongues say. A reckless thing that will risk pain to snatch pleasure."

"I think I'd prefer you to enthuse about my eyelashes now," she replied, though she could barely hear her own words for the thrumming of her heart. She wanted his touch desperately, and knew now that this fervent need had nothing to do with Mrs. Ferrers, Washington, or her father's safety. She was lying on her back, skirts pulled up, legs spread, for the pleasure of Bayard Caide, her enemy. And she wanted it all the same. Mrs. Ferrers had known.

She cried out when his hand covered her sex, the palm pressed firmly to her sensitive flesh. She writhed, unable to resist the friction.

Then he withdrew his hands to capture both of hers and pin them above her head. With his left hand he held her prone, while his right hand returned to worry her softening nipple.

"Lie still, Lydia, and I'll give you what you want."

"But I don't know what I want," she gasped. He could not possibly know the depth of her confusion. But he seemed to know the depth of her need.

His fingers returned to the entrance to her body and circled, making a slick inspection of her contours. She gave herself up to it entirely. Then without warning, he slid two fingers inside and turned, with a small motion of his wrist, her world upside down.

He stroked his fingers in and out, curling and uncurling them until she could no longer stay still, but thrust her hips up and down in time with his ministrations. He chuckled low in his throat and she opened her eyes once more. "My love, my joy, my Lydia, you're doing all the work."

Her body tensed like a bowstring. The next calculated swipe of his thumb released her. She subsided into
his arms, wrung out and replete. He reclined beside
her, and twined damp fingers in hers. Kate realized that
this was the sort of lust, the sort of inappropriate desire,
that had ruined the Hessian Colonel Donop.

She became aware of his erection, pressed against
her thigh, and shifted to bring herself flush with it. She
knew what she wanted now, and it had nothing to do
with love.

She shifted again, and he groaned. "Stop that, Lydia.
I'm not made of stone. And I'm not foolish enough to go
further without some kind of assurance I won't be court-
martialed for it."

He released her hands and laid his fair head on her
breast, like a child seeking comfort.

"What do you mean?" she asked, stroking his hair,
unnerved by his sudden tenderness.

"What are your parents like?" He sounded tentative, boyish. He was a baffling contradiction, this man.

She realized there was no reason to lie. "My mother
died when I was twelve. She was witty and sensible in
equal measure."

"Like her daughter."

"I suppose so," she said, finding more irony in the
context.

"And what of your father?"

Her father, her sources told her, was with Washington, and playing merry hell with Howe's supply
lines. She could picture him, ambushing Regulars in
the backwoods of Pennsylvania in his fringed buck-
skins and beaver hat. "You might find him . . . rustic.
He doesn't tolerate fools."

"Do you think he would like me?"

"Not a bit. Why do you ask?"

He lifted his head from her chest and tugged her chemise and gown into place. "Because I intend to present myself and declare my honorable intentions, so next time I have your skirts up I can have you without fear of hanging for it. There is only one thing you must know first. I'm a bastard."

She laughed. "So I have been told."

He sat up. "The truth is rather more literal than that. My mother became pregnant with me when she was fifteen. She would not name her seducer. Her family bought her a dupe of a husband, so I am, in the strictest sense of the law, legitimate, because I was born in wedlock. But my mother's husband did not take kindly to the deception. He beat her, so she ran away from him. 'Caide' is my mother's surname. I have no desire to use his. My mother's cousins took us in, or we'd have starved. My great-grandfather was drawn and quartered for treason, and I myself am not exactly beloved in the country hereabouts." His clever hands moved on her again. "But I think you want me anyway," he said, then went about proving it once more with ruthless skill.

That day at the playhouse was the first and last time he made any mention of his family, and never did he speak of a connection with Peter Tremayne.

Their engagement, tentatively approved by the Valbys, waiting a letter of confirmation from Lydia's supposed ship's captain father, followed a week later.

With it came entrée to Howe's inner circle. And everything Kate heard, Washington heard. He used her intelligence to tighten his grip on the rivers and roads, and within a month the occupation was a siege. A month more, and the river would freeze. Howe would be starved out of Philadelphia, Lydia Dare would disappear forever, and Kate could go home to Orchard Valley.

And not a moment too soon. She feared she did not have the heart for espionage. She'd lived in a state of fear for weeks. Of exposure, which would be deadly. And of her physical attraction to Caide, only barely held in check. Which could prove ruinous. She'd had enough of jewels and silks and fine entertainments, and she wanted to go home to pots and pans and the siren song of drafty, well-loved rooms and bristly groaning chairs. Her goal had been within reach just a few short hours ago.

Until Peter Tremayne came back.

Seven

Philadelphia, October 20, 1777

Peter Tremayne was not insensitive to the pleasures of music. Under other circumstances, he might have enjoyed a concert. As it was, he was acutely aware that less than thirty miles from where the musicians sat tuning, Washington's army lay hungry, cold, and vulnerable.

"How can you stand it?" he asked Bayard Caide, who was scraping his boots meticulously free of mud on the porch outside Howe's High Street mansion. The grand residence that Mary Lawrence Masters had built for her daughter not ten years before had stood empty since Congress dispatched her son-in-law to London with the luckless Olive Branch Petition. It was the largest house in Philadelphia, and when General Howe finally entered the City of Brotherly Love, after nearly a month spent delaying at Germantown, he had immediately commandeered it for himself.

"I have other consolations than war, cousin." Caide sidestepped the water running freely from the roof of the portico, the gutters choked with decaying autumn leaves. "Howe should see to the damned gutters," he added under his breath. "The rain stopped half an hour ago. Half the city's been sacked already and the rest of it is falling to pieces."

It was true. In the week that Tremayne had spent there, he'd fended off two attacks by Regulars attempting to pillage the small clapboard house where he'd found quarters. Caide had offered him digs with three other officers, but the atmosphere had felt more like a brothel than a barracks, and Tremayne chose instead the establishment of a bachelor reverend and his spinster sister. The pair had held out against quartering soldiers early in the occupation, and with good reason. The Regulars occupying the Old Barracks shat in the stairwells. But by the time Tremayne arrived, and real privation was being felt in the city, the reverend and his sister welcomed him, and his access to military stores and protection from uniformed looters, with open arms. The cleric was not associated with any of the more radical churches in town, though Tremayne suspected he was a deist. The house was small but warm and tidy.

Howe's residence, on the other hand, was spacious enough to accommodate his personal household, and those officers on his staff he felt closest to. This did not include the charming Captain André, the author of the evening's entertainment, whom Tremayne spied through the crowd, ushering guests to the neat rows of chairs in the front parlor. André had taken up residence in the abandoned home of Benjamin Franklin. Revolutionary or no, Franklin was a much-loved figure on both sides of the Atlantic. To occupy Franklin's house was a show of cheek typical of André.

"It's maddening," Tremayne said. "Howe has the advantage and he will not press it. He could march on Washington's forces and put an end to the war tomorrow."

"He marched on Breed's Hill and lost a thousand men," Caide said. "He won't risk it again. And the entertainments aren't all frivolity. It keeps the officers out of trouble, for the most part. Although I'll grant you, it takes its toll. Some poor sot passed out in Howe's icehouse and froze to death last week. Go on inside. I should wait for Lydia, make sure she isn't doused by water from these gutters."

"What do you want a wife for anyway?" Tremayne asked, sounding, he realized, altogether too testy on the subject.

Caide laughed at him. "You don't like her, cousin? What does any man need a wife for?"

And that, Tremayne decided, didn't bear thinking about.

"I'm going home." Tremayne turned on his heel. He would have taken a swing at any other man attempting to stop him, but when his cousin clapped a hand on his shoulder he checked his temper.

"You're going inside. You're going to flirt and make small talk and toady to André because he toadies to Howe. And you're going to find that blasted bitch who unmanned you on the road to New York and get your command back."

Caide was right, and Tremayne said as much. "But this is no way to win a war."

"Have patience, cousin. And be sure to flatter the little Huguenot. He has Howe's ear."

The little Huguenot had spotted them. André's savoir faire and dark good looks made him a favorite with the Philadelphia ladies. The concert was early enough that many of them, unmarried, still in their teens, and tottering under the ludicrously tall hairstyles so popular in London this season, flocked around him. André shed them like rainwater and emerged from the house to embrace Caide like a long-lost brother, pressing a small paper-wrapped package on him.

Caide fished in his purse. "I'll have to owe you the rest," he said to André, passing him a gold guinea. Whatever was in the package was expensive. Tremayne preferred not to know.

"You can bring me the money at the theater. We're opening as soon as we can rent enough chairs," André said, scanning the crowd.

Caide slipped the package into his tunic. "You'll have to contend with both Peggys tonight, I'm afraid. Chew and Shippen. Lydia tried to stop it but she couldn't dissuade the one because the other was already going."

"No matter. So long as I seat them at opposite ends of the room, we should survive the first movement." André turned his attention from Caide. "I have someone I would like you to meet, Major."

"Go on, Peter," Caide urged. "Women are always late."

Tremayne followed André through the brightly lit rooms to the pretty green and gold double parlor where the doors were thrown back to reveal musicians in the smaller rear chamber. The players were a mixed assortment, half civilian and half soldiery.

André led him to a chair in the middle of a short row, quite near the front, and impossible to escape from once the concert started, blast the man.

The Hessian seated there, formal, exquisitely turned out in the scarlet-faced green of the Jaeger Corps, rose stiffly and bowed to André. Tremayne realized with sinking heart who this man must be: the officer largely believed to be responsible for losing Trenton, who had dallied at Mount Holly with the Merry Widow for three fateful days.

"May I present Colonel Carl Emil Ulrich Von Donop of Hesse-Cassel," André said in the French of his fathers.

"It is an honor, Colonel," Tremayne said in the same language.

"Colonel Donop. Major Peter Tremayne, Viscount Sancreed," André said, completing the introduction.

The Hessian count inclined his blond head: a calculated acknowledgment of Tremayne. "I am acquainted," Donop said, "with your cousin." His accented French did not entirely disguise the ambiguity of the statement.

"I think you two will find you have much in common," André said, and left.

The timing of his exit gave Peter Tremayne little choice. The row of chairs filled in behind him like the incoming tide. If he made polite apologies to the colonel, if he turned and fought his way upstream and out of the parlor, all eyes would be on him. As it was, he knew André was watching. He could do nothing that would draw attention to this carefully orchestrated tableau of two officers brought low by the same woman.

Donop appeared similarly discomfited and resumed his seat.

The musicians struck up. It was Purcell, mediocre and maudlin.

Donop fidgeted, crossed his elegant legs and recrossed them, every discordant note seeming to afflict him. The Hessians were notoriously vain, and their colonel appeared to be no exception. Tremayne judged Donop to be perhaps five years older than himself. He was tall, blond, handsome, and the polish of his boots, the gold wire on his coat, and the quality of his buttons indicated an independent income.

After the fifth discordant note, the colonel spoke, once more in French. "The little captain means to do us a mischief, I suspect."

Tremayne was uncertain how to respond. "Do you mean the music, or some other matter?"

Donop cast him a sly glance. "I do not care much for your English composers. But I was not speaking of the music. Howe has set you like a dog on the Widow's heels. You will not find her. I have searched the Jerseys for the lady for the better part of a year."

So they were not to speak of music. "Howe has offered me my command if I find her."

"I was not searching for her for General Howe." It was a rebuke.

Tremayne accepted it as such. "Have you no thought for your career, Colonel?"

"I will earn that back, honorably. I advise you to do the same." The Hessian's voice was low and icy.

"She deceived and disgraced you. You owe her nothing."

"How long have you been in America, Major?"

"Six months."

"I have been here more than a year. I have suffered bad food, bad company, and poor entertainment. Only the hunting is any good. But I had three exquisite days in Mount Holly with the most beguiling woman I have ever met. What have you had?"

He should not have looked away from the players. He should have kept his eyes fixed on them, or their instruments, or perhaps examined the paintings, the ersatz Titian over the fire. Instead he turned and found her, across the aisle, absorbed by the music despite its inadequacies. She seemed small and fragile beside Caide, who lounged in the chair next to her, ignoring Purcell entirely. His cousin's hands rested lightly on her knee and neck, and the possessiveness of his pose drove Tremayne to hot and irrational anger.

And the awareness that André was watching him.

He looked away. Donop had been observing him as well, his expression more quizzical and less frosty than before. "What did the lady look like?" Donop asked him, all amused curiosity.

He was speaking about Mrs. Ferrers, and Tremayne found that his memory of her was inexact. It was Kate he remembered in exquisite detail, but he did his best to recollect. "Tall, slender, handsome rather than beautiful. Fair-haired, I think, though that might have been a wig."

"I thought as much," Donop said with quiet satisfaction, and chuckled to himself.

"What?" Tremayne said, irritated with the turn the evening was taking.

"You were not intimately acquainted with the lady. Unless, of course, she kept her wig on. Is that an English custom?"

Tremayne's anger fled. He smiled, then laughed, and decided he rather liked the colonel. "I didn't go to bed with the lady. No."

"You are a poor judge of beauty. And you are not in love with her, which gratifies me," the colonel said with some satisfaction. "I will do what Howe should have done the instant he disembarked at Head of Elk. I shall attack Fort Mercer, and the river will be opened, and the city will be British for the winter. I will redeem myself in the eyes of my prince, and then I will find the lady."

Tremayne had reconnoitered Mercer with the Royal Engineers. They hadn't liked what they'd seen. Mercer was built on high ground. It was a solid, defensible position, and with some work, it could be made very costly to take indeed. Tremayne said as much.

Donop smirked. "The Rebels have many strong positions. In my experience, they abandon them at the first sight of our colors. During the last campaign we took Fort Washington in under an hour. They fled Fort Lee before we could send them our drummer. The poor man had to chase them. In any case, your engineers' opinion should be taken *cum grano salis. Professionals* might differ with their appraisal of the works."

"Howe cannot put Breed's Hill behind him. He won't risk the British lives Mercer would claim."

"No, Major. But I think he has come to a point where he will risk Hessian lives." It was said with unconcealed disdain. "He is approaching the problem of the river backwards. He attacks Mifflin, because it is conveniently on our side of the river. He can watch the bombardment in comfort. But Mercer is on the Jersey side. He must venture across the river, which the Rebels control with their flotsam and jetsam of a navy. It is a day's march, through hostile territory. But Mercer is the supply point. Take Mercer, and Mifflin falls. Howe risks nothing, and gains nothing. I will risk much, and gain glory, and honor, and the freedom to pursue a certain lady."

"You are willing to risk your career and very probably your life for a woman you knew only three days. What kind of woman is worth that?" Tremayne asked, imagining the ramparts of Fort Mercer.

"The only kind worth having, Major," Donop said, as the music ended. He stood, bowed once more, and cast a glance at Kate that Tremayne prayed André would miss in the suddenly bustling room. "As I think you already know. Good evening."

Tremayne realized it was his opportunity to depart. He sped for the door, only to be cut off by the ever-solicitous André.

He was carrying, impossibly, six punch glasses in his two hands, and deposited one in Tremayne's palm such that Peter either had to grasp it, or let it shatter on the marble floor. "That's for Miss Dare. Would you be so kind, Major?" And off he went.

Frustrated, Tremayne threaded his way through the crowded parlor to where Kate stood talking with one of the musicians. He handed her the glass and warned away the cellist with a dark look. She accepted the drink with obvious surprise. "Thank you, Major Tremayne. How have you been enjoying Philadelphia?"

"I have not. André doesn't trust me. His little maneuver with Count Donop was intended to embarrass one of us."

"It is impossible to embarrass Colonel Donop. He is Hessian and in love, poor man."

"Yes, with your dear aunt Angela," he said, for her hearing alone. "The count searched for her for a year."

"And you think you can find her in the next two weeks," she replied, just as softly.

"I would have thought you'd have slunk away by now, Peter." Bay appeared at his shoulder, slipped an arm around Kate's waist, and pulled her close. "Good for you that you didn't. You'd miss all the fun."

"What fun?" Kate asked.

"Howe's in a snit. Donop's been stirring up trouble again, writing letters to his princely employer, the Landgraf of Hesse-Cassel, about Howe's mismanagement of the campaign. Howe has a mind to give Donop what he wants and let Careless Carl make a fool of himself attacking Mercer."

"You said that fully manned, Mercer was impossible to breach from the land side," she said, sliding from Bay's grasp.

"Yes, but it isn't fully manned. Our reports say the fort is down to two hundred men. The size of that place would require fifteen hundred to defend. A thousand at the very least. The Americans always build too large." He kissed her forehead, lingering with his face buried in her hair. "It's nothing to worry about, my love. The Hessians will be out front in the van. Howe won't commit British troops until the thing looks like a victory."

Tremayne tried not to look at Bay's hands, which roamed too freely over Kate's supple body. Had he made love to her? Would she let him, knowing what he was? Could she feel some attraction to him? Too many women did.

"Peggy and I must go. Will you see us to our carriage, Bay?"

"I'm afraid he can't." André appeared behind Tremayne. "Howe wants to see you, Colonel Caide."

Bay planted a chaste kiss on his fiancée's hand. "I'll be back shortly," he said, and left with André.

"Will you see Peggy and me to our carriage, Major?" she asked sweetly.

"So you can slip away and relay the news about Mercer to your accomplice?" he asked quietly. "Certainly not. Are you sleeping with him?"

She blushed prettily and used her punch glass to hide her flushed face, drinking off the contents and depositing the glass on the mantel.

"I take that as yes."

"I'm sorry, what was the question?"

"Are you sleeping with *my cousin*?"

"That is none of your business."

"I'm afraid rather it is. I told you the price of my silence."

"You were so eager to secure my consent when you thought I was a naive farm girl, and now you care for it not at all. Do you really want me in your bed by blackmail?"

He stepped closer, smelling the rum, sugar, and lime that still lingered on her lips. "I want you in my bed by any means necessary, but I won't have you fresh from his."

He saw the flicker in her eyes, the frisson of desire that passed through her body, saw her master it, and damned her for her self-control.

"Then you won't have me at all." She turned on her heel to leave, but he caught her by the elbow. She clearly knew better than to cause a scene, and smiled and laughed for the benefit of anyone watching them. But her eyes weren't smiling. Neither were his.

"Why do you say two weeks?" Tremayne asked. "Why do I have only two weeks to find the Widow?"

"Howe's predicament is no secret. That is all the time you have left in Philadelphia. Maybe less. The river will freeze, the city will starve, and Howe will be forced to surrender to Washington. Your search will be moot."

"You're overconfident. And in danger. André doesn't trust me. He sent me to bring you punch because he wanted to see us together. Which means he suspects *you*." And then, because angry as he was, jealous as he was, he had to speak, he added, "Get out of the damned city, Kate. Do it tonight, before something happens."

"Would you care? If something happened to me?" For just a moment, her face seemed unguarded, her eyes wide, vulnerable, entreating. *Lonely.*

But he had to remind himself of what she was. "About the fate of a creature who could open her legs to a man like my cousin, condemn a city to starvation, and damn an army to destruction, all for her politics?

Not a goddamn bit. How could I? What kind of a fool do you take me for?"

*K*ate watched Peter Tremayne's retreating back. She hated herself for asking him, because she'd known the answer. Her actions, no matter how many American lives they saved, were a betrayal of her Quaker beliefs. Her "inner light" had led her to this place, and she now wondered what it was that burned in the lamp.

But self-recrimination was a luxury she could not afford tonight. Fort Mercer must be warned. They were indeed down to only two hundred men, and could not stand against Donop's thousand unless they were reinforced. She had to make her rendezvous with the Widow. With Caide detained at Howe's pleasure, and Tremayne unable to stop her—because if he exposed her, he exposed himself—there was nothing to prevent her from feigning exhaustion and calling for the Shippen carriage to take her home.

In truth, Kate did feel strangely exhausted. Her eyes felt dry, her head had begun to ache during her conversation with Peter Tremayne, and while earlier she had put it down to the strain of sparring with him, she now felt uncertain that this was the cause.

She was not the worse for drink. Intoxication had been one of Mrs. Ferrers' categories of instruction. She had taught Kate to build up a tolerance, to know how much she could imbibe and still keep her wits about her. To abstain entirely would bar her from the liquor-fueled gaming tables and dinners, where no one enjoyed the presence of a teetotaler. To appear to drink more than she had was a necessary art, but tonight she had consumed a single glass of punch. She should not be feeling any ill effects.

She reached for her discarded glass, but a hand was there before hers.

André.

"Miss Dare. You look like you could use some air. Let me take you to the garden."

"I'd prefer to go home, Captain André."

"John, please. Call me John."

The candle flames bent and blurred in her vision. When she tried to fix on André's eyes, the pale gold flecks danced like pinwheels. He slipped a hand around her waist, curiously impersonal, and she realized that he was supporting her. "Let me help you, Miss Dare."

She tried to free herself, but his grip was like iron and her fingers felt numb and boneless. "Please, my carriage."

He was leading her toward the door. "Not tonight, Miss Dare. Though I would love to know where you were going, there's too much to be done. And you're flushed. I'll take you somewhere cooler. The icehouse perhaps."

The icehouse. Where the man had frozen to death last week. She stumbled, looked around desperately, and saw Peter Tremayne. He was watching her. She tried to fix her gaze on him, tried to communicate her distress, but André whirled her down the hall. An icy draft from the back door brought her temporarily to her senses and she dug her nails into his flesh and tore away from him.

Without his supporting arm, the room spun, the floor rose up to meet her, and then didn't. The embrace that saved her was warm, familiar, and decidedly not Bayard Caide's.

"I have you, Kate," whispered Peter Tremayne. "Try to stand, lean on me. Smile. I'm going to get you out of here."

"I was just taking Miss Dare to the garden for some air." André's voice sounded far away to Kate. She knew she was standing, knew that her knees would buckle but for Tremayne's protective grasp.

"I'll see her home, *Captain*." His emphasis on André's lower rank was decisive.

"Yes. Yes, of course. The worse for drink, I should expect. She'll sleep till dawn. Safest thing for her. She could do with a visit to the country, I daresay. Clean air. The city vapors can be deadly."

It was a threat. There was no mistaking it.

His retreating footsteps rang like church bells in Kate's head. "I'm not drunk," she managed to say, but the weight of her words unbalanced her and she spun once more toward the floor.

And then Peter was carrying her in his arms, and she felt like a child in her father's embrace, her cheek pressed to the soft wool of his tunic.

"Of course not, you silly bitch. You've been poisoned."

The knot of drivers, servants, and footmen gathered around the fire behind Howe's stables betrayed no surprise when a British officer carrying an unconscious girl demanded the use of the Shippen carriage. It was the first time Tremayne had felt even remotely grateful for the dissipation of Howe's staff.

Inside the carriage he laid Kate on the bench, removed her gown, and unlaced her stays. She swatted at him ineffectually, then started up quite suddenly and found the strength to push the carriage door open and vomit into the street.

She collapsed onto the floor of the box in a heap, and lay looking up at him with glassy, dilated eyes.

"I told you that you were in danger. Now do you believe me?" he asked, coming to sit on the floor of the carriage beside her.

"Is the worst of it over?" she asked, wiping her mouth on the handkerchief he offered.

"I don't know. There's no way of knowing how much André slipped in your drink. Enough to put you out for the night. He was clever to pass you the glass through me, but I doubt he's an expert with the stuff. He doesn't seem the type. You probably only expelled the excess, which is fortuitous, because too much will kill you."

"What was it?"

"Opium, I think."

"But Bay takes more than André could have put in a single cup of punch."

"Cousin Bay has built up a tolerance to the stuff."

"André didn't mean to kill me with the drink. He meant to leave me in the icehouse. It would have looked like an accident."

Tremayne felt a hot white stab of anger. "I'll call him out and kill him."

"Brilliant. Then we'll both be revealed and hanged as traitors."

She was right. He could do nothing to Captain André without exposing himself and Kate. "Are you sleeping with Bay?" he asked, wanting the answer to be different this time.

"No. Not entirely."

"Not entirely? What the hell does that mean?"

Despite her distress, she managed to roll her eyes at him in exasperation.

"Never mind," he said. "I would prefer if you didn't elaborate. But you won't be able to put him off forever."

"I know," she said. And there it was again. The steely-eyed determination that she'd shown in that moonlit room upstairs at Germantown, the fortitude that must have carried her from the sleepy farm where she had been raised to the glittering court that was Howe's dissolute circle.

"You would allow him to be the first?"

"It is a small matter in the scheme of things."

"Not to me it isn't."

"Yes. As I recall, you've already offered to do the honors yourself."

"Stop it, Kate. It doesn't have to be me, but it damned well shouldn't be Bayard Caide. If you think it's such a trifling matter, that's only because you've never done it. You can't disengage your emotions at will."

"My fiancé would beg to differ with you," she said dryly. "I understand he disengages his emotions with alarming frequency, and with women far less willing to sacrifice themselves than I am."

"Is that what it would have been with me, at Grey Farm? A sacrifice?"

"No."

"Then for God's sake, Kate, leave the city tonight. You heard André. He's ruthless. He cannot move against you openly without evidence, which I will not give him, but he can certainly arrange another *accident* like tonight. Leave, or he will kill you."

"I will take greater care in future," she said, fists clenched against another wave of nausea.

"If he cannot remove you by assassination, he will find a way to arrest you. And God knows when one of the other officers who dined with us at Grey Farm might not turn up in Philadelphia—and recognize a certain Quaker girl behind Miss Dare's exquisite facade."

"I cannot leave."

"You can, and you will. I'm taking you home now to rest. In a little while, after the party is done, I'll return to Howe's for my horse. I'll get a pass, and we'll ride out of the city together. I'm supposed to be protecting the houses in the Neck from looting. The guards will assume I'm taking my mistress there for a tryst, but once we're out of the city I can take you wherever you want to go."

"I have to stay. I have to . . ."

Her voice was fading, and Tremayne realized she was succumbing to the effect of the drug.

"You have to stay awake, Kate." If she fell asleep, if she allowed the drug to take her now, she could stop breathing and suffocate. He'd seen it in battlefield hospitals, the killing dose, a mercy to the mortally wounded. How much had André given her? He had no way of knowing. Her best chance lay in remaining conscious and vomiting up as much of the stuff as possible. Tremayne shook her hard. "Lecture me on your damned Rebel politics, or rattle off your recipe for piecrust, *but for God's sake stay awake.*"

Her eyes snapped open. "You patronize me by suggesting they are of equal importance." She swayed, fought to keep herself upright.

He smiled. She couldn't resist an argument. "I flatter you by speaking plainly, as I would to one of my peers. Politics or piecrusts. In a year's time, the one will be as inconsequential as the other."

He watched a wave of nausea pass over her, reached out to comfort her, but was swatted away. "Your peers? You think I'm your inferior because of a ludicrous accident of birth." Her eyes narrowed, and he could see what it cost her to summon from memory the words best suited to her purpose. " 'To the evil of monarchy,' " she quoted, " 'we have added that of hereditary succession; and as the first is a degradation and lessening of ourselves, so the second, claimed as a matter of right, is an insult and imposition on posterity. For all men being originally equals, no one by birth could have a right to set up his own family in perpetual preference to all others for ever, and tho' himself might deserve some decent degree of honours of his contemporaries, yet his descendants might be far too unworthy to inherit them.' "

"Yes. I've read 'Common Sense,' Kate. And while I have every reason to know that Paine's observations are entirely true—I'm not fit to hold my title, lands, or fortune—there are others who are even less fit than I. And I am acutely aware of the fact that it doesn't matter. It never did. It never will. My great-great-grandfather was not the man who earned those honors.

Bayard Caide's was. Do you know *why* I am Viscount Sancreed, and not him?"

Something about his tone must have penetrated her drug-induced haze, because her eyes cleared and she looked straight at him. "No."

He smiled bitterly. "Bay's great-grandfather Edmund Caide was a Roundhead, and was guilty of regicide. He rode out with Cromwell's New Model Army. He participated in the trial of Charles the First. He even consorted with your Quaker founder, George Fox, and his followers. He believed in equality, universal suffrage, and the rights of his fellow man, but when his fellow man could not sustain the burden of self-governance and invited Charles' son back to the throne, Caide was hanged, drawn, and quartered, his head impaled on a spike at Westminster.

"Before he was executed, though, Edmund Caide was attainted traitor, stripped of all his lands and possessions, and forced to watch while everything he had earned and held dear was passed to a cousin—my great-grandfather William Tremayne—who had remained, if not steadfastly loyal to the Crown, if not valiant or honorable, then at least judiciously absent from the field and fray. Your revolution will end no differently."

He had meant to keep Kate awake with argument, not torture her with his own guilt and self-loathing. But with his confession, the fight had gone out of her and he had no heart to torment her further. "How Bay must hate you," she said simply, and slumped to the boards, eyes glazed, hands clenching and unclenching as waves of cramping and nausea passed through her.

Peter lifted her from the floor. She made no attempt to stop him. She curled on her side on the bench, and subsided with her head in his lap. She was half naked, and her painted lips were only inches from his cock, but he felt no stir of lust, only a desperate desire to protect the plainspoken girl who had reemerged on the carriage floor.

She was sick once more on the way to the Valby mansion, and he prayed she'd vomited up enough of the stuff. When they reached the house she was deeply unconscious, but her breathing was even and her pulse strong.

He carried her past the scandalized servants, who explained that the Valbys were out and attempted to bar him from Kate's rooms, but he ignored them and deposited the girl on the bed, issuing orders for hot water and clean towels and a fresh fire.

He turned his back while the maid removed her stays, and got her settled under the counterpane. The housekeeper appeared and attempted to eject him from the room, but he wasn't going to leave Kate until the worst of it was over.

She was sleeping comfortably now, but it wouldn't last long. Tremayne had tried the stuff himself. Bay liked it for the dreams, feverish transports and horrific nightmares that fed his art. Tremayne could only imagine what kinds of visions a girl who had just narrowly escaped an icy death would have. He could not leave her yet.

She woke screaming an hour later and struck at the bed curtains like she was fighting off an attacker. He knew she was blind, still dreaming, lashing out at phantoms. He climbed onto the bed, caught her flailing arms in his, and held her while she cried herself to sleep once more.

He had dozed off himself, stiff and uncomfortable in the chair beside the bed, when the door opened.

He expected Mrs. Valby, or one of the servants, demanding that he leave.

Instead, it was Angela Ferrers.

He might not have recognized her in a crowded room. Her hair was bound tightly under a mobcap, her face was free of cosmetics, and the tiny lines around her eyes, which had been artfully concealed at their last meeting, were naked in the firelight.

No wonder Kate had refused to leave the city. She had planned to meet the Widow and pass on what she had learned about Mercer.

"What happened?" Angela Ferrers asked dispassionately.

"André. He slipped opium into her drink and tried to abandon her in the icehouse."

The Widow made no move to come closer to Tremayne or the girl in the bed who lay between them. She barely glanced at Kate.

"Why? What is happening tonight that he wanted so much to conceal?"

"Damn your politics. *She almost died.*" Tremayne thrust the chair back as he rose and it screeched across the floorboards.

Angela Ferrers didn't move an inch. "But she didn't. And now she can't tell me what André didn't want me to know. But you can."

"No, madame, because I am not a turncoat, and have

no intention of becoming one. I am loyal to my king, and to my country, and to my commander, and for that reason, I am taking you now to General Howe."

He advanced on her and she dropped languidly onto the footstool beside the bed. "No, you are not. If you take me, I will expose Kate. And then she *will* die. And not prettily, in her sleep."

He stopped in his advance as though she'd physically struck him. "You wouldn't dare."

"Try me, Major. I would have nothing to lose. It's not an idle threat. You obviously don't want to see her harmed. If you betray me to Howe, you sign her death warrant."

"You're both mad."

"We're both women of conviction."

"And where do *your* convictions come from, Mrs. Ferrers? An ill-done-by husband? A murdered son? Do I detect a brogue beneath your clipped consonants? Whatever tragedy shaped you, whatever miscarriage of British justice made you the treacherous whore you are, it has not befallen Kate. *Yet.* She's an innocent. And I'm going to see her clear of this mess and safe from you. Before she becomes what you would make her."

"If you would save her, then take her place. I'll send her back to her adoring father tonight. He's probably getting suspicious by now anyway. He might even know she's not home at Grey Farm."

"I will not spy for you, woman. I won't betray my country, no matter how incompetently it prosecutes this war."

"Then I'm afraid you have no choice but to leave Kate Grey to the fate she has chosen for herself." She stood. "Now, get out. She's fine. And I have no patience for ineffectual romantics. Kate has the courage of her convictions, Major, and you do not. She deserves better."

"She doesn't deserve Bayard Caide."

It was the first and last emotion the Widow betrayed. "No," she said softly, her eyes flickering to the girl in the bed, "she does not."

She turned to leave. He moved faster than she anticipated, wrenching her arms behind her back. "You'll do me the courtesy of not screaming. Your discovery here, as you have taken pains to point out, would condemn us all."

"Let me go, Major."

"So you can warn Washington? Not a chance."

"Warn him of what?"

"There's only one thing important enough for André to risk murder. You guessed the moment you walked in this room. It's the river forts."

He ripped a strip from one of the bed curtains and worked quickly to tie her hands. She struggled briefly to get away from him; then, to his horror, she stopped struggling and pressed herself hard against him. "Is that your pleasure, Major? Does helplessness arouse you?" she asked, clearly offering herself, bound, to him.

His reaction sent her sprawling to the floor, but she must have realized even before he hurled her away from him that he was not in the least aroused by her offer.

"I'm sorry, Major," she said from her unceremonious seat on the carpet. "Clearly that is not your preference. But you must know"—she made no move to rise—"*that it is Bayard Caide's.*"

She might as well have punched him. It took all the air out of his lungs. On the bed, Kate stirred feebly, and Angela Ferrers struggled, hands bound, to her feet. "Let me go tonight, and I'll take Kate with me to the Continental lines. Give me Mercer and Mifflin, and I will give you her safety."

It was a decision he would regret all of his days, no matter which way he chose.

In the end he tied Angela Ferrers to the chair beside the bed, gagged her, and locked the door behind him.

*T*he hour was long past Howe's curfew and Market Street should have been deserted, but the pavement teemed with horses and men, and the windows of Howe's mansion blazed with light.

Bay met him on the steps of the house. "Good God, Peter. What did you do to antagonize André?"

Tremayne stiffened. "Why? What's happened?"

"André needled Donop about his folly with the Merry Widow at Mount Holly. Then Donop went off spoiling for a fight and picked an argument with Howe and Howe gave Donop his wish. He's leading the attack on Mercer. Tonight. Now. And you're going with him."

"Why me? There's no use for cavalry on that ground, and I'm no engineer." But he knew why before he said it. Because André wanted him out of the way so he could deal with Kate—to arrange another accident, this one fatal.

"You reconnoitered the fort last week, and you

speak French. You're to be the count's interpreter. But you're going because André wanted it. I did tell you to toady to the man. But you've gone and wounded his vanity somehow, and so he's cooked up this piece of nastiness for you."

There was no way to tell Bay *why* André had cooked up this particular nastiness: that he wanted Tremayne out of the city to be free to dispose of Bay's fiancée. But perhaps Bay could protect Kate, if he thought André posed another sort of danger. "It was Lydia," he said, her false name thick on his tongue. "André spiked her drink and tried to get her alone."

Caide snorted. "André? Don't you know, Peter? She's not his type."

"How can you be so sure of that?"

"Because *I* am his type. Don't look so shocked, Peter. Everyone does it at school, then pretends later that no one does it at all."

"Does Howe know?"

"I expect so. Howe has his own peculiarities, so he's disinclined to throw stones. In any case, André is nothing if not discreet."

"Bay, I don't know why he was trying to get her alone, but it was for no good purpose. Keep her away from him."

"You don't know Lydia. She's more than a match for the little Huguenot, whatever he's up to. I'm off to deliver the orders for the bombardment to the *Augusta*. Supposedly they've cleared two of the chevaux out of the river. Enough to plot a course around the obstructions and warp through on tow lines, if the tide is right. Or run aground and miss the fort altogether. For God's sake, Peter, be careful out there. I don't care what the oddsmakers say. Howe's sending a thousand men to take a fort that could swallow twice that number. It's going to be Breed's Hill all over again."

Bishop and rook. André was clearing the board to take the queen, to take Kate. Removing Tremayne, and removing Caide.

Tremayne felt desperate. "I can't go with Donop. I'm supposed to be searching for the Merry Widow."

"Yes, you were. But tonight you are ordered to Mercer with Donop. André has taken against you, Peter. If you fail to report, he'll have you arrested for desertion."

He was outmaneuvered. And Kate . . . Kate was alone, and helpless. He could not return for her now, could not spirit her away to safety.

Caide misinterpreted his expression. "Cheer up, Peter. You'll be back in two days. The Widow will keep until then. And you won't have to hunt her alone. I've hired you a beater to flush her out." Bay pitched his voice to the street behind him. "Bring Lord Sancreed's horse."

In the crush of men and drays filling the street, Tremayne's chestnut mare was unmistakable. So was the young officer who held her: Phillip Lytton.

Eight

Philadelphia, October 21, 1777

A canopy floated overhead. Hers at Grey Farm was white. This one was blue. Kate closed her eyes, then opened them again. It was still there. She must be at the Valbys', then. Devout Friends were not given to voicing profanities, but she had learned a number of choice oaths since coming to the City of Brotherly Love, and she swore them now in the privacy of her mind, and wished herself home at Grey Farm, where the scuffed floors would not show the stains from what she was about to do.

She threw back the Valbys' fine chintz counterpane and vomited over the side of the bed. It had the feeling of finality to it. She did not think she would be sick again, if only because there was nothing left in her stomach. At least the carpets here were not hers to beat clean.

She'd been so stupid, so besotted with Peter Tremayne that she'd drunk poison from his hand. The man had a knack for throwing her off balance. Whenever she encountered him, practical Kate Grey of Grey Farm fled, and she was not replaced by cunning Lydia Dare, agent of the Merry Widow. She was replaced by a dunderhead who made terrible mistakes.

Like turning to him for help.

She'd had no reason to hope for his assistance, but she'd obeyed some instinct that told her to reach out to him in her extremity. They'd met only twice since his return to Philadelphia, and neither meeting could have been termed a success. Just moments before she was stricken, she'd misjudged his mood and appealed to him with a bit of imbecilic coquetry for which she'd been instantly ashamed. He'd turned on his heel and left.

And then saved her life. She was alive because of a man she should count as her enemy.

Or at least she was half alive. And some drama had unfolded here while she was unconscious. The patterned curtains at the foot of the bed were torn, and shreds of knotted blue chintz hung from the arms of the chair beside her bed.

Whoever had been here, whatever had transpired, Tremayne had seen her safely through the night. Now she must see herself safely through the day. Because he had promised to come back for her. And she had made her decision. Lydia Dare's career as a spy was over. When Peter returned, it would be Kate Grey who would leave with him.

She swung her legs over the side of the bed but when her feet touched the floor, her legs buckled under

her. She crawled to the washstand. There was fresh water in the pitcher, and tea—a luxurious concession to
her infirmity—and sugar by the kettle. She grasped
the cool iron pot stand and pulled it to the edge of the
brick, extracted a warm coal from the brass box nestled
against the fireback, kindled a small blaze, and lay
down to rest on the floor.

The morning passed in a series of similar battles
with the weight of the kettle, the brightness of the sun,
the chill of the washbasin. Every completed action was
a tiny victory.

Mrs. Valby knocked on her door twice, and asked
in a worried voice if she was feeling well. Kate called
back to her, claiming a headache caused by overindul-
gence. She knew better than to endanger the Valbys by
sharing confidences with them.

Finally, at noon, she was clean and dressed, with a
stomach full of sweet tea and a delicate equilibrium
that suggested she unlock the door and attempt the
stairs, *slowly*.

By the time she reached the bottom, her knuckles
were whiter than the ivory cap of the newel post.

She went straight to the henhouse, punched two
holes in an egg, blew the contents out, and slipped a
tightly rolled note inside. The egg she marked with a
cross and placed at the back of the top shelf where Angela Ferrers knew to look for it. Then she returned to
the house and ordered the maids to wash her blue silk
petticoat and hang it immediately up to dry in the
garden.

It was her signal flag. The Widow, or one of her
agents, would see it and come for the message in the
egg. Howe and André and their minions were wise to

invisible inks, experienced in cracking codes, expert at interrogation, but they could not, if their lives depended on it, imagine that anything normally found in the henhouse or laundry could be important. It was a failing Kate had determined to use against them.

Even the short trip to the garden had tired her, but she knew she mustn't spend the day in bed. There might be talk, and talk, when you were a spy living under an assumed name, could prove fatal. So she forced herself to join Mrs. Valby in her bedroom for an hour of sewing. Despite the older woman's stream of pleasant chatter, Kate had to fight to stay awake, jabbing herself with her needle whenever she started to nod off.

When the doorbell rang in the early afternoon the maid brought her a note from a gentleman who, she said, was waiting on her answer. The card was unsigned, but the writer desired an audience with her to tender his apologies for last night.

It could only be Tremayne.

Kate hurried to the parlor and made a hasty attempt to improve her appearance, but she quickly realized that nothing would put roses into her pallid cheeks, and chose a seat by the hearth so she might at least borrow the glow from the fire.

In the end, it didn't matter. Her caller, when the door opened, was not Tremayne.

It was John André.

*S*he is a keen hunter and an excellent shot," Donop said of the Merry Widow, as they marched through the Jersey woods at the head of the

Hessian column. "As well as a beauty," he added, eyeing his companion challengingly.

Tremayne had had no choice but to come. He could not help Kate from a deserters' prison. His only option was to join Donop on this debacle and pray that Angela Ferrers had not escaped her bonds last night to take a warning to the Rebels; that Fort Mercer remained undergarrisoned, and would surrender without a fight. The sooner the business was done, the sooner he could return to Kate. Lytton trailed silently behind them, and Tremayne hoped he did not speak French.

"The Merry Widow is a known agent of foreign powers, in the pay of the French most likely. You can't keep her with you if you're attached to the army," Tremayne reasoned.

"What," Donop asked, "is the point in being a count if I may not do as I please? The lady shall get no intelligence through me, and she shall be too well occupied on her back to make other mischief. If there is difficulty with your government, then I shall marry her and there will be an end to it."

"She is hardly a suitable countess." Nor was Kate.

"I thought, Lord Sancreed, that your ancestor was a famous Leveller. You have not inherited his egalitarianism."

"That was my cousin Bayard's forbear, not mine, and he paid dearly for his principles. He was drawn and quartered and stripped of his lands and title. That is why I hold Sancreed and not Bay. You, on the other hand, are not an egalitarian. You're just pigheaded on the subject of this woman."

Donop laughed, the short, sharp bark of delight that Tremayne was coming to recognize as characteristic of the man, whose gusto was infectious. "Hah! Maybe so. Your cousin strives to regain his ancestor's status through arms. Caide is a famous name. His uncle amassed a great fortune and attempted to buy back the title and disinherit you, did he not?"

Tremayne was not surprised by the count's depth of knowledge. With its fractious, fractured peerages and patchwork states, the German aristocracy had an insatiable appetite for genealogy and disputed successions. Tremayne spared a glance to be sure Lytton was not paying attention, then said, "Bay does not share his late uncle's obsession with Sancreed. There is no enmity between us over the title. We were raised together."

"Still, I always thought it peculiar that his uncle should labor and politic to reclaim the title, when he had no son to pass it on to."

Tremayne treated Donop to a frosty silence.

"I have trespassed. Forgive me, Major," Donop said.

"Howe refused your request for more guns."

The count allowed the subject of Tremayne's family tree to drop without further comment. "Your general meant to provoke me into disobeying him. He thinks we Germans are cowardly and weak, and that without every convenience of war, we will cower in Philadelphia. But we will show him otherwise."

He'd pitched the last to be heard in the column behind them. His Jaegers, the elite Hessian riflemen, cheered. Donop waved his showy Hessian tricorn. The peridot on his cockade winked in the sunlight—and shattered into a thousand glittering fragments.

Tremayne, by instinct and training, turned in the

direction the bullet had come from. Thick woods on all sides. Perfect for hiding snipers.

What you wanted to do was fold yourself up no wider than one of the surrounding trees, close your eyes, and pray no one hit you. Lytton was already doing a very fine impression of a Dutch elm, but Tremayne had been a soldier long enough to know that death would find him if it was looking hard enough, and all he could control was how he met it.

Donop didn't so much as flinch. He poked a finger through the bullet hole in his hat and nodded appreciatively. "A good shot. An excellent marksman. But we have better." He barked a set of orders in German and his Jaegers parted like the Red Sea, dividing down the center of the road and taking up positions in the tree line on either side of the way. They were the cream of the Hessian infantry, and it showed.

More shots rang out. Lytton remained frozen in the middle of the road, asking to be hit. Tremayne could have solved a great many of his problems by leaving him there, but he pulled the boy into the tree line instead.

"He's mad," Lytton said, watching Donop stroll down the center of the road, a glittering target in blue silk and silver lace. It was the sort of lunatic bravado Tremayne could not help but admire. He was coming to quite like Carl Donop.

A few more shots were exchanged. The skirmish was over almost as soon as it had begun, and the march resumed. Two hours later Donop fell into step beside Tremayne once more and asked, "What do you make of our friends in the woods?"

"They are keeping pace with us, and they are being led by a professional," he replied.

"Just so," said Donop. "It is a pity you recruited so many colonials in your last war with the French, then denied them commissions in your army. I understand Washington is just such a man."

"Hindsight is eagle-eyed," Tremayne said evenly. But it was true. The tactics employed against their column were exactly right for a small band of militia facing a much larger force on home ground. The Americans knew what they were doing. Say what you liked about the Rebels, and Tremayne often said a great deal, but these particular men were well led, most likely by someone who had served with the British against the French and Indians. There was no shortage of such men in America, but most of them likely mirrored their counterparts in the British Army, and were competent if uninspired tacticians. This unseen adversary was something different. There was a keen intellect, a talent for war, at work somewhere in the Jersey woods.

Donop shared his opinion. As they talked, largely in French, Tremayne found that they had much in common. They were of a similar age, social class, and martial inclination.

But Donop possessed the autocratic arrogance of his race. He spoke now without caution or delicacy, enumerating the deficiencies of the brothers Howe. "They are Whigs. American sympathizers, Black Billy and Black Dick. When the general last stood for Parliament he stated publicly that he would refuse service in America. He is only here because your king personally persuaded him to come. He has no stomach for fighting the Americans; still holds out hopes of negotiating a peace. Only a fool like your secretary of state, Lord Germain, would send such men to prosecute this war. You also, I suspect, have Whig sympathies, Peter. Why, then, did you request service in America?"

Tremayne studied the rutted surface of the road. It was littered with sweet-gum sticker-balls, brown, spiked, and damned uncomfortable beneath his boots. "Because I thought it offered greater scope for advancement." But what he meant was that he hated his station in Ireland, because he had no desire to uphold laws that were abhorrent to him.

At Haddonfield, Donop found quarters for himself in a trim little farmhouse and camped his men under canvas on the heights overlooking the town. It was then that they realized yet another consequence of Howe's impulsive orders: the Hessians had no rations. Men could not trek for miles and fight on an empty stomach. Flour and apples might be purchased from the farmers of Haddonfield, but something must be done if the men were to have any meat that night.

Turkey were abundant in the Haddonfield woods, so Donop ordered his Jaeger captain, Ewald, to organize a hunting party, and retired to his quarters to confer with his battalion officers. Since Tremayne was not needed as a translator, he left Donop closeted in the cramped and smoky kitchen of the farmhouse to smoke his pipe in the orchard outside.

He was not alone for long.

"Major." The energetic Captain Ewald, with his martial bearing and dashing eye patch, who Tremayne noted was only a few years younger than himself, came striding out of the farmhouse, the picture of Hessian professionalism. The man had somehow found time to restore the gloss of his mustache and the shine of boots after the march, no doubt with the same blacking. "The colonel presents his compliments. He wishes that you should not miss the sport." He handed Tremayne a rifle, longer than the typical Jaeger weapon, and lighter as well.

"This is one of Ferguson's. How did Donop get hold of it?"

Ewald's lips twitched. It was not quite a smile. "The count is a man of resource. And he likes his hunting. You have heard of the gun?"

"I've heard it may be fired six times in a minute."

"Just so. And yet your General Howe will not make use of the weapon."

Tremayne wouldn't touch the remark about Howe, but he wondered, not for the first time, what it must be like to be an ambitious junior officer without title or fortune, serving beneath a man like Donop, or for that matter, beneath a man like himself. "What is Donop like in the field?" Tremayne asked, flipping open the breech and admiring the smooth motion of the spring.

Ewald, he noted, did nothing so unbefitting his Hessian dignity as to turn and look into the trees behind him, but his eyes did scan the empty fields on either side before he spoke. They were quite alone. "He is as you have observed. Cool under fire. Brave to within a hairsbreadth of recklessness."

"Just so. And?" Tremayne prompted.

"He has only two faults, Lord Sancreed, and only one of those is likely to get us killed tomorrow. He is proud, and exceedingly fond of the fair sex."

"I'd rather thought we were here for both reasons: his pride and his amours."

And now Ewald did turn to look at the farmhouse behind him, and did smile. "You may be interested to know that for a man who rarely denies himself pleasure when it is offered, the count has been curiously temperate these past months. He has not had a woman, that I know of, since Mount Holly."

Ewald bowed and took his leave to organize the hunting party.

And that was how Tremayne found himself, dogged once more by Lytton, advancing with the ambitious young Jaeger captain, Ewald, and sixty hungry riflemen through the Jersey woods at dusk, the moon already up and night coming on fast.

Turkeys gobbled in the distance. The Jaegers gobbled back, attempting to draw them, but the birds would not come out, and the party was forced to drive deeper into the woods.

Tremayne needed to speak to Lytton privately, before they returned to the city, and this was likely to be his best chance. Having arrived in Philadelphia only the previous day, the young lieutenant had not yet had time to meet Caide's fiancée and identify her as the spy of Grey Farm. The boy had to be sent back to New York, before he exposed Kate.

Tremayne stopped Lytton at the top of a ravine as the Jaegers descended, gobbling and clucking. When they had passed, Tremayne said, "Has Caide told you why he brought you to Philadelphia?"

"Yes," the boy said, but he sounded uncertain. "To help you hunt for the spy who stole your dispatches at Grey Farm."

Kate's name lingered unspoken between them.

"I don't want your help. After Mercer is taken, you're going back to New York." It sounded like a curt dismissal, but Tremayne couldn't help that. He could not explain himself.

"I can't. I was cashiered when your troop was disbanded. Your cousin allowed me to purchase a captaincy in his regiment."

Tremayne hadn't known, hadn't given another thought to Lytton after the court had dismissed him. The boy had been under his command, had been his responsibility. He should have made it his business to see him clear of the whole mess. He had been callous, and now Kate would pay for it. Lytton would expose her. She would be arrested, and hanged.

"You disapproved of my morals at Grey Farm, Phillip. You'll like my cousin's even less. Sell your commission or transfer to another regiment before Bay puts you to the test and you find that you cannot stomach his orders, because it will come to that. You will be forced to betray yourself, or your commanding officer."

"I'm afraid that I can no longer afford such scruples. I mean to make my career in the army, and after what happened while I was under your command, no other regiment will have me."

And here was the crux of the matter. Tremayne was already perilously close to treason himself. He was consorting with a known spy, concealing her presence from Howe, in direct violation of orders. This, all for a woman he had once kissed fleetingly in a stifling farmhouse many months ago. He had no right to ask another man to dally with treason.

"I may be the author of your misfortune, Phillip, but I have no intention of handing a lady over to Howe for espionage, no matter what she has done. No gentleman would."

There was something cold and brittle in Lytton's eyes, and Tremayne recognized it as hurt pride. He recognized also that had he behaved with anything like the chivalry Lytton had unsuccessfully championed at Grey Farm, Kate would not be in danger now. But it was too late. Tremayne had stolen her letter, attempted to seduce her. He had embittered the callow boy standing before him, and placed an innocent girl at the mercy of John André.

Lytton spoke coolly now. "Miss Grey is not a lady; she is a traitor."

"Howe isn't looking for Miss Grey. He wants the Merry Widow, Mrs. Ferrers."

"Then I will advance my fortunes twice as quickly by bringing Howe two spies instead of one."

"You don't know what you are talking about, Lytton. This thing is more complicated than you understand. Trust me. If you discover Miss Grey, you will find no friends in your current posting." Caide would not love any man who brought him proof of his sweetheart's treachery. Whatever else his cousin might be, Tremayne had no doubt that in his own strange, obsessive fashion, Bay was in love with Kate. But everything Bay touched, he destroyed. Tremayne would not allow him to destroy Kate.

Below in the ravine, the Jaegers whooped and huzzahed. A giant tom turkey, eyes glittering in the moonlight, breast puffed and wattle trembling, tore from the brush. The angry gobbler clucked and flapped his wings, then rushed at the Hessians. The Jaegers pointed and laughed, and the enlisted men fell back and encouraged Ewald to take his shot.

Lytton stared at the crazed turkey. "It's attacking. Stupid bird."

"No," said Tremayne, understanding dawning too late, "it's running away."

But not from us. It was an ambush.

Most of the Jaegers were now in the bottom of the ravine, with little or no cover. Heavy fire erupted from the trees ahead and above. Some of it was buckshot, to judge by the sound of it. Ungentlemanly, but a particularly good choice in the fading light.

The Jaegers hadn't been following turkeys into the woods. They'd been drawn by the gobbles and clucks of the Rebels.

Clever. Very clever indeed. The Jaegers were in an indefensible position. The Americans poured their fire into the bottom of the ravine, which would soon prove a killing field.

Fortunately, Ewald was no fool. He and his men had been after turkey tonight, not Rebels. Mercer remained the real goal, and to take Mercer, Donop must get his force intact to Red Bank. The young captain ordered a hasty retreat, and the Jaegers began to scrabble, tree to tree, back the way they had come. Professionals to a man, a few paused, when a convenient tree or position permitted, to return fire—hoping to unsettle the unseen ambushers and cover the withdrawal.

Tremayne motioned for silence and led Lytton to an outcropping of rock. He lay down flat over the cold stone with the Ferguson beside him. Lytton did likewise with his own gun.

The Americans were nearly invisible in the twilit woods. Tremayne would have liked to pick off their officers, but he could find none; no gold braid or silver lace to mark his targets.

Tremayne passed the Ferguson to Lytton. "Here. Give me yours." Muzzle-loading a rifle while prone was difficult but not impossible, and Tremayne was likelier to do it quickly than Lytton was to master the art in the next few moments.

They could hear the Rebels calling to one another. The Americans knew the Jaegers were retreating, and there was clearly some disagreement about whether or not to follow. A horse whinnied. "That is the sound of a target, Lytton. An officer. Whoever is sitting that mount is paid a good deal better than the poor bastards on the ground. Kill him, if you please."

The boy scanned the trees. There was a single rider on a massive gray horse, his face invisible beneath a crumpled brown hat. Lytton looked through the sights of the Ferguson, and took aim. The rider removed his disreputable headgear, and for Peter Tremayne, the world stopped.

Tremayne had never set eyes on the man before, but even in the moonlight there was no mistaking the quirked mouth or the peculiar set of the stubbled jaw.

Lytton drew back the trigger. Tremayne had no time to think. He hurled himself against the boy, knocking the rifle over the rock. The gun went off and the two men tumbled down the incline together, striking every root and stone in their path and fetching up at the bottom of the ravine.

Lying on his back, the wind knocked out of him, bleeding from a dozen cuts, Tremayne heard the horse crashing through the trees, knew the rider would be on him any minute.

He climbed to his feet. He left his saber hanging at his hip, unlaced his neckcloth, and when the rider was within twenty feet, held it aloft in surrender and called out, "Colonel Grey, I have an urgent matter to discuss with you."

"Who the devil are you, sir?" Arthur Grey was not a handsome man, even in the kindness of moonlight. But his face, unlovely and masculine as it was, bore the same stamp as his exquisite daughter's softer features.

"My name is Peter Tremayne." He hesitated, then added, "Viscount Sancreed. I'm an officer on Howe's general staff. And I must tell you that your daughter is in danger."

"Title or no, if you are threatening my home, I'll shoot you in cold blood." Tremayne felt the temperature drop considerably. Kate Grey might espouse pacifism, but her father held no such beliefs.

On the ground a few feet away Lytton stirred and groaned. Tremayne was running out of time. Arthur Grey was quite possibly the only man in the world who could help Kate if Tremayne did not return from Mercer.

"Your daughter is not at home. She is in Philadelphia, with the Merry Widow, the woman who calls herself Angela Ferrers. She is spying for Washington. Howe knows there is a traitor in his midst. Howe's spymaster suspects it is Kate."

Arthur Grey said nothing, so Tremayne went on, willing Phillip Lytton to remain dazed for a few minutes longer. "There are only two men at present who can identify her. Myself and Mr. Lytton here. He wishes her caught so he may advance his career."

"If my daughter is with Angela Ferrers—and I'm not saying I believe you, mind—then she is in no danger. I knew the lady during the last war. She is a resourceful woman, more than capable of keeping Kate safe. And my daughter is not given to wild exploits."

"Angela Ferrers has allowed your daughter to become engaged to Bayard Caide."

Arthur Grey laughed out loud. It was not the reaction Tremayne expected.

"You, sir," said Arthur Grey, "are either mistaken, or a madman. My daughter is not the sort of woman to attract the attention of a man like Butcher Caide."

In Tremayne's mind was a picture of Kate as she had appeared the day they met. She stood beside the elegant, silk-clad Widow on the wide porch of Grey House, her faded skirts singed, pie crumbs in her hair, and a singularly unimpressed quirk to her mouth as she scrutinized him and his men. No, the Kate her father had known would not be of interest to Bayard Caide, but the woman she had become in Philadelphia was of interest to any man with a healthy carnal appetite. This, however, was not an observation calculated to win over a woman's father, particularly when that father was leveling a loaded rifle at your chest and your own allies were slipping fast away into the woods.

"I am afraid, sir," said Grey, pointing his gun at Tremayne, "that if you can offer me no better proof of your claims, I will feel obliged to take the surest route to protect my family, and kill you."

In answer, Tremayne reached into his tunic and

drew out a crumpled length of green ribbon. It was proof of his acquaintance with Kate Grey. And evidence that Arthur Grey ought to shoot him anyway. Because he had eaten this man's salt, and drunk this man's whisky, and sheltered beneath this man's roof.

And then tried his damnedest to debauch this man's daughter.

Nine

Kate sat frozen in her place by the fire.

John André bowed deeply in the parlor doorway.

As he rose, his gold-flecked eyes surveyed her. He was scrutinizing her, she realized, for the lingering effects of the opium. Anger put color in her cheeks. She surged to her feet in one smooth movement, and stood with the practiced grace Mrs. Ferrers had taught her.

It was a challenge, and André read it as such. He cocked his head in answer, a smile tugging at the corner of his mouth. For a fleeting second Kate detected in his eyes something entirely unexpected: approval.

Then Peggy Shippen was bounding past him like a puppy and the moment passed. Kate sat down with relief. The room had begun to swim when she stood so quickly.

Peggy did not sit. She circled the hearth rug in a dizzying pattern. "John is designing costumes for the new theater. My father says I may not model for him, but he says you're already engaged to Colonel Caide so nothing you can do can bring you lower."

André draped himself over one of Mrs. Valby's silk damask chairs. "Charm, in the Shippen family, does not skip generations," he drawled.

Oblivious to the slight, Peggy basked in the attention, but André's eyes were fixed on Kate. "I'm so happy to see you recovered from your indisposition, Miss Dare."

Something in his tone must have reached even the dim consciousness of Peggy, who disliked being out of the spotlight for even a moment. "Everyone says you were so drunk that Lord Sancreed had to take you home so as not to embarrass their family."

It was a nasty thing to say, but there was no sting in it for Kate. Peggy was in love with André, and he had barely spared her a glance since arriving. Today, as before, Kate noted how curiously impersonal was André's interest in the girl. "Yes," Kate said. "It was imprudent of me, to drink as I did. I'll take greater care in future."

"André says you would make a fine Kate," Peggy offered, trying to take hold of the conversation.

André's gold-flecked eyes flickered briefly to Peggy, then returned to Kate. He was still watching her, gauging her reaction. If he had arrived at her door with a squadron of marines and a warrant, she would have been on firmer ground. "Flattering, but of small consequence. My parents are no longer taking suggestions on the subject of my name, Captain André." It struck her then, the reason André kept Peggy at arm's length. *Cinaedus*, Hamilton had called him. A lover of men. She had thought the slur just an insult, not a literal descriptor, but now she understood. "Although yours, I suspect, might have done better to choose Alcibiades."

He smiled openly now. "I am more Critias than Alcibiades, I suspect." He leapt up, took her hand, and pressed it to his lips. "And I was making reference to the character in *The Taming of the Shrew*. You would make a fine Kate, but we are staging *No One's Enemy but His Own* instead. Will you come model my costume for Lucinda? Mr. Black assures me he has fifteen yards of spangled muslin, and his wife is, I believe, reputed to be the best dressmaker in Philadelphia."

Anstiss Black was indeed the best dressmaker in Philadelphia. That is why Mrs. Ferrers had chosen her to outfit Kate for the role of heiress. Kate realized it was possible that André knew this, and was still testing her. His playfulness in the parlor did not mean he had forgone the option of clapping her in irons, or breaking down her door in the dead of night.

She could not recall whether Mrs. Ferrers had ever used her real name in front of Anstiss Black, had no idea how deeply the woman might or might not be in the Widow's confidence. She must gird herself for a tricky encounter; but the burst of anger that had sustained her in the parlor dissipated in the carriage. Her fatigue returned as she sat hemmed in by bolts of cotton lawn and watered silk, the bench littered with paper-wrapped packages and spools of tasseled trim.

Fortunately André had at last turned his attention to feeding Peggy Shippen's infatuation. The pair sat on the bench opposite, André's fine-boned hands a supple blur. He was weaving cat's cradles out of silver lace for the giggling girl, seemingly unaware of Kate's discomfort.

Mrs. Black greeted Kate with the warmth reserved for a favored customer. She drew Kate into a back room and helped her into the confection André had ordered.

"She will meet you at Du Simitière's at seven thirty," Anstiss Black whispered as she tugged the gown over Kate's shoulders.

When Kate emerged from the back room in the spangled muslin, André applauded and Peggy sulked. The seamstress was unused to being directed by a man, but once Kate was up on the block, professional instinct took over and Mrs. Black draped, pinned, and basted with the exacting skill for which she was famed.

The muslin was frost blue and stiff with sizing, and scratched Kate's arms, which ached as she held them spread wide for Mrs. Black to pin the sleeves. The final concoction was a sort of polonaise, body-skimming and tied at the waist, but curiously tight through the shoulders.

Kate tried to lower her arms. The row of pins extending from her wrist to the sensitive flesh along her ribs twisted and bit into her skin, and she instantly jerked her arms upright again.

"If you want the sleeves that tight, Captain André," Mrs. Black pointed out, "you'll have to sew it on your actress the night of the performance."

André stood up and made a slow circuit around Kate. "It is really quite good, Mrs. Black, but it lacks the color and panache required for the stage." He turned to Peggy, who was still attempting to duplicate one of André's cat's cradles, and ruining at least three yards of Mrs. Black's best beaded lace in the process. "I know just the thing. Peggy, dearest, would you nip out to the carriage and find that spool of tasseled cord we bought this morning?"

Peggy's face lit up, and she jumped to do her master's bidding. Kate hated to see it, knew by training and instinct that such slavish enthusiasm was the surest route to losing a man's interest. But then, if Kate's surmise was correct, Peggy had never had a chance of capturing André's real affections.

When Peggy was gone, André's gracious smile faded. He turned to Mrs. Black. "Get out." His voice dropped an octave from the musical tone he had used with Peggy.

"I should like to be unpinned first," Kate said, her arms aching.

Mrs. Black looked from Kate to André, picked up her skirts and hurried from the room.

Kate stood pinned like a butterfly on a card while André locked the door. When he turned to face her, there was none of this morning's good humor in his countenance.

"And now, Miss Grey, let us discuss how matters stand between us."

"Why, Captain André, I believe there must be so many ladies vying for your attention that you have begun to mix us up. My name is Dare."

"It does suit you better than Grey. Are your arms getting tired?"

She was beginning to feel faint, but she wouldn't give him the satisfaction. "I'm quite comfortable, thank you."

"Good. I wish to apologize for my behavior at the concert, and to give new offense while doing so would defeat my purpose. You see, I thought you quite an ordinary little eavesdropper, as decorative and useless as you appear. The Merry Widow has a knack for training butterflies."

"Is that what you are doing with Peggy?"

André laughed. "Not quite a butterfly, is she? More like a spaniel."

"It's cruel. She's in love with you."

"And Bayard Caide is in love with you. Or is cruelty acceptable in his case?"

"What is it you want, Captain André? If you have the proof to move against me, I wish you would do so, as my arms are getting tired."

"I have all the proof I need to make you disappear forever, Miss Grey."

"Bay wouldn't like it."

"No, proof wouldn't sway him. But if he knew you were sleeping with his cousin, he'd wield the knife himself."

"I barely know Peter Tremayne. I've only just met him," she countered. She was prepared to face her own fate, afraid though she was, but she would not drag Tremayne down with her.

"Please, Miss Grey. I wish this to be a new beginning between us, and for that we must have honesty. As soon as I saw you with Tremayne at the concert, I knew. It was the work of a few hours to retrace Lord Sancreed's steps the day his dispatches were stolen. And Quakers, with rare exception, have no talent for prevarication. Your name is Katherine Grey. You are the only daughter of Arthur Grey, who was known in the last war as the Grey Fox. A very capable commander at present absent from home and believed to be serving with the Continentals, despite his adoptive faith. You have a very pretty friend named Milly who survived some rough handling from a party of dragoons and has just been brought to bed of a healthy baby boy. Sadly for the child, his father is imprisoned in the State House for treason. And it was not Angela Ferrers who distracted Tremayne the night he lost the dispatches. It was you."

Kate refused to faint. Her tired arms were sagging, the pins scoring her flesh, prickles of blood beginning to well, but she continued to meet his golden gaze steadily. "Then arrest me, and be done with it." It would, she realized with a sickening sense of fatalism, be a relief. It must be how Angela Ferrers faced death with such calm, because it held the promise of an end to the gut-wrenching tension and fear.

"I have no desire to arrest you, Miss Grey. I wish, instead, to employ you. The Merry Widow has a rare eye for talent. To find amidst the rye and barley fields of New Jersey a girl who could captivate not only Peter Tremayne but also Bayard Caide is testament to the Widow's acumen. And your nerve. Few women could stomach the two of them, knowing their relationship."

"Their grandfathers were cousins. They are distant relations," she said.

"They are surely more than that, Miss Grey. Only close kinship could produce such congruity of form and figure. And the eyes, Miss Grey. Such strikingly pale blue eyes are rare. Neither Bayard Caide's mother, nor Tremayne's, had such eyes."

She realized that he was talking about more than

illegitimacy, which was common enough. He had her at a disadvantage, knew some secret about this ancient family that he hoped to use against her, so she said, "No man is responsible for the circumstances of his birth."

"Quite so. And yet he must live with them nevertheless. I am an ambitious man, but I labor under the taint of my proclivities, with which I assure you I was born, and of my French blood. Through you, I could wield power over the Tremaynes. It is a difficult choice: to make you the mistress of a lord with the ear of the king, or the wife of a coming man who might rise even higher."

"My services are not for sale, Captain André."

"No? Then consider this. You have been under constant surveillance since the concert. When the Merry Widow next tries to contact you, my men will take her. You will be alone. If you try to leave the city, you will be arrested. You were, until a few months ago, the spinster daughter of a man loyal to the king. Now you are the daughter of a traitor, and living under an assumed name. You have only the skills of a spy or a courtesan, and to practice either craft you must have a protector. Work for me, Miss Grey."

André stepped back, inspected Kate dispassionately. "Become my agent, or the next garment I fit for you will be a shroud."

"And Mr. Lytton?" Donop asked, when the turkey had been eaten. They were seated in the Haddonfield farmer's snug kitchen, around a table littered with the remains of the crazy-eyed gobbler from the woods.

"Taken by the enemy," Tremayne replied smoothly. The turkey had tasted like ashes in his mouth. He'd handed a man under his command over to the enemy. Arthur Grey had agreed to take Phillip Lytton prisoner, and let Tremayne go. In return Tremayne had sworn to return to Philadelphia to rescue the man's stubborn daughter. Tremayne wondered what Kate would think of the sacrifices made in her name.

"Too bad," said Donop, with no sympathy whatsoever. "But he is a gentleman of good family, and will no doubt endure confinement in comfort until he is traded back to us. Besides, he seemed a bit of a prig."

Then the brandy was passed, the merits of the Ferguson were discussed, and no further mention was made of Phillip Lytton.

When Mercer came into sight the next day, crisp and neat in the midday sun, with the river sparkling silver through the trees, Tremayne cursed. Two weeks ago the fort had been a tumbledown pile of bricks buried in orchard groves, but the Rebels had been busy. Now it stood in an efficient clearing, devoid of cover, the felled trees put to wicked use as an abatis.

Donop surveyed the works through a spyglass. "You do not think I should attempt it, Peter." It was not a question.

Tremayne answered anyway. "Not without a crack team of engineers equipped with axes to cut through the abatis." They'd used apple trees, probably cut down a whole orchard. It was a technique as old as war, to fell trees and ring forts with their tangling branches. Fruit trees, apple, pear, and peach were best, with their small but closely growing branches. It would take hours to clear that ring of snarled boughs.

Donop offered him a small fatalistic shrug. "We will use our artillery."

It was not a job for a small battery of artillery. Donop's guns would only blow a narrow hole in the abatis and the wall behind it. A bottleneck. The worst possible way to attack a fortification. The Hessian must know it, but could not, with honor, turn back now.

It was late afternoon by the time the lines were drawn up and ready for attack, and Tremayne's impatience must have showed. Donop smirked at him and said, "Are you eager to attack, or eager to get back to the girl, my friend?"

"What girl?" Tremayne said.

"The small one who is fucking the cousin of yours who should be Lord Sancreed." And that was about as plainly put as the matter could be.

"She isn't sleeping with him."

Donop slapped him on the back. "Very well. There is no girl, and she is not fucking your cousin." He made a sweeping gesture toward the fort. "Tonight, this shall be called Fort Donop, or I shall be dead."

He ordered the artillery crew to open with their guns, and the gravel from Mercer's rooftops flew black against the orange sunset, like the crown of an exploding volcano.

The bombardment lasted less than ten minutes, consumed the bulk of their powder, and blew a hole twenty feet wide in the east wall, at the end of the two-hundred-foot extension that ran parallel to the river. Then the Grenadier battalion, five hundred strong, charged through the breech, screaming.

Tremayne and Donop followed. They emerged in a long, narrow enclosure filled with shouting Grenadiers.

There were no Rebel defenders. The extension was abandoned.

Tremayne turned to the east, where von Lengerke should have been coming over the bastion wall with another five hundred Hessians, and where the barracks and powder sheds should lie. Instead, there was another abatis, and behind it another set of walls. A fort within the fort. Which made the area they were standing in a killing ground.

"*Mein Gott.* If you have not the men to defend the perimeter, then build smaller walls within. *Ja.* It is what *I* would do. I am impressed," Donop acknowledged.

"Don't be." Tremayne felt only disgust. "The Rebels didn't build this. This means they have French engineers. And French powder. And French guns. Turn back. The odds are changed. Honor does not demand this."

Donop shrugged, noted his subalterns' efforts to impose some order on the milling Grenadiers. "The odds might be different, but the stakes remain the same. In any case, I prefer the French as adversaries. At least they are professionals. Shall we?"

They were halfway to the second abatis and the little inner fort when the American gunships on the river announced their presence with a volley of grapeshot, driving the Hessians toward the landside wall. Tremayne didn't like it, the men massing so close under the breastworks, but Donop pressed on: undaunted, invigorated if anything by the chaos of the battle, the smell of powder, the din of shot and shell.

With military engineers trained to deal with enemy field fortification—or even with good axes—an abatis was no impediment, but the Hessians had neither. The Grenadier column of five hundred men, already squeezed tight to escape the deadly fire from the river, began to coil like a spring behind the obstruction.

There was nothing to do but go forward, so Tremayne began hacking a path through the trees with his saber. A wiry Grenadier sergeant with the look of an old campaigner, his mustache and boots both a fine, sooty black, fell in behind Tremayne nodding and offering what Tremayne believed to be encouragement in German.

He was almost through the first ring of trees when he turned to check the progress of their advance. The abatis was crawling with men making similarly slow paths.

On the parapet of the south wall, something glittered in the setting sun, and a rank of Rebel gunmen, musket barrels glimmering, rose up and fired on the Hessians.

It was the purest form of slaughter Tremayne had ever seen. The Hessians were penned like cattle by the fire of the naval guns. There was no cover from the muskets on the rampart above. The men who survived the first volley threw themselves into the tangling trees, only to die there, limp bodies hanging like macabre scarecrows.

To turn back was certain death, and pausing to return fire at the occasional Rebel face or arm glimpsed through the smoke of powder was folly. The Grenadier sergeant understood this as well, and had continued hacking, cool as you please, without a glance behind him or up at the rampart.

They pressed on until Tremayne heard the drum

and the bugle that could mean only one thing: retreat. He turned to his companion, and opened his mouth to speak, but the Rebel artillery spoke instead. A shell sang through the air overhead and ripped a hole in the abatis that no amount of saber work could have accomplished.

The explosion deafened him. Hot pain tore through his right cheek, chipped his front tooth, and hurtled out his mouth, leaving behind the peppery tang of powder and blood. After that, everything moved with dreamlike slowness. He heard, as from a distance, the branches twang and snap as he fell into them; felt the burning impact of another bullet tearing through his tunic and into his arm. Then the soft quiet closed in around him.

Ten

Kate was being watched not by one man but by two. The ruffian who observed the front door of the Valby mansion was difficult to spot at first, but when the crowd in the street had changed several times over, when the knife grinder had come and gone, and the boy who sold the *Gazette* and the tinkers and peddlers had finished their trade for the day, a lone figure in a beaver hat still lingered.

The man at the back was easier to spot, because the Valby cook did not like layabouts and any man loitering in her alley who did not take up a broom or a barrel for the coin offered was set upon in short order by the groom, who knew on which side his bread was buttered.

Kate must reach the Widow, and she must not be followed, but by seven she still had no idea how she was supposed to evade the men André had set to watch her.

While she stood hesitating in the parlor window, a fight broke out. There were four toughs, dockworkers by the look of them, all three sheets to the wind, singing at the tops of their lungs and taking good-natured swipes at one another, staggering down the street. When they came level with Beaver Hat, they tried to sweep him into their party and off for a dram. When he refused, they cajoled. When he demurred, they took offense, and a punch was thrown.

Kate snatched her cloak and was out the door and up the street without a backward glance.

She arrived at Mr. Du Simitière's lodgings in Arch Street, just above Fourth and around the corner from Christ Church, at exactly half past. She had never been to visit the peculiar artist and antiquarian before, and was surprised when he asked, however politely, for a sum of fifty cents for the pleasure of calling on him.

"It is for the support of my museum, my collection. For I must devote myself," the plump, bespectacled Swiss said in perfect but odd English, "to the acquisition, cataloging, and display of these artifacts to the detriment of my earning a living."

Such devotion was also plainly to the detriment of his personal appearance and housekeeping, but Kate felt compelled, now that she had paid for the privilege, to investigate the exhibits. His rooms were stuffed full of natural and artificial curiosities.

"Your work as an artist must provide you with some income," Kate said. The man had been commissioned by Congress to commemorate the Declaration with a medal, and to provide the new nation with a suitably grand seal. Surely he could afford a brush for his coat.

"Alas, Congress and Mr. Adams are more generous with suggestions than with cash."

Du Simitière opened an English cabinet, black with age and carved with that peculiar combination of the geometric and organic favored by the Jacobeans. "My Indian department is deficient, particularly in representative pieces from the tribes of the more northerly states, and those of Canada. Should you be traveling north, might I prevail upon you to keep an eye open for any such collectibles as may appear? The governor of New York was formerly a reliable source of information and artifacts, but I have sent him three missives in the last month about my need for information on the diet of the Cayuga people, and he has failed entirely to respond to me."

"I daresay he's rather more occupied with General Burgoyne at the moment, Mr. Du Simitière. There is a war on," she replied, but she was fascinated despite herself. The cabinet was lined with baize and stuffed with tomahawks, war clubs, pipes, bowls, baskets, and arrowheads. He was in possession of quite the largest stone hatchet she had ever seen. She thought she detected bits of bone and dried blood clinging to the blade. "Goodness. How did you acquire that?" she asked.

"I write letters to people and ask them to send me things."

"I find it difficult to believe that this axe's owner was much of a letter writer."

"The hatchet was unearthed on the farm of the late Dr. John Kearsley on the Frankfort Road, about four miles outside our city," replied Du Simitière. "I'm confident its owner had no further need of it," he added brightly.

"You mean he was unearthed along with it."

Du Simitière was elated by her conclusion. "Quite so! Are you a student of antiquarianism, Miss Dare? I believe that much could be learned from studying America's native peoples with the discipline that Herr Winckelmann has applied to the ancients. Grave goods can tell us much about how a people lived. Do you not agree?"

Kate wasn't certain she thought grave robbing was a legitimate form of scholarly inquiry. She agreed, however, that it might be informative, then demurred firmly when he tried to press upon her the loan of a copy of *Geschichte der Kunst des Altertums*.

Delighted to have an appreciative visitor and eager to find more wonders to please her, he begged her to follow him into the next room, where his most recent paintings and drawings were on display.

Du Simitière showed her quarto volumes of clippings detailing the progress of the revolt, from broadsides about the Stamp Act to engravings depicting Boston's Tea Party. Sketches and miniatures of famous men on both sides of the conflict were bound together in his books, as they would never be in life. He was an impartial chronicler, preserving for posterity the Americans and British alike.

She stopped at the easel of a portrait, only half finished, of a handsome, dark, young lieutenant in the scarlet coat and blue facings of the 7th Foot. Something about the gold-flecked eyes and full lips of the subject gave her pause.

"Ah! That is a new commission. For Captain André. A portrait of his younger brother."

"You know Captain André?" she asked, attempting to keep her tone light and conversational, as she wondered if she had stumbled into a trap of the captain's making.

"Mr. Du Simitière knows everyone," said Angela Ferrers, standing in the open door and dripping lightly on the compass rose painted floor. She wore homespun and coarse linen stays beneath a briny apron drenched with oyster liquor. "Your supper, Mr. Du Simitière," she said with unusual cheer, setting a newspaper-wrapped parcel on a wobbling gateleg table.

"Delightful! I shall endeavor to build my own shell mound like our native peoples on the shores of the Delaware!" Du Simitière snatched the soaking package away from his precious drawings and unwrapped the parcel. He produced a knife from his pocket and began shucking and slurping oysters with quiet murmurs of appreciation.

"I had a message for you last night. Where have you been?" Kate asked, hating the petulance that crept into her voice.

Mrs. Ferrers ignored the tone of her question. "Shucking oysters on the dock."

Her disguise was brilliant and practical at the same time. Kate couldn't help but marvel at the woman. "Is that how you got into the city? With the fishing boats?"

"Howe cannot afford to turn away any catch now. We control the roads and the river. There are almost no supplies reaching the city, save what we let pass. I must say"—the Widow smiled at Mr. Du Simitière, carefully removed her sopping apron, and drew Kate into the next room—"America is proving to be a second education for me. Who knew that opening mollusks required such skill?"

"Anyone who has ever lifted a hand in the kitchen," Kate said sourly.

Angela Ferrers laughed musically. "I wonder if you'll be quite so eager to take up your role by the hearth when you return to Grey Farm, after such a glittering winter."

"Howe means to attack Mercer," Kate said.

"Yes, I know. I came to your room last night. I knew that the troop movements I observed in the city and André's attempt on your life must mean an attack on Mercer. Your work allowed me to put it all together and get a warning to Washington last night. By this afternoon, Mercer will have been reinforced, and Colonel Donop will find the road to Red Bank hazardous. Enlisting Tremayne to aid you was resourceful. You did well to get away from André that night, but you didn't tell me Peter Tremayne was back."

The news that the Widow had been in her room when she was unconscious surprised Kate, and now the change in subject took her off guard. So she struck back. "You told me Peter Tremayne and Bayard Caide were cousins. André hinted that they are closer than that, but he did not say how."

Angela Ferrers leaned back and made a critical inspection of Kate. She wasn't fooled by the carefully applied cosmetics, because she had taught Kate to use them.

"Really? Did he happen to mention that while he was poisoning your drink? That was very careless of you, by the way, to take a drink you didn't pour yourself. I taught you better."

"No. He told me today, when he offered to fit me

for a shroud if I didn't come work for him. He means to track you through me."

Even in sea-drenched rags, Angela Ferrers moved with a supremely confident swagger. She twirled in her tattered skirts and settled gracefully onto a threadbare stool. "How much do you know about the connection between Caide and Tremayne?" she asked.

"I know that their grandfathers were cousins, and that they were raised together. That Bay's mother, Ann, fled her abusive husband. And that she and Bay were taken in by Peter's father. And that Peter's title was once held by Bay's great-grandfather Edmund Caide. The Caides lost Sancreed when he was attainted for treason."

"All of that is true. But it is not the whole story," Angela said. "Edmund Caide's descendants were embittered and twisted by the loss of Sancreed. None more than Ann's brother, James. And James Caide lacked the principles that both ennobled and destroyed his grandsire. He spent most of his life trying to wrest the viscountcy back from the Tremaynes. When he feared he might never succeed, he abducted and raped Sancreed's wife, Tremayne's mother, to ensure that at least his child—and his own blood—would hold Sancreed again."

"And Peter was that child?" Kate said. "Does he know?"

"I have no doubt," said the Widow.

Kate could not imagine what it must have been like to grow up with such knowledge. "If the facts of Peter's parentage were known, why was he allowed to inherit?"

"The late Viscount Sancreed was a man of principle. James Caide counted on as much. He knew the viscount would not be persuaded to divorce his blameless wife, Emma, or disown her innocent child. Indeed, that he would raise it as his own. He loved her, you see. To quiet rumors, the viscount even went so far as to acknowledge Peter specifically in front of the king. Peter's legitimacy is now a lie accepted at the most exalted levels, which makes it fact."

And a tragedy. "What became of Peter's mother?"

"Emma Tremayne was, by all accounts, a loving mother while her son was a boy. But it was widely known that after enduring James's touch, she couldn't abide the touch of any man, including that of the husband she loved. "

Angela paused, studied Kate's face a moment. "But none of that is your concern. You can't involve yourself with Peter Tremayne. And you and I cannot meet in person again unless you have news that cannot be committed to a ciphered letter. John André is playing a deeper game than you are."

"How so?" Kate asked.

"He is thinking beyond this theater and this conflict. Spymasters can become powers in their own right. Sometimes the power behind a throne. André has the talent and ambition for it, but he also has certain liabilities."

"He admitted to me that he prefers lovers of his own sex," Kate said, wondering just when she had become the sort of woman who discussed such things with candor. "He did not seem to regard the knowledge as a liability."

"He is careful, and so long as he is discreet, Howe will turn a blind eye. But if Howe were to receive certain letters detailing André's relationship with a young man he met while he was a prisoner last year, such a thing could not be ignored."

"André would hardly write such letters. He is, as you said, careful."

"But his young lover was not. I have brought his letters. You may find them shocking, but you must read them now and commit their contents to memory. Be ready to quote them if André threatens you again, and warn him that if you disappear, he may be certain they will find their way to Howe."

Kate turned the stack of letters over in her hands. André had tried to kill her, had threatened to try again if she did not comply with his plans. And yet she hesitated to untie the bundle. Instead, she voiced the question that had been worrying her since the Widow had arrived.

"You came to the house that night. You knew André had tried to kill me. Why did you leave me there?"

"Because if you disappeared, André would know Mercer had been warned, and the Hessians would have been recalled."

"But that," reasoned Kate, "would have saved Mercer from any attack at all. With no blood spilled."

"For a day. Perhaps even a week. And then Howe would have moved in earnest. He'd make a fresh reconnaissance and plan a well-ordered attack. He'd do things right, and win. Instead he has sent the cream of the Hessian infantry into the jaws of an ambush. The British think Mercer is an oversized fort with an undersized garrison. But in the two weeks since their engineers saw the works, it has been rebuilt from the inside, and gunships positioned to support it from the river. Tell me, are you in love with Peter Tremayne?"

Again, the sudden change of subject. Kate understood the Widow's game. She didn't trust Kate to answer honestly where Tremayne was concerned. It was
her reactions the Widow was gauging, her hands, her
eyes, her breathing, in the seconds before she answered. "He saved my life."

"That's no answer. Tremayne acted out of instinct.
Given time to consider what he was doing, time to
make a decision, he might not have acted as he did. He
has too much to lose: money, lands, title. If he pre-
served your life, it was only for one purpose, and when
he has what he wants from you, the connection will
end." There was no unkindness in her voice, only a
weary pragmatism.

It rankled all the same. "Really? Did Tremayne tell
you all this while I was unconscious?"

"It is the way of powerful men, Kate, and no judgment of your value, or your virtue. And mostly we
talked about the attack on Fort Mercer."

"He was aware that you knew of the attack, and he
let you go?" Kate was incredulous.

"No, he was too patriotic to let me go. And unfortunately for his masters, too gentlemanly to truss a
woman properly." Angela Ferrers favored Kate with a
sidelong glance. "Escape is an art you would do well to
master. You may have cause to need it."

At least that explained the torn curtains and the
strips of chintz tied to the bedside chair.

Kate lowered herself stiffly onto a mustard-colored
settee, which, like everything in Mr. Du Simitière's
hodgepodge of a house that was unrelated to his collection, had seen better days. She picked at the flaking paint.
"Whatever Tremayne's motives," she said, remembering

the safety she'd felt in his arms, "I am alive because of Peter." His Christian name, with which she had never addressed him, felt strange on her tongue.

"Yes. And because of that, André has sent him to Fort Mercer with Carl Donop."

For a moment Kate forgot to breathe. Tremayne had saved her life, carried her bodily away from danger, risked himself for her, and she had sent him into an ambush, into the waiting guns of Fort Mercer. While she had sparred with André this afternoon, Peter might have been dying.

Angela Ferrers' voice, melodious and cool, brought her back. "Mercer had to be warned, Kate, no matter what we might have at stake personally."

We, not *you*, Kate noted. It was like a lock tumbler clicking into place. "You're attached to Count Donop." Kate hesitated to use the word "love" in relation to Angela Ferrers. She had never met a woman more in control of her emotions. "You care about him, but you still disgraced him at Mount Holly. You're the reason he's determined to take Mercer."

"And I am the reason he will fail. I am sorry, Kate, but there is no room for sentiment in our work. By saving you from Captain André, Peter Tremayne implicated himself in treason. André now has a hold over him. Those letters will give you a hold over André. Read them," the Widow ordered.

The envelopes felt like dry leaves, the dead husks of a love affair. She did not want to open them.

And she did not want to confess to the Widow, but lying to Angela Ferrers had not so far produced pleasant results. "I was going to leave with Peter. He offered to take me out of the city. If he had come back for me, I would have gone with him."

Angela Ferrers' smile was sly and knowing, as it had been on the road to the Ashcrofts'. "But you survived on your own."

She had. She'd survived the poison and its aftermath and, as she was coming to realize, had held her own against André. And she could do so again, if she must.

"And when Peter returns?" she asked.

"He saved your life. If he survives Mercer, you must return the favor. Keep him at arm's length. You are a Rebel, a spy, and to him and his, a traitor. If you turn to him for help again, you'll put a noose around his neck."

Eleven

It was the cotton wool sleep of the nursery, of warm summer afternoons and tame English landscapes, deep and untroubled by dreams. It lingered, until the numbness of waking became the numbness of cold and Peter Tremayne came back to himself lying faceup on a packed-dirt floor.

There was a blanket, or a greatcoat, spread beneath him. His shirt was missing and he could feel the weave of the coarse wool printing itself on his back. It hurt to swallow, and he could still taste powder in his mouth. He remembered the bullet tearing through his cheek. He probed gingerly with his tongue, then stopped abruptly when he felt a line of stitches running down the left side of his face, and a curious, elastic quality to the skin there.

He knew better than to try to move his left arm, which throbbed painfully and was thickly bandaged. "Where am I?" he croaked to the room at large. He did not expect an answer.

"We are inside Fort Mercer, my friend," said Carl Donop, from somewhere off to the left.

Donop spoke a few words in German, quite softly, and Tremayne found his mind wandering, thinking that the guttural language could have a pleasing sibilance . . . when the gaunt, mustachioed face of the Grenadier sergeant who had hacked that torturous path through the abatis with him loomed overhead. He pressed a flagon to Tremayne's lips, and dabbed gently when some of the drink escaped through the stitches in Tremayne's cheek. It burned like hell.

It was brandy, fiery and warming, and for a few minutes it was all Tremayne could focus on. When he turned his head as much as the pain in his shoulder allowed, he discerned a small room, a guardhouse most likely, with roughly plastered walls and an unfinished ceiling. Wan daylight filtered through a single dirty window. There was a camp bed and a pitiful fire. From his place on the floor Tremayne could not see the occupant of the room's only bed, but it must be Donop.

They were not the victors, then. Not if he was lying on the floor in a poorly heated cell. Tremayne addressed the bed, where he presumed his friend to be lying. "How bad is it, Carl?" he asked in French.

"At last count, four hundred dead, but the American colonel thinks the number will be as high as six hundred when they search the wood for bodies."

"Dear God," was all Tremayne could manage. The cream of the Hessian infantry, slaughtered. They'd left Philadelphia with more than a thousand men, the better part of them Grenadiers and Jaegers. *Six hundred dead.*

"And captured?" Tremayne asked.

"A few dozen, mostly dying. And twenty officers killed."

"And the Americans?"

"Eight killed," Donop said with grudging approval. "Bachmann here," Donop went on, "pulled you from the abatis. He dragged you to the shelter of the wall and watched over you during the night. He surrendered on your behalf to the Americans this morning. I hope you won't hold it against him. He probably saved the buttons on your coat from looters, at the very least."

"I seem to have both arms. Tell him I'm grateful for that as well."

Donop spoke softly in German once more and the Grenadier nodded at Tremayne. Then Donop said, "The bullet passed cleanly through your shoulder, but lodged in your arm, and took some digging to remove. You lost a great deal of blood, but the American doctor says the wound is clean and the bone untouched. But your face, Peter, will be the envy of every man in Philadelphia. A very good scar. Very attractive to the ladies."

"But sadly not to my lady. She is a pacifist. Or likes to think she is," Tremayne said, sitting up slowly and doing his best not to bend his arm. He had to return for Kate. Had to get her out of the city. He'd been gone too long already. "Sergeant Bachmann here has not, I take it, given the Americans my parole?" If the Hessian had already offered Tremayne's word as a gentleman that he would not try to escape, he was bound to honor it.

He levered himself to his feet with the help of a

nearby table, then crumpled to the ground in a bone-less heap.

There was amusement in Donop's voice, and something else, when he spoke next. "Ja. We are fifteen miles from Philadelphia, it is forty degrees, you have no shirt and have not eaten today, and you mean to attempt an escape. Forgive me for turning your own words against you, but what kind of woman is worth that?"

The kind who can argue politics with me from the floor of a moving carriage while casting up her accounts, thought Tremayne. Who is resourceful and brave and who trusted me to save her; who is a traitor and a spy, and engaged to my cousin. But he could tell Donop none of this. So he said, "Can you swim?" and mounted another attempt to get to his feet.

"To Philadelphia?" Donop lay propped up in the bed on an improvised bolster of flour sacks and rolled blankets. His blond hair had uncurled and was bound loosely in a scrap of silver lace at the back of his neck. He looked pale, and something about his posture in the bed was wrong.

"To the *Augusta*. She was supposed to be standing off from the fort. We should be able to get over the wall on the river side." The land assault might have been a disaster, but the *Augusta* was a sixty-four-gun dreadnought, the biggest ship they had brought to Philadelphia. Mercer's guns would not be enough to scare her off; American gunboats she could reduce to splinter and kindling, if their captains were fool enough to stand and fight.

A chancy business to reach the *Augusta*, but though

Tremayne had spent fewer than three days in Donop's company, he already understood the man well enough to know he'd be game for such an exploit. For the Hessian, it would almost be fun.

"Ah, yes, the mighty British Navy, which was supposed to support our attack. You might be able to get over the wall, my friend, but I cannot."

The blanket that covered Donop's legs was boiled wool. It lay in stiff folds, but this did not account for the unnatural angles beneath it. "My hip and thigh are shattered."

Tremayne was stunned. "I am sorry, Carl," he said, lowering himself into the chair at Donop's bedside. Even in his dishevelment, Donop retained his native elegance, but the pain had to be nearly unbearable, and it told in the set of his jaw and his tightly clenched hands. A broken femur could be crippling, even deadly.

"Do not be. I am in the hands of honor itself. Their second in command is a Frenchman. They have brought a doctor to tend me. I have no fear of mistreatment. You must not stay on my account, although I do not think the *Augusta* will be your salvation. The Frenchman, Du Plessis-Mauduit, tells me two British ships ran aground last night, and one of them is burning."

Tremayne felt light-headed, and while the throbbing in his arm had receded, it was replaced by a strange trickling warmth. He looked down at his bandaged arm and saw the spreading crimson, knew his wound had reopened.

"My friend, you are bleeding, and your lady, should you get so far as Philadelphia, will not thank you for soiling her carpets." Donop called for Bachmann. There was shouting, in French and in German, and then finally in English, but it all sounded a long way off to Termayne, and the room blurred as two more men entered and someone—a doctor, he supposed—helped carry him to his pallet and began unraveling bandages. He could not make out their muffled words, so he lay unresisting while they worked busily to staunch the blood.

Then there was a noise. The floor shook, the windows blew in, showering glass, and Tremayne's ears suddenly cleared.

"What was that?" he asked, from his place on the still-trembling floor.

"I suspect," said Donop, "*that* was the powder magazine of the *Augusta*."

They were moved to a private house, just outside the walls of the fort, later that afternoon. By then Tremayne had realized escape was unlikely. He had lost too much blood. It might have been possible—just—to slip away in the confused hours immediately following the attack, but he had been too weak then and by the time he was conscious they were well guarded. And Carl. Carl was not going anywhere.

Donop had been silent as they carried him, lying flat on the camp bed, into Ann Whitall's pretty brick house. To give the Americans credit, they'd set six men to lift the Hessian. The doctor, Tilden, had supervised the effort and done everything in his power to keep the bed and his patient level, but by the time they were settled, Donop's face was as white as his linen. Tremayne knew that the Hessian's injuries were worse than he was letting on.

Tremayne himself had been weak and dizzy but able to walk with the assistance of Bachmann, under heavy guard.

Carl had told him the casualties were high. He had seen the devastation for himself inside the extension, the bodies of the Grenadiers hanging limp in the abatis like scarecrows, but he was not prepared for the sight that met him outside the walls. The Mirbach Regiment had attacked the front gate, and also had been slaughtered. Bodies were heaped in the ditch, and the smell of blood and excrement was choking. It was almost impossible to believe that beyond this carnage lay the fragrant forest they had marched through the day before, and that across the river, smelling of oranges and cinnamon, was Kate.

But that wasn't quite right either. When he closed his eyes and thought of her, it was of her wrist in his grasp, powdered and scented, at the foot of the stairs in Howe's Germantown mansion. Or of her skirts bunched in his fists in that closet, or her head pillowed against his chest as he carried her out of the house where André had tried to poison her. But she was not warm and safe and scented now. She was likely suffering just as much as he was, recovering from the opium, and the lengths to which her body had gone to expel it.

Ann Whitall's house was not soft and feminine and scented. It smelled of blood and sulfur ointments and the herbal taint of home remedies and backwoods doctoring. And godliness. The woman was a Quaker matron of the old school. She spoke in "thees" and "thous," as only the sternest Friends still did. Tremayne could not place her age. She might have been anywhere between fifty and seventy. The simplicity of her dress mimicked the simplicity of her home, which was clean, sparsely furnished, and organized around seasonal work.

On their first morning in her house, which was filled with the dead and dying, most of whom were not afforded the privacy Donop and Tremayne shared in the parlor, she subjected both men to an herbal draught that if nothing else, obliterated their sense of smell for the next several hours. She proceeded to read the Bible to Donop for forty minutes. Her preference was for Revelation, and the blood and thunder of the Second Coming.

The French engineer, Du Plessis-Mauduit, turned out to be much younger than Tremayne had expected. Twenty-five, handsome, and wearing, with some affectation, American homespun, he visited with them for several hours. They conversed in French, and strove to outdo one another with courtesy. Tremayne complimented Du Plessis-Mauduit on his resourceful defenses, Du Plessis-Mauduit complimented Donop on his brave attack, and Donop thanked Du Plessis-Mauduit for rescuing him from the ditch where he lay most of the night on his shattered leg. It was the politeness with which the fighting men of Europe papered over the brutality and misery of their calling.

They were joined by Colonel Greene, who brought tea and brandy and sat stiffly while Tremayne translated his inquiries into Donop's well-being, and received, with clear discomfort, the Hessian's compliments on his gallant defense of the fort.

When the interview was concluded, Tremayne followed Greene into the kitchen garden to smoke a pipe of tobacco. The scent of rosemary and mint masked the smell of death here, and with the river sparkling behind them it was almost possible to forget for a moment the carnage that lay on the other side of Ann Whitall's house.

"Will he live?" Tremayne asked. "Your surgeon will not say."

Tremayne had thought at first that Greene was older than himself, but out in the light, he decided that Greene was only in his early thirties. Command, which Donop wore so naturally, lay heavily on this man.

"You have my permission to stay with him in the house," Greene said. His evasion of Tremayne's question spoke for itself.

"That is very good of you. But I cannot give you my parole." Whatever honor he had left seemed to require such frankness. Tremayne knew that no matter what Kate's danger, he could not leave Donop while the man lay dying here among strangers, but afterwards . . .

Greene snorted. "Run and you'll be shot. It's as simple as that. I don't want your parole. It's a damned stupid practice. I'm not giving you the run of my garrison because you're lord of something or other, and you give me your word you won't attempt to escape."

"You surprise me, sir. Your care for the count has been exemplary. I took you for a man who observed the niceties of civilized warfare."

"There is nothing civilized about war. I cannot afford to offend the Frenchman. He insisted on bringing both you and the count into the fort. Donop is crippled.

You are another matter entirely. You've seen the strength of my garrison, the condition of my walls, the size and number of my guns up close. You pose a threat to us. I don't like to shoot a man in cold blood, but I can't waste a man guarding you. If the count dies, you'll be locked in the empty magazine until I can figure out what to do with you."

As an officer Tremayne was entitled to genteel—if spartan—lodgings during his imprisonment, but as a practical matter, this was entirely up to the discretion of the officer who held him. Tremayne understood perfectly what Greene was telling him: he would prefer not to kill him, but confinement in the powder magazine was only death deferred. Windowless, unheated, and damp, it would kill him just as surely as a bullet, only more slowly.

Greene let himself out the garden gate, then turned, the river sparkling behind him. "I am sorry, Major, but I am not fighting a gentleman's war here."

I should like you to deliver a letter for me, Peter," Donop said.

"Of course." Tremayne did not need to ask to whom it would be addressed.

"Can you reach her, through the girl you wish to steal from your cousin?"

Donop had lingered in good spirits but in agonizing pain for five days, but now most certainly he was dying. The time for subterfuge was over. "How did you know she was an agent of the Merry Widow?"

Donop's face grew wistful. "A lovely creature, your lady. Too young for my taste. I prefer a more seasoned woman. But there is a resemblance between them. If you look carefully, you can often detect something of the mistress in the maid. And, of course, Angela spoke to me of her protégé."

Donop's dalliance with the Widow had taken place last December, almost a year ago. Tremayne did not believe for a moment that Kate had been the Widow's protégé at Grey Farm in August. Which meant . . .

"When, exactly, did you speak with her, Carl?"

"We met at Head of Elk, in the summer. And at Germantown. I have seen her several times in Philadelphia. Delightful occasions, if too brief. I offered to make her my mistress. She refused. So I offered her marriage. Morganatic, of course."

"Of course," Tremayne said dryly.

Donop shrugged. "You English disapprove of the practice, but it solves many problems."

"Marriage is a tricky business at the best of times, especially where a succession is concerned. Best not to tinker with it."

The bitterness in Tremayne's voice betrayed him. Donop's amusement fled, and he said softly, "Tell me, Peter, is it true? You are not the last Viscount Sancreed's son?"

He had never admitted his bastardy to anyone, but Donop was dying, and however brief their acquaintance, Tremayne now counted him a friend. "Yes. It's true. I am not the late viscount's son. My real father was James Caide. The same Caide whose Roundhead ancestor was attainted by treason and lost Sancreed, and the same Caide who spent his life trying to wrest the title back from the Tremaynes."

There. He had said it. He waited for Donop's appalled reaction. Not just to his bastardy, but to his true parentage. It was well known that James Caide had been a vicious man.

"I am sorry," Donop said, with no trace of pity whatsoever.

Here was a man Tremayne might have counted a friend all his days, and he was dying. There was finally someone he could speak with about this, and the man was leaving him. Tremayne poured forth his story, sordid and painful. "James Caide spent his life and fortune attempting to reclaim Sancreed. Finally, after decades of trying, he realized he could not buy or litigate the title back. There was only one way he could be certain that a child of his blood would be viscount."

"By forcing himself on the viscount's young wife, your mother, and getting her with child. There was talk of an abduction," Donop said.

"He held her for a month, until he was certain he had succeeded." How strange to speak of his hateful conception so dispassionately. He'd only learned the details, pieced together from the hushed whispers of servants, as a young man. But when he thought of his smiling, delicate mother, Emma, his mind skittered away from what she had endured. She had been a warm and affectionate parent until he'd gone away to school; the summer he was fourteen he left a boy and returned a man, and his mother never touched him again. She did not, he later learned, touch any man after James Caide raped her.

"But under such circumstances, surely the last Viscount Sancreed might have obtained a divorce and removed you from the succession. And yet he raised you as his son."

"He loved my mother. He could never put her aside."

"He also took in the disgraced sister of James Caide, along with her dubious child, did he not? A generous man, the late viscount, to be so charitable toward the sister and nephew of the man who despoiled his beloved viscountess."

"The late viscount was a good man," Tremayne agreed. Bay's secrets were not his to share.

Donop's sly smile returned. "I think I would have liked the last Viscount Sancreed very much. No matter your true relationship, you are very much his son." Donop handed him the letter. "You must read it, of course, or you could not in good conscience deliver it. There will be no British secrets in it. I wish you to know that the Widow had no intelligence from me at any time. My only folly was tarrying so long with her at Mount Holly. In all our other meetings I was discretion itself."

"I thought you said you searched the Jerseys for her for a year."

"I did. I never found her. She always came to me on her own terms, at times of her own choosing. I flatter myself that she took some care to protect my tarnished honor."

It all made sense. Donop's single-minded quest to regain his honor, his compulsion to take Mercer and be free of the stain of Trenton, his desire for liberty to pursue the Widow—all these were not passions born out of single tryst more than a year old. His certainty that she would accept him if he could find her and was in a position to make some kind of permanent offer spoke of an established romance.

Donop's breathing had become shallow. He lay very still.

"Do not pity me, Peter. I have few regrets. I worry, of course, what the Landgraf will say. I lost so very many men. And they died so far from home. I should like to be buried with them, not apart. I underestimated the Americans. Greene is not a gentleman, but he has the mettle of a soldier. Had I to do it over again, it would not be in my nature to behave differently. My only regret is that I have not the opportunity to offer for her again."

"You think the answer would be different this time?"

Donop's voice was weak now, but he went on doggedly. "In the beginning, I did not trouble to inquire too deeply into her past, for fear I would not like what I found. But then I thought better of it. How lowborn could such a woman be? She rides and shoots like one born to such a life. So I made inquiries. There was never any need to offer her a morganatic contract. She holds a title in her own right, though she has taken great care to obscure her real identity. This time I would have offered properly for her, and if your young lady was coming along as she hoped, I believe she would have accepted me."

The idea of Kate following in the Widow's footsteps, of taking up her furred mantle and marching through an endless succession of wars, turned Tremayne's stomach. But he could not resist asking. "Who is she, Carl? Who is Angela Ferrers?"

There was no answer. Carl Emil Ulrich Von Donop was dead.

*A*t the end of October reports of a crushing defeat began trickling into the city. Kate listened, breath held, for news. Six hundred men lost. Twenty officers killed. Donop missing. Donop wounded. Donop captured. But no mention of Peter Tremayne.

She did not see Bayard Caide for nearly a week. The failed attack and its aftermath plunged the high command into turmoil. Messengers came and went at all hours, and the lights in Howe's mansion burned late into the night, until there were no more beeswax tapers, and Black Billy was forced to read by rush and tallow light, like everyone else in the starving city.

Then Caide wrote to her: a short note asking her to come to Howe's and join them for an outing to the Neck. Hungry for news, she agreed at once.

On the cobbles in front of Howe's mansion Kate encountered three liveried footmen scrubbing the outside of the Loring carriage in studious silence. A rouge smear told where much of the graffiti had been removed, but blazoned across the door of the box was the gist of the Rebel sentiment: WHORE.

She thought the scene outside awkward, and hurried past the poker-faced footmen, only to be confronted by an even more confounding scene in the parlor. The house was clearly in an uproar of some kind, and the maid didn't bother to knock when she showed Kate into the best room at the front of the house.

She walked in on them. Not on Mrs. Loring and

Howe, which would not have embarrassed her in the least. They made no secret of their carnality. But on Mrs. Loring and Mr. Loring. It wasn't a lewd embrace, which somehow made it all the more shocking. It wasn't even all that intimate. He had only his hand on her shoulder, her forehead bowed to his chest, but the way they started when the door opened made it clear that Kate had intruded on something deeply private.

Up to now she'd felt only scorn for a man who pimped his wife and a woman who allowed herself to be sold, but the sight filled her with a sudden and unwanted pity. Mr. Loring sketched her a hasty bow and left the room. Kate did not know how she ought to feel, had no idea what to say. It was Elizabeth Loring who spoke first. She offered Kate tea.

The brew was watery and left a black sludge in the bottom of Kate's cup. There was no fire, and the room was decidedly cold. The situation was not improved by Mrs. Loring's insistence that the parlor doors remain wide open. She did not mention the epithet scrawled on her carriage door, and while she made pretty small talk, Kate was certain that their conversation commanded only a fraction of the woman's attention and that Elizabeth Loring had, at all times, one ear cocked to the ceaseless activity in the hall.

Kate recognized most of the Hessians, many of them injured, all of them haggard, who filed into the house as the morning wore on. The British officers were less disheveled but far more tense. Caide could spare her only a curt nod. She had never seen him so anxious.

Captain André arrived late. Kate did not blanch when she saw him. They knew each other now, had made their respective positions clear. Soon he would press her for an answer, and she would be forced to use the letters. She did not like it, but when he stopped in the parlor doorway and acknowledged her with an elaborate bow, Kate was struck with a curious irony: the people who knew her best in this strange life of subterfuge were all opponents of one kind or another. It was easier, with that in mind, to see how Angela Ferrers might love a man she had set out to disgrace. Easier to understand why she herself cleaved to Caide.

Howe's mistress suggested a game of piquet to pass the time, and Kate agreed. Now that the men had gone into their meeting, Kate offered to close the parlor door against the draft.

"It would be better for you if we were not seen conferring behind closed doors, Miss Dare," said Elizabeth Loring, dealing cards over the green baize table.

Kate thought of the graffiti on the carriage. "Peggy Shippen has already informed me that I can sink no lower, now that I am engaged to Bay."

Elizabeth Loring raised an artfully tinted eyebrow. "That is convenient, as I was about to warn you that there is no chaperone who could make our outing respectable for you if I am included."

She proceeded to play like a taproom cardsharp.

Then the door to Howe's private office opened and an argument in highly idiomatic German, French, and English spilled into the hall. Both women forgot their cards.

"Enough." Billy Howe didn't shout. His voice carried. And the noise stopped. "Thank you for your advice, gentlemen. I'll take it all under consideration." Kate heard the impatience in Howe's tone, saw the anxiety printed across Elizabeth Loring's heart-shaped face.

Kate studied her as the men made their grumbling exit. Kate's own allure was half artifice: the gloss of high fashion; the careful highlighting of her best features; the camouflaging of her worst. But Elizabeth Loring would turn heads even in a flour sack.

Howe's spurs rang across the polished marble hall. Just before he appeared in the doorway, Elizabeth Loring donned a smile wholly feigned but entirely convincing.

Howe's thin answering smile was less persuasive, but he seemed determined to put the morning's conference behind him. "Let's be off. Where's Caide? He was here a moment go."

André hovered in the doorway. "We must talk about Burgoyne," he said softly.

"Not now." Howe waved him away like a mosquito and ushered the two women out to the yard.

Kate assumed they would go by carriage, but when they emerged from the house the Lorings' rig was gone, and the footmen were leading three horses up the drive.

"Have you missed me?" Caide asked. She turned to find him lounging against one of the pillars of the porch. A fey smile quirked the corners of his mouth.

She knew it was a betrayal of Peter Tremayne, but she *had* missed Caide. Perhaps because in many ways the two men were so alike. True, Caide was fair and mercurial and had sly artist's hands, while Tremayne was dark and serious and had a wry, fleeting smile, but they were struck from the same mold, and she was drawn to them both. Her mouth felt dry. Somehow she knew that if she spoke the words, said, "I have missed you," she would fall further from grace. As things stood, she had made no declarations of love. Caide had offered for her and she had accepted, but the attraction was not one-sided, and he knew it.

"I don't have a mount," she said.

"Soon to be rectified. But in the meantime, I bought you a horse."

He led her out to the street. "Do you like her?" he asked.

The chestnut mare stood clean-limbed and freshly groomed on the cobbles. Caide's hulking lackey, Dyson, whom she did not like at all, held the reins.

It was a lavish gift. Horses were scarce in the occupied city. And there was more: a saddle with a red velvet seat, leather flaps tooled with acanthus, and a dainty black whip.

She had never owned a mount of her own, and tack, in the Grey household, had been an amalgam of secondhand bridles and saddles from her father's service in the French and Indian War: heavy, cumbersome, and built for a man. This saddle, though, was sized for Kate, elegantly decorated, and as supple as silk.

It was seductive, as Caide had intended. "At least I'm getting something between your thighs today," he murmured in her ear. He caressed the leather of the seat, but it was as if she could feel his hands on her. He knew, of course, and he enjoyed watching her respond. "You'll be hard-pressed to find fodder for her in the

market, so I'll stable her for you until the river is opened."

He was right. She had only to glance at the scrawny nags passing in the street to know how little fodder was reaching the city. And all of it was going to the army, whose horses were stabled in the "seditious" churches: Methodist, Lutheran, Presbyterian, and Baptist.

Their little party set out: General Howe on his charger and Mrs. Loring on her strawberry roan, with Bay and Kate following, trailed by Dyson and the general's servants.

Before the occupation, the Neck had been a pretty suburb of garden cottages where the rich retreated from the bustle of the city, but now it was abandoned. Splintered fences marked where soldiers had foraged for easy fuel.

When Howe halted in front of a handsome stone cottage, larger and more impressive than its neighbors, the rest of the party was obliged to do likewise.

Caide looked at the house and swore under his breath.

In chalk over the lintel was a faded warning: UN-DER THE PROTECTION OF GENERAL HOWE. Across the door in black paint was a more permanent and effective admonition: UNDER THE PROTECTION OF BAYARD CAIDE.

Though the garden was ruined, the house was untouched, down to the black iron shutter dogs.

Howe snorted.

"It's Peter's idea of a joke. On me, not you," said Caide. "You *did* put him in charge of discouraging looters here."

"As though I needed further reminder of my impotence," Howe said. "So kind of your cousin to oblige.

Major Tremayne would have done better to focus on that other business I entrusted to him."

Kate attempted to keep her face bland, her eyes fixed on the ostentatiously rustic cottage. She counted the quoins over the windows, the dentils over the door.

"He was ordered to Mercer with Donop," Caide said evenly.

Kate counted the slate tiles of the roof, the stones in the foundation.

Howe sniffed and turned his mount back toward the road. "I gave the man a task, and he allowed himself to be diverted from it. What the devil was his quarrel with André?"

"A private matter," said Caide, quite softly.

Howe shot him a sidelong glance and Caide added hurriedly, "Nothing like that."

"Captain André has his uses," Howe said, "but at times he overreaches. I sent my surgeon to look at Donop before he died. He also treated your cousin's wounds. The Americans would like to trade Tremayne for some of their prisoners in the State House, but André advises me against it. What do you say?"

Caide turned to look at her, and she did her best to keep her face blank.

"The Americans will make better deals in the spring when they're desperate for officers for the new campaign."

Howe turned his horse toward the river. Kate realized she had fallen behind, and Caide with her.

"It's not your fault," Caide said.

She'd been lost in her own thoughts, which were entirely of Peter, and that was dangerous, with Bay watching her.

"What isn't?"

"André sending Peter to Mercer over whatever happened at the concert. He's always been a chivalrous idiot. I told Peter you were perfectly capable of handling the little Huguenot," Caide said, with a pride she found oddly flattering.

"Then why didn't you press the general to trade him back?" She was courting danger by asking, and she knew it.

"Can't you guess? Surely you noticed Peter watching you at the concert. My dear cousin wants you. And he's had *everything* that should have been mine, including Sancreed. He won't have you. Don't pity him, Lydia. He is a viscount. He'll be well treated. And by the spring, when he's traded back, you and I will be married and he'll see that you are the one thing he can't take from me. Besides, if he'd had his way this past summer he'd be with Burgoyne now, and no better off."

"In New York?" She knew of General Burgoyne's plan to attack Albany from Quebec, and his strategy to separate New England from the southern Colonies. She knew also that Howe liked neither the plan nor its author. She did not know why they were talking of Burgoyne.

"You'll hear soon enough. It can't be kept secret. We didn't just lose a battalion strength of Hessians at Mercer. We lost the entire northern army. Burgoyne surrendered to Gates and the Rebels at Saratoga six days ago."

An army of eight thousand, defeated. Kate could not take it in. There was nothing to compare with it. Up to now, the Continentals had won only skirmishes like Trenton. It had been a war of retreat and survival, not battles and victories.

"What will happen now?"

"Burgoyne's entire force will be sent home to England. Under the terms of surrender, they can't fight again in this conflict. It was Burgoyne's plan, and Burgoyne's fiasco, but Howe will be blamed because he didn't throw his army away supporting Burgoyne's madness. Howe will resign, naturally."

It had not occurred to her that a general could resign. Her father couldn't. If Arthur Grey left the army, if he returned home, he'd hang as a traitor. Resignation was a British luxury.

"Howe hasn't any choice now," Caide was saying. "He can't go on coddling Washington, or he'll face an inquiry, maybe even a trial, back home. He'll have to take Mercer and Mifflin no matter what it costs, or we'll be starved out of Philadelphia. It would be best if we married now, in case the city must be evacuated."

She'd never thought of the engagement as real. It had always been a ploy, an achievement that elated her when she told Angela Ferrers. The marriage was an eventuality that would not, could not come to pass. "But my father is not yet returned," she said carefully.

"But you are of age, and of an independent turn of mind," Bayard Caide observed, his blue eyes hungry—and startlingly vulnerable.

"What if you married me and then my father turned up and you discovered him to be a hopeless rustic?"

He shifted his gaze for a moment, checking distances and proximities like a soldier. "Lydia, your father is long overdue. Howe issued a landing pass more than a month ago. Nothing can get near the coast without encountering a navy ship, so he must know he has permission to land. And that prices are sky-high in the city. There are only two kinds of merchants who would not land their cargo under such circumstances. A dead man, or a Rebel."

She didn't bother to deny it. "What will you do?"

"I don't care a fig for your father's politics. Or yours, for that matter. Though I must insist you keep your views private. I'm not unambitious. I've never hidden that from you. My family is only a few generations removed from the taint of treason. I cannot dabble in it here. You understand?"

"Yes." She understood perfectly. She had been risking her life to safeguard Mifflin and Mercer for weeks. She'd sacrificed Peter to the cause. Now, when it seemed she might have succeeded, she would have to sacrifice herself to Bayard Caide.

*T*hey buried Donop, as he had asked, in the mass grave with his countrymen. The Americans rendered him full honors. Colonel Greene was in grudging attendance, but Du Plessis-Mauduit traded his homespun for a suit of white satin with blue facings. He was the picture of Gallic military splendor. Donop would have been pleased.

After the service was concluded, Greene took Peter Tremayne aside to ask a series of gruff questions about his family and military connections. Tremayne answered those few he felt did not violate his trust as an officer, and Greene left, more quizzical than satisfied.

That afternoon, Ann Whitall removed the stitches in Tremayne's face. She grasped his chin in her bony hand and turned his head this way and that, then declared, in her outmoded Quaker patois, "Thou'll do." Later, he inspected himself in the shaving mirror over the basin. The scar was ugly, bisecting his cheek and pulling up the corner of his mouth. Yes, he would do. His expression seemed frozen in wry amusement. He supposed it was better than a perpetual scowl.

Colonel Greene summoned him to the fort the next day. The Hessian sergeant Bachmann was not allowed to accompany him, and he was advised against wearing his red tunic. Greene, he surmised, did not have total control of his men, could not ensure Tremayne's safety if the Rebel infantrymen felt inclined to mischief. A month ago Tremayne would have insisted that the Americans could not triumph without adopting British discipline. Elected officers and volunteer soldiers did not, in his experience, win battles. At Mercer he had been proved wrong.

Tremayne had thought the squalid guardroom in Mercer insultingly poor accommodation, but Greene's own quarters were no better. His desk was pulled up in front of a camp bed. He offered Tremayne the only other seat in the room, a chest riddled with bullet holes.

"I have a letter here," Greene began with no preamble, "from my cousin, begging me to release you. I should like to know how you are acquainted with him."

"Who, sir, is your cousin?" Tremayne had few American friends. He wondered if Kate would consider herself among them.

"Major General Nathanael Greene."

Tremayne did not know the general, and said as much.

"I thought you might be one of his Masonic connections," Greene said. "A widow's son in need of aid. I can conceive of no other reason why he might ask me to let you go. You appear to be a capable and experienced officer. You have seen how things stand with us here. You know the strength of our garrison. Your release could do us a great deal of harm, so I must ask you: why does the Fighting Quaker want you freed?"

Like many of his brother officers, Tremayne was a Freemason, but was not acquainted with Greene, did not even know to which lodge the man belonged. The Fighting Quaker. There were only so many involved in the American cause—these men disowned by their faith—and most of them surely knew one another. If Greene was known to Arthur Grey . . . "Might I ask what your cousin has to say in his letter?"

Greene passed Tremayne the missive, but he must already have known its contents by heart. "My cousin begs, for the sake of a personal matter of the most delicate nature and involving an old and valued friend of his, that I provide you a horse, a servant, coin—which he encloses—and a pass to see you safely to your own lines."

Tremayne handed the letter back.

"An extraordinary request. He leaves the decision up to me, as the safety of my garrison is at stake."

"Would it make a difference to you if I assured you

that I am pursuing no military purpose by returning to Philadelphia? That I intend to put right a personal matter involving an American lady whose welfare has been endangered by my absence?"

"No, Major. It would not. In any case I would be extremely unlikely to believe you, save that today I received another letter, from a lady who is herself a particular friend of Washington, and who desires me to keep you here at all costs. She also cites the welfare of an unnamed lady, though she avers that this woman would be put at hazard by your return to Philadelphia."

The lady who had written could only be Angela Ferrers. She would not give up such a well-placed spy as Kate so easily. Grey must have discovered his daughter missing and Tremayne captured. Perhaps he had approached Angela Ferrers first. He was a direct man. Unfortunately, Angela Ferrers was a subtle and devious woman, and Arthur Grey could not possibly know how valuable his daughter had become to the Merry Widow. And forewarned, Angela Ferrers must have made a countermove. Tremayne's only hope was that she could not be everywhere at once, that he could reach Grey without her interference. "Might I be permitted to write a letter myself?"

"I've already informed your commanding officer of your presence here," Greene replied curtly. "I've received no offers for a trade."

And none would be forthcoming if André had anything to do with it. "The letter I would like to write is to one of your own commanders. Colonel Arthur Grey."

Greene raised a single querulous eyebrow. "What a lot of American friends you have made in your short

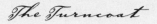

time in our country, Major." He gave him paper and ink, but no privacy, and Tremayne was not fool enough to think the letter would reach Grey without passing through many hands. He must be discreet.

Later the guard came to remove him. He was not surprised when they turned away from the open gates of the fort. He knew where they were going. They marched him into the dank brick walls of the fort, along a corridor lit only by the fractured beams of the gun slits, to the black depths of the powder magazine.

*T*hey had given him back his coat, and for that he was grateful. Tremayne knew as soon as the door shut behind him that the chill, dark powder magazine was meant to be his tomb, a convenient solution to Colonel Greene's problem. He did not intend to die in the cold and darkness, so he set about the business of survival as soon as his eyes adjusted to the dark.

Only the barest sliver of light entered beneath the batten door, which was reinforced on both sides with iron plates. He took care not to look directly at it; in this blackness it would blind him like the sun. He stood soaking up the darkness, breathing in the chemical smells of old powder and fresh mold, and reining in the panic that threatened to overwhelm him. It was like being underground, being buried. The unseen vault must be at least three stories above him, and the emptiness held all the childhood terrors of the night, and the decidedly adult terror that came with the knowledge of all the ways a man might die in such a place.

He wanted to sink to the paving where he stood,

wrap his arms around himself and withdraw into his own mind. But he was determined to live, to inconvenience the coldly practical Colonel Greene, to get back to Philadelphia and Kate.

He forced himself to pace the outer wall of his prison, running his hands along the masonry. When he had gone thirty paces, he felt the liquid splash of water beneath his boots, and discovered the jagged run of brickwork where the magazine was broken. This, then, was why it was empty. The foundation must have cracked during the brief bombardment from Donop's guns, and let the river in. When the water became ankle-deep Tremayne retraced his steps and retreated toward the door. Cold and damp were his enemies, and there was a putrid smell to the water that indicated it might filter through a rubbish tip—or worse—before reaching here. He felt along the shattered wall for loose bricks and rubble, anything that might be of use if he were to attempt an escape.

He searched the rest of the magazine thoroughly, but found nothing else. Then he withdrew to the corner farthest from the water.

He had no way of marking the time, but he judged that a day passed before the door opened. He was blinded, as he knew he would be, by the lantern, and by the time he was able to see clearly, his guards were gone. He'd seen enough, though. They were smart enough to open the door and shine the light in first, then one man entered and covered him with a rifle while the other set something down on the ground.

They'd brought him a tin bowl of some kind of gruel. He ate it, licking the bowl clean like an animal because he knew that water was vital and he must not drink the stuff pooling in the darkness unless it was his only choice. On a single ration of gruel, he would grow weaker every day. If he were to escape, it must be now, before the cold and hunger sapped his strength.

When they returned the next day he was waiting behind the door. He had spent the past twenty-four hours learning every inch of the space just inside the entrance, and now he made good use of his knowledge. He hammered his fist into the kidney of the man with the lantern, and brained the rifleman with a broken brick. He made it as far as the guardhouse, where the shift was changing. There were six men on duty, and they took their time beating him. When they dragged him back to the magazine they took his boots, his shirt, and his coat.

After that he lost track of the days, slipping in and out of consciousness, trying to keep as much of his bruised body off the cold stone floor as possible. When he was lucid once more, he began to hear the shelling. It was like a distant thunder that rose and fell in volume, but never stopped. Not an attack on Mercer, then. It had to be Howe bombarding Mifflin, across the Delaware, on the Philadelphia side. And for the sound of it to reach him here, on the other side of the water, behind such thick walls, Howe must be blasting the fort from all sides.

Listening to the roll and report of the ordnance, Tremayne knew it would be only a matter of time before Mifflin fell. Nothing could hold up under that kind of fire. And then Howe would turn his full attention on this garrison and it would fall as well. Colonel

Greene was a competent commander and a realist, and must know by now that the fort's days were numbered, so Tremayne was not surprised when the door opened, three days after the bombardment started, and he was dragged from his cell. It only remained to be seen whether Greene was going to release him or shoot him.

Twelve

Philadelphia, November 26, 1777

"Where do you go to do it?" Peggy Shippen sat in front of her dressing table, admiring her freshly coiffed hair. It was teased up and plumped with wool padding, and framed by golden ringlets that perfectly matched Peggy's own. The style towered atop her head like an over-risen loaf.

"Do *what*?" Kate asked, stifling her impulse to tell Peggy what she thought of her hair. Elaborate, chandelier-scraping styles were all the rage in London, of course, and Philadelphia's Tory daughters strove to outdo one another in their Englishness.

"*It*," Peggy Shippen hissed, her coiffure wobbling dangerously. "John André says you and Bayard Caide can't be going to the theater anymore because the players rehearse there during the day."

Sometimes Kate forgot how young Peggy was, but

in the sunlight streaming in the window, without cosmetics, it was plain that she was still a child, barely eighteen, and trapped in a prolonged adolescence by wealth and comfort. The reminder of her connection to the calculating Captain André was more poignant still.

"We don't do *it*, Peggy, and even if we did I'd hardly go advertising the address for our trysts in the *Gazette*."

"No one believes that," insisted Peggy. "Everyone says Sir Bayard is debauched and that you must be as well, no matter how demure you act in public."

Kate decided it was fruitless to argue. Better that the world thought she was already sleeping with her fiancé. No one would believe the truth: that since his initial seduction at the playhouse, he had not touched her. He treated her with an uncharacteristic delicacy, a reserve that spoke of passion under heavy rein.

Bay's urgent desire to marry her, thankfully, had passed with the fall of Forts Mifflin and Mercer. After Donop's failed attack in late October, Howe had concentrated all his guns on nearby Mifflin. The bombardment lasted nearly a month and reduced Mifflin to a heap of indefensible rubble. But the Rebel garrison still did not surrender. The wily Americans had infuriated Howe by abandoning the fort in the dead of night and slipping away across the river to Mercer. When Howe turned his attention there, the Rebels spiked the guns and blew up the magazine, leaving Howe nothing but a wrecked shell.

And control of the river. With the Rebel guns at Mercer and Mifflin silenced, there was nothing to stop Howe's brother, the admiral, from clearing the chevaux-de-frise from the river and warping his frigates

through. With the city firmly in British hands for the winter, no doubt Caide felt more certain of her.

Peter Tremayne had been right. Her espionage had not prevented the taking of the forts and the river—it had only delayed it. She should have prayed for Mercer to hold out. She'd sacrificed her safe, respectable future in Orchard Valley to keep the river American and drive the British out. But when the navy guns announced their presence in the river, when the *Cerberus* and the *Roebuck* fired their salute, rattling her windows and waking her from an uneasy sleep, she'd wept with relief. She would not have to marry Caide. And Peter Tremayne would be free. She only hoped he would go home to England, away from her and all the trouble she had brought him.

"And no one imagines," Peggy prompted, "that Sir Bayard is a man who would long be content with kisses."

Of course they didn't. Few people understood Bayard Caide. And just as well, Kate thought. Admitting to corruption was clearly the only way to end this conversation. "Then thank goodness I'm engaged. Otherwise I would be quite ruined."

"Not if you took precautions," Peggy suggested carefully.

Kate suppressed a sigh. "What are you planning, Peggy?"

"Captain André and I have an understanding," she said, blushing.

No doubt André wished her to think so. If only Kate knew what purpose the spymaster had in mind for Peggy. If only she could keep the girl away from him. It occurred to her that André was handling Peggy the way the Widow handled Kate. The only difference was in their respective levels of awareness. Kate understood the danger she was in.

"Is this an understanding you would be willing to tell your father about?"

"Yes, of course, but John and I agree it's best to wait until after his promotion to tell my father. Only I'm tired of waiting. Tell me what to do so I won't get pregnant."

Kate did not, herself, have any practical experience in the matter. What she did have was a small wooden box with an assortment of sea sponges, left for her by Angela Ferrers in their agreed-upon drop spot, since they no longer dared meet in person. She could not possibly give one to Peggy. André would know where they had come from.

And while André had admitted that he preferred lovers of his own sex, Kate suspected he was quite worldly when it came to women. Espionage, she was coming to learn, was a study of the human condition. André was unlikely to leave such a fundamental experience untried. Still, she could think of no reason he would want to compromise Peggy, so she asked, "Is this your idea, or his?"

Peggy bristled. "He is too much a gentleman to broach the matter."

"And Caide is too much of an aristocrat to leave me unbroached?" Peggy goggled at her crudeness, but Kate plunged on. "If you are planning to become his lover, then discuss the matter with him." Then she added, with genuine concern, "But Peggy, you would be better off not to—at least not without some formal promise from him. You might be left disappointed, or worse."

She had been lectured, in occasionally shocking and often humorous detail, on the perils of intercourse. Angela Ferrers had tutored her in all the means available to prevent pregnancy and disease. Unfortunately for Peggy Shippen, the Widow had no recipe against heartbreak.

Which was a pity, because when Kate returned home to the Valby mansion that afternoon, Peter Tremayne was waiting for her in the parlor.

*T*remayne had seen very little of the Valby house on his last visit. He remembered only a darkened hallway, an impression of grandeur about the double staircase, and shadowed swaths of drapery. The parlor he was shown into today was elegant and modern, if somewhat provincial in scale and ornament. The faux Titian over the fireplace gave away Kate's equally false aunt and uncle for what they were: merchants with pretensions. Exactly the sort of people who shouldn't be swept up in a revolution. The Indian cotton, Turkish carpets, and Chinese wallpaper said it plainly: they'd done well under the present regime. They had too much to lose. Like Kate and her father. Coming on the heels of Donop's disastrous assault on Fort Mercer and Burgoyne's defeat at Saratoga, it was worrying. A people who would not be cowed easily. Another Ireland waiting to happen.

Tremayne was so busy studying the room, lost in his own thoughts and misgivings, that he did not hear the door open. He had dreamed of Kate, in the cold dark of the powder magazine. Not the sophisticated coquette in silk he'd encountered at Germantown, but the farm girl from Orchard Valley whose cotton skirts carried the kitchen scents of nutmeg and vanilla.

Today she was everything clean and soft and domestic that he had longed for. Kate wore a striped polonaise in blue and cream sateen. The color set off her coffee eyes and chestnut hair; the pattern emphasized the neat curves of her body. The irony of a real country girl dressed as an aristocrat's notion of a milkmaid was not lost on Tremayne, but he discovered then that his imagination lagged behind the reality. Kate now belonged to neither world, had transcended her rural upbringing and Angela Ferrers' tutelage to become something entirely original.

She closed the door gently behind her and they were alone.

He had had a month to rehearse speeches for her: in the cold dark of Mercer; in the guardroom, where they allowed him to wash and dress, with the imperturbable Sergeant Bachmann assisting him, as the Rebels spiked their guns and prepared to abandon the fort; on the road home to Philadelphia, where the countryside had smelled of wood smoke and apples instead of gunpowder, mold, and rotting flesh. And now he was speechless.

He smelled her perfume: citrus and spice and vanilla, like a Christmas pastry. He remembered the feel of her fevered body, as she thrashed in the grip of the opium and he held her close on the bed upstairs. At the time, protectiveness had swamped lust, but now the memory came back to him colored with desire.

"Thank you," she said, taking another tempting step closer to him, "for saving my life. It's long overdue, but I am more grateful than I can say." Her eyes lingered on his scar, still livid across his cheek, but there was no pity or horror in her expression.

It was his cue. He could take her in his arms now and taste her mouth, run his hands over her supple body, whisper all the things he planned for them in her ear. He reached for her, but she sidestepped him.

"But you must leave. And we cannot meet again." The words left her mouth in a rush.

"Why the hell not?" The first thing he had said to Kate in a month's time. And the very last thing on earth he could have imagined saying to her after weeks of captivity and deprivation. He'd come expecting gratitude. Sweet words, soft, yielding flesh, and ultimately, her carnal surrender. Not a curt dismissal. "Madame, the warmth of your welcome leaves something to be desired. I rather thought you were partial to me."

"You know I am. And so far my partiality has gotten you court-martialed, lost you your command, and sent you into an ambush. Imagine the consequences if I loved you." The last was said in a throaty voice that made his cock stir. He could imagine a great deal. He was about to tell her so in more than words when she slipped past him to the window. "Captain André has me watched. He will know you were here. You must leave now. A short visit from my fiancé's cousin will arouse suspicion in no one but those who already know what I am. A long one will tempt André to scheme."

"He knows who you are?"

"He knows who I am, and what I am doing here. The only reason I am not dead is that he wants to catch the Widow. He thinks he can trace her through me. He wishes to recruit me. His dilemma is whether he would wield greater influence if I were Caide's wife or your mistress."

Tremayne swore. "What a bloody mess. Come away. I can get you out of the city."

"No. Howe is planning something. He has already written to the king, asking to be excused this duty, but he does not want to return to London in disgrace. He means to attack General Washington's army in winter quarters and salvage his career before it is too late. I cannot leave now. My father is with Washington."

"Then let me take you to him. He was a distinguished officer in the last war. You could convince him to resign his commission and accept Howe's amnesty. You could both go home to Orchard Valley."

"André knows my real name. I can never go home to Orchard Valley. Not while the British hold Philadelphia. And my father will not desert Washington, even for me and my safety. The only freedom you can offer me is the freedom to see him hanged."

"When we met, at your father's house, you argued tactics with me like a drawing room general. It was an intellectual abstraction for you then. Something has changed."

"The dragoons came after you left."

Her words washed over him like ice water, colder than the fetid dark under Mercer. He had given no thought to what might have happened to her later that night. He'd returned to Grey Farm and found her and his papers gone, and he'd burned with humiliation and anger. But his had not been the only troop of horse abroad that night. The political arrests he'd declined to take part in were midnight affairs of broken doors and broken bones and other, less palatable acts. "Tell me," he said, dreading what he would hear next.

"The Widow would not allow me to stay at Grey Farm. She took me to my friend Milly's, and planned to leave me there, but she couldn't. Because the dragoons came, and they took Milly to the barn. She was pregnant. There were apples," she added. Her eyes were fixed on some faraway point, and he knew she was reliving events in her mind. He led her to a chair and she floated down, a dandelion puff on the breeze. He would not force her to go on. He could guess the rest. He knelt beside her, careful not to come too close. "Did they touch you?" If someone had, there would be a death in it.

"No. They didn't know we were there. The Widow, she made us hide. I wanted to help Milly, but Angela wouldn't let me."

"And quite right she was too. Has your friend brought charges?" he asked her gently.

"Milly's husband is a prisoner in the State House. She doesn't dare bring charges. Who knows what might become of him?"

It was just as well. Court-martials for rape and plunder had become a nearly daily occurrence in the city. He'd sat in on his fair share before his capture. If the girl was pretty, there were plenty of officers who were not above condemning her rapist to hang, then dicing to determine who would offer her "protection."

"They kept Milly for three days," she said, as though finishing the story were her penance for running away, "and then abandoned her on the side of the Germantown road. Mrs. Ferrers' people found her."

"And the babe?" he forced himself to ask. He feared the answer.

"Delivered premature but safely. Mother and child are in hiding." Kate stared at him, defying him to defend his countrymen. He had no excuses, and was not callous enough to tell her that this was the way of war, that she and her countrymen had brought it on themselves. He had only a desperate desire to take her someplace safe and see that she stayed there. And to do that, he was beginning to realize, he must break her formidable resolve.

He reached out, careful to keep a distance between them, careful not to loom or threaten, and tucked a stray lock of her hair behind her ear. "Keeping Washington's army in the field for another season will not keep the dragoons from your door. You think you have experienced oppression. This is nothing compared to what will follow if this conflict drags on. If you continue to provoke Parliament, we will do here what we have done in Ireland. You will find yourselves barred from government, denied education, and turned, in a generation, into serfs. What happened to your neighbors will become commonplace."

"Unless we win."

"You cannot win against the Crown."

"No one has told General Gates that."

He laughed. It was a relief to see her wit surface. "Now that is the Kate Grey I met in Orchard Valley."

She arched a plucked brow. "You prefer me with singed skirts and crumbs in my hair?"

"I prefer you safe, Kate. Let me take you to your father."

"You can't. André will arrest me if I try to leave the city. I'm being watched."

"Yes. By a brace of ruffians," he said, crossing to the window. He folded back a shutter to look down into the street. "I saw one of them outside. I presume there is a second at the back gate."

"There are three of them, actually, since yesterday." She slipped past the spinet to join him at the window and stare down at Beaver Hat and the newcomer; a lean, mustachioed man in a clean but threadbare brown serge coat.

"Ah. The third ruffian is Sergeant Bachmann. He belongs to me. Or at least I inherited him and no one seems to have demanded him back."

"I should have realized. He did not skulk as well as the others."

"Hessian Grenadiers are notoriously unsubtle," he said. "But Bachmann can handle your watchers, and I can handle André. Will you come?"

She shook her head. "No."

"I came back because I wanted to see you to safety, Kate, and because I had to see *you*. I can't force you to go home to your father, but if you are determined to remain in the city, then I am not above blackmailing you into my bed."

"You wouldn't," she said carefully. She was trying to convince herself. "You are not that kind of man."

If she cried, he wouldn't be able to go through with

it, but she met his eyes, and only her lower lip quivered, so subtly he might have missed it were he not studying every breath she took. But she did not cry. And he was resolute in his purpose, so he said, "You will meet me tonight, Kate, or I'll turn you over to André myself."

*S*he picked her way through the Valbys' vegetable garden in the fading light, careful not to tangle her shot silk gown in the overgrown rosemary beside the gate. If this were Grey Farm, the bush would be trimmed, the excess branches drying in the kitchen, or adding fragrance to the fire. The wild plots would be cleared and organized with the most often used herbs—the parsley, rosemary, and sage—growing closest to the kitchen door. That she could still think this way, robed in pale blue silk, on the way to such an unwelcome assignation, was a peculiar comfort. No matter what happened tonight, she would still, somewhere inside, be Kate Grey.

Kate heard him before she saw him, the clop of hooves on stone, sure-footed in the darkness. Sound carried differently in the city. At Grey Farm his horse would have thudded softly over the packed earth. In the city, its shoes rang claxons on the cobbles. There were finer distinctions too. She could tell the difference between the sound of a horse and rider, a mellow, lasting note, and an unmounted beast, high-pitched and brief; so she was not surprised when Tremayne appeared around the corner leading his chestnut mare.

He wore his dress uniform, the scarlet a shade richer than his ordinary coat, the wool a finer weave. There was a froth of Mechlin lace at his collar and cuffs, silvery white in the fading light. His hair was loosely braided at the back of his neck and tied with a black silk ribbon. She remembered it falling free over his shoulder at Grey Farm, and felt the prickle of tears. Tonight would not be like Grey Farm. She blinked the tears away. They would streak her powder.

"You've come dressed for battle," she said lightly.

He looped his horse's reins over the saddle and used both hands to push back her muffling hood. He parted her furred cloak, and settled his warm hands over her collarbone, studying her. "So have you."

She knew what he saw. She'd used the skills the Widow had taught her to armor herself. She'd dressed her own hair. It had taken an hour to curl the sides and braid the crown, then loop and pile her handi-work with mother-of-pearl combs. She had rouged her cheeks, blackened her lashes, and stained her lips berry red.

"Enchanting," he said, but there was something wistful in his voice. If she did not know better, she might almost call it regret.

Unsettled by his tenderness, she pulled her furred cloak tight around her. "We shouldn't linger." She darted a glance at the lit windows of the service ell. "Someone might see us."

"The Valbys are not in your confidence?" he asked, giving her a leg up onto the mare.

"I endanger them enough just by being here. The less they know of my activities, the safer they are."

"If you are arrested, what will they say?"

"They will say I was an imposter. That they had not seen their niece since she was a girl. I've taken care to protect them as much as possible."

He sighed, guiding her hands to the pommel. "And who will protect you, Kate?"

Before she could answer, he slung himself up behind her.

She was immediately aware of the easy grace of his body in the saddle, of the size and strength of him at her back. He was a professional horseman, of course, so this should not surprise her, but there was an unexpected intimacy in riding with him. It was more than the feel of his thighs pressed against hers, tensing and relaxing as he guided the horse. It was the understanding that she was being admitted to the private world between horse and rider where he often spent much of his day.

They followed the alley to another, and emerged on a side street Kate had never seen before. She realized how little she knew of Philadelphia outside the fashionable center. Here the houses were smaller, older, brick and stone giving way to painted clapboard and finally the weathered gray post-and-beam hovels of the poor.

The narrow streets were empty. It was a city under martial law, and only officers and rich Loyalists were exempt from Howe's curfew. The ramshackle houses, with their shake roofs and bottle glass windows, were dark and forbidding.

Anything might happen in such a place. And no one knew where she was. The Valbys were not in her confidence. Peggy Shippen was little more than a child and too much under André's influence. The Widow no longer met with Kate in person. If she did not come home tonight, no one would know where she had gone, or with whom.

There was light and music up ahead, and when they rounded a corner Kate recognized the name of the public house that loomed in front of them: a many-gabled, hardscrabble affair, notorious for the cheapness of the ale and the women. Jaded hussies in rude leather stays, merchants, and dockside laborers spilled out into the street, here where the guard did not bother to enforce the curfew, because that would curb their own entertainments.

Kate closed her eyes and remembered to breathe. It was going to be sordid. She had been hopelessly naive. Angela Ferrers had tried to warn her on the road that night. A privileged, powerful man like Tremayne had only one use for a country girl like her. There would be no pretense of courtship or romance. She would have to spread her legs for Tremayne amidst the smells of stale beer and urine. She'd lie on a sour mattress and he would grunt and shout above her, like the men in the barn with Milly.

She was not going to cry.

They drew level with the tavern and Tremayne tensed. "Easy, Kate. We're not stopping here. It's just the straightest route to where we're going."

She realized only then that she had been trembling.

"Do you hear me, Kate? I don't want you to be frightened."

"Yes, I hear you." But she didn't believe him. For all of Angela Ferrers' lectures, Kate's practical experience of intercourse was limited to what had occurred between her and her suitors, Tremayne and Caide, in the relative safety of parlors and drawing rooms. And what had happened to Milly in the barn.

The trembling became a shuddering that she could not control. Tremayne swore inventively, then threaded his hands beneath her cloak to circle her waist.

"Lean back against me, love," he coaxed.

She knew she should not allow her guard to drop, but his hands were warm and reassuring.

"What I said in the parlor . . ." he began, but she shook her head, and didn't want to hear whatever he was going to say next.

"Save your flowery words. We both know what this is."

"Would you have come if I offered you any other choice?" he asked.

"No," she replied honestly.

"Then reserve your judgment for the morning. I promise that when we reach our destination, I will do nothing you find distasteful."

"Short of taking me home now, you will not be able to fulfill your promise."

His sigh ruffled her hair. "There may be nothing I can say that will make you believe me, but in the morning, I hope you will feel differently."

They rode in silence until they reached the first sentry, and Tremayne bade her pull up her hood and hide her face from the red-coated sergeant who challenged them. Tremayne spoke the password then, and made a laughing remark about his business for the night, which was to relieve a sorely tried officer. Himself, of course. Tremayne's hands slid over her in a lewd caress that she knew was meant for their audience, the sergeant and soldiery clustered about the picket fire. She fought against enjoying it, but found herself drinking in the scent of Tremayne's cologne—rum and lime—and leaning back into the warmth of his chest. And she was shamelessly gratified by the way the muscles in his thighs twitched in response.

They continued their journey. She shut her eyes and tried to imagine that the last few months had never happened, that this was still that night at Grey Farm, that she was still that girl. That she had never writhed beneath his cousin on a sun-strewn stage. Enveloped in the fantasy, her mind began to drift, her dreams fueled by the very real hands that now traveled her body, half soothing, half caressing. The rhythm of the horse lulled her and became the rhythm of Bayard Caide's caresses at the Southwark, but the figure beside her on the chaise was now Peter Tremayne. She woke drugged with sleep and sensuality to find Tremayne looking down at her with that secret smile playing over his lips.

They were challenged once more, but this time he murmured to her not to stir, and kissed her hair softly, speaking the password in hushed conspiratorial tones, as though not to wake her.

The air freshened, the night closed in and became cooler, and she smelled the Delaware, not fouled as it flowed through the city but fresh from the countryside. When she opened her eyes they were riding slowly up to the low stone wall of a cottage, and she realized when she saw the chalked door that it was the same place she had come with General Howe and Caide. They were in the Neck, the abandoned neighborhood of pleasure cottages and private docks where the wealthy retreated from the city for rustic weekends. In truth it was as pastoral as her polonaise dress, a citified version of Arcadian life, but charming all the same.

She blinked sleepily in the light spilling from the

house. Tremayne slid lightly from his horse, then set his hands about her waist and lifted her from the saddle.

A man appeared at the gate. Kate recognized him as Bachmann, her new watcher. Impassive and efficient, he seemed a fine accomplice for such sordid business. With a nod for Tremayne, he took the reins of the horse, and led the animal away. Then they were alone in the chill night air, the cottage beckoning.

She expected Peter Tremayne to lead her directly inside, but instead he stood looking down at her, his hands resting gently on her shoulders. "I will always wonder how things might have been different," he said.

His words were baffling. Stranger still, he took a fine lace handkerchief from his pocket and gently wiped the rouge from her cheeks. He rubbed the stain from her lips with his thumb, then said, "Damn it all to hell, I'm no saint." Then he kissed her.

There was nothing gentle or teasing about it. This was not a prelude to seduction. And it was not rape. She opened her mouth to his thrusting tongue and decided that no matter the circumstances that brought them here, she wanted this man, and she was going to have him. When he drew away, her lips felt bruised, her throat parched, and she wanted more, wanted everything, but he made no move toward the house.

She didn't understand his hesitation, wondered if there was some gesture she ought to make, words she ought to say. She knew so little of lovemaking, and now she regretted her ignorance. She found she wanted to please him. "Should we go inside?" she asked.

He didn't reply. She turned toward the cottage, but Tremayne still hung back, reluctant to enter. She picked up her skirts and pushed open the gate. The rosebushes that had bloomed only two weeks ago were now bare. Their bruised petals carpeted her path. She climbed the granite steps and wiped her silk court shoes on the straw mat just inside the door. The diamond buckles twinkled in the moonlight. A pretty compass rose floorcloth radiated from the center of the hall and Kate turned left, and according to the floor, east, toward what she presumed to be the parlor.

When she opened the door, the air was wood-scented and warm, and the cottage was not empty. The cheery yellow parlor was papered in Chinese silk, a fantasy landscape of birds and branches and flowering trees. There was a fire burning, and two needlepoint lolling chairs pulled up beside it.

One chair was empty. Waiting patiently in the other was her father.

Thirteen

Tremayne knew he ought to allow them some privacy, but he trailed Kate into the cottage like a faithful dog. He could not bear to be separated from her. Not now, when they had so little time left.

She rounded on him at the sight of her father. "You tricked me."

"Yes," Tremayne agreed. "I did not like doing it, but I could see no other way to bring you here. I could not convince you to leave Philadelphia, but I hoped your father might."

The look she gave him was full of regret and longing. He supposed it was the same expression he had worn outside the cottage when he kissed her. Then she took a deep breath and turned to face her father.

Arthur Grey was much as Tremayne remembered: grizzled, lanky, forbidding. He wondered if Grey had ever been truly accepted among his Quaker neighbors. There was a steady hum of violence about the man. Or perhaps that was just the circumstances under which they met. In the Jersey woods they'd been on opposite sides of a nasty firefight. Tonight, Tremayne suspected, would be the same.

Arthur Grey rose as his daughter approached, and Tremayne observed the old campaigner, who had terrorized the French a decade ago and remained very much a force to be reckoned with, doff his cap and hunch his shoulders in the presence of a beautiful woman.

He didn't recognize her.

Then Arthur Grey took another look. An uncomfortable thing for a father, Tremayne realized. Harrowing, even: to have a daughter, and see her for the first time as a woman.

An alluring woman. Not *pretty*, actually. Kate would never be anything so simple. Her features were even and regular, her eyes a glory to behold, chocolate swirling in the cup. But it was her poise, her wit, her bearing, the intelligence sparkling behind those eyes that would draw men to her for the rest of her days. He'd seen this at Grey Farm, these qualities that others had missed. Like a perfect stone stuck in a dull bezel, she had lacked only the proper setting to bring out her sparkle.

"It suits you, Kate," her father said at last, with unexpected gentleness. "The finery. Would have suited your mother too."

Tremayne could not see Kate's face, but he heard her controlled, even voice. "I never meant for you to see me like this," she said.

"I wasn't born in Orchard Valley, Kate. I have nothing against finery." Arthur Grey opened his arms to his daughter, and she flew into them.

For a moment, Tremayne hated Arthur Grey.

Hated a man who had not recognized just how extraordinary his daughter was. Had kept her at home, in that dull backwater, where she could find no occupation, no man worthy of her.

But he had no business being angry, should not be here at all. Kate was no longer his. She would go away with her father, resume her quiet life in Orchard Valley. He could not follow her there, no matter his fantasies of seeking her out and making her his mistress. Nor were the secrets, the quiet murmurs between Arthur Grey and his daughter, of Angela Ferrers, of Mercer and Mifflin, of Washington's winter plans, his to bring away. He would leave here tonight empty-handed, report his failure to Howe, resign his commission. He too would go home.

"And what is this man to you?" Arthur Grey asked of Kate, when the conversation turned at last from armies and generals to more personal matters.

She turned to look at Tremayne and said softly, "I have wondered that myself, but I think now I can safely say he is my friend."

He didn't want her as a friend. He wanted her in his bed, crying out beneath him, but by bringing her here tonight, he'd forfeited that pleasure.

Arthur Grey snorted. "A damned dangerous friend. Men like him don't make friends with country misses."

"You're entirely right," Tremayne said. "Until tonight, my intentions have in truth been less than honorable, but also less than successful. You can take her home without shame."

Arthur Grey stiffened.

"I'm not going home," Kate said, perching on the other armchair with regal grace.

Her father poked the fire. "Orchard Valley isn't safe, but you could come with me, Kate. It will be a lean winter with the army, but there would be plenty of work to occupy you. Washington is short of clerks."

She blinked. Tremayne damned Arthur Grey once more for a fool. She would never go with him now. Philadelphia, of course, was not London. In London she might have found scope for her formidable talents, become a rich and influential courtesan, a patroness of the arts, a political power as the mistress of an important man. But even here she had tasted power, moved events, become part of something larger than herself.

"Clerks copy reports and orders," she said coolly. "My intelligence makes them."

"Your mother always said pride would be my downfall," Arthur Grey replied evenly, "but we never suspected it would be yours. Your damned fool lover is right. It would be best if you came away with me tonight."

"Lord Sancreed is not my lover," she said impatiently, sounding more than a little like Angela Ferrers. "But pray tell me where you met."

It was a trap, but Arthur Grey, wily old campaigner though he was, didn't see it. "In the woods near Haddonfield," he replied.

"On the road to Mercer, you mean." There was a gleam in her eye that quickened Tremayne's pulse. She was remarkable. "Where my intelligence dispatched you," she finished.

"Yes," her father agreed. "Where your intelligence, as relayed by Angela, dispatched me. Though I did not know the source at the time. Washington refused to speak about it with me. It was his secretary, Hamilton, who confirmed what Sancreed here told me in the wood. That you'd gone to Philadelphia with the Widow. Hamilton says you code the cleverest messages he's ever seen."

Grey paused a moment, and Tremayne saw at last how much alike these two were. Neither would hesitate to use the weapon to hand. "Six hundred men died at Mercer, Kate. I have been a soldier most of my adult life, save the years I spent in Orchard Valley with your mother. But you were born there. The weight of those deaths is not something you will carry lightly, when all this is done. And in the game you're playing, you won't be able to do all your killing at second hand. Angela Ferrers could tell you as much. There will come a time when you will have to choose between your life and that of the enemy who would take it from you. If you haven't the resolve to take that life, then what you do here is martyrdom, not patriotism."

"I will not leave," she said.

Arthur Grey rose from his chair. "If that is your decision, then it is time for me to go."

"Good God, sir, what kind of father are you?"

Kate gasped. Arthur Grey rounded on Tremayne. They had forgotten he was there.

"What would you have me do?" Grey challenged. "Carry her out the door kicking and screaming?"

"I am asking you to exercise a little paternal authority," Tremayne said icily. "Captain André thinks he can use her now, but when she crosses him again, as she surely will, he will have her dragged from her bed in the middle of the night and hanged without a soul to witness. And I will be able to do nothing—nothing—to stop it."

Arthur Grey picked up his battered hat and strode to the door. He paused to look back at his daughter, but he made no move to touch her, and for a second Tremayne thought the man a coward. Then he recognized it for what it was: a love that ran so deep it could not be overridden by self-interest. Arthur Grey had the power to break his daughter's resolve, to keep her safe—and a child—forever. But he loved her too well to use it. "Take care, Kate," he said, and walked out the door.

Kate did not move from her stance by the fire. Tremayne hesitated only a moment before following Grey outside. He ran to catch up, around the side of the house, down the grassy hill, to the small dock at the bottom of the lawn. Bachmann was there already, speaking quietly with the boat pilot. When he saw the two men coming, he retreated into the shadows.

"Sir," Tremayne began, but quickly realized that everything had already been said.

"*Are* you her lover?" Grey asked suddenly from the boat, as the pilot made ready to cast off.

"No," Tremayne admitted. He owed this man honesty. "But I intend to be."

"Angela Ferrers had the nerve to tell me this was all my fault. That I should have found Kate a husband. Made her a farmer's wife. But she's more than that, isn't she?"

"Much more," Tremayne agreed. "I can't marry her, of course."

Arthur Grey snorted. "Of course."

"You are a man of the world. You must recognize the unsuitability of such a match. But she would want for nothing. You heard her. She won't go back to Grey

Farm. But she would be happy in London. Admired, influential. We could come to terms."

Tremayne had bargained for women before, because that was how the world worked. He was taking a risk, of course, because Americans were infatuated with equality, tended to be unsophisticated about the arrangements of privileged men, and Grey might take mortal offense at being offered a settlement for his daughter's protection. But it was the only recourse left him.

Grey said nothing for a long time. Then finally, "Any arrangement you wish to make must be with my daughter, not me."

So Grey would not pimp his daughter, but he was a political animal, and would not scorn her if she became Tremayne's mistress. Well and good. The family might need a friend on the right side of the law when peace was concluded.

Tremayne knew he ought to feel some satisfaction. This was what he wanted. Kate for his own. He had not succeeded in sending her to her father and safety, but he would have her in his bed tonight. In the morning she would have no choice but to accept his protection. But all he felt was self-loathing and disgust. Which was why he suddenly said, "I care for her."

"If I didn't believe that," Arthur Grey said quite softly, "I'd have shot you at Haddonfield." Then the little boat was swept out into the current. It carried no light, because it had no business being there, and before Tremayne could frame a reply, it disappeared into the night.

Sergeant Bachmann waited on the back porch of the little cottage, drinking whisky from a flask. The

Hessian held it up wordlessly and Tremayne took a swig, grateful for the liquid courage. Then he mounted the stairs and let himself in the back door of the small, neat house where Kate Grey waited for him, and where he intended to break every promise he had ever made her.

*K*ate was staring into the fire when he returned. She didn't dare look at him or he would see her weakness, might carry her bodily down to the dock and recall her father's boat.

"He treats you like a man," Tremayne said. "I suppose that is the way of men without sons."

"He treats me like an equal," she said, relieved that her voice did not betray her. "But I have noticed you are inclined to confuse the two."

"Not so," he countered. "I treat very few people as equals. Sex doesn't signify."

"What does then?"

"Courage, which you have, and kindness. Loyalty, which you inspire. Honesty, which has been in somewhat short supply between us."

"You tricked me into coming here. You've no right to expect honesty from me."

"Don't I? I won't pretend my intentions were honorable at Grey Farm, but you and your aunt lied to me, trapped me, damned near got me hanged. And you've been lying to me ever since."

"I didn't lie to you at Grey Farm."

"You split hairs with extraordinary delicacy. That's how you reconcile your pacifism with your espionage, isn't it?"

"I didn't steal your plans. By the time I knew it was done, you were already gone. I was going to wait for you to return, explain that it wasn't me and . . ."

"And offer up your body as proof of your lies," he finished for her.

"That's not how it would have been."

She could barely see him for the tears blurring her vision, but she felt the air move and knew he was coming for her. His arms were around her before she broke down and sobbed.

"No," he said. "That is not how it would have been."

She felt safe and warm in his arms and so she let the tears come, as he whispered soothing nonsense in her ear. When the wracking spasms subsided, he said, "Let me call your father back."

"No. I don't want to leave." But she wasn't sure if she was talking about Philadelphia, or Tremayne's arms. She reached up and drew his face down to hers. She felt hot, thirsty, desperate, and she did not want to think. She brushed her lips against his. They remained closed. She tested the seam with her tongue, pressed, then found entry.

He gave in and kissed her, his tongue diving into her mouth, his hands in her hair and at the small of her back. She knew a sudden rush of exultation. She'd never been the aggressor before, but now suddenly she discovered that she held the same power over him that he held over her. She could make him want her.

He pulled away, gasping. "Kate, you don't have to choose between this and your safety. You don't have to stay here for me. There is another boat. I'll take you to your father. In the spring, when this madness is done, I'll come to you."

Kate didn't want words and promises, and she didn't believe she had a future beyond this winter. There was only now. She fitted her body to his, sighed when she felt the evidence of his arousal pressed against her belly.

"Stop, Kate. Or we'll end up on the floor, and I'll do this all wrong."

She couldn't imagine how to do it wrong, only how consummation would somehow sever her from the decision she had just made, divide now from then, put decision and need both firmly in the past, allow her to go on.

He grasped her wrists and held her at arm's length. "This is shock, Kate. The aftermath of great emotion. It is not how we should begin our affair."

He backed her to the armchair she'd been sitting in earlier and pushed. She fell onto the cushion in an undignified tangle of skirts and petticoats, but the tortured expression on his face told her that her dishevelment was alluring, that her bruised lips and exposed ankles tempted him. He looked down at her and ran his hands through his hair; tension was plain on his face. She started to rise from the chair.

He groaned in exasperation and backed away. "Wait here." He left the room and returned a few seconds later with a flask, rummaged in the pretty china cabinets beside the fire for glasses, and poured her a dram of whisky. She drank it. Desire fled.

Exhaustion replaced it. And desolation. "You must have planned this rendezvous with my father days ago. You never meant to seduce me tonight."

"You sound almost betrayed."

"I came rather overdressed for a rowboat." And she felt foolish.

He smiled at that, and took the chair opposite her, his long legs stretched before the fire to cross with hers, his empty glass dangling from his fingertips. "You're also overdressed for the other options available to us."

She rolled her eyes heavenward. The man blew hot and cold. She'd just offered him that and he'd demurred. Besides, it felt oddly companionable, just sitting here with him, and she found herself starved for companionship.

He leaned across the distance between them, removed her glass, and took both her hands in his.

"Shall we make love, Kate?"

Her voice caught in her throat. Heat bloomed in her. He could have had her already, but he'd refused. He could have told the court-martial in New York about her, but he'd refused. He could have turned her over to André at Germantown, but he'd refused. And he'd risked his life to bring her father here.

They had talked of making love, but never of falling in it. She knew better than to speak of it now.

"Why didn't you want me a few minutes ago?" She suspected, but she had to know.

"I did want you. Desperately. But not unadvisedly, lightly, or wantonly."

They were not part of the Quaker order of service, but she'd attended English weddings since coming to Philadelphia, knew where Peter's words came from, and what he was trying to tell her. He was not offering her marriage, but he didn't want her in a mindless frenzy, or for just one night.

"I need a moment alone first," she said. In her mindless frenzy she had almost forgotten.

He quirked an eyebrow.

"Mrs. Ferrers advised me to take precautions," she explained.

Tremayne sighed. "I can only imagine what she told you to do."

"No imagination is necessary. It's an entirely prosaic item," she said, drawing the small wooden box from the practical pockets she insisted on beneath even her most impractical gowns. She held it up in the palm of her hand.

He removed the lid. "Have you used one of these before?"

"Of course not. But the theory seems sound."

He capped the box, then covered her hands with his own. "Put it away. You don't need it. There are other ways."

"Yes. But the other ways all depend entirely on your goodwill."

"And have I ever given you reason to doubt it?"

"Mrs. Ferrers says—"

"I'm not making love to Mrs. Ferrers, at the moment. I intend to make love to you. Is it so impossible for you to trust me?"

She swallowed. "I want to."

"Kate, I'm not placing my pleasure ahead of your safety. I know how those things are prepared. Boiled in vinegar and soaked in brandy, yes?"

"It makes sense if you think about it. Nothing grows in a pickle jar."

"And have you ever gotten vinegar or brandy in a cut on your hand?"

She was beginning to see his point. "Mrs. Ferrers said I probably won't bleed. I'm too old."

"She is a font of knowledge on the subject, I'm sure, but since we are being indelicate, I can tell you from experience that age alone does not ensure that it will be painless for you. Even if you don't tear, you'll be sore, and removing the thing once we're finished might make the occasion memorable for you in an entirely different way than I intend."

"Oh." She subsided into her chair. Speaking so frankly of such intimate matters with Tremayne was bizarre, and somehow quite natural. "But I've brought nothing else."

"We don't need anything else. I can withdraw."

She said nothing.

"You don't need to rely on my goodwill in this. A child would be equally inconvenient for me as for you. Charming as you are, I will manage to control myself. I'm not an overeager schoolboy or a loutish farmhand."

"I want to trust you—"

"—but you have not been able to trust anyone for a very long time. I know. Trust me, now."

He held out his hand.

She took it. She felt very small beside him as they crossed the cozy parlor together and ascended the stairs.

It was an old house, like Grey Farm, but far more fashionable. The stamped wallpaper upstairs was fresh, delicately colored and pleasingly classical. The carpets were thick and bright. A fire was ready to be lit in the largest bedchamber, and Kate fleetingly thought of Bachmann, Tremayne's loyal Hessian, camped downstairs. Not the po-faced conspirator she had imagined, perhaps, but what must he think of her, his master's lover? She put it from her mind.

She'd realized in the first few weeks of her adventure in Philadelphia that no matter what the outcome of the war, she had transgressed. There would be no place in polite society, neither the learned salons of Philadelphia nor the forgiving parlors of Orchard Valley, for a woman who bartered her body for secrets. It was simply too sordid.

But this bedroom, borrowed though it was, was not sordid. It was the private retreat of proud parents. There were penmanship and embroidery samples on the wall, framed and hung with care. In the corner was the dressing table of a lady fine enough to receive visitors during her toilette, but not so fine as to banish the toys abandoned beside her chair: the cup and ball, the hoop and stick some toddler must have chased around the room just before they were forced to flee the house.

The bed was hung with cream wool and crewel embroidery. It was decades out of date but well cared for and obviously much loved. A fitting place to part with her innocence.

But now that she was in the room, she had no notion what to do. It had all seemed so easy in her bedroom at Grey Farm, when he had taken the lead, and even downstairs, less than hour ago, when she'd rushed headlong at him.

"I don't know how to begin," she said.

There were logs laid on, and a tinderbox. He knelt beside the hearth. "*Beginning* has never been our problem. It's seeing the deed through that has eluded us. I half expect someone to start pounding on the door at any moment."

She laughed, and he smiled up at her, and Kate realized that for tonight at least she would put her faith in him. Then he lit the fire. The next step, she knew, was to disrobe, but these were not the practical garments she'd grown up in. Her gown fastened in front, but the lacings of her stays required a maid's assistance. Or a lover's. She found herself blushing furiously, and when she looked up, he was draping his fine red coat over the back of a chair, removing his silver gilt gorget and leather neck stock, and placing them carefully on the dressing table.

He smiled when he realized she was watching him. "You're blushing. Do you like watching me undress?" he teased, unfastening the buttons on his waistcoat.

Her mouth felt dry. The elegant flourishes of his uniform were not just for the benefit of the guard; they were for her. The silver buttons on his coat and Mechlin lace at his cuffs. The sweet lime and rum cologne. They were to entice her, to please her.

How shockingly adult it all was. She'd been living among strangers under an assumed name and committing treason for months, had experienced a taste of intimacy with Bayard Caide, but only now, to her surprise, did she feel anything like a grown woman.

She forced herself to swallow. The room was warming quickly. Or maybe that was her own body. "Yes," she said. "I want to see your hair down."

"Yours first, I think," he said, gently freeing the tortoiseshell combs and laying them beside his gorget on the dresser. They formed an intimate still life, her ornaments lying beside his regalia. Then he threaded his hands through her hair, unwinding the elaborate coils and loosening the tight curls, until it fell free over her neck and shoulders.

She closed her eyes, and felt his lips brush against

hers, slow and patient, not seeking entry, only contact, until her mouth opened of its own accord and their tongues met.

When he finally broke away she felt dizzy. Everything around her, the carpets, her gown, the very air, felt cushioned and cloud light, as though she could float away.

She watched him shrug out of his waistcoat and fold it neatly. She tried to unhook the front of her gown, normally the work of a few moments, but the hooks kept slipping from her clumsy fingers.

"Let me help." He covered her hands with his own and brought them to his lips for a brief kiss, then lowered them to her side. He made quick work of the hooks on her bodice, then untied the tapes cinching her skirts, and when both were open, he took her hands and steadied her as she stepped out of the circle of pooled silk.

He fingered the laces on her stays. "May I?"

She nodded, her heart pounding. He turned her to face the glass of the dressing table. She could see him, darkly handsome, standing behind her, the scarred side of his face lost in shadows, his eyes on hers in the mirror, his hands invisible but busy at her back. She was breathing in shallow gasps, the rapid rise and fall of her chest clearly visible in the glass.

Then the back of her stays parted and she felt cool air on her skin. He appeared to know better than to pull the laces out. He left them loosely plaited and drew the garment over her head. She wondered fleetingly how many other women he had undressed, then put it from her mind.

In the mirror she was naked and vulnerable before

him, her gossamer shift transparent in the firelight. She could see the hunger in his eyes. His hands rested lightly on her shoulders, then slid down to cup her breasts through the cloth. He lifted them, tested their weight, then gently thumbed her nipples. She felt them tighten, saw them in the mirror, budding pink through the sheer fabric.

She was trapped between his body and the dressing table, every move visible in the tilted glass. Every involuntary twitch of her hips, triggered somehow by the play of his hands on her breasts, was visible both to him and to her.

She understood suddenly why he'd turned her to face the mirror. He wanted her to see, to know, to acknowledge that this was him and not his cousin. Him and not Bayard Caide.

He needn't have worried. She knew the difference between the two men. Caide had played her body skillfully, driving her before him to knowledge and pleasure. But Tremayne, she now understood, was determined they should go there together.

She whimpered when he abandoned her breasts to untie the lace at her collar, then trace the lines of her collarbone, her neck, her jaw. When she felt the pads of his fingers pressed to her lips, she gave in to instinct and flicked her tongue out to taste him. She heard his sharp intake of breath, and when she opened her mouth to his questing fingers, she heard him groan. She suckled, and felt his hips shift, felt him press his arousal into the small of her back.

When he touched his wet fingers to her aching breasts she felt a coiling pleasure between her legs. He continued rolling her nipples between his thumbs and forefingers, moistening her chemise until it was damp and transparent, the pink of her nipples showing red in the firelight. Her breaths were coming shorter now. Every muscle in her body tensed. She closed her eyes. If he only squeezed her nipples once more, surely she would—

He stopped. Cool air swirled around her thighs and her eyes flew open. Back to the mirror. He was drawing up her chemise.

One hand held her hem, the other fingered the neatly trimmed hair at the juncture of her thighs. "Very pretty. The Widow's grooming, I presume?" he said.

"She insisted." Kate gasped as his finger slid through the curls.

"Did she help you, or did you do it yourself?"

She'd never thought of the procedure as erotic before, but she could tell the thought of another woman touching her intimately excited him. "She helped me the first few times. Then I used a mirror."

"Did you part yourself and look?" he said, spreading her open with his fingers.

She shook her head.

"Did you touch yourself like this?" He found the bud that pulsed there, then circled.

"No!"

He stopped.

"No? You wish me to stop?" he asked playfully, dropping kisses on her shoulder. "Or no, you did not touch yourself?"

"I didn't touch myself."

"That's a pity." The circling resumed, light and deft. "But other times, you explored yourself?" he asked, persistent.

"Yes," she admitted. She felt curiously unashamed.

"And did you bring yourself to climax?"

She shook her head. "No. I've never . . ." But that wasn't quite true. "Bay did."

His hand stilled. He dropped her chemise and it fluttered back into place.

She met Tremayne's eyes in the mirror, expecting anger but finding only amusement.

"Bayard Caide, Angela Ferrers," he said. "What a lot of people we seem to be bringing to bed with us."

"He didn't . . ." She groped for words.

"Make love to you?"

"No. He just . . ."

"Pleasured you," he finished for her.

"Yes."

"With his hands?" he asked, drawing her hem up once more. "Like this?"

"Oh," she cried out as he found her again, his touch cool against her heated flesh.

"Or with his mouth?"

The thought nearly undid her. She looked up at his face in the mirror, his eyes intent, his hair falling over her shoulder. She needed . . .

But his hands slowed, pulled her back from the brink, turned her gently to face him. "I'm determined to banish all thought of Bayard Caide from your head. And in the event that my attentions aren't frequent enough for you, my passionate pearl, I'll teach you to take care of yourself in the interim."

"Show me," she said hoarsely.

He picked up the hand mirror lying on the dressing table, and led her to the bed. They climbed on together, and she sat uncertainly with her legs folded beneath her. He knelt beside her and began kissing her mouth. Long, languorous, tongue-tangling kisses. He dragged her chemise off her shoulders, used the weight of his body to guide hers back against the pillows, and chuckled with satisfaction when her legs fell open and she drew her knees up of her own accord.

Then, still in his breeches and shirt, he knelt between her legs and spread her sex with his long, skillful fingers. She gasped when she felt the cool air touch her heated folds. "You are pink and lovely and, I am sorry to say, decidedly virginal. We should go slowly, Kate."

"How can you tell?" she asked, genuinely curious and wildly impatient all at once.

He placed the mirror in her hand and helped her angle it until she could see herself. It was bizarre to think there were parts of her own body she had never seen, could not actually, with her own eyes.

She watched as he traced a finger around her entrance. It was the most erotic thing she had ever seen, and the tiny quivering muscles in her thighs made obvious her desire.

Down, around, and up he traced, then he stopped on the downswing and applied gentle pressure to the flesh there. It became taut when he pressed. "If I go slowly, it should stretch, not tear."

"Oh." It was a detail Angela Ferrers had left out.

He mistook her tone. "Are you afraid, Kate?"

She shook her head. "Not of the pain." Of the intimacy. Of where it would lead.

"Would it be such a terrible thing for us to fall in love?" he asked.

Of the way he could read her so easily.

"Ask me again in the morning."

His eyes, so unguarded a moment ago, became shuttered now, and she knew he was going to bend all his formidable skills to procure the answer he desired.

He circled the nub at the top where so much tension centered. "Do you know what this is called?" he asked, with a wicked gleam in his eyes.

"Tell me," she said breathlessly.

He did so. Then he bade her touch it herself. "It's so small," she said, amazed that such a tiny thing could so rule her desires when touched like this.

"It swells more when you are very aroused," he said. "Let me show you."

Before she could protest, his head dipped between her thighs and he sucked the swollen nub into his mouth, worried it with his tongue. When he relented, her eyes were closed, her head thrown back, her legs splayed wide.

"Now look," he said, holding up the mirror.

But she was done with playing. She batted aside the mirror, desperate for relief. But his fingers resumed their play. She arched shamelessly into his hand.

"I see you know what you want," he drawled, stretching out to lie beside her, one hand propping up his head, the other stroking her, as if he could do this all night. "I was thinking about killing Bay for touching you, but now I think I might have to thank him for awakening you. It's breathtaking."

Finally he ceased teasing and settled into a rhythm that stole her breath. She climbed fast toward the peak. Then his touch changed, slowed. She writhed in frustration. "Please."

"Please what? Open the window? Put out the light? You'll have to be more specific."

She whimpered. "Please."

He laughed. "You don't know what it's called, do you?"

She blushed. He had his hand between her legs and he was pleasuring her with practiced skill, but only now did she blush and turn away.

"The French call it the little death, *la petit mort*. The Spanish say they are going to run, *correr*. The Romans used to say they were hastening, *festinus*, to the finish. But in English, we say we will come. Come for me now, Kate."

She did.

When her body started to calm, when the thud of her heart in her chest was finally louder than her ragged breathing, her eyes fluttered open to find Tremayne looking down at her, swallowing hard.

He'd loosened the flap on his breeches. Her eyes widened. She'd never seen one before, had not expected the sight to make her feel . . . hungry . . . thirsty . . . ravenous.

"I want to see all of you," she said, realizing he remained clothed out of deference to her innocence. He hesitated, but she was struggling out of her chemise and the sight seemed to snap his control. He shucked his clothing quickly, and Kate stared in wonder at the glory of his body. He was broad-shouldered, flat-stomached, and narrow-hipped, like a statue of a Greek god in one of Mr. Du Simitière's engraving books. Except for the scars. Not just his wounds from Mercer, but others as well. He was beautiful, but he had led a soldier's life, and she should not be here with him.

She might have turned skittish, might have bolted, if he had not settled his body over hers at that moment, and threaded the fingers of his left hand with her own. His right hand, she could feel spreading her. Then he was poised at her entrance, and with the gentlest nudge, he slipped inside, and she was lost.

Her hips surged to meet him, to engulf him, but he drew back, just out of reach. Then he dipped back inside her, and she was running, hastening, on the verge of dying once more, but the contact she needed remained out of reach.

"Peter," she said. "Please."

He groaned. "Slow and gentle, my love. Trust me."

She didn't want slow and gentle anymore. She wanted all of him. She wrapped her legs around his waist, dug her heels into the small of his back, and rose to meet him.

*H*e had not anticipated seducing her. If he'd thought ahead to what might happen at the cottage, he imagined himself kissing her farewell before she stepped into the boat with Arthur Grey.

But they were maddeningly proud and stubborn, father and daughter, and she did not board the boat.

He ought to have returned to the house and taken her on the floor of the parlor when she offered. Should have used her fast and hard with no regard for her innocence, and bundled her tearful and torn into the waiting shallop. Instead, he had taken her hand and talked of lovemaking.

There was no other word for it, this shared journey. He'd been nervous, leading her up the stairs, afraid he would hurt her or, much worse, disappoint her. He ought to have seduced her, courted her pleasure with a rake's tricks and driven her before him to climax, if he wanted to make her pliant. But he could not bear to insult her that way. They must go together, he realized, or not at all.

Her boldness had delighted him, stirred him to a degree he scarcely remembered feeling since he and Bay were teenagers, set loose on London with too much money and too little sense. His determination to go slowly with her had proved the right course. She responded so artlessly and honestly, he needed no further stimulation than the sight of her, head thrown back, hips pumping, to bring him to aching hardness.

He'd stopped twice after entering her shallowly to prolong his erection. He had promised her he would not spill inside her, and he was determined to bring her to pleasure again before he spent outside her body.

She surged up, her wet warmth engulfed him, and he froze. He retained control, but only barely. Her eyes were wide with pain.

"Kate," he said, "I didn't want to hurt you."

"I wanted to remember this. Always."

When her grip on him slackened, he began to move again, and said, "You will. I promise."

Then there were no more words for some time, until she had run, hastened, died, and come for him again, and lay tangled between Tremayne and the bedclothes.

He'd done everything in his power to stay hard but not come with her, and now he faced a dilemma. He was still sheathed in her, still painfully erect. To thrust inside her while she lay nearly insensate seemed caddish, and also dangerous. He did not think he would have sufficient warning—or will—to pull out. But to withdraw from her body and groan and stroke himself in front of her seemed awkward, out of the question. He must turn away and finish into the bedclothes, silently.

He withdrew from her as gently as possible, but a tremor of aftermath shook her small frame, and her eyes fluttered open to hold his. Before he had a chance to move, she reached out and took him in her hand.

He was slick with their mating, and shocked when she displayed no distaste. Her fingers closed around him and stroked. A lush, liquid sound. Her hand felt scorching hot, her touch artless and devastating. He would, at that moment, have done anything for her.

"Harder," he begged, ashamed and exhilarated by his capitulation. She tightened her grip, stroked again, then once more, and he came, crying out and spurting into her hand and onto her pale belly.

He'd been neither discreet nor silent. He had no idea what to do next, but she was smiling up at him, her fingers playing over his still-twitching length, and it seemed the most natural thing in the world to collapse on his back beside her and laugh.

"Dear God. Where did you learn that? Angela Ferrers again?"

She turned her head on the pillow and kissed him, openmouthed and as generous with her tongue as she had been with her hand. "No," she said, pulling away with laughter in her eyes. "Pure instinct. Was it correct?"

"I'm not sure I have words for what that was."

She looked sidelong at him. "Is it always like this?"

He shook his head. "No. It's usually enjoyable, but not like this." This, he realized, had been more than enjoyable. It had been important. And it could not, must not, be the last time.

He rolled to face her. "I'm sorry about that," he said of his seed on her stomach. "Rest here a moment and I'll bring a cloth."

There was a washstand with a full basin, courtesy of Bachmann, who had clearly planned for all eventualities. Tremayne washed himself, then dampened a cloth and returned to the bed. "In case Angela Ferrers did not inform you, it's terribly discourteous for a gentleman to come on a lady."

"But they like to," she observed shrewdly.

"Yes, we do. I suppose it's like an animal marking his territory: this is mine."

But she was not his. Not yet.

They lay drowsing on the soft down mattress, curled on their sides facing each other.

"I like this room," she said, running her fingers through the fringe on the bed curtains. "Whoever lived here must miss it. I don't think you could be unhappy in a house like this."

He'd noted the toys beside the dressing table, the penmanship samples on the wall. "It feels like a home," he replied. "Sancreed was too grand to have rooms like this. Too formal. I can't imagine my mother hanging my penmanship samples on the wall."

"Was your handwriting so poor?" she teased.

He laughed. "Perhaps. But I will wager yours was no better. I saw no proud examples of your accomplishments hanging on the walls at Grey Farm. And I looked, I assure you."

She groaned. "That is because I have no accomplishments. I was a failure at drawing, painting, and needlework. Music is my only talent, I'm afraid."

"And tactics," he reminded her. "If battlefield

strategy was an after-supper entertainment for ladies I am certain you would excel. In any case, I would love to hear you play. I noticed the harpsichord at Grey Farm. I had always thought Quakers rejected worldly pleasures like music."

"Not all Quakers. It is a matter of individual conscience. My mother taught me to play. My father taught me to sing."

"They enjoyed music together, then."

"That, and reading. My father liked to read to my mother. Sometimes he came to the table early for meals so he could read to her while she cooked. You should know you were accorded very special treatment, taking dinner in the dining room at Grey Farm. We usually eat in the kitchen."

Her stomach growled, and she laughed. "I'm sorry. It must be all this talk of cooking."

"Bachmann thoughtfully brought a hamper. If I can find something to read to you, will you prepare us something to eat?"

They searched the rooms for books and descended to the kitchen like children let to play in an empty house, she in her shift and stays and he in his shirt and breeches, and dove into the hamper Bachmann had left for them.

"This is *butter*," she said, with something halfway between suspicion and delight. "And it is fresh. How did you come by fresh butter? The navy ships aren't even unloaded yet. Nothing has gotten through the blockade for weeks. Even the Valbys are cooking with tallow these days."

"I am as surprised as you. But Sergeant Bachmann

is an old campaigner. He forages with preternatural skill. I hope you are not too patriotic to share it with me?"

"My stomach has no scruples, I'm afraid."

"What else is there?" he asked, imagining with a growing appetite the things fresh butter could complement.

"There are potatoes. And some ripe cheese. A package of salt." Then she plucked out a string of sausages and examined them suspiciously. "Even the joints that reach Howe's table are tainted. You will pardon me if I will not trust sausages."

Tremayne laughed. "Our Hessian allies hardly recognize meat unless it is ground and stuffed into a casing. But of that humble form, they are connoisseurs. If Bachmann acquired them, they are quite safe, I promise you."

"Very well. Now then, what have you found to read to me?"

"Our unwitting hosts have catholic tastes. We have here *A Dissertation Concerning the Nature of True Virtue*—"

"Not the best choice, considering I've but lately surrendered mine."

"Regrets?" he asked.

She stood on tiptoes to kiss him, soft and fleeting. "No."

Thank God.

"What else is there?" she asked.

"Novels." Tremayne sorted through the small stack. "We have *The Castle of Otranto*—"

"What's that one about?"

"Young ladies being stalked by dangerous gentlemen through a dark old house."

She stopped, potato in hand, mid-peel, and raised a plucked eyebrow. "Perhaps a little too close to my current predicament as well."

"I suspect our hosts took their favorite books with them. We have here the dregs of their library," he informed her. "Your choices are sermons, ghosts, or three-month-old copies of the *Gazette*."

"The *Gazette*," she said, pushing a pile of cubed potatoes to the side and beginning to slice sausages. "Advertisements, please."

"Wouldn't you rather have a story?"

"Oh, there are stories in the advertisements. If you know how to read them."

She was right. "'Mr. James Wheelright,'" he read aloud, "'farmer, begs assistance in apprehending his wife, who ran away, a month ago, on his mare. He very generously offers that she will be restored to his affections once more, if she will only bring back the horse.' Do you always practice divorce by newspaper here?" he asked, incredulous.

"Only when circumstances warrant. The Marriage Act has been rather slow to reach the hinterlands. Has the wife responded? Check the next day's paper."

Tremayne scanned the next day's edition, then the next, then found what he was looking for. "Indeed. The lady responded three days later. The horse, apparently, came with her into the marriage, and she feels it is only right that it carry her out of the marriage."

Intrigued now, he paused and scanned farther down the page. "It seems his wife has gotten the better part of the bargain in keeping the horse. Mr. Wheelright is also advertising for the return of a bondservant, a girl of fourteen years, at least six months pregnant—no doubt courtesy of her employer—believed to have run away to the city."

"I wish Mrs. Wheelright joy with the horse," Kate said dryly.

"Would you like to hear about Dr. Kelley's most efficacious cures for venereal diseases?"

"Is it likely I will be needing them?" she asked.

"Good Lord, no. I haven't been a saint, but I have been careful. You need have no worries on that score."

"Thank goodness. You wouldn't like me to tell you about Mrs. Ferrers' prescriptions. Not before we eat." She paused, considering. "Or *ever*, really. Should I be jealous of these paramours you were so careful with?" She said it casually, but he hoped the answer mattered to her as much as it did to him.

"There is no one else but you, Kate."

She smiled, and kissed him once more on her way to the hearth. He watched her tie the hem of her chemise up and then wet it down. She blew the dust out of a pan, set it on a stand, and kindled a small fire from the waiting coals. Everything she did was deft and efficient.

He wondered how long it had been since she'd done something as homely as cook. The sausages sizzled when she dropped them into the hot pan, the potatoes likewise when they followed a few minutes later. It was deeply satisfying to sit at the table and watch her, to know that he was going to enjoy a meal prepared by her hands.

He imagined her in the kitchen of the little cottage at Sancreed where his father had kept his mistress. Before they were old enough to understand the role of the quiet widow who lived in the gatehouse, he and Bay used to slip off to visit her. Alice made treats for them, buttered muffins and toast smothered with blackberry jam. It was warm and wonderful and a world removed from the bustling, businesslike kitchens at the main house. Those were the domain of the servants, ruled over by a tyrannical cook who knew her place in the hierarchy, and that of the young masters. He and Bay were not welcome there.

But *Alice* had welcomed them. Sometimes they went fishing and brought her their catch, or hunting and brought back a brace of game. She was always home, it seemed, and only shooed them out if they lingered too long into the evening, when they knew Tremayne's father came to visit, although they did not understand, until they were older, why.

And by that time Tremayne understood the distance between his parents, knew something of what had happened to his mother. He'd stopped visiting Alice, but he had seen them together, his mother and his father's mistress, sitting in companionable silence in the cottage garden, neither woman entitled to a whole happiness.

And he knew all at once that he did not want that for Kate. He didn't want her in that cottage, a swift gallop away, with a wife, or anyone else, to come between them. Nor could he imagine her tucked away in a discreet house in London. She was not his social equal, but as Donop had pointed out, what was the point in having money and power if a man could not have what he really wanted?

And *this*, what they were sharing here, now, was what he wanted.

He caught her up in his arms as she crossed from the hearth to the press cupboard, and pulled her laughing into his lap.

There was an obvious solution to their difficulties. "Marry me."

Fourteen

She slid from his lap. It was like leaving a warm bed on a cold morning: wrenching, but necessary.

"No."

She had no regard for hereditary privilege, but he had been raised with it. He was offering to lay aside the prejudices of a lifetime. *There is no one else but you, Kate.* Her chest constricted with grief, as she had felt when her mother died, for this future that would never be theirs. She held his gaze. "You do me a great honor. It is not every day that a viscount proposes to a farm girl. But marriage between us is impossible."

"You have never been just an ordinary farm girl. Even in Orchard Valley, you were already more than that. Are you so afraid of John André? His silence can be bought."

"For how long? He could dangle a noose over our heads for the rest of our lives. There might be no end to his blackmail."

"Marriage would put an end to it. I am the principal witness to your actions at Grey Farm. If we married, I could not be called to testify against you."

"I have been living under a false name since I came to Philadelphia. Everyone in your world knows me as Lydia Dare. If we married, it would be a union built on lies." And she could barely stand the ones she was living with already.

She retreated to the safety of the hearth, but he got up from the table and followed her there.

"Do you need to hear the words? I've never said them to anyone before. I love you. I desire you. I want you for my wife. There has to be a way."

There was. A way for them to marry without lies. "Come with me to the Continental lines." There, she'd said it.

"Kate, you know I cannot."

Of course he couldn't. It gave her a little strength, this limitation of his; enough to push him away. "Then you do not love me enough."

"You ask too much."

"You ask no less. *To give up everything.*"

"It is not the same, Kate. You're a woman. Marriage to a man with a title and fortune elevates you. But if I were to run away and play at rebellion with you, I would be dragged down. My lands and titles would be stripped from me."

"You would still be the man whom I loved. But the reverse would not be true if I went to England and lived a lie with you. I would not be the woman you fell in love with. I'm sorry, Peter, but tonight is all we will ever have."

"This cannot be the end." There was something desperate and reckless in his tone now. "If I can't have your hand, we can at least meet again—like this. It is not so difficult to arrange."

It was the first she'd troubled to think of the arrangements he'd made. She'd become good at this life of deception. She'd mastered charm and manners and fashion. The Widow had thrown her into deep water, and she'd learned, out of necessity, to swim. But she still had difficulty thinking out all the consequences. And when she did not, men died.

"What did Bachmann do with André's spies?" she asked warily. "The ones watching the house. Beaver Hat and Alley Loafer."

"I am not a murderer, Kate. They are alive and well, but detained at His Majesty's leisure. Montresor has been put in charge of building gun emplacements on Mud Island. The ditches flood nightly. The conditions are so bad that the soldiery will not stand for it, and the civilians will not work for the wages offered. So he press gangs his work crews. It will be at least a day, perhaps a week, before your unwelcome friends turn back up. We could come again tomorrow night."

She wanted to. She wanted to spend her days looking forward to nights like this, but she couldn't. "No. The Widow is right. If we continue to meet, sooner or later I'll put a noose around your neck."

"The Widow is a hypocrite. Donop wrote a letter before he died. I promised to deliver it. It is addressed to Angela Ferrers. But you should read it."

He led her back upstairs and found the letter in his coat pocket, then pressed it into her hands. He took up a seat at the elegantly feminine dressing table, and Kate had to banish the easy domesticity of it from her mind. This would never be their future.

She climbed onto the bed with the letter. Which was a mistake, because somehow the scene took on an even more intimate aspect. But nothing to do with the Widow could be homey, so she read the letter. Then she read it again.

"They were lovers for nearly a year," she said, trying to take it in, to reconcile the contradiction that was Angela Ferrers.

"Yes. Before you knew her, and then afterwards, while she was living in Orchard Valley. Even here in Philadelphia she managed to come to him. Always, as he said, on her own terms."

"He wanted to marry her. He addresses her as *his marchioness*, but Donop was a count." She was coming to realize that everyone had secrets, but the Widow's were deeper than most.

"Carl told me she was once a woman of name and note. I suspect she has good reason for obscuring her origins."

"I think she did love him," Kate said. *As I love you.* And if she continued to meet him, they would end the same way. "But Angela took the warning to Mercer, all the same. She knew what might happen."

"He didn't blame her, Kate. They were both adults. They understood the rules of the game."

"And you think we should play the same game. But, Peter, the difference is that I *would* blame myself."

*B*itter as it was, Peter Tremayne tried to stay away from her, but it proved impossible.

He did not want to dine or converse with Howe, and Howe's pretty mistress, and Howe's pretty mistress's pandering husband. He did not want to listen to Montresor and his engineers carp about their lack of money and men, or endure the bitter smiles of the Hessian officers who resented Howe's part in Carl Donop's death and assumed Peter to be an ally because he'd had the decency to remain with the count to the end. He did not want to share a table with Captain André, who had tried to kill the woman he loved, or with Caide, whom he had just cuckolded. Most of all he did not want to dine with Kate, who had rejected his offer of marriage. But the river was open, and Philadelphia, at least that portion of it that was loyal, was rejoicing. Refusing Howe's invitation to celebrate was out of the question.

The banquet was being held upstairs at the City Tavern in a private room painted pale green and hung with damask curtains of wheat gold. Kate was seated not three gilded chairs away from him—opposite Caide and flanked by the dashing Hessian Jaeger Captain Ewald and the Engineer Captain Montresor—talking gaily and flashing smiles at Howe, her fiancé, and the Hessians in equal measure. Her eyes, he could not help but note, glittered with more fire than the garnets at her wrist and ears.

Tremayne knew that just a week ago flour had been unavailable at any price and even salt pork had been scarce. Tonight there was roast beef seasoned with rosemary and salt, warm crusty bread with the sort of fresh butter Kate had swooned over at the Neck, duck in cherry sauce, apple tart and soft local cheese. He ate everything and tasted nothing. She ate very little. He saw her refuse the beef and accept only a slice of the

duck. He noticed everything she did, his gaze returning to her like a bird to roost, over and over, until he
had to force himself to fix his attention on the heart-
shaped face of Mrs. Loring, who ignored the husband
seated to her right and fed choice bits of meat to the
lover seated on her left.

The conversation first bored, then disturbed him.
Complaining about local conditions was the small
change of military life. The casual dismissal of the
Rebel army's prowess was willful blindness. It had
taken five thousand men, in the end, to capture Fort
Mercer, and even then it could not be counted a total
victory, because the Rebel garrison had spiked the
guns and slipped away in the middle of the night.
Three hundred Rebels had held two tumbledown fortifications against more than seven thousand British
and Hessian Regulars for a month, and nearly every
man of them lived to tell the tale.

Before the cheese was cleared he heard the music,
drifting up from the open windows below. When their
party moved downstairs to join in the dancing, Tremayne found himself trailing behind his cousin and
Kate, Bay's arm about her shoulders, his hand caressing her neck, impossible to ignore. When Tremayne
realized he was staring and forced himself to look away,
he found the Hessian Ewald at his side, his eyes studiously averted.

He supposed that to a country girl like Kate, raised
a Quaker and unused to finery, the ballroom must be a
dazzling spectacle. After ten weeks of dwindling supplies, chronic shortages, scarce provisions, and tainted
meat, Philadelphia suddenly had every necessity—and

a great many luxuries—in abundance. The chandeliers in the main hall were full of beeswax tapers, infusing the room with a faintly cloying aroma, but infinitely preferable to the stinking tallow that had become commonplace in even the wealthiest homes. The rum punch was strong, even if the limes were old and bitter, and the sugar had borne a faintly musty shipboard taste with it into the bowl. He was not tempted by the pastel iced cakes or the sweets frosted and glittering with castor sugar, but the brandy, although he had to leave the main room and seek it out in a tiny parlor filled with card tables, was excellent.

It surprised him to find Kate dancing when he returned. Nothing about her midnight blue silk *robe à la française* betrayed her Quaker origins, and she moved with the grace of a gypsy. Not in the mincing style of London dance masters, but with the full commitment of her entire body. First with a young lieutenant he dimly recollected to be titled and rich and named something birdlike, perhaps Sparrow or Finch. Then with Howe, who seemed to fancy himself in the role of doting uncle. Then with the altogether too handsome Ewald, who, Tremayne noted, had been watching her with his good eye all night. Ewald was harmless, but all the same, Tremayne would have to have a word there.

But of course he couldn't. She was not his.

Her next partner was not harmless. And the man had not sought her out. She'd gone from the floor and returned with him in tow. If Tremayne lived to be a hundred, and the damned woman lived past this winter, he would never be able to predict her. She was at a large public event, well chaperoned, and had no reason to endure the attention of any man she did not wish to, let alone one who had tried to kill her. So why the hell was she dancing with John André?

I have come into the possession of certain letters," Kate said, as she passed close to her partner.

She'd expected André to pale or stumble or express some surprise. Instead he turned her smoothly and executed his steps with a graceful flourish.

"Delightful," he said. His gold-flecked eyes twinkled, and he smiled broadly. "Now you are supposed to hint at the dark secrets contained therein. Next, I blanch in terror, whilst you, to press your advantage, quote a salacious line or two."

"You're mocking me," she said sourly.

"I am. I apologize. Blackmail is a serious business. By all means let us be dour and grim. Go on."

"They are from a lover," she said.

"Really? How droll. Please credit me with the good sense *not* to write compromising letters, and to instruct my lovers not to do so either."

"The letters are filled with the effusions of first love for a man somewhat older than the sender, and they were written quite recently."

"Forgeries," he replied smoothly.

"There are drawings, informal sketches. They are intimate."

He did not blanch, but the smile faded from his full lips, and Kate thought she detected something bittersweet and quickly buried in his gold-flecked eyes. "I can only presume your dear aunt sought out the writer, and encouraged this communication, no doubt vowing to see the missives delivered herself."

It had not occurred to Kate how Angela Ferrers might have come into possession of the letters; that she might not have found them but encouraged their writing. The thought made her uneasy. "Something rather like that, I expect."

"Oh, Miss Grey," he scolded. "You don't have the heart for this, do you? I resent and regret the card you've played, but I would expect no less. You can save your empathy. I assure you, I would have little enough for you if our positions were reversed. What do you think to demand in exchange for these letters?"

"I have no intention of handing them over to you. They are not in Philadelphia."

"Very prudent. Next you are going to say that if you die or disappear, they will be sent to Howe. And perhaps the broadsheets?"

"Yes."

"Also shrewd. But the difficulty with blackmail, Miss Grey, is that it is a weapon that can be fired but once. I grant that you have a loaded pistol pressed to my heart, but whom will you choose to save? Yourself, or Lord Sancreed?"

Her feet failed her. She nearly tripped, then stopped short, snarling the line of dancers for a second. Then André tugged her hand and turned her smoothly back into the steps. "Peter has done nothing," she said when they next passed close.

"Nothing? He turned Phillip Lytton over to the enemy at Haddonfield, and held private parley with a notorious Rebel officer whose skirmishers and raids have plagued our supply lines for months. Recently it seems he slipped that same officer inside our lines for a private tête-à-tête at a small cottage in the Neck. But of course you know this, because you were there. I admit, had I known the Grey Fox was visiting our fair city, I'd have had a squadron of dragoons shadowing Tremayne."

She felt suddenly queasy at the thought that one or more of André's henchman had followed her and Peter to the Neck, had watched the cottage while they'd made love. "And if I give you the letters, what guarantee do I have of Peter's safety?"

"None whatsoever, I'm afraid. The viscount's safety rests upon your good behavior. I have plans for you, Miss Grey, and these no longer include Peter Tremayne. You must not see him again. Or I will make dead certain he hangs."

She swallowed. She'd feared this, and now it had come to pass. And it would only be harder to give Tremayne up now that she knew what it was like to lie with him—to love and be loved by him. With relief she realized that the music was ending, and soon this harrowing interview would be over. "I think we understand each other."

She tried to leave the floor, but he held her hand fast. "Not quite," he said. "I wish you to know that my relationship with the boy went no further than the bounds of propriety, at least in a physical sense, but that my feelings were and are deeply engaged."

She forgot her fear for a moment. "Why not?" She had failed utterly to anticipate her enemy, and she was beginning to realize that it was because she did not understand him.

"I was captured by your countrymen in Canada at

the fall of Fort St. John. Myself and my fellow officers were marched to Pennsylvania and given our parole and the freedom to roam up to six miles from Lancaster, but it was not uncommon to be waylaid and beaten by gangs when we went about town. Those of us forced to shelter at the local inn were particularly vulnerable to attacks. The Cope family was kind enough to take me in and suffer the opprobrium of their neighbors for it. I could not abuse their hospitality by seducing their youngest son."

"But you flirted with him," she said, recalling Tremayne's careful teasing at Grey Farm. He'd been a guest in her home, courteous but forthright in his desires. She did not believe André had more scruples than Tremayne.

"He was old enough to woo," André replied, "but too young to bed."

She knew there was more to it. "I have read the letters. He is seventeen. Girls marry at such an age, and no one thinks the worst of it. And you are not yet thirty. It is not so great an age difference."

"Ah, but let us say we had consummated our love. The experience might have proved the forging of his preference, and not the expression of it. Virginity is a tricky beast."

To her horror, she blushed. Had her hand been free she would have snapped open her fan and hidden her face, but a new song had begun and André's grasp was like iron. He studied her as the steps of the dance carried him around her in a circle. "Oh, Miss Grey," he said softly. "So the fruit was picked only recently. Was Peter Tremayne a gentle lover? Did you go to him willingly, or did he blackmail you into his bed?"

"You presume too much, Captain."

"I asked you to call me John."

Now it was her turn to circle him. "I seem to recall that you were attempting to kill me on that occasion. Forgive me if I took the request as stock villain's banter."

"The exigencies of the moment compelled me, but now we are in accord and can speak as friends. And I can admit that my admiration for you only grows. I assumed you'd bedded Tremayne in Orchard Valley, but now I learn that instead of besting him with your wiles, you blindsided him with your purity. A ruthless stratagem I cannot help but applaud. Come work for me, Miss Grey."

"I will never work for you. And we are not friends."

"Are we not? We are of an age. We have both had cause to reinvent ourselves. We alone know each other's secrets. If not friends, what does that make us?" He dropped her hand at last, and Kate realized the music had ended. André did not wait for her answer, but bowed and allowed himself to be swept up into the press of men and women selecting their next partners.

He was wrong, she told herself as she sought the fresh air of the stairwell, and when even that proved too stuffy, the cool dark of the back porch where the crowd spilled noisily into the yard. Perhaps she was the only person in Philadelphia privy to the secrets of André's heart, but he was *not* the only man in Philadelphia privy to hers.

Peter.

She'd tried to ignore him at dinner, but whenever her eyes lighted on him, she'd felt stripped bare, as though everyone who looked at her could tell that she'd

given herself to him. They'd lain together naked like
Adam and Eve in the Garden, and sweated and cried
out and been as vulnerable as newborns in each other's
arms. And tonight they sat swathed in silk and lace at
opposite ends of a mahogany table and pretended not
to know each other. They drank wine and talked with
other people who seemed to Kate to have all the sub-
stantiality of ghosts.

He'd betrayed Phillip Lytton for her, and committed treason as damning as her own. Every time their
lives touched, she brought him danger and dishonor.

"I know a place where we can be alone. Will you
come?"

She thought at first that she had imagined his voice
in the dark of the garden, but then she realized that he
was standing behind her. She did not turn to face him.
She said nothing. Her breath came fast, making a mist
in the cool night air. He told her how to find the place,
his directions precise and succinct, and then he was
gone.

She resolved not to go to him and threaded her way
back through the crowd in the yard. It had coarsened
since she'd come outside. In the back hallway she noticed that the sound had changed subtly. Early in the
night, all of Philadelphia had been abroad celebrating,
but now the very young and the scrupulously virtuous
had gone home. It was past midnight, and tipsy flirtation and mild wagering had given way to drunken
propositions and high-stakes gaming. If she turned
into the taproom under the stairs, she knew, she would
find Caide betting on a fight, or stripping to the waist
to take part in one.

The fall of Mercer and Mifflin, and the opening of

the Delaware being celebrated tonight, had destroyed everything she had worked for since coming to Philadelphia. But it had bought her one priceless thing: time. She did not have to marry Caide right away. Pray God she did not have to marry him at all.

She ought to float to Bay's side on a tide of rustling silk and admire his skill or his winnings, allow him to show her off the way he liked to when the company was becoming informal. He might draw her down to his lap and balance his glass on her busk, the condensation running in rivulets down her breasts.

Instead, she opened the door to the cellar. At the bottom she found a long brick corridor painted shimmering white, stretching the length of the tavern from back to front. She followed it past haphazardly stocked storerooms, disordered by the recent influx of goods from the supply ships. Behind one half-shut door she heard the fervent urgings of a vigorous tryst, and hurried farther, until she reached the door Tremayne had described.

Batten oak and brined with age and the proximity of the docks, it nonetheless opened silently on oiled hinges. A smuggler's passage; two hundred narrow feet of smooth paving lined with boxes of contraband. It led straight to the river.

There was already a light burning in the tunnel, though there were no beeswax or spermaceti tapers here. It was rushlight, stinking of tallow and smoking like a forge. Her lover—and she realized with shock that was precisely what he was—lounged in the middle of the passage, ankles crossed, head down, shoulder negligently grazing a stack of wine crates. He looked up when she approached, and his expression of hope mixed with hunger gripped her like a vise. "I wasn't certain you would come," he said.

"I shouldn't have. Peter, André had us followed to the cottage. He knows what you did to Lytton, and about my father's presence behind your lines. He will destroy you if I do not give you up."

She'd never observed him in such a confined space. He was all coiled emotion and violent passion held in check, but he didn't move until she did.

She realized at once that it was a mistake. She sought his arms, desperate for comfort, but his hands on her waist were not gentle. He backed her into the crate behind her, and lifted her to sit on its edge. He gathered her skirts into a froth about her hips. "I'm not afraid of John André."

But Kate was. Afraid for herself, afraid for Peter. She braced her palms against his chest. "Don't."

They were frozen like that, his hands beneath her skirts, hers on his shoulders, when the tavern door at the top of the stairs swung open and disgorged two men dressed in white, carrying canvas sacks. They pulled the door shut behind them and made it almost to the bottom of the stairs before they realized they were not alone. They stopped on the bottom step, the older man shielding the boy behind him.

Tremayne stepped in front of Kate, but not before she got a good look at them: soldiers, from their snowy stocks and gaiters, but the man in the lead was portly, balding, and red-faced, and would never see forty again, while the boy was wide-eyed, carrot-topped, and scarcely fifteen. And their coats were not white. They were red, like Peter's, but turned inside out to show the cotton lining.

Tremayne was so close to her that she could feel the change in him, the way his body tensed and his center of gravity shifted when he took a second, smaller, but more calculated step in front of her to draw his sword. It echoed like a bell in the brick-roofed chamber.

The boy said something thick with consonants in a language she did not understand, but his fear was plain in his high-pitched voice and wide, panicked eyes.

Before the older man could answer, Tremayne spoke. "The boy has the right of it, Sergeant. You should go back to your barracks now."

"Who are they?" Kate asked. She could not place the language, though she knew she had heard it before.

"Deserters," spat Tremayne, "from the Royal Irish." He was vibrating with anger. And something else she didn't recognize.

The older man didn't flinch. His drew a pistol from his bundle and curled his lips into a nasty smile. "You have a bit of the Gaelic, to be sure, my lord. All the better for slapping down them that speaks it. But I'm afraid we can't oblige you. There's a boat waiting for us at the end of this tunnel."

"I cannot let you pass."

"But you will, my lord. Because I know something the boy here doesn't. That fancy piece you're about to tup doesn't belong to you. Better to let us meet the boat that's waiting than bear tales back to them that might be interested."

Caide. The threat chilled Kate to the bone. The man thought he was dealing with simple cuckoldry.

"Where will you go?" she asked the sneering sergeant.

He seemed surprised to hear her speak, then shrugged

and answered her. "The boy was never cut out for a soldier. He has family in Lancaster who will take him. It's the farmer's life for him. Me, I favor a billet with the Continentals."

"I'm sure you do," Tremayne scoffed. "For long enough to collect the shilling. A man who will desert from one flag will desert from another."

But Kate was already fishing through her pockets for the bag of coins her father had given her at Orchard Valley. She'd never needed pocket money since becoming the Widow's acolyte. She did not need it now. She tossed the bag high into the air and the rogue caught it, suspicion writ large over his coarse features.

"And what would this be for?" he asked.

Kate placed her hand on Tremayne's sword arm. "To speed you on your way," she said, praying Tremayne would lower his blade.

"Kate," warned Tremayne, never taking his eyes off the sergeant, "you cannot trust men like these."

"They are better out of the city than in," she said. "Lower your sword."

Tremayne shrugged. "Just as soon as he lowers his pistol."

The sound of the pistol being uncocked was as loud as a gunshot. Tremayne lowered his blade. The stocky sergeant sketched Kate a mocking bow as he passed close to her in the narrow hall, tugging the goggling boy along after him. They were lost quickly in the shadows at the far end of the tunnel, but a wash of cool air and the smell of the river told her that they had found the exit.

Tremayne was still standing over her. She saw the

pulse beating at his throat. His sword lay unsheathed on the crate beside her. She felt strange. Hot and restless. She reached for him. "Peter, I . . ." She didn't know how to describe it.

His hands rested lightly on her thighs. Her skirts were still drawn up over her knees, but he made no move to lift them. "It's the threat of violence," he said thickly. "The nearness of death."

She saw now that his hands were trembling. She touched him through his breeches.

"Don't," he said. His jaw was clenched.

She ignored him. The buttons popped free between her fingers. His flap fell open, and he sprang thick and heavy into her waiting hand.

"You won't like it. Not like this," he warned.

But she did.

*K*ate exited the cellar ahead of Tremayne on shaky legs. She'd done her best to repair her appearance, but she knew she looked like she'd been ravished, so she waited for the Shippens in the dark of their carriage. Peggy breezed in sometime later without noticing Kate's dishabille, but Mrs. Shippen ran an assessing eye over her, and pursed her lips in distaste. No doubt she attributed Kate's dishevelment to Bayard Caide. She thanked God for her fiancé's louche reputation.

Peggy's chatter on the ride home had a single theme: John André. Captain André was reopening the theater. Captain André was planning a ball. Captain André was building sleds for pleasure outings in the

Neck. And while Peggy's mother might be an indifferent chaperone, she was not a foolish woman. On the subject of John André, Mrs. Shippen was strategically silent. Canny city Quakers like the Shippens didn't fraternize with soldiers so their daughters could marry lowly captains without name or fortune.

Listening to Peggy prattle on as the hot bricks on the floor of the carriage cooled and the chill night air crept in, Kate felt her chest tighten until she could barely breathe. Washington had told her to consider carefully what she might be giving up to become the Widow's eyes and ears in Philadelphia. And she had considered. She'd considered that she would never see Tremayne again, and yet she could not imagine another man to suit her.

By the time the Shippen carriage deposited Kate at the Valby residence, she craved the solitude of her room, and took the stairs two at a time.

But her room wasn't empty when she reached it.

"Kindly close the drapes and light a candle or two. I'm tired of sitting in the dark," Angela Ferrers said. She sat in a shadowed corner, well away from the windows. Her appearance tonight was as surprising as ever. She was not the Quaker Widow of Orchard Valley, or the wiry groom of the Valby stables, or the oyster monger of Du Simitière's museum. And she was certainly not the exquisitely turned-out lady who had tried, and failed, to seduce Peter Tremayne. This woman was a bourgeoise, a comfortable merchant's wife, to judge by the richly figured velvet of her gown, too heavy to carry off its ruffled style, which ought to droop elegantly at the wrists and hem, but instead added bulk to her slim frame. It was a calculated lapse in taste, de-signed to relegate her firmly to the background of any gathering. And it would work. Amidst the overdressed burghers of Philadelphia tonight, Kate would never have given her a second glance.

"I thought we weren't to meet again in person, An-gela." Kate found a hot coal in the firebox. The candle flared, then became a pinpoint of light in the deeper dark as the drapes fell closed.

"I had no choice but to come. You and André's watch-dogs disappeared for an entire night."

Kate felt the hairs on the back of her neck prickle. She had not mentioned those events in her last dis-patch, in the masked letter she'd deposited, two days ago, in the dead drop at the Haymarket. "Are you also having me watched?"

"Of course. Where did you go?"

"On a private errand."

"You can expect no privacy. You are a spy. You watch and are watched in turn."

"*Quis custodiet ipsos custodes.* Where I went is no one's business but my own."

"It is if you are working for John André."

The suggestion stunned Kate for a moment. It was almost laughable, if it weren't so plausible. André *had* attempted to recruit her. To a jaded spy like the Widow, who clothed herself daily in lies, mistrust and suspicion came naturally. And Kate had fed it unwittingly.

"I'm not working for André," Kate said carefully. "I spent the night with Peter Tremayne."

The Widow rose and stalked to the cold hearth. She crossed her arms, leaned against the mantel, and took a deep breath. "At Grey Farm I said you were either very clever, or very stupid. Facts begin to weigh toward the latter. Bayard Caide might be besotted enough with you to forgive a great deal, but not, I think, that."

"There is more to this tension between Peter and Bay than the fact that they are closer cousins than society thinks. What aren't you telling me?"

"You're right. There is more. Their family tree is gnarled like an oak, and only a fool would place herself between those two men."

"Tell me what they are to each other and allow me to decide for myself."

"If you knew the truth, you wouldn't be able to conceal your knowledge from Bayard Caide. Believe me when I say that you are better off not knowing, and that you must give up Tremayne."

Kate knelt at the hearth and used a penknife to loosen a brick in the fireplace. She withdrew a sheet of paper and held it out to the Widow. "As you gave up Carl Donop?"

Angela Ferrers made no move to take the letter. "What foolishness is this?"

"The count wrote to you on his deathbed."

Angela Ferrers accepted the folded missive from Kate's hand and carried it to the candle. Kate thought she meant to read it, but the Widow held the folded paper to the flame.

"No!" Kate snatched it, the corner just beginning to burn, and threw it on the hearth. She dropped to her knees and smothered it with the loose brick.

The edges were singed but the message remained intact. Kate rose from the floor, brushed the soot from her skirts, and held out the letter once more. "You were loved by a man who was willing to die for you. Who *did* die for you." Kate laid the letter on the table between them.

The Widow made no move to touch it. "I advise you against following my example. Don't take up with a man who will die for you. Find one who will kill for you instead." But after a moment, Angela Ferrers reached out to finger the singed edge of the letter. "I cannot leave here with this," she said. "It is too dangerous."

It took a moment for her meaning to penetrate. The Widow wanted to read the letter here and now, but alone. Kate picked up the water jug from the washstand and went out of the room. She wondered, not for the first time, if anything touched Angela Ferrers, if the woman had any feelings at all, and decided that given tonight's display, the answer was a resounding no.

When she returned from the kitchen pump with fresh water, a chill wind met her at the door. The sash was up. The shutters were thrown back. Moonlight slanted into the room.

Angela Ferrers stood in the open window for anyone to see. She wore her fur-trimmed mantle, the hood casting her face in shadows. Kate could see nothing of her expression, but the Widow's hands were visible resting on the sill, white and trembling.

"Where did you get it?" the Widow asked.

She meant the letter, now ashes on the hearth.

"From Peter Tremayne."

Kate caught only a glimpse of the Widow's face as

she passed on her way out of the darkened room, but it was enough to tell her how very wrong she had been.

*I*t was the patter on the stairs that woke him. He was up and wrapped in his banyan before the reverend's bony sister knocked on his door.

Tremayne's first thought was of attack. The Rebels had crept up on Trenton last year in the dead of night, in the bone-rattling cold, and on Christmas Eve no less.

"There's a woman downstairs." Not an attack then. The reverend's sister stood barefoot in the corridor wrapped in a patchwork quilt. She had exceedingly large feet for a woman, he noted, recalling Kate's perfect proportions.

It must be her downstairs. Kate. He knew no other woman in Philadelphia who would seek him out in the middle of the night.

His room beyond the bed curtains was chill, the hall outside even more so, but the reverend's sister hesitated there, her message delivered, and Tremayne knew what she must be thinking.

"I'll be down in a moment. Thank you," he said. He dressed hastily, wishing there was a glass in his room. He was afraid for Kate, of course. Nothing but disaster, most likely in the form of imminent arrest, would bring her to his door at this hour. But he was also relieved. The crisis was come. There might yet be time to spirit her away. If not, he would intercede for her. No one liked to hang pretty young women. Howe had a soft spot for her. And no one would be surprised if a rich lord saved her from the gallows to install her in his bed. It was the way of the world.

She was waiting in the reverend's tiny parlor, but he knew before she threw the hood of her furred cloak back that it was not Kate. Even in the bulky velvet gown, the Widow was taller and more slender than Kate, boyish almost. He could think of only one reason why she might be here. "What has happened to Kate?"

"Nothing, my lord. She's safely tucked in bed, though it would please me immeasurably if in future you refrained from joining her there."

"Are you warning me off?"

The Widow looked suddenly older than he remembered, and bone-weary. She took a seat in the carved chair by the fire—a relic of one of the reverend's Pilgrim progenitors—and it creaked beneath even her slight weight. "We both know I'm a hypocrite, Major Tremayne. But Kate would be safer if she would do as I advise, rather than as I have done."

"I will not give her up," he said flatly. "Is that all you have come for?"

"No." She reached into her cloak. He recognized the folded paper and the bold, flowing hand, though not the scorch mark that now marred it. "You were with him at the end. *Tell me.*"

After what the woman had done to him, he did not think he could possibly pity her. If she had cried, he would not have. But Angela Ferrers sat perfectly still in the ancient chair. It would have given away her slightest motion with a plaintive creak. And he did pity her.

There was no sound in the room but his voice, and faintly, from the hall, the irregular tick of the battered case clock.

She listened to it all. Donop's delight in the

Ferguson, his admiration of the Widow's skills with a rifle and her seat on a horse, his determination to take Fort Mercer, to regain his honor, the details of his terrible wound, and his deepest regret upon dying: that he would never see his beloved again.

Tremayne wanted to offer some words of comfort, but he could find none, and he was very close to an unseemly display of emotion himself. The Widow clearly did not permit herself the luxury of weeping, and he rather doubted she had much patience for the shedding of manly tears. So he swallowed the lump in his throat and ignored the tight feeling behind his eyes, which was as much for what he feared he was doing to Kate as for what had befallen Carl Donop and the Widow, and made the only safe gesture left to him: he stood up and offered her his hand.

She never took it. The sound of booted feet outside the window froze her for only a second, then she was up and scanning the room for exits.

There was only one, and before she could reach it, the front and back doors of the house were battered open by the carbine butts of a squad of dragoons.

The parlor door opened, Captain André strolled in smiling, and the Widow adopted a pose of murderous rage and smacked Tremayne hard across the face. "You told me you loved me, Peter. That you would marry me. That you would take care of me. All to lure me into a trap."

Tremayne was stunned. André looked intrigued. And General Howe—following the little Huguenot in with the expression of a pleased parent on a school visit, studiously ignoring the shabbiness of the house and furnishings—looked delighted.

"Well done, Major." Howe clapped his hands and darted quick glances around the room. "Clap her in irons, Captain André, and then we must have a glass of brandy."

"Yes, very well done, but I'm afraid the celebrations must wait, General. We need the names of the Widow's confederates before they are alerted to her capture."

Howe nodded, willfully ignoring the nastier implications of André's statement. "By all means. Let's have done with it."

"Not here, I think," André said, inclining his head toward the reverend's sister, and the reverend himself, who was blinking sleepily in the doorway.

"She is entitled to a trial," Tremayne said.

"Perhaps. If she were an Englishwoman. Are you?" André inquired of the Widow.

She said nothing. André smiled, and Tremayne realized with certainty that John André, like Donop, was privy to some secret intelligence, knew who the Widow really was, and would not say. And neither, it was clear, would she, even if her rank or the circumstances of her birth could save her from torture and imprisonment, or entitle her to a trial by a jury of her peers.

They did not clap her in irons, but she made a break for it in the street and took down two men, who would not be addressing attentions to their sweethearts anytime soon. It took four to subdue her. André bound her hands with rope himself, and then once she was mounted pillion behind a dragoon, he tied her feet to the stirrups as well. Through all this Howe looked away, vaguely embarrassed, and fell back on praising

Tremayne for his efforts. "A new command in the spring, Major. You can rely on it."

They expected him to join them, he realized, as the detachment mounted up and prepared to depart. He could feel the furtive eyes of the neighbors peering through their shutters. With scenes like these, he wondered how many loyal subjects would be left in the city when this winter was done.

He did not want to go with them, for what was certain to be an interrogation, a trial, and an execution. He wondered if the dapper André did his own dirty work, or left that to others. He tried to beg off, pointed out the vulnerability of the reverend and his sister with both their doors off the hinges, but in the end André detailed a guard to protect the house and Tremayne had no choice but to accompany them.

They rode in silence, because their errand was secret and, to Tremayne's mind at least, shameful. The route was different but he recognized their destination long before they reached the Neck. He could not inquire whether the idea was André's, who had, he knew, traced him with Kate to the pretty stone cottage, or Bay's, who stood languidly waiting for them in the door of the house beneath the chalked warning that bore his name.

THIS HOUSE UNDER THE PROTECTION OF BAYARD CAIDE.

Caide was not alone. The dragoons, of course, had been his. André chose well. A dirty job, for men who would not ask questions. But even Caide had some scruples and Tremayne did not think his cousin was capable of torture.

That was why Dyson was there.

They bundled the Widow, still silent, into the kitchen, André taking the lead and Dyson padding in after them like the predator he was. Howe nodded and strode out the front door of the little cottage, distancing himself from the proceedings until they achieved the desired result. Tremayne watched the kitchen door close and turned to find Caide scrutinizing him.

"I didn't think you had it in you, Peter."

He didn't, of course. He'd told Kate he would give them the Widow in her place, but he'd never have gone through with it. He'd seen torture, and knew what the low voices, the scrape of furniture over floorboards, the soft snap of the fire all meant.

He had no illusions about what was taking place behind that door. Everyone talked under torture. The best he could hope for was that Dyson was clumsy or cruel, that the Widow died before naming Kate.

Tremayne was poised on a knife's edge. He could ride to warn Kate now, and give her away for certain. Or he could wait and pray God the Widow did not break.

John André had proved himself more clever than they had realized. Tremayne had noticed Kate's watchdogs. He could not fail to. Beaver Hat and Alley Loafer made no attempts to hide. And so Tremayne had not suspected that he himself might be watched by more subtle agents.

Caide returned from the parlor with a flask, and the same delicate cut glasses Tremayne had shared with Kate. Peter was thankful that his hands did not shake when he took his.

"We should get drunk," Caide offered, with rare sympathy.

"Afterwards," said Tremayne.

They waited.

Caide, never squeamish, sat beside him in the cold dark hall. But he was not unaffected. Bay was not ordinarily a man to drink purposefully toward oblivion, but he did so now, neglecting even to offer Tremayne the flask again.

Then the door opened, Howe was summoned, and the door closed again.

Tremayne and Caide waited once more, listening to the low voices and the occasional hoarse, shuddering moan. It could not go on much longer.

It didn't. Captain André opened the door, looking, for once, suitably grim. "My lord, matters are near a conclusion and your presence would be helpful." He oozed polite deference. His linen, Tremayne noted, was spotless, but there were dark glistening speckles patterned over his boots.

Bay followed Tremayne in. He could only be coming out of solidarity. Under other circumstances, Tremayne would have welcomed his support, but not tonight. If Angela Ferrers broke, if she told them what she knew of Kate, and if Bay heard it, if he learned that his adored fiancée was a spy and, more, Tremayne's lover, her life would hinge on who reached her first, and whether or not Tremayne could kill a man who had been raised as—and whom he still considered—his brother.

They must have tidied the room and the prisoner before admitting Howe. Angela Ferrers wore her shift, but it was bloodstained in telling places. She was tied to a straight-backed chair now, but bloodied ropes still dangled limply off the edge of the pine table.

Dyson had not tidied himself, and Howe took pains not to let his eyes light on the man. "I am sorry, Peter," said Howe, "but you must remember what she is, and what is at stake."

The lives of at least twenty thousand British soldiers and an equal number of loyal civilians. He knew it too well. They had fallen for her ruse at the reverend's house. Of course they had. Her performance, her outrage—the way she had slapped him—had been thoroughly convincing, worthy of Drury Lane. They thought he'd made love to her and was witnessing the violation and torture of a woman who had taken him into her body. And he might as well have been, because all he could see when he looked at her was Kate.

"Mrs. Ferrers has already been kind enough to give us the names of her couriers and the locations of her dead drops," André explained, in a voice an octave deeper than the dulcet tones he favored with the belles of Philadelphia. "We are trying to establish now the events of the night the lady entertained you in Orchard Valley. We need to know who else in that house was working with the Widow. And whom else she might have working for her here in Philadelphia."

"Orchard Valley. Was that the name of the place?" Tremayne replied, trying to keep the emotion out of his voice. "It was a provincial backwater, a hamlet full of dour Quakers. I cannot believe Angela had accomplices there."

André shrugged, and Caide's brute, Dyson, took his cue. He stepped forward, blocking the Widow from Tremayne's sight. Tremayne knew he had a knife, suspected what he was doing with it, knew for certain when he heard her muffled cry. He could not control the muscle in his cheek that spasmed at the sound.

"This will go on until you give us names," André advised the Widow. "And your suffering pains Lord Sancreed almost as much as it does yourself. Have some pity on the man and bring this to an end. You *have* other agents in Philadelphia. Who are they?"

Dyson stepped close again.

"Give her a chance to answer first, man." Howe looked decidedly uneasy. Tremayne sensed there were deeper currents running here, that André and Howe were not after the same thing. He forced himself to look at the Widow.

She curled her lips into a snarl. "Which lord did you mean, Captain André? Peter Tremayne, or his cousin, who is surely *twice* as entitled to be called Sancreed."

Bay tensed beside him. The room became dangerously silent.

"You have an accomplice in the city, Mrs. Ferrers," André persisted. "A woman who is feeding you information. Give us the name or I will clear the room and allow Lieutenant Dyson to persuade you."

Howe looked stricken and anxious. "I think that's enough, Captain André. The woman has nothing more to tell us. She's just spewing bile now."

"Oh no, General, I have more to say. But first . . ." It was as though a dam had burst and what had been withheld might now be revealed.

The Widow turned her face to Caide. "It was you I was waiting for in Orchard Valley, Colonel. I'll confess, I was relieved when your cousin came instead. Tell me, does your pretty fiancée know what her chil-

dren will be? If so, she has a stronger stomach than I.
Children? Sickening enough just to lie with a bastard
whose—"

Tremayne guessed what she was doing a moment
too late. "Don't," he said, but Caide had already smashed
the delicate glass in his hand against the table. Dyson
twisted with a tigerish grace out of his master's way.
And before Tremayne could reach him, Caide jerked
his arm down in a graceless arc.

Tremayne heard the hiss, but mercifully he did not
see the glass slice through the Widow's throat. There
was a gurgle. The ropes groaned. The chair creaked.
Then all was silence.

For a second no one moved.

Then André shoved Caide aside and bent over the
Widow. "You imbecile," André spat at Caide. But Bayard Caide didn't hear him.

Bay stood trembling beside the chair, and by the
time Howe placed an arm on his shoulder and turned
him, shirt spattered in a thick red line, away from the
body, that is what it was. Angela Ferrers' eyes were
closed. Her chemise was soaked, the blood saturating
the silk and dripping in a steady stream from her torn
hem onto her bare feet.

The woman was dead. Tremayne knew he should
see to his cousin. But Howe was doing that, herding
Bay toward the door, calling him "my boy" and mur-
muring that it was all very understandable and that the
woman had goaded him.

And so she had. To protect Kate. The Widow had
known, or hoped, what Bay would do.

Dyson threw the corpse over his shoulder like a sack
of meal and strode out through the summer kitchen.

André watched him go with visible distaste. "Do not think I enjoy this," he warned Tremayne, wiping his boots with a kitchen towel.

Tremayne shut the door to the hall and turned to face Howe's spymaster. "Let us speak plainly. What is the price of Kate's safety?"

There was genuine surprise in André's gold-flecked eyes. "Plain speaking indeed, my lord. But that is what it always comes down to for your sort, isn't it? Money. You think you can buy anything or anyone. But you could not buy a woman like the Widow."

The bloodstained chair stood in mute testament.

"You sound as though you admired her," Tremayne said, light-headed with revulsion and anxiety.

"I did. I had never met her equal, except perhaps Miss Grey. She may be as great as the Widow, some-day. And that is why you have nothing to fear from me. I do not wish Kate Grey dead, and now that I have broken the Widow's network, I do not need her dead. But make no mistake, Major. Miss Grey is mine."

"I was given to understand that you have little use for women, Captain."

"Not so. I esteem them greatly. I even bed them when necessary. But my passion I bestow elsewhere."

"Tastes such as yours can be expensive to conceal," Tremayne said, hating the idea of blackmailing the man for this. Bay was right. A great many men of their class engaged in buggery as youths, the practice sancti-fied by the cloistered air of the public school. Some even continued the practice into adulthood, hiring link-boys in Drury Lane, or accommodating servants. But the privileged prosecuted their inferiors when they dared follow suit.

"If money does not tempt you, Captain, then tell me how I may be of service to you. Invitations, introductions to men of power and influence. In exchange for the liberty of one rather ordinary girl."

André laughed out loud at his last statement. "The 'girl' in question is anything but ordinary, as you have cause to know. Still, there might be another I could groom to take her place in my plans. I shall consider your offer, my lord. Only tell me, how are you so certain she won't betray you? *Again.*"

There was no point, Tremayne decided, in lying. "I'm not."

Fifteen

General Howe's winter revels proceeded with the forced gaiety of a cuckoo clock, and Kate found herself trapped in the works, called upon to twirl hourly like an automaton. The playhouse opened shortly after Christmas. The deep January snow ushered in sledding in the Neck. And ice skating. And toboggan races. Between Smith's City Tavern, the private subscription clubs formed by the officers, and Howe's own appetite for conviviality, there were dances at least three nights a week. The Quaker City had never known such merriment.

The Valbys said nothing about it, of course, but there was the problem of money. All Kate's expenses had been paid publicly by the Valbys, but were reimbursed privately by Angela Ferrers. The money stopped coming at the same time as her instructions, the day after the Widow's midnight visit. For her own safety and theirs, Kate did not know the Widow's other agents in Philadelphia, but after two weeks passed in silence, she called upon the only person she knew to be in

Angela's confidence, Anstiss Black—only to discover that the dressmaker and her husband had also disappeared.

It was February, and Philadelphia was shingled with ice, when she remembered what the Widow had said in Washington's headquarters at Wilmington. There was another agent in Philadelphia. *Still with Howe, but trapped like a fly in amber.* Now Kate was trapped as well.

To her great relief, Caide was much away on business for Howe, foraging, and when he was in Philadelphia, he was attentive but distant. Something had changed in him since the Widow had disappeared, though Kate was hard-pressed to name exactly what.

Since their reckless encounter in the tunnel beneath the tavern, Kate caught only glimpses of Peter Tremayne. She understood that he continued to work to stem the tide of vandalism in the Neck and looting in the city, and that he protected the property of absent Rebels with the same zeal as that of absent Loyalists. Angela's disappearance strengthened Kate's resolve to stay away from him. Whatever had happened to Angela, Kate knew it could be nothing good. She did not wish the same upon Tremayne.

Then it was March and the news spread like wildfire: General Sir William Howe was being replaced. The British planned to withdraw from Philadelphia. It was as though the entire Loyalist population woke up from a winter-long drunk with a spectacular hangover. They'd been so confident when the Rebels fled—so quick to offer their absent neighbors' houses to the British, even pocket a few items, or an entire business, for themselves, when Howe invested the city with twenty thousand men. Now, in the harsh morning light of retrospect, some of the Loyalists' actions appeared unwise.

In April, the ground thawed but the local inhabitants grew frosty. If Howe's officers noticed a certain coolness, they ignored it. The general's staff was too busy anyway, planning his farewell celebration. A river flotilla, a tournament with knights and ladies and jousting, a ball, a dinner, fireworks. It sounded fit for a conquering Roman general, rather than a defeated one. Captain André had dubbed it the Mischianza, a medley, a bit of everything.

In the first week of May, Kate found that she was to play a leading part in the entertainment. If she did not drown first. She returned from a rainy rehearsal bedraggled and choking under twelve yards of sodden cotton tulle. She dripped up to her room at the Valbys' and knew a moment of déjà vu. She looked into the shadows between the window and the fireplace, but no one was seated there. But her instinct had not been wrong. There was someone in the room with her. She realized what it meant a moment too late.

A strong arm fell over hers like a bar, and a man's hand smothered her cry. This was it then; André had decided he did not need her after all. At least it would be her death and not Peter's. But she was afraid. When André had poisoned her, she'd had no time to be frightened. But pinned in the dark, she had the unwanted leisure for fear.

"Easy, Kate. It's me."

Peter.

She sagged in his arms, and he went from holding her prisoner to holding her up. He led her to the bed, placed her hands on the counterpane to steady her. "Stay here," he said. He knelt at the hearth and lit the fire. "You look like a drowned rat. And you're shivering. We should get you out of those wet clothes. Good God, what are you wearing?"

"It is one of André's costumes for the Mischianza," she said of the transparent polonaise plastered to her breasts. "I'm to play one of the Ladies of the Blended Rose, and Captain André is to be my champion. It was supposed to be Peggy, of course, but her father withdrew his permission, and now here I am." She curtsied, and the turban fell from her head, releasing her dripping hair.

Tremayne laughed, and she smiled wearily back at him, and he reached for her laces. She'd been holding on by her fingernails, alone and threatened from all sides, for months. And now Peter was here in her bedroom. One by one he peeled her sodden garments away and then she was naked. His finger followed a drop of water as it fell from her hair, ran over her breast, and formed again over her nipple. "This isn't precisely why I came here," he said, circling the hardening bud.

She couldn't speak. Fear and relief were all mixed up inside her and she couldn't sort them out because her body was not her own anymore. Not with him so near.

He backed her to the bed, the wool of his breeches absorbing the moisture on her thighs. He threw off his jacket as her calves hit the bed; then his shirt was plastered to her dripping breasts and there was no place that their bodies, hers naked, his clothed, did not meet.

"You should stop me," he said, his breath feathering her cheek.

She shook her head, slipped her arms around his neck, drew his mouth down to hers.

He reached between them to free himself from his breeches and test her readiness. Then he lifted her by the knees, perched her on the edge of the bed, and slid inside.

Kate hadn't spoken since he first touched her, but he could not possibly mistake the tenor of her cries, low and throaty and needful, as he rode her. The wool of his breeches scratched her damp skin, an erotic contrast to the wet glide of his body inside hers.

It was only the third time she had done *this* with a man, but she sensed by his grip on her thighs, the speed of his thrusts, the fierceness of his expression, that he was going to reach his peak before her. She didn't care. She just wanted to be close to him, intimate with him, like this.

He slowed, then stilled, and she expected him to pull out. Instead, he unwrapped her arms from about his neck. "Lie back."

Her perch on the bed was precarious. She leaned back tentatively. He held on to her wrists, lowering her back to the mattress, watching her eyes intently.

"Oh." The sound popped out of her mouth as she felt the angle change deep inside her. She meant, *how wondrous*. He was hitting her there. In a spot he had not taught her a name for, but he'd found with unerring skill the first time they made love.

"Yes," he said, a little smirk of triumph kissing the corners of his lips. "Like that, my love."

He thrust.

"Oh," she said again. This time she meant, *Don't stop.* And it was as if he heard her.

*H*e was a bastard. She still hadn't asked him why he'd come; was too sated to inquire, staring up at him dreamily, her legs sprawled open over his arms.

They'd never even locked the door. He disentangled himself and rolled her onto the bed. She lay naked and drifting, still damp from her adventures outside and in some places a good deal damper than when she'd started. He wrapped her in the counterpane, mounted the bed beside her, and gathered her cocooned body into his arms.

She needed sleep. He'd seen the signs of strain in her, these past months, watched from afar as the smile she wore burned brighter, like oil near the bottom of the lamp. He wanted to let her doze, felt a deep and instinctual satisfaction at her dreamy relaxation, but he could not risk being caught here. "I've secured your freedom from André."

A moment ago she'd been a loose, warm bundle, down in a pillow. Now she was a tied spring. She sat up, holding the blanket over her breasts. It was a small gesture, but one that pained him, when she'd been so trusting and bare before. "What have you done?"

"Would it help to know that no actual money changed hands?"

"What did you give André in exchange for me?"

She would not make this easy. He should have known. "I have promised him an introduction at court. I've written letters to the War Office, and to General

Clinton, who will succeed Howe. In that, at least, I have not compromised myself. I wrote that he has been an exemplary intelligencer, and that he bested the Merry Widow, a spymistress who had compromised operations in Philadelphia to an intolerable degree."

Kate swallowed hard, and he knew what her next question would be. He did not want to be the one to tell her. He'd hoped she'd known, made peace with it, but it was clear that she hadn't. "What happened to Angela Ferrers?"

The details, even now, sickened him. He wanted to spare her, but she needed to hear it, if she was ever to see sense. "The night we all dined at Smith's, she came to my lodgings. She had Carl Donop's letter, I presume from you. She wanted to know about his last days. I told her."

He stopped, steeled himself. "André stormed the house with a troop of dragoons. They took her to the cottage in the Neck where you and I made love, and they tortured her. In the end, she gave them names, and dates, and places. Her entire network. But she did not give them you. She chose to die rather than reveal your name."

Kate was so very still, he could barely see the rise and fall of her chest.

"I have been pressing André to release you ever since," Peter said. "He has an eye to his future, decoupled from his patron, Howe. And so, today, he accepted my terms. Now you must honor the Widow's sacrifice and allow me to see you to safety."

"To my father?" she asked. But she said it in a small, frightened voice. He should have been glad. Finally, she was broken. So frightened and alone and cornered that she would follow him out of the labyrinth. The harsh truth was the only way to save her. He knew that. And he still hated himself for speaking it.

"No, Kate. To England, with me." He took the papers out of his pocket.

She untied them, then stopped to finger the ribbon. It was the tie from her jacket. The one he'd taken at Grey Farm. She looked up at him, confused.

"Read them."

She did. "This is a marriage license."

"Yes. It permits Lydia Dare to marry Peter Tremayne in the Church of England. We will be married, Kate, and then you will be safe. From John André and from Bay."

She looked again at the license. "It is dated May nineteen. The day after the Mischianza."

She suspected already, so he confirmed her worst fears. "André would hardly let you go before the attack on Valley Forge. Howe's last grand gesture, a parting shot that might restore his reputation."

"The night of his ludicrous party. That's why you won't take me to my father. That's what has been keeping Bay out of the city so much. The attack will take place *during* the Mischianza."

"André wants you in his sight while the attack takes place. I have a pass permitting you to leave the city with me after midnight."

"He thinks I'll try to run, to reach Washington. What makes you think I won't?"

"Because I'm responsible for your good behavior. If you flee, I will pay the consequences. I flatter myself that you prefer not to see me hang."

"But you haven't asked for my word on the matter."

"Would you give it, Kate?"

"No."

"Do you love me?"

"Yes."

"Then I place my life in your hands."

*I*f she was wrong, it was the last mistake she would ever make.

She was shown into the front parlor of Howe's Market Street mansion after only a short wait in the hall. She remembered when she'd come to see Elizabeth Loring, all those months ago, and interrupted that puzzling scene between the notorious lady and her cuckold husband.

This afternoon Elizabeth Loring was the picture of English gentility. She sat before her needlework frame, scrutinizing a painted design of flowers and birds. Her husband lounged by the fire, seemingly a gentleman at leisure, but Kate sensed a watchfulness in him. Howe had made Joshua Loring commissioner of prisoners, and rumor had it he skimmed funds and pocketed money while Rebel prisoners starved. Even if Kate had guessed right about Mrs. Loring, she may have guessed wrong about him. And if so, she would never have the opportunity to sample the man's dubious hospitality. She would die quietly, in a back room, like the Widow. She suddenly wished the fire were larger. The parlor felt chilled.

"To what do we owe the pleasure, Miss Dare?" asked Howe's mistress, her fingers sorting through bright silk yarns. Her heart-shaped face was still and beautiful in the slanting afternoon light.

Kate waited until the maid closed the door behind her, then said, "I think you know that isn't my real name."

Elizabeth Loring's hands stilled. Joshua Loring strolled to the center of the room, placing himself between Kate and his wife. "And why should she know a thing like that?"

Kate stood her ground. "Because I believe we are related, after a fashion, through my late aunt."

Elizabeth Loring rose with a familiar, practiced grace Kate should have recognized the first time she saw her. She crossed the parlor and laced her hand in that of her husband. The gesture was unmistakable. They were husband and wife, and lovers, and this man had not sold his wife to Howe for money or power. Kate's own sacrifices paled in comparison.

But Joshua Loring, it was clear, felt no answering sympathy for Kate. "How do we know you aren't working for André? You two are thick as thieves of late."

"You don't."

"You should leave, Miss Dare." It was a dismissal.

"I need your help. The Mischianza is a cover for an attack on Valley Forge."

"You think we don't know that? We see and hear everything, and can do *nothing*. Elizabeth is watched. I am watched. We have been trapped since New York. John André ingratiates himself with Howe by politely ignoring the fact that he caught the general's mistress spying. It is all so very gentlemanly and courteous. But make no mistake—if either of us attempts to leave, the other *will* hang. We can do nothing for you, Miss Dare, or whatever your name is."

He dropped his wife's hand and retreated to his place

by the fire. Unburdening his frustration and anxiety seemed to have left him hollow.

Elizabeth Loring remained standing in the middle of the room, her perfect stillness, her practiced calm so like the Widow's. "In New York," she explained, "I discovered a British plot to poison Washington. André intercepted my letter to Angela, broke my cipher, and arrested both Joshua and me. Fortunately, I had sent the message by two other routes. One of my missives got through, and Washington was saved. But my husband and I are alive only because of the affection Howe bears for me."

Kate saw Joshua Loring swallow hard and shut his eyes at that last.

They had already risked—and lost—so much. Now Kate was asking them to do more. "If I do not warn Washington," Kate said, "if Howe overruns Valley Forge, all your sacrifices will have been in vain."

The silence stretched. Then finally Elizabeth Loring said, "There is a way."

"Lizzie," Joshua Loring warned softly.

"There is a rendezvous. Angela Ferrers arranged it before we left New York. There is a man who waits around the clock at the King's Arms on the Post Road, ready to ride for Valley Forge at a moment's notice to warn Washington if Howe stirs from Philadelphia."

"And André very likely knows it," Joshua Loring snapped. "The Widow was tortured for hours before she died. She gave them Anstiss Black and who knows how many others."

"But she did not give him Miss Dare."

"How can I reach this man?" Kate asked. She had an inkling of what they were asking her to do.

"You must get yourself out of the city. Then there are several changes of horse posted along the way."

Joshua Loring's voice was icy cold. "Which André may also know of. To undertake this ride is suicide, plain and simple."

"But the Widow would have done it," Kate said, considering everything she had known of her enigmatic mentor. Even if André waited for her on the road. She would have shot her way through. Kate had seen her do just that. She'd brought down two dragoons with an unfamiliar gun on a moving horse in the dead of night. Kate wasn't certain she could do the same, but she doubted the Lorings would disclose the route if she admitted as much. So she forced herself to relax her shoulders and affect a tone of bored insouciance that the Widow would have approved, and said, "I shall need a map. And a pistol."

Sixteen

Philadelphia, May 18, 1777

Peter Tremayne was filled with a pleasurable sense of anticipation. Tomorrow morning he would wake up next to Kate Grey. He must learn to call her Lydia, of course. It chafed a bit, having to call his wife by a false name for the rest of his life, but it wasn't as though she must live with an entirely assumed identity. She would be taking his name anyway in two days' time, and there wasn't really so much difference between Kate Tremayne and Lydia Tremayne. It was a matter of syllables, nothing more.

He did not plan to wait for morning to set out. The pass was effective at midnight. They would leave directly from the Mischianza, before it had even run its course. He'd stabled two horses at the Wharton Mansion this morning, and sent the resourceful Bachmann ahead with his things. There was an inn in South Jersey where he had once stayed. It was clean, steadfastly loyal, and on the road to New York. Once they reached Manhattan, maybe even before if they found a willing parson, they could marry, and even if his cousin Bay pursued them, Kate would be safe. Then they could sail for home.

With all this before him, he found it shockingly easy to enjoy the pageantry. Or maybe it was just because he'd picked her out of the waiting crowds and he enjoyed watching her. The costume was slightly less fetching when dry, but only slightly. The turban and veiling hid her face and hair, and something about the body-skimming cut of the gown hampered her natural grace. Perhaps Kate felt awkward, being so much on display in such a revealing ensemble. Perhaps she grasped the peculiar eroticism of a bared body and a hidden face. Whatever the reason, the result was a slight hesitation in her step, a fussy stiffness when she sat, that suggested she'd like to pull her neckline up and her hemline down at the same time.

The Ladies of the Blended Rose and the Knights of the Burning Mountain, a bit of doggerel that smacked of André's invention, did not have to wait for the galleys with the hoi polloi lining the river. Someone had erected a platform adjacent to the dock, topped with a faux marble arch and draped with bunting. He was able to pick out one or two other familiar forms, if not faces, in the group. There was Peggy Chew, the Shippen girl's frequent rival for André's affections, unmistakably top-heavy in her ensemble. Kate seemed to steer clear of her. The Knights were unmasked, so it was easy to pick out Montresor, who surprised Tremayne by going in for this sort of nonsense, and

Banastre Tarleton, who did not. Neither of them came off particularly well in the orange and black Turkish getups André had designed for the Knights, though perhaps that was André's intention, as the color scheme suited the spymaster's dark coloring admirably.

The little Huguenot himself appeared on and off here and there like a lightning bug. For the myriad parts of the Mischianza hung together only with the constant attention of its impresario. One moment he was instructing the galley captains, the next he was directing the crowd. Tremayne noticed that for once, Kate was acting sensibly and avoiding the man.

It took an hour to load the boats, and another two to make the trip downriver to the Neck. He could see now why André was so insistent that Kate take part in the pageant. The route was lined with navy boats, the *Cerberus* and the *Dauntless* and the *Roebuck*, and there were marines stationed on every galley. An honor guard, they would appear to the blameless guests. A prison detail, they must seem to Kate.

The disembarkation was a fussy affair. Wharton's private dock was draped in silk bunting, and the broad way to the jousting ring and stands was festooned with swags and garlands and punctuated by two triumphal arches. André had managed to cobble together nearly an entire orchestra out of at least eight disparate military bands, and Howe had wasted a fortune attempting to dress them uniformly. There was a good deal of trumpet fanfare alternating with Handel, meant to sound vaguely medieval.

The Knights and Ladies and well-heeled guests processed to the jousting lists. As a professional horseman, Tremayne enjoyed seeing a bit of trick riding,

and the way the Knights handled the unfamiliar bag-
gage of gilt shields and gilt plaster breastplates. André
himself was passably good. Tarleton was spectacular
but brutal. He seemed not to have grasped that the tilting
was entirely for show, and managed to unseat his opponent, a red-faced major who refused to shake hands
afterwards and stalked from the field dragging his broken lance. Tremayne made a private vow to avoid Tarleton for the rest of the night. The boy was obviously
spoiling for a fight and Tremayne had no intention of
being drawn into a senseless duel, not now.

There was a bit of stagey drama when the Ladies of
the Blended Rose stood up as one and begged the
Knights of the Burning Mountain to leave off their
contests. Their favor was won, they declared, and they
would unveil.

But they could not go directly into dinner yet. The
Knights and their Ladies were to lead the way into the
banqueting hall, miraculously constructed in under a
month and outfitted, it was rumored, at a cost of six
thousand pounds. Each Knight in turn was to ride to
the viewing stand, receive his Lady's favor, watch appreciatively as she unveiled, and then escort her in to
dinner. The business was going to take forever, which
was regrettable, because Tremayne hadn't eaten since
breakfast.

Servants dressed as pages had been coming and
going all night, and Tremayne had paid them little attention, but now there was one climbing the stands directly toward him. "For you, my lord," the boy said,
depositing an oilskin package in Tremayne's hands and
departing the way he had come.

The unveiling was proceeding painfully slowly.

Only a quarter of the Knights had claimed their Ladies when Tremayne opened the oilskin package. He knew Kate's writing at once, though he had never seen it before: bold, neat, and graced by unexpected flourishes.

Only the first page was in her hand. It was brief, and to the point. Where she had gone, André would be waiting, but she had no choice but to try. To get a message to Washington, of course, Tremayne knew, heart sinking. The contents Kate had enclosed, if he kept a copy, would ensure that André did not trouble him further.

There were only three Ladies left on the platform, including the one he had assumed to be Kate. He leafed quickly through the rest of the letters in the packet. From a boy. To André. Detailed and damning. The price of Tremayne's safety. He had put his life in her hands, and she—she had handed it back to him.

He looked up then to see John André approach the stand, lower his javelin, and come alongside the platform. His Lady stepped forward, laid a laurel wreath on his head, and lifted her veil.

Tremayne did not need to see her face. He saw the ripple of surprise that ran through André. Then the spymaster laughed. Openmouthed, appreciative, and not at all welcome to the girl who stood on the platform, who had clearly been expecting an altogether different reaction.

Because the lady was not Kate. She was Peggy Shippen.

*I*t had not been difficult to convince Peggy to take part in the deception. She already owned the dress. Her scandalized father had withdrawn his consent only at the last moment, and that was when Kate was drafted to take her place.

It helped that Peggy had been growing desperate. The expected proposal from André had never materialized. He'd seemed to her singularly unconcerned when she'd told him she was barred from attending the Mischianza. He was slipping through her fingers.

Kate doubted very much that Peggy would win André's favor with this escapade, but she could not afford to worry about one spoiled girl's broken heart. She had sent Peggy off to the docks, turbaned and veiled, assuring her that she was a veritable Cleopatra, sneaking past the guards rolled in a rug to meet her Caesar. Kate refrained from mentioning that the Egyptian did not come to a good end.

She waited until the galleys shoved off, because the Widow had taught her that lies are most successful when they contained a grain of truth, then ran to the Presbyterian Church, where Bay had stabled her horse. She was out of breath and in a hurry and desperately needed to get to the Neck, because she was one of the Ladies of the Blended Rose, and had missed her boat.

They believed her, of course. She was wearing one of the scandalous costumes after all, and no well-bred lady, not even Caide's lady, would run around in such a thing in broad daylight to no purpose. Her acting, she realized later, did not have to be of the first quality, because the quantity of calf and bosom on display guaranteed that the grooms and stable hands were not looking at her face.

She was astride in a matter of minutes, mounted on the horse Bay had bought her, seated in the saddle he'd had made for her, using, with purpose if not with skill, the dainty black leather whip.

Her destination was north of the city, on the road to Valley Forge, but she could not ride in that direction. Not yet. She was supposed to be going south to the Mischianza. So for a while, she did. It was easy to pass the sentries on the main roads below the city, because so many people were attempting to do so: caterers and carters and brewers and drapers all hurrying last-minute goods to the party. She was a last-minute good as well, and threw saucy comments back at guards who winked and complimented and wished her luck arriving at the Wharton Mansion in time for the joust.

Then, when she reached a quiet stretch of road with no one to witness, she turned her horse down a narrow lane, barely a cow path, overgrown with new spring grass and wildflowers, and cut across to a smaller, less-traveled road, and began heading north. It took her an hour to get clear of the city, and then the trouble started.

The first sentries, posted by Howe to keep messengers from alerting Washington to the attack, swallowed whole her story about rushing to the Mischianza, and politely pointed her in the right direction, back the way she had come. She cut across country again to avoid them, and got a few miles farther north, when she encountered another line of pickets. They were equally polite but much more firm, and assigned a gawking young ensign to escort her back down the road.

He was much taken with her, and difficult to shake, but eventually he was persuaded to leave her. She cut across country again and found her way to the farm where she had been assured by the Lorings that a change of horse waited, but she knew her luck would run out sometime soon. She said a silent prayer of thanks that she had memorized the route, and carried no maps or documents, because if she was taken, she would be searched. And soldiers would fall on the little farmhouse with the wide red porch and the sky blue ceiling where the tan-faced boy sat peeling apples.

The boy was no more than twelve, she guessed, and growing bored with a responsibility that had seemed awesome in November, palled by January, and appeared entirely ludicrous now that it was May and the hated British were leaving anyway.

But the skinny boy knew at once who and what she was. Ladies in nearly transparent dresses silvered with spangles were not a common sight hereabouts. Especially not beautiful ones, with elaborately piled hair that matched the silken sheen of their chestnut mare.

He stood up and dropped his apple, but not his knife, because this was a dangerous business in which even pretty ladies still needed passwords.

She spoke it. And he ran. Straight into the barn. He emerged so quickly that she knew the horse must have been kept ready at all hours. Exercised, no doubt, regularly, because it would be ridden fast. Bored or not, the boy and his family had not shirked their part in this.

And if she failed them, if she did not warn Washington, these people would suffer for it, the way Milly and Andréw had suffered. If Howe destroyed the Continental Army, if the British were allowed free rein here, reprisals would be inevitable, and there would be nothing to keep the dragoons from their door in the middle of the night.

It was the work of a few minutes to change saddles, and as Kate watched the boy, she weighed her chances of reaching the King's Arms. They were not good. Still, it was one thing to risk her own life, another to risk that of a child. Yet these were the kinds of decisions the Widow must have made all the time.

Then the Dutch door on the porch opened and a man strode out, lean, hard, and sun-browned, his features stamped with the same imprint as the boy's. His father. But he was not in awe of her costume or her beauty. "Where is the Widow?" he asked.

"Dead," Kate replied. And she was a poor substitute, she knew. "Howe is moving against Valley Forge tonight."

"The roads are crawling with dragoons," he said. "Do you have a pistol?"

She was a terrible shot, but she did have a pistol, the muff-size gun the Lorings had provided her. He held his hand out, and she retrieved the tiny pistol from her saddlebag. He held out his hand again, and she passed him the ball and the powder horn. He loaded it, primed it, and placed it in her trembling hand.

She knew she would not be able to fire it.

She tucked it in her saddle and strode into the barn, where the boy had gone to brush down the horse Caide had given her. She gave the boy a ruby, fat as a pigeon's egg, from around her throat, and a message that would, if it reached the right ears at Valley Forge, wake a sleeping army. She watched him set off running across country, then returned to her mount to face the opprobrium of his father.

He said nothing. Merely gave her a leg up into her saddle. But as she turned her new mount toward the road, he spoke. "The boy has a better chance cutting across country on foot than you do on the road, whether or not you make good use of the pistol."

Night was coming on fast when she passed the last of her memorized landmarks: a wooden bridge crossing a small stream built beside a rock as tall and wide as her horse. The King's Arms lay three miles up the road.

The galleys would have docked at the Wharton Mansion by now. When the joust was finished, in a few short hours, her deception would be revealed. There was no going back. She would never see Peter Tremayne again. But he would be safe. She had sent him the letters that would buy his freedom from hanging and André's blackmail.

Another mile passed, and then she saw them, a line of red and silver glinting in the moonlight strung out across the road. No ordinary picket, then. Joshua Loring had been right. André knew of the rendezvous at the King's Arms. Her only chance now was to do as the Widow would have done: shoot her way past them and ride on to Valley Forge.

She drew out the pistol, wondered if it was better to shoot straight into the middle of their ranks and scatter the five horsemen, or aim for their flank and try to skirt them at the side of the road. Angela Ferrers would have known.

And the Widow would have crouched low over her horse and fired, even when she recognized the man who commanded them.

Kate slowed, then stopped, the dragoons less than twenty feet in front of her.

"Miss Grey, please lower the pistol," said Phillip Lytton, with a gravity he had not possessed at Grey Farm. She wished then he had a weapon in his hands. She might be able to shoot him. The rest of the dragoons were armed, four carbines leveled at her breast.

"Tell your men to lower their guns and stand aside, Mr. Lytton," she replied. "Or I will shoot you down."

His mount pranced. Even if Lytton had learned to hide his nerves, his horse could sense them. But he was no longer the boy he'd been a year ago. "Shooting me will serve nothing, Miss Grey. You cannot outrun four well-mounted men. And we have orders to take you alive. The charges you face are serious enough without adding murder to them."

She heard a burst of hysterical laughter and realized that it came from her. "We both know I will not face any sort of charges, Mr. Lytton, because I will not be tried. All in all, I think I should prefer a bullet."

Phillip Lytton went rigid. "I spent five months a prisoner in your father's custody, Miss Grey. I have dined at his table. I give you my word as a gentleman that you will not be mistreated."

He wasn't lying. He meant every word he said. And because of it, she couldn't shoot him.

She lowered her pistol. He walked his horse forward and took it from her, along with the reins of her mount.

"Mr. Lytton," she said, as he led her horse toward the lights of the King's Arms. "Whatever happens to me tonight, please don't ever tell my father the details."

"I gave you my word, Miss Grey. Though you are a spy and a traitor, I promise you will not be molested.

Your fate is for a court to decide. More than this I cannot say."

Still, she knew there would be no trial.

The King's Arms reared up on their left, a three-story stone, cross-shaped house with two projecting wings and a great walled yard. She could hear music and men and horses on the other side of the wall. The yard was bustling with dragoons. An entire troop in buff and scarlet. There was some regular custom as well, but the locals sat in quiet groups in the shadows, while the soldiers gambled and drank in raucous abandon. Lytton led her past the elderly innkeeper, who looked white and drawn, up the stairs and down a long hallway. It was quieter here, the sounds of the common room muffled.

He reached the last door at the end of the corridor and scratched before entering. Then he opened the door and led her in.

Her heart stopped when she saw the man standing in the window. His back was to her. Moonlight limned his silhouette, and in the silvery light all was shades of black and gray. And she thought: Tremayne. Then he turned and dispelled the illusion. She struggled to breathe. And her heart started again with a single, painful stroke.

"Hello, Kate." It was her fiancé. Bayard Caide.

*P*eter Tremayne swam upstream through the dancers in the vast, temporary banqueting hall. A hundred mirrors, borrowed, and in some cases stolen, no doubt, from the householders of Philadelphia, gave back the light of a thousand candles. The air was perfumed with flowers and beeswax and costly scent, and every surface was painted to look like something it was not. Plaster painted to look like marble, pasteboard painted to look like mahogany, and cloth painted to look like blue, cotton-clouded sky.

It was a carpentry simulacrum of his world. The merchants of Philadelphia playing at being English aristocrats. And the English gentlemen playing at being chivalric heroes. Everyone pretending to be something they were not. Except for one girl, who was not here, because she was no longer playing at being anything but herself.

His progress was halted when the fireworks began, and the orchestra put down their instruments, and the tide of dancers turned in his direction and flowed out onto the lawn, leaving him a path to the end of the hall where Captain André sat with one particular Lady of the Blended Rose drying a tear-streaked face.

"I thought you would be happy to see me," Peggy Shippen murmured. André murmured something soothing in return.

Tremayne didn't bow or offer any kind of greeting. "A word with you."

Long-lashed, gold-flecked eyes looked up at him with more sympathy than they had mustered for the teary girl. "In private, I think," replied André.

The Shippen girl pouted miserably and André chucked her on the chin. A brotherly gesture, or something one might do to a favorite dog. Tremayne did not know why it disturbed him so.

There was a room, or a closet really, at the end of the hall, lit by sconces too utilitarian for the ballroom, and piled with bunting and building supplies and broken chairs. Painted double doors, most likely "borrowed" from someone's home in town, divided it from the ballroom. André gestured for Tremayne to precede him in, closed the doors, twitched the skirts of his black coat behind him and sat, gracefully, on the only unbroken chair.

Tremayne remained standing. "We had an agreement."

"In which I kept my part," replied André smoothly. "Please don't mistake me for a twopenny villain. I do nothing without a purpose. There are twelve thousand men marching through the dark for Valley Forge. Honest soldiers in scarlet coats who do not disguise their business. Balance them—and the Crown's will— against the life of one girl, who is, I must remind you, a spy."

"And you are a spymaster."

"But like Anubis, the weigher of hearts, I am not obliged to place my own upon the scales. She was a fool to make the attempt. Brave, but a fool. We captured her several hours ago."

Tremayne's worst nightmare, come to pass. "She is an English woman. She deserves a trial."

"You would bring her back here just to see her hang?"

"I would use every ounce of influence and my entire fortune to see that she did not. What have you done with her?"

André regarded him with something akin to pity. "I will not tell you, my lord, because while your political support might advance my career, your disgrace could destroy it. And if you follow Kate Grey, there is only one end for you. On the gallows. The king will have little love for the man who put you there, so I find that I am obligated to save you from yourself."

Tremayne drew the packet of letters out of his pocket and handed them to André. "In exchange for Kate."

He had not seen them before, that much was obvious. André swallowed, and it was the first unconscious thing Tremayne had ever seen the man do. Brushing his finger over the careful slanted script was the second. The gesture was imbued with all the sensuality that had been absent when he touched Peggy Shippen.

André wanted the letters. Not to burn. Though he would have to.

"Where can I find her?"

André looked up at him. "She is by now with Bayard Caide." He said it with the same intonation as if the words had been "She is dead."

"Where?"

"He may have already killed her."

"Bay is many things, but he is not a murderer."

"The Merry Widow might beg to differ, if Caide had not opened her throat."

"You and I both know Angela Ferrers goaded him into doing it, to save Kate."

André still held the letters lightly, reluctant to take full possession. "Consider carefully, Lord Sancreed. Miss Grey has been gone more than twelve hours. You will not be arriving in the nick of time like the hero of some tawdry stage play. If nothing else, he has had her by now. She will not be the same girl you knew."

It was true, and Tremayne knew it. Was prepared for it. But he was not prepared for what André said next. "Colonel Caide has always been bent on self-destruction, but I did not expect to find you so ready to reenact your parents' tragedy."

The music struck back up then, and the doors shook under some invisible onslaught. When Tremayne did not reply, André slipped the letters into the breast pocket of his waistcoat. "I beg you to consider some other way I might pay you for these letters."

The doors burst open, revealing a glittering tableau. The ensigns had been running races across the dance floor, with a drunken embellishment: skating the final few yards on the gilded wooden shields of the Knights of the Burning Mountain. Two of them had overshot the finish line, broken through the doors, and fetched up at Tremayne's feet.

He experienced it all with the dreamlike slowness of a ballet. The bright-eyed women in their towering hair and shimmering silk, pouring a starting line of sugar across the dance floor. The young men taking their places for the next meet. The slipping and sliding as they ran and dove onto their improvised sleds. The casual lewdness at the fringes of the crowd, promising more direct encounters in the dwindling hours.

And John André, standing at his shoulder, speaking in his ear like a coryphaeus. "If you leave tonight, my lord, I will not be able to keep your name out of it. You will lose everything. Title, lands, and fortune. There will be no turning back."

*P*hillip Lytton laid her pistol and her dainty black whip on the baize-covered table and retreated to stand beside the door, blocking her escape. Bayard Caide rose from his seat and strolled to the table. He picked up the pistol and removed the flint and emptied the pan. With care, he slid the ramrod down the muzzle and fished out the ball. Then he set the harmless weapon down and brushed his fingertips over the whip with the same care he reserved for his paints and his brushes, and his adored fiancée. "Thank you, Mr. Lytton," he said, his eyes finally searching out Kate's, and holding them. "You may go."

"I gave Miss Grey my word," said Phillip Lytton unwisely, "that she would not be mistreated."

A smile quirked the corner of Bayard Caide's mouth, and for a moment he looked more than ever like Peter Tremayne. She willed herself not to flinch.

"And I gave you an *order*, Mr. Lytton." His eyes didn't leave Kate's. "Now kindly shut the door and leave us."

"She needs a chaperone," insisted Lytton. "One of the barmaids, or the innkeeper's—"

"That will do, Mr. Lytton."

Lytton stood hesitating in the doorway.

"Thank you for your concern, Mr. Lytton." She hoped that would pass for absolution. She did not want to be on anyone's conscience but her own.

"I am sorry," the young officer replied. He retreated from the room but did not close the door, and she heard Caide sigh behind her. He crossed to the door and shut it himself, then turned to face her.

He looked tired. And dangerous. "I don't even know what to call you," he said. "Are you Kate, or are you Lydia?"

She didn't know. "My name is Katherine Lydia Grey."

"Who were you for Peter?"

"Kate. I was always Kate for him."

He leaned back against the door and thrust his hands into his hair. "I began this day thinking the end was in sight. That we would take Valley Forge, and the war would be done. That you and I would marry. Then André came to me this morning and told me you planned to run away with Peter. But if you did not, if you made a run for the Rebel lines to warn Washington, I must deal with you. I scarcely knew which outcome was more desirable, or deserved."

"I am sorry."

"Sorry? You made a murderer of me, Lydia. I killed her for you."

There was suddenly not enough air in the room. "Who?" But she knew already.

"The Merry Widow. Angela Ferrers. I slit her throat. To keep her from speaking your name."

"But," Kate said, her voice almost a whisper, "how did you know I was working for her?"

"I didn't, not for certain. Not until that night. It all made a terrible sense then. The way Peter always watched you so intently. His inability to find the spy in Philadelphia. I could tell he wanted you, but I convinced myself it was the same old rivalry—and that *you* had chosen me. Do you know what the worst part was? Howe thanked me. For killing the Widow. He thought I did it for him. Slit that woman's throat to protect his precious mistress, Elizabeth. Mrs. Loring's spying is an open secret on the general's staff. But I didn't do it to keep Howe's paramour safe, *Lydia*. I did it for you."

"What will you do with me?" she asked. She sounded braver than she felt.

"I haven't decided yet."

"My father," she began tentatively, "is less than ten miles from here. Let me go to him."

"No." Absolute and final. "Of all the men in Philadelphia, for God's sake why did it have to be Peter?"

"I love him."

"Some things," he said, crossing the room and turning her roughly to face the window, "aren't about love."

The courtyard below was filled with dragoons. There were thirty men, and only half a dozen women scattered among them. Some must have been professional whores, and willing, but the rest were not.

She tried to back away from the sight, but he was there behind her, blocking her escape and pressing her forward until her shins barked the window seat and she was forced to grip the molding to steady herself. They remained frozen like that, his chest pressed to her back, her knuckles white on the fluted woodwork, the scene below playing out an awful prelude to what she knew was to come. His breath danced in her ear. "It's better this way, I've decided. Now we need be no one but ourselves."

His fingers settled over the neck of her immodest gown, gripped, and tore, splitting the flimsy gauze easily down the middle. He lifted her gossamer skirts, piling them around her hips, positioned himself, and entered her. He had done nothing to court her pleasure, but found a slick, shaming welcome in her body all the same.

He worked her methodically until he coaxed a response. She broke and shuddered for him, openmouthed, rigid and wordless with mortification. Her legs buckled and his hands seized her waist, held her in place. He was still as her heartbeat slowed and her skin cooled. Waiting for her to become aware of the intrusion of his body in hers. The thick pulse of his cock lodged inside her.

Then she felt it. His spasm of release, held deliberately in check, because he'd wanted her to know this moment fully. It came in total silence. He didn't groan or cry out. Only a rush of liquid warmth inside her, humiliating and final.

He slipped, still hard, from her body, and she sagged against the open shutters, pressing her cheek to the cool wood there. She felt his hands busy at the hooks and laces on her back, his touch all solicitousness now that he had shown her what she was. *You may be tempted, because of your upbringing, to despise and punish yourself for what you have become. Do not use Bayard Caide for that purpose. No man or woman deserves that.*

Angela Ferrers had understood Kate only too well. Kate did despise herself. She had betrayed Peter Tremayne when she rode out of Philadelphia, and her father when she failed to shoot Phillip Lytton in the road. And this was exactly the reckoning she deserved.

He stripped off the tatters of her clothes and led her by the hand, naked, to the edge of the bed, and bent her over the quilted counterpane. He was skilled, even with the dainty little crop, whose weight and contours must have been unfamiliar to his hand. He placed his strokes precisely, feathering them down her back in a neat pattern that kissed her shoulders and mimicked the print of her absent stays. Only the first few strokes were painful. The rest were something else. She heard his breathing grow uneven, in the utter silence of the room. And then he stopped and turned the whip hand over to her.

Seventeen

A little after dusk the pickets on the line south of Valley Forge were interrupted at their dinner. A boy came running into their midst. Skinny and panting. He stopped to catch his breath and spoke two words. They sent a man each running in opposite directions, one to the next picket just over the hill, and another down into the valley, straight to Washington's headquarters.

Persephone rising.

The same words turned out the Life Guard, Virginians chosen for height and strength and skill at arms to defend the commander in chief. They brought the battalion commanders running and woke the general's staff, including the man known to so many as the Grey Fox, and sometimes the Fighting Quaker, Arthur Grey.

It took no more than an hour to muster the sleeping army that had weathered that unkind winter, and when the British scouts advanced to within rifle range of Valley Forge, they discovered an unbroken line of blue coats and bluer steel, and turned back. Howe's commanders lacked the men and materials for a pitched battle. There would be no surprise attack, and thus no attack at all, on Valley Forge.

The Rebels remained in their lines through the dark watches of the night, just to be certain that General Sir William Howe had really abandoned his attack, and with it his career, in earnest. By dawn every other man was allowed to stand down, and a few hours later only a heavier than usual guard remained.

And Arthur Grey. He was not waiting for an attack. He was waiting, without hope, for a single rider, because he had known in his bones the moment he heard those two words who had borne that message out of Philadelphia.

But she did not come.

Eighteen

She woke in pain. She was lying on her stomach, her cheek pressed to a pillow stuffed with more quills than down. Someone had built the fire up, which was a mercy because she was bare above the waist.

She opened her eyes to find Caide sitting in a deep chair beside the bed. It was still night, and the room was dark. His face was lost in shadows; his hands rested palms up on the upholstered arms. She did not know if he was awake, but he had dressed himself carefully while she was unconscious, and she was acutely aware of the brightness of his linen, the polish on his boots, and the shine of his buttons.

She tried to lever herself off the bed, but fiery pain shot down her back and she gasped with shock.

"I cleaned the stripes on your back," said Caide from the shadows, "while you slept."

Which explained the smell of strong spirits. And the burning, blinding pain. She wondered if he had tended similarly to his own marks. His back, when he had offered it to her, had told of long acquaintance with the whip. "What happens now?" she asked, but her mouth was dry and it came out a hoarse whisper.

"André told me you were mine to dispose of as I saw fit, so long as you never trouble him or the British Army again. Which means we cannot stay with the army, or I in service. But I see no reason why anything else should change."

Then, in answer to her silence, he added, "I didn't mean to hurt you last night. You mustn't let me do it again. I would have stopped, had you asked it."

She'd thought he was her punishment for all the things she had done, was ready to allow him to destroy her. But she hadn't understood him—or herself—until last night. And the truth was worse than anything she had imagined. They would destroy each other. And that was not a fate she could submit to. "André won't just let you keep me."

"He won't have a say in the matter. This war is going to be over in a matter of days. I'll keep you out of sight until Howe is done mopping up at Valley Forge, and then I'll resign my commission, and we'll go to India. I found the life there congenial enough. So will you. And I'm not opposed to being a company officer."

"What about Peter?"

"He won't want you back."

"Because you're his cousin?"

"No." He paused. "Because he is my brother."

It fit. It explained their extraordinary resemblance, the way she could close her eyes and mistake the touch of one man for the other. An affinity that went deeper than physical similarities. A family tree, the Widow

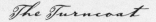

had said, more gnarled than an oak. And if what she deduced was true, it meant only one thing: incest.

Caide must have read her face, even in the near darkness. He'd stripped her bare in more ways than one tonight. "He didn't tell you, did he?"

Her voice wouldn't come, so she shook her head.

"Dear 'Uncle' James spent his entire life trying to wrest Sancreed back from the Tremaynes. When he finally understood it wouldn't happen in his lifetime, he took steps to ensure that no matter what, his blood would succeed to the title. He abducted Peter's mother, Lady Sancreed, and raped her until he got her with child. And then he seduced his own sister and got a child on her as well."

"Your mother."

"My mother," Caide agreed. "James wanted an heir, because there was always a chance one of his suits would succeed and the title would revert to the Caides. But no respectable family would tie their daughter to him. To a man like that, seducing his own sister and buying her a husband to legitimate the child must have seemed an elegant solution to his dilemma. I doubt he lost much sleep over it.

"But guilt drove my mother mad. She was always highly strung. So loving, so gentle. So sad. Perhaps if I hadn't been born she might have made some life for herself, but, for all the love she tried to show me, I was a constant reminder of her weakness, her sin. She drowned herself in the lake at Sancreed when I was twelve."

"It's monstrous," Kate said, wondering how her pillow had become wet, then realizing she must have been crying for some time.

"My father was a monster," said Caide simply. "There's a glass by the bedside. It's wine, with something to dull the pain."

"I won't take opium."

"I measured the dose carefully. It's only enough to help you sleep. André didn't know what he was doing when he tried to drug you."

"You know about that too?"

"The Huguenot bastard told me. I expect he thought he was enlisting me against you, that my jealousy would ensure my cooperation. But all I could think while he was talking was all the myriad ways I might enjoy killing him. I *will* kill him, for you, when the time is right. But for now I need to get you someplace safe and out of the way. Most of my men are camped at the Kearsley Farm on the other side of the river. I had Dyson round up the patrols and pickets once you'd been intercepted. Dawn is only a few hours off. If you don't sleep now, you won't be able to ride in the morning. Drink the wine."

She hadn't been able to take the opium. The spicy scent of the drug swirling in the glass had turned her stomach. Her body remembered the stuff, and it bore a grudge, even now, when the poppy promised relief rather than destruction. She slept fitfully, waking to the sound of movement in the room and opening her eyes to the cold dawn light. She guessed that no more than three hours had passed. The skin on her back felt stretched as tight as a drumhead. She moved stiffly, and dressed with the help of a battered girl who must have been one of those women pressed into unwilling service in the court-yard last night.

Kate had the girl lace her stays as loosely as possible, but she still nearly blacked out from the pain when the silk met her back. She tied on her petticoats, and pinned the tattered gown together as best she could. Her cloak was plain heavy wool. She'd chosen it to cover her outlandish costume once she was out of the city, in the hopes that the homely garment would make her inconspicuous and keep her warm. The weight of it on her lacerated shoulders would be agony, but she brought it all the same, because she had no intention of baring herself before Bay's men. And because today, on the road, offered her best chance of escape.

Phillip Lytton met her at the door. She knew that in the light of day the gown was nearly transparent, and she felt a stab of pity as Lytton tried to find a safe place for his eyes to rest that did not require him to look into hers. "I was to be one of André's Ladies of the Blended Rose," she said, by way of explanation and because the situation beggared almost every avenue of conversation.

"I wanted very much to be there," answered Lytton, and he was once again the theater-mad boy she had met at Grey Farm. "Knights and Ladies and jousting." But only for a moment. Then he remembered that he was her jailer and sobered. "I am a poor Galahad, Miss Grey."

He took the cloak from her arm. She tried not to wince when he settled it on her shoulders, but she must have failed because anguish was writ plain on his face. "You should have shot me on the road," he said bleakly, and then he bound her wrists together and pulled her cloak closed so that no one would have to see her shame.

They didn't speak after that. Lytton led her down into the courtyard, his hand discreetly beneath her arm, supporting her and sheltering her from the press of men and horses, and servants frantic to see these soldiers gone.

The yard smelled of stale beer and horse.

She shrank when she saw Caide's creature Dyson, whom she had always instinctively disliked, holding her mount and smirking. She clutched frantically at Lytton. "Would you give me a leg up, Mr. Lytton?" She did not want Dyson to touch her.

And blessedly Lytton offered no false reassurances, because she was certain she would have begun screaming if he had. Instead he helped her into the saddle while Dyson held her mount, and lingered, checking her girth and her stirrups with meticulous care until he could find no further pretense for delay, and finally had to leave to see to his own horse.

Which left her alone with Dyson. His cold eyes appraised her. She saw hatred. The venomous kind possessed only by very young children and madmen. She pulled on her reins and tried to back away, but the brute had her horse by the bridle, and her struggles only made him smile. "You thought you could humiliate him," he said, his hand slithering around her ankle. "But look at you now. I'm looking forward to my turn, woman. You'll think you can't sink any lower when the colonel's through with you, but I'll show you different. Like I did for the other one. The jaded bitch thought there was nothing she couldn't stomach, but she was wrong."

Even without the opium, Kate was sure she was going to vomit. What had happened with Caide last night had been inevitable. What Dyson promised was beyond her ability to endure.

"Take your hands off her, Lieutenant." Caide's voice cut across the tumult in the yard. "No one touches her." He'd pitched it to include all those in the yard, but he was looking straight at Dyson. "Is that clear?"

Dyson released her ankle. "As you say, sir," he said calmly, but his eyes, as he strode off into the throng, promised no such obedience if he chanced to get her alone.

Caide took the reins out of her bound hands and tied her wrists to the pommel. When he tied her ankles to her stirrups as well, she knew she had no chance of escape on the road today. His voice, now low for only her to hear, came light and ironic as he mounted up on the animal beside her and began leading her horse. "I'll teach you to ride and to shoot properly in India. And how to defend yourself from rogues like Dyson. It took four men to subdue your impressive aunt Angela when they took her." He smiled. "Of course Dyson wasn't one of them."

"She offered to teach me to fight, but I was brought up a Quaker."

"Were you, by God?" He laughed, and turned to her with the same look of delight he'd so often favored her with during their courtship. "You might be the first person in my sorry life that my Roundhead ancestor would have approved of."

They'd been on the road for an hour when Lytton drew up level with them and spoke quietly to Caide.

"The men are growing restive. They don't like being cut out of the attack on Valley Forge to chase your doxy across country." And here he had the good grace to cast Kate an apologetic glance. "Their words, not mine."

Caide was unperturbed. He'd been keeping an eye on her, as they rode, and had slowed the pace incrementally as the night began to catch up with her. But he'd never been less than fully aware of the men riding behind them. "They've no cause for complaint," he said evenly. "They've had beer and bawds and a night under cover instead of tramping through the woods. And it's because we ran down 'my doxy' that the attack proceeds and prevails."

"Nevertheless," said Lytton.

She expected Caide to dismiss him as he had last night, but the appraising glance he gave the younger man reinforced her opinion: Lytton had grown up over the past year. That some of his maturity was due to months spent with her father was a strange irony. It had given him the will to face her down on the road.

"They can have an afternoon of organized bloodshed. Just the thing. Have Dyson set up a boxing match when we reach camp," said Caide. "But try to discourage the deeper sort of betting. It only leads to bloodshed of the disorganized kind later."

It was midafternoon by the time the detachment reached the farm. It was the kind of smallholding so common in these parts. Not a great acreage like Grey Farm, but a reasonably substantial one. Enough to support barley and rye, some fruit trees, kitchen vegetables, and a few pigs and goats. Or at least it had been. The fields were lying fallow. There was no sign of livestock in the yard or the barn, and the broken shutters on the two-story stone house with its sloping Dutch roof and wide, comfortable porch spoke of a winter of neglect.

Kate was surprised to find the ground floor tidy, but suspiciously short on furniture. She paused at the bottom of the stairs, looking up the banister and wondering how she could compel her aching body another step, when Caide bent at the waist and lifted her over his shoulder like a sack of grain. And pathetically, she was grateful for it. She wanted only to be at rest, somewhere, anywhere. And if he had lifted her any other way, her back, which had quieted since she'd gotten off the bloody horse, would riot with fresh pain.

He carried her upstairs and set her down in a bedroom overlooking the fields behind the house, and cut her bonds. He helped her out of her cloak, and she was too sore and weak to reject his aid out of pride. It occurred to her then that she had not eaten since breakfast yesterday morning. Though she felt no hunger, she knew she wasn't safe here, and should try to keep up her strength. But the thought of food made her head ache.

All this passed through her mind while she stood surveying the room, taking in the solid pine bed with its dusty blue wool hangings, the matching curtains on the windows, the single chair by the fire, the iron kettle and pot stand. This had once been someone's home. The easel in front of the window told her it was now Caide's. And the Chinese paint box sitting on the floor beside it, which she had bought him all those months ago, told her she was now Caide's as well.

She must have swayed slightly, because his hands

were suddenly beneath her elbow and around her waist and his voice was cutting through the blackness, raw and panicked. "Sit down, Lydia."

She couldn't remember sitting but suddenly she was in the chair and Caide was kneeling beside her, tipping her head up and looking into what she knew must be her glazed eyes. He looked worried. "I warned you that you wouldn't be fit to ride this morning without more sleep. Let me give you something for the pain." He was touching her cheek, and if she closed her eyes, she could pretend he was Peter. She leaned into the caress for a moment, tried to draw some strength from it.

Then she opened her eyes and shook her head. "No." To be drugged and helpless here with Dyson and those men outside would be madness. And she needed her wits about her to escape.

Caide swallowed hard, unhappy with her resistance. "I could force you to take it," he threatened.

"But you won't," she chanced.

His shoulders sagged. His eyes fluttered shut and he lowered his head to her lap. She brushed his hair from his face. He was not Peter, and she did not love him as she loved Peter, but she felt something for him, a strange sort of kinship. "I didn't mean to hurt you so badly," he murmured into her lap. "You should have cried out. Asked me to stop."

When she didn't reply, he captured her hand, pressed it to his mouth. "I must see to the men. Don't try to run, Lydia. Not even I can control them when their blood is up, and a chase would rouse them like nothing else at this point. You'll be safe enough in here with the door locked."

He got to his feet and shouted into the corridor. "Lytton!" The young man appeared instantly in the doorway, his face carefully blank. "Make her comfortable. Bring her anything she asks for." Then he favored her with an apologetic smile. "Apart from a pistol and a horse." Then he was gone.

And she could take refuge in practicalities. "A needle and thread, Mr. Lytton. And pins. As many as you can find. And something to eat." Lytton nodded, then left.

She watched the door close and listened to the key turn in the lock. That was another skill against which she had stood on her principles and failed to acquire. If she knew how to pick a lock, she might be away and across the fields by now.

The windows at least offered some hope. She tested the casement nearest the bed. Nailed shut. As were the others.

When Lytton came back he brought her a carpet needle, scarlet thread, and a rattling wooden box full of pins, along with a few slices of stale toast and a pitcher of water. He lit her a fire and locked the door again when he left. She stripped off her gown and petticoat, and loosened her stays but left them on. She was too stiff to lift them over her head, and she didn't think she could get them laced again later on her own. She washed in the water provided, tied her stays and petticoat back on, then sat down beside the fire and began pinning her tattered dress back together. The gown was so delicately constructed and so badly torn that she quickly emptied the box of pins.

While she worked, the sounds from the yard changed in tone. The clatter of horses and the jangle of tack were replaced by the hum of a crowd, pierced by occasional shouts. The boxing match. The noise rose and ebbed in time with the fight.

The door must have opened on one of the swells, because she never heard the key in the lock. Just the heavy tread of Dyson crossing the room.

She put down her sewing and stood. Dyson was the kind of predatory animal that could smell fear. "What do you want?"

"Cooperation." He struck fast like a snake, seizing her wrist and yanking her off balance. His strength was frightening—her shoulder felt wrenched from the socket.

She tried to run, but that was a mistake. She should have screamed. He clapped a sinewy hand over her mouth, and kicked her legs out from under her. She fell, her knees cracking against the floor, and he followed her down, his body a deadweight on her back. *No no no no no.*

"Shut up," he snarled.

Kate couldn't have stopped screaming if she'd tried, but his hand muffled her sobs. She thrashed and kicked and bit until she tasted blood in her mouth and he cursed her. She felt his weight shift, and he reached for something.

Then he stiffened and screamed. His grip loosened and she twisted away from him. She scrambled toward the hearth and seized the black iron kettle. She turned to find him kneeling and holding out a handful of bloody silk bristling with pins. Her sewing. He'd meant to gag her with it.

"You bloody bitch." He lunged at her. She hefted the kettle and brought it up in an arc that caught him on the jaw. He tottered, and she struck him again. He sprawled on his back and twitched, and she brought the kettle down again. And again. And again.

The afternoon light was already waning when Tremayne reached the outskirts of the farm. André had given him the location of Caide's new camp in exchange for those damning letters.

The sound of a raucous crowd met him at the gate, washed over him like a wave of sickness. But he checked his urge to gallop in and walked his horse, as if he had every right to be there, straight up to the ring of shouting, surging men.

They parted for him and silence fell. A boxing match. Thank God. And Bay, presiding over it like a Roman emperor, enthroned on the low stone wall that circled the house and yard.

He leapt down from his perch, but didn't come any closer. "Turn around and go home, Peter."

"I've come for Kate."

"She isn't here."

There came a single, high-pitched, bloodcurdling scream from the little stone house, abruptly cut off. Tremayne slid from his saddle and strode to his brother.

"Fine," said Caide. "She's here. But you're not taking her."

"She isn't safe here."

"That scream was Dyson, if I'm not mistaken, and it sounds like he got what he deserved for disobeying me. Now turn around and go home, Peter. You can't fight thirty men."

"I'm not here to fight thirty men. I'm here to fight you."

"Leave it. Content yourself. You have Sancreed, and I have Lydia."

"Her name is Kate. And I would trade Sancreed for her if I could."

"But you can't. It's yours. And now she's mine."

"She doesn't love you."

"That didn't matter last night," Caide said quite softly. "She didn't flinch. *Not even when I whipped her.*"

Tremayne drew his saber. It was a poor weapon for a duel, graceful on horseback for a cavalryman's slashing cuts, but cumbersome as hell on the ground. A pistol would have been the wiser choice, but he knew he could not level a gun at Bay, at the brother he had protected since boyhood.

"My sword," Caide said with a sigh, opening the fingers of an outstretched hand expectantly.

Tremayne, with sinking heart, recognized the young man who brought it. "Lytton," he said.

"My lord," acknowledged the subaltern.

"You see, Peter. You can't keep her. Too many people know what she did. She'll hang. Or worse." He flicked the blade, like a negligent leveler cutting tall poppies down to size, and smiled at his brother.

"If I win, she leaves here unharmed." Tremayne said it loud enough for the crowd to hear.

Caide shook his head. "She won't leave with you. Not after what we did last night." He made a tentative feint at Tremayne and fell back when steel met steel. "I didn't have a birch, so I used the little black riding whip I bought her."

Tremayne lunged. "She was your prisoner. She didn't have the power to stop you."

Caide sidestepped neatly. "Ah, but she did, you see. *She could have stopped me with a word.*"

He knew what Caide was trying to do: get him angry, throw him off his guard. But he had a purpose, and he would not be deterred. "Only a fool or a madwoman would have fought you," he replied evenly, drawing back a pace after one of his brother's economical attacks.

Caide smirked. "I would show you my handiwork, Peter, if you had any appreciation for the whip, but her back isn't the real masterpiece. No. If you want to see something extraordinary, *you should see mine.*"

Tremayne rushed him. They were so well matched, in speed, in age, in skill, that Caide should have sidestepped easily. But he didn't. He froze, his eyes fixed on something beyond Tremayne's shoulder. At the house. Tremayne didn't look. Whatever it was could wait. He drove the point of his sword into his brother's shoulder.

Caide looked down, then sank to his knees without a sound. And Tremayne turned to see what had captured his brother's attention.

The door to the farmhouse was open. Kate stood on the porch, swaying, her eyes blank. Her white damask stays and gray silk petticoats were spattered with blood. Her bare arms hung limply at her sides, and a black iron kettle, barnacled with bits of hair and bone, dangled from one hand. She wove unsteadily down the steps and into the yard.

"Kate," he said gently.

She looked up at him, but her puzzlement was plain.

Then she looked down at herself. "Don't worry," she said dreamily. "It isn't my blood."

But it would be soon if he put a foot wrong now. He surveyed the crowd warily. Hard-bitten men, by birth and circumstance, as well as Caide's sterling example. They were stunned for the moment, but that wouldn't last long. And Caide . . .

"Take her and go." Caide was kneeling on the ground, covering his wound with a hand that looked freshly dipped in crimson paint. He was bleeding, his shirt wet with blood, but it was impossible to know how bad the wound was. He might live. Or not.

Lytton crouched beside him, surveyed the wound, then looked up at Tremayne. "No one will detain you, my lord. I'll see to it."

Caide laughed, the sound a little strained. "Poor Mr. Lytton. Always trying to do the honorable thing."

Tremayne crossed the remaining ground between himself and Kate, and loosed her grip, one finger at a time, from the grisly kettle. He had to place her hands on the pommel, and shove her up onto his horse. When he mounted up behind her, and his arms circled her waist, they slid through the gore on her petticoat.

He didn't dare look back. He spurred his horse out of the yard and sped from a trot to a canter once he was on the road. Kate was as limp as a rag doll in his arms, bereft of wit and senses. Or so he thought, until he turned his horse off the road and began cutting through an orchard budding with new fruit.

"Where are we going?" she asked.

"I'm taking you home to your father."

"We'll never make it past the British lines."

"There *are* no British lines, Kate. The attack failed.

Your warning made it through. Howe's troops have withdrawn to Philadelphia to begin evacuation."

He waited for her reaction, but there was none. Her flesh felt cold. Too cold. And the weals patterning her shoulders clearly continued down her back, beneath her stays. He did not know what else might have happened to her, but she was deep in shock. She needed clothing, shelter, and food, and he was at least sixteen miles from Valley Forge. They would never make the journey before nightfall.

He rode for another hour or so with her clutched tight to his chest, because he could not risk stopping so close to Caide's camp. She stirred when he lowered her to the ground, and he wrapped her in his coat while he built a fire. Then he pulled her into his arms, trying not to touch her back, and dribbled brandy from his flask into her mouth.

Her eyes opened. "I didn't mean for him to die," she said.

"He may yet live," Tremayne said.

"Not Bay. Lieutenant Dyson. I killed him."

That explained the bloody kettle. "Dyson deserved his fate. A mad dog. The man . . ." Tremayne knew the awful truth offered Kate absolution for the death of Caide's henchman. "He tortured Angela Ferrers." And I did nothing to stop him, he reminded himself.

"Bay is your brother," she said. It wasn't a question. She knew.

"Yes."

"How long have you known?"

"Since I was fourteen and he twelve. The year his mother died."

"And how long has he known who his father was?"

That Kate could still care about anyone or anything but herself was astounding, when she lay spattered in the gore of the second man who'd tried to violate her in the space of as many days. Tremayne owed her nothing less than the complete truth. "Bay has always known."

She tried to sit up. Her skirts rustled like paper, stiff with dried blood. She looked down at the stains. "Does it ever get easier?"

"To kill a man?" He considered carefully. "Yes. That is the mercy and the horror of it. It becomes all too easy."

She nodded. "You can't come all the way to Valley Forge with me."

He took the coat from her shoulders and turned it inside out, then slipped it back over her arms. He knew better than to wear scarlet in the territory they were traveling now. "You are an exceedingly stubborn woman. I've made my choice, and I have no regrets."

She shook her head. "I won't allow you to make the sacrifice."

"It is the same one I asked of you," he pointed out gently.

"And you were right when you said I had far less to give up. Take me to within a mile of Washington's camp."

"They'll hang me if I go back. I have nothing left to bargain with. André told me where to find you in exchange for the letters."

"But I can give you something new to bargain with. Elizabeth and Joshua Loring are American agents. Howe knows, and he will protect you if you keep his secret."

It wasn't possible. "Loring can't be a spy. He is Commissioner of Prisoners. Everyone knows the man's been starving his American charges all winter and siphoning the money into his own coffers. Even I've seen the numbers of Rebels leaving the Walnut Street jail in pine boxes." Even as he said it, he saw the brilliance of it.

"They weren't all dead, were they?" he said. "He was smuggling prisoners out."

"Yes. And the supplies he diverted have gone to Valley Forge. I didn't know any of this myself until last week, when I remembered something the Widow had said about another spy, caught like a fly in amber. I guessed—hoped—it might be Mrs. Loring, because I needed her help to escape the city. Howe knows she is a spy. André holds this information over him, but the general will not give her up. Now you know too. It means you can go home. To Sancreed."

"My home is with you." He only realized how true it was now that he said it, but her expression told him he had far to go to convince her. She looked like she might make further argument, but he hustled her back onto his horse. They had a great deal of ground to cover, and he did not think her burst of lucid energy would last.

He was right. She was limp in his arms again inside of an hour. Despite his coat, which kept falling from her small shoulders, her skin was cold and clammy to the touch.

The moon was full; otherwise, keeping hold of a half-conscious girl and controlling his horse over rough terrain would have been impossible. They were in deep woods now, the road they were following no more than a cart track. Even so, he should have heard them. Would certainly have heard ordinary soldiers.

But not these men. His horse was rearing and a bayonet pricking his throat before he even saw their faces. Backwoodsmen in forest green and deerskin boots.

One demanded his name and his purpose. He would have told them, but before he could utter a word, the motion of his restless horse pitched Kate from his arms and to the road below, where two of the men caught her. His coat slipped from her shoulders, and the moonlight showed clearly the red of his regimentals, and the deeper crimson staining her tattered skirts.

They pulled him from his horse. He begged them to see her safe to Arthur Grey, but they paid him no heed. He caught a glimpse, as they surrounded him, of Kate, limp and unconscious, being carried away in the arms of a hulking Rebel scout, her bloody skirts trailing on the forest floor. Then they began clubbing him with the butts of their rifles.

"Washington will want him alive for hanging." The voice of their leader, bandy-legged, unshaven, and armed to the teeth, halted the rain of blows. The man placed a foot on Tremayne's chest and asked, "Does the name Nathan Hale mean anything to you?"

Hale. The young schoolteacher Howe had hanged in New York last year, without trial, and in the face of Washington's most heartfelt pleas. It was well known that Washington had vowed to return the favor. And Tremayne, an officer and an aristocrat, would make an ideal object for the Rebel general's retribution.

The American grinned widely. "I can see it does."

Tremayne was under no illusions about his predicament. He'd been captured, out of uniform, behind Rebel lines. It would not speak in his favor that he was in possession of his regimentals, since they were wrapped around the abused body of one of their most beloved commander's daughters.

Tremayne's captors bound him hand and foot and slung him over the back of his horse. They traveled a mile like that through thick forest. Then they reached the perimeter of the camp.

He had read the reports coming out of Valley Forge, heard of the staggering losses to cold, privation, and disease. Influenza, typhus, and dysentery had run wild through the camp. Every intelligence the British had received painted a picture of a rebellion on the brink of collapse.

Tremayne saw no evidence of that now. Admittedly, his was not the best vantage point for making accurate tactical observations, slung as he was over the side of his beast and mildly concussed. But what he could see—row upon row of rude log huts—was neatly laid out and solidly built. There was the sound of a military drill, crisp and precise, somewhere in the distance, and he recalled a bit of gossip he'd heard from Ewald over the winter: that the Americans had acquired a mountebank Prussian who styled himself "Baron von Steuben" and had undertaken to teach them proper warfare. From the sound of that drill, the Prussian's military training, if not his pedigree, was genuine.

His captors cut his bonds and deposited him in one of the log huts, a little removed from the rest. They barred the door from without. It was a more comfortable prison than the powder magazine at Mercer, but a prison all the same. Dirt floor, brick chimney, plank bunks. There was no fuel, no light, no tinder. No mattress or even a blanket. The day had been pleasantly warm, but the May evenings were still cool, and in only his shirt and breeches, the night would be chill indeed.

He lay down on his side on one of the bunks, nursing a sore head and bruised ribs, and curled up to contain his bodily warmth. He did not want to die, but he could not regret the step he had taken today. Provided the Americans did not try him as a spy and hang him, as they very well might, he knew that he and Kate could build a life together, wherever fortune dictated. The passion they felt now might one day be tempered by time, but the joy they took in each other's company, the life of ideas they might share, would not fade with the passing years. He had only to win through the next few days.

When the bar was lifted and the door opened a few hours later, he knew it would be more difficult than that. Arthur Grey stood silhouetted in the torchlight, his face a grim and forbidding mask. Of course it was. No doubt he'd seen the state in which Tremayne had returned his only daughter

"Kate?" It was the first word out of his mouth. Everything else could wait.

"My daughter will live," said Arthur Grey. "You, sir, are another matter entirely."

Nineteen

It was a kitchen. She knew that before she knew anything else because she knew the sounds of kitchens. The low ring of the spoon in the pot, the clink of stacked plates, the pat of shoes on hearth tiles.

It was warm, and there were quiet voices, but she wasn't ready to make sense of them yet. It was so very good to feel warm. She wanted to stretch and turn over on her back, but then she remembered. Everything.

And because she had not been waking up in good circumstances lately, she schooled herself to remain still, to breathe evenly as in sleep, and to listen.

"Isn't there anything else you can do for her?" A voice, female, low, cultured, mature. Not a girl, a woman. Who spoke with the drawling cadences of the Southern states.

"Someone's already cleaned her stripes as well as I could have." A man's voice. Smug.

"Something for the pain, then. You must have opium." The woman again, firm, patient.

"Madame." He didn't mean *madame*. He meant *woman*. And he said it like *bitch*. "Madame, I have two hundred men dying of fever and infection in my infirmary. I can't spare opium for some lobsterback's whipping whore."

Silence, during which Kate could hear only the snap of the fire and a third person moving about the kitchen. A servant, then, because they did not have the leisure to stop or the status to take part in the conversation.

At length the woman said, "You are misinformed, sir."

He snorted. "The whole camp knows she came in half naked on the horse of a Redcoat. And it's plain she went willingly under the lash. I've treated men who weren't whipped half as badly and their wrists were bloody from the ropes. Hers are as fine and unmarked as swan's down."

"Nevertheless. If you cannot spare some opium, then we can broach the general's supply."

Kate had heard enough. She was home, she was safe, and no one had lied to her about how hard it would be. She no longer had the Widow to turn to, but she did have her example. "Opium," she said, clutching the sheet to her breasts and rising from the cot, "will not be necessary. But a glass of watered rum would not go amiss."

It was smaller than her kitchen at Grey Farm, and the clutter told her it was serving a larger household than intended. Her champion was a woman decidedly past forty, sensibly and expensively dressed, but without style. There was a black serving woman as well. Kate noted that she didn't pause for a second about her tasks but took quiet note of every spoken word. A slave, then.

The man was middle-aged, overdressed for the country in gray silk, and no friend of Kate's. She was acutely aware of the way he looked at her in her state of undress, in a bedsheet, wrapped togalike, and she stood to put distance between herself and this man, who had, she realized with revulsion, touched her while she slept.

He failed to take the hint. He slapped her rump and laughed. "See. The slut will be on her back again in no time."

She knotted the sheet and lowered her hand, because she did not want to appear to cringe in front of this creature. "I think it only fair to inform you that the last man who touched me without leave is wearing his brains on the side of a cast-iron kettle."

"Have a care, then, Doctor. This is an exceedingly well-equipped kitchen." A new voice, from the top of the stairs leading into the house.

Hamilton.

She'd met him only once, months ago, but they'd corresponded all winter, their words masked, ciphered, and sometimes written in invisible inks.

He bowed to her. "My lady."

The old coot snorted again. "She's no lady. And if she's well enough to be on her feet, then you should send her on her way. I've enough men sick, and she'll only spread disease."

For the first time since she'd woken Kate heard the serving woman stop in her tracks and listen as her mistress drew a breath to speak. Hamilton beat her to it.

"That will be all, Doctor. Your services are no longer required."

"About time. I've better things to do than treat whores."

"You misunderstand me." Hamilton's voice was icy. "Your services are no longer required at Valley Forge. Collect your pay and depart, immediately."

"You jest, sir."

"I am indeed known for my sense of humor. Alas, the Life Guard are not. They will escort you to the perimeter."

When the doctor—outraged but outfaced—had gone, Kate asked Hamilton the question that had been on her lips since she woke. "Where is Peter?"

"You'll see him soon. First, if you are well enough, the general would like a word."

"We could not rescue your petticoat, but your stays might be salvaged if you dye them. They're too fine to give up on entirely," the middle-aged woman said. Kate realized at last who the lady of the house must be. Washington's wife.

Hamilton eyed the bloody heap of clothing lying in the washtub. "There is a trunk outside as well. It belonged to Angela Ferrers. She left instructions that it should be yours. I'll have it brought in. There might be things you can use."

The trunk turned out to contain Angela Ferrers' Quaker ensemble from Orchard Valley, a sack gown in cherry floral stripes fit for strolling the gardens of Versailles, and an extraordinary sum in gold coins. Because the trunk had belonged to the Widow, Kate looked for, and found, a false bottom. In that she discovered a pouch of uncut gems, a pair of pistols, a set of lock picks, and a silk roll of throwing knives. There was also a packet of letters, some coded, others not, in every language spoken in Europe and several not.

The clothes and weapons might have belonged to any of the personas the Widow had adopted, but the cloak Kate found lining the bottom of the trunk, she suspected could only be the Widow's own. A genuine relic, perhaps the only one, of the real Angela Ferrers. The hood was wide and edged with snowy foxtails. The felted wool was soft as a sheep's belly, dyed midnight blue, and fastened with a silver brooch of delicate Celtic knot work.

Kate considered the plain Quaker dress. It was comforting, familiar. And no longer for her. If she was going to be branded a harlot, she might as well play the part.

She ate a bowl of thin oatmeal with sugar and salt, and it was the very best thing she had ever tasted. Then she washed and dressed in the striped gown. The general's wife lent her an iron to curl her hair, and she found tortoise combs and a box of cosmetics in the trunk.

Then she wrapped herself in the Widow's dark blue mantle and went outside.

*Y*ou own a château on the Loire," Washington said, reading from the report on the desk before him. "A fine house in Paris, and significant lands in Burgundy."

Tremayne was surprised at the breadth and depth of information Washington possessed. The American general was, if nothing else, exceedingly well informed.

Tremayne found him inscrutable. But whatever reversals of fortune and political trials the general had weathered over the winter, he was very much in command now. The parlor of the little stone house from which he directed his new-minted army was well appointed and pin neat. And from what Peter Tremayne could see, the camp ran like clockwork.

Arthur Grey eyed Tremayne with the same wary detachment he'd affected since rescuing the younger man from imprisonment that morning. Tremayne had passed the whole night in that comfortless log hut, wondering if he was to be tried as a spy. Washington, it turned out, was indeed determined to hang the next British agent fool enough to be caught behind American lines. But Arthur Grey had been able to convince the general that Tremayne's intention had not been espionage—approaching the Rebel encampment with the Grey Fox's bloodied and beaten daughter across his saddle hardly facilitated spying or covert reconnaissance.

No doubt the question of Kate's future had entered into their deliberations. They had not yet allowed him to see her.

Tremayne was also acutely aware of the fact that he was wearing Arthur Grey's second-best suit. Black velvet with silver buttons and a coat cut wide enough for a corsair. And that he had failed the man. He'd rescued Kate too late, proven himself a poor protector for the Grey Fox's daughter.

"And you have been received at the late King Louis' court," continued Washington with the same bland cordiality. They'd offered Tremayne brandy, and been gruffly approving when he'd asked for whisky instead.

His saber, his pistols, the pass, and the marriage license he'd procured all lay on the sideboard beside the decanter. But he couldn't believe that all this talk of France was leading toward a marriage settlement, though God knew he'd have nothing of his English fortune to offer Kate shortly enough.

"My holdings in France come through my mother." Who would suffer for what he had done. He did not regret rescuing Kate. He knew now that he could not live without her. He would not regret losing Sancreed. He *would* regret that his mother might become an outcast, that she would be forced upon the charity of her relatives if Sancreed reverted to the Crown—as it surely would when he was tried for treason in absentia.

Washington turned a page of the closely written report and went on. "You have served with the cavalry since you were fourteen but made a particular study of artillery and small arms and were detached repeatedly to the Royal Corps of Engineers. It is plain you intended to marry Miss Grey, but you are not a man likely to beat his sword into a plowshare. And you could not, with honor, serve me against the men you lately fought beside."

Arthur Grey eyed him with unconcealed skepticism. "That is, if you still intend to marry my daughter."

"I do, sir. If you will allow it."

Washington stood up and paced to the window. "You may put your proposal to Miss Grey, under the following conditions. I have been forced to send glum lawyers and mercurial eccentrics to Paris to beg arms from the king of France. Like most of us 'Colonists,' they drive excellent bargains but do not know a mortar from a howitzer. I can send them instructions, but they are an ocean away and lack a professional's understanding of the materials of war. I require a man in Paris who can advise them."

It was a tempting offer: an opportunity to use the skills of his calling in the service of Kate's cause, without bearing arms against his countrymen. It should not have surprised him. Tremayne knew the Americans were woefully short on professional military expertise. Most of their commanders, like Washington, had not seen service for twenty years. Career soldiers were in such short supply that the Americans had been forced to import foreigners like Von Steuben, who did not, Tremayne had discovered just that morning, even speak English, to teach them the basics of drill. He did not doubt that Washington could use him. What remained unclear was why Washington thought he could trust him. "And your conditions?" Tremayne asked.

"You may not take your new wife, should she accept you, to France. And you must leave tomorrow."

The air was soft with spring. Hamilton stood leaning against the house and holding the reins of an enormous draft horse. "He's gentle and slow," explained the young man. "And I thought you might not be up for climbing the hill quite yet."

"When can I see Peter?"

"After you've spoken with the general."

"He rescued me and was beaten senseless for it."

"It is unfortunate, but appearances were against him. And the major is an enemy officer. No matter what he did for you, even now his status here is not quite that of a guest."

Which was not something Kate could argue with. She was hardly up for climbing onto the horse, but she managed it with the aid of a mounting block. Hamilton led them up a steeply wooded slope, past row after row of rude wooden huts.

"The men sleep mostly under canvas now that the ground has thawed, but I assure you, a six-man log hut was a great luxury in December."

"Did you sleep in one?" It was odd to think of him living like that while they were writing to one another.

"I confess I did not, although General Knox did, just for the principle of the thing." And seeming to read her thoughts, he continued, "I enjoyed our correspondence very much, Miss Grey. Mind you, it was hair-raising sometimes, having Washington standing over my shoulder while I tried to puzzle out your inventions. Alluding to the Three Graces in your surface letter, indicating that I should cut a new mask in such a shape was exceedingly clever, once I figured it out. And got the proportions right. But until then I looked like an utter fool."

She took a surprising amount of pleasure in having challenged him. "I enjoyed my return letters from 'Cousin Sally' enormously. And it took me no time at all to determine that your search for the correct quantity of green ribbon for your bonnet meant Jaeger green and an approximation of their numbers."

They teased one another like brother and sister as he led her horse into a clearing where Washington waited. He was seated on a spirited white charger that looked exceedingly put out to be standing still for any length of time, and she realized that Hamilton had taken great care in coddling her on the ascent. She'd hardly noticed, which meant she'd needed it.

The general doffed his hat. "Miss Grey. I am glad to see you well."

"Well enough, sir," she said carefully. She'd met Washington only once, months ago, but something had changed. Perhaps it was her.

"I am sorry to drag you out of the warm, but there is something I would like to show you."

They left Hamilton behind in the clearing and rode side by side on a narrow path through the trees. She was grateful for the even ground. She could hear fife and drum music ahead.

"It was a winter of sacrifices," he said after they had proceeded in silence for a few minutes. "Yours . . . and others. I am in your debt."

"Many sacrificed more." Elizabeth and Joshua Loring, and the Widow, whose cloak was resting on her scarred shoulders. The soldiers fallen to hunger and disease in this camp. "And it was all for nothing. We lost Forts Mercer and Mifflin and control of the river. Howe kept Philadelphia and his army. It was all for nothing."

"Not for nothing." The music grew louder and became distinct: a martial tune. "You will want a favor of me today, which I cannot grant."

They broke out of the trees on a vast plain, green as only the Jerseys were green in May, buzzing with locusts, lush and sweet-smelling like an herb garden in the sun. As far as Kate's eye could see stretched lines and lines of blue coats and bright steel bayonets, men drilling in formation, advancing and wheeling in the bright morning light. "But anything else in my power is yours for the asking. Because your sacrifice, alongside that of Mrs. Ferrers' and others', was not in vain. It bought me an army."

*H*amilton waited for her in the clearing. He took his stewardship of her very seriously, so she allowed him to lead her horse and they descended in an easy and amiable silence. Somehow, through their letters, and a few brief conversations since, they'd arrived at a comfortable camaraderie.

Until he broached an uncomfortable subject. "What will you do now, Miss Grey?"

She had no idea.

The silence stretched. He broke it. "I am sensitive to the difficulties in which women find themselves. Things would doubtless have been easier for my mother and me had she a husband."

"Oh." Oblique though it was, it was the third proposal she had received in her life, and this from a man she scarcely knew.

"His Lordship will make you an offer, but I wished you to know it was not the only choice."

They'd reached the bottom of the hill, and were standing once more beside the narrow stone house. "Thank you." She sifted through her mind until she found the right words for the occasion, because this man was not offering her passion, but a shield, and it was breathtakingly generous. "You are uncommonly kind."

He laughed, and his shoulders twitched in a graceful, self-deprecating shrug. "But alas, kindness rarely stirs the feminine heart. Go and speak with Peter Tremayne, Miss Grey, but bear my offer in mind."

*P*roposals of marriage, it seemed, came in flavors, like pies. She'd been offered a union of tortured spirits with Bayard Caide, a lifetime of lies with Peter Tremayne, and a platonic alliance with Alex Hamilton. But today was the first time she'd been offered a marriage without a husband.

"Your father and Washington need a man in France with my expertise. It is an opportunity for me to prove my loyalty and usefulness," Tremayne was saying from his place on the carpet.

He was kneeling, like some chivalric knight, and after the idiocy of the Mischianza, she found it more than slightly ridiculous. "Do please get up," she said.

They retired to the settle together, like some courting couple. "Your father and Washington are pragmatists. War makes men so. They know that once I am in France my countrymen will send emissaries, make overtures, try to woo me back. And failing that, they'll do their damnedest to catch me and hang me. Your father and Washington are right to keep you here—both as surety that I will not be tempted to betray them and to keep you safe from harm," Tremayne said. "Do you want to be my wife? You will have other offers, from your own countrymen; of that I have no doubt. I am going to lose Sancreed and the viscountcy. There is money in France, but not a great deal of it. You will be ordinary Kate Tremayne, not the fine lady I wanted to make you. But we will be together."

"You will be in France. For a year. At the least. We would have to marry today."

"Yes."

And then he would be gone. "I can't. Not yet. Not today."

"I am not expecting a wedding night, Kate," he said gently.

"It isn't that. I mean, I know your mother was never able to . . . that is to say . . . what happened with Bay will not haunt me. I knew the risk I was running, was already prepared to endure it. But, Peter, he did not withdraw. I could be carrying his child. It would be better if we waited until you returned."

"It is something of a family tradition, raising another man's child."

"This is not a joking matter."

"Then let us *be* serious. I am embarking for France tomorrow, Kate. I have to cross three thousand miles of ocean controlled by the country I just betrayed. I may well die. If I do so *before* I am tried, any male issue of our union would inherit Sancreed. And there might be some safety there for you if the war goes badly, to be the mother of a viscount. If I am tried, and Sancreed gone, then there is money and land in France to keep you, and the child if any. Please, Kate. I have failed in every effort to protect you. You may be pregnant. It would give me great peace of mind to know you were provided for. Let me give you what little I have."

"That was almost the least romantic proposal I have ever heard," she said. It was also the most welcome.

"Almost?" he asked.

"It is neck and neck with Hamilton's. He thought my life might be easier with a husband."

"Did he kneel?"

"No."

"Then I beat him by a head. Let me get on my knees again and I will beat him by a furlong."

He knelt and took her hands in his. "You refused me at the cottage because you would not lead a life of lies. You were right to refuse me then. You left me in Philadelphia because you had a duty to warn Washington. You could not have done otherwise and been true to yourself. But you are wrong to refuse me now, because even if the worst comes to pass and we cannot rediscover desire together, we have something more abiding than physical love to unite us: amity and equality of spirit. Kate, marry me."

"Yes."

She had no idea until he stood up and kissed her tears away that she had been crying.

They were married twice. Once, in the Quaker way, which had always been of dubious legality with the English courts, and then once more in an Anglican service to satisfy Tremayne and the laws of succession.

Reverend Matthis had not read Kate or her father out of the meeting, because he had not returned to Orchard Valley. He'd stayed on at Valley Forge, and was tickled to witness a wedding for the first time in nearly a year. Kate and Tremayne made their promises in front of him and an hour later, a Church of England divine was brought at gunpoint by Arthur Grey from a neighboring township. He proved entirely happy to perform the ceremony once Tremayne produced the license.

And by that time it was afternoon, and Peter and Kate retired with her father's grudging blessing to a garret room made available to them, in one of the little houses that dotted the bottom of the valley. It was hot and stuffy under the eaves, and she stripped down to her chemise without pretense to either seduction or modesty, while he watched from the bed.

She came no closer. "About Bay," she began.

"You have nothing to apologize for."

"You said you wouldn't have me fresh from his bed."

"He forced you."

"I didn't fight him."

"You were his prisoner," he said decisively. "You were alone and friendless and in his power. You didn't choose what happened to you. We often don't."

"I chose not to shoot Lytton on the road. I chose not to fight Bay in that inn room. And I did the things he asked me to. And I . . ." She couldn't say it.

"You responded to his cruelty because you thought you deserved it. And you responded to his touch because this was a man with whom you had already resigned yourself to intimacy."

"And because he is so like you," she whispered.

"None of that changes the fact that you were raped, even if you can't bring yourself to think of it that way."

She wrapped her arms around herself and shuddered, despite the airless heat of the room.

"My love, all of that is behind us."

"All I want is to lie with you to prove that true," she said, without one ounce of desire in her entire body.

"You might be brave enough to reopen your wounds for the sake of consummating this marriage, my blushing bride, but I've been beaten to within an inch of my life and beg your forbearance."

"Liar."

"Good God, woman, I hope that isn't what you're going to say anytime I fail to spring to attention and salute your beauty. I've married a virago." He laughed and opened his arms. "Come here."

Kate climbed up beside him. "This is our wedding day. We can hardly troop back downstairs. Some poor officer gave up his lodgings so that we might have some privacy. Washington would be insulted, and it would raise questions about our marriage."

"I thought," Tremayne said, "that we might spend the afternoon reading to each other."

She laughed. "Peter, I would like nothing better, but I suspect books are scarce in an armed camp, and we can hardly go from hut to hut asking if anyone has a three-month-old copy of the *Gazette* they can spare."

"In most other camps, you would be quite right. But Washington, true to baffling form, has put a bookseller in charge of his artillery. These are General Knox's quarters. I found a rather extensive library downstairs." From the floor beside the bed he produced a saddlebag stuffed with books.

She narrowed her eyes at him. "That *bookseller* drove fifty-nine guns from Ticonderoga over three hundred miles of ice and snow to force the British Army out of Boston."

"Yes. Howe should have fortified Dorchester Heights when he had the chance. It was not one of our finest moments," Tremayne agreed. "But I can't be sorry for it. If Howe had remained in Boston, I might never have met you. Shall we see what the bookseller general has been reading?"

She couldn't resist.

And the next day he was gone.

K ate did not return immediately to Orchard Valley. Tremayne had spent their last morning together writing instructions for his stewards, his bankers, his lawyers—and his wife. She had trouble thinking of herself as anyone's wife, but there it was.

He'd asked her to remain with the Continental Army until the British were truly gone from the area. "If something happens to your father, go to Hamilton."

"That might be awkward. He did propose to me."

"That only proves his taste and perspicacity. He would not be a bad choice if I don't come back."

She didn't want to talk about this. "You will come back."

"You must be prepared to carry on if I don't. Depending on what story Bay tells, you may be branded a murderess. Though Dyson won't be much mourned. It is a far easier thing to arrest and hang you for murder than for treason. André will likely suggest as much if the fact escapes my brother's notice. Stay behind the American lines at all times. And for God's sake, don't set foot in New York."

"I have no intention of going to New York," she told him, "but I hardly see what makes it more dangerous than Philadelphia."

"Loring wasn't the best Commissioner of Prisoners, but it seems he kept his charges alive as often as not. If you're taken in New York and end up on one of the prison hulks in the Hudson, you're as good as dead. They are floating caskets."

"Prisons ought to be places where character can be reformed." It was a popular Quaker notion, and sprang to her lips unbidden.

"That is not the view held by the military government in New York. Stay off Manhattan, Kate."

"You are the one who is going to be in danger, from almost the moment you leave this camp."

"Yes. But I am willing to take another life to safeguard my own—I've done it before, with less at stake. Whereas you are not. Promise me you will stay out of New York."

She promised.

And immediately after Tremayne left, she took out the false bottom of the Widow's trunk and carried the pistols, the knives, and the lock picks to Hamilton. "I want to learn how to use these."

He didn't bat an eye. He taught her, patiently, to shoot accurately with a pistol. He knew a little of knives, and nothing of lock picks, so he found a raffish, gimlet-eyed man among one of the New York regiments who did. And a brusque, ill-mannered cavalry officer from Massachusetts who improved her seat on a horse, though she suspected she would never ride half as well as the Widow.

When she did ride, at the head of an army, back into Philadelphia a month after she had left, she discovered herself no longer a pretend heiress but a real one. She'd gone to the Valbys' to repay their kindness with cold cash from the Widow's store, and collect her wardrobe, and found a lawyer waiting for her. Middle-aged, soberly but expensively dressed, he treated Kate with an unexpected deference. He treated her as Washington had treated the Widow.

"Mrs. Angela Ferrers has bequeathed to you her entire estate. Her holdings were, of a necessity, diversified, as collecting income in some countries becomes impossible when one is acting for others. But at present, you are receiving revenue from a sugar plantation in the West Indies, orange groves in Spain, olives in Italy and Greece, wheat and grapes in France, and barley and rye in England, though that income is, as you might imagine, uncertain now. And there is cash." He named a sum. Kate blanched.

"You may wish me to act for you, or you may wish to hire someone else," the lawyer, Mr. Sims, was saying. "Angela believed in land, but I suggest you consider broadening your outlook and investing in manufacturing."

"Who was she?" Kate cut in. "Who was Angela Ferrers?"

He shrugged. "She trusted me with her land, her money, and at times, her life—hers was a far-ranging and fascinating career—but she never trusted me with her origins. It was not important to her, where she had come from. Only what she had become."

Kate remained in Philadelphia long enough to settle her affairs with Mr. Sims, and to observe Peggy Shippen's defection from the departed John André to the newly arrived Rebel military governor, General Arnold. He was almost twice her age and before the summer was gone, was accused of using his office to enrich himself. Kate wished them joy.

She also sought, but failed to find, Elizabeth and Joshua Loring. Sims informed her that the couple had departed for England with Howe and the other Loyal-ists. "Mrs. Loring's role as Howe's mistress was public. Even if her private patriotism became widely known, few of her countrymen would thank her for it. It is a peculiarity of our American character that homicide is more forgivable than adultery."

Kate retired to Grey Farm, and with the income provided to her by Mr. Sims, immediately took up the web of international correspondence spun by the Widow and rent by André, and wove it back together. Through the network she learned, before his first letter reached her, of her husband's arrival in Paris. His own report arrived a few days later.

> *We were stopped once, by a naval frigate, searching for that traitor Tremayne. They could not handle us too roughly as we flew a Dutch flag, but they brought all the passengers up on deck to be inspected by a young man. Lytton, of course. What a tangled web, etcetera. In any event, he passed me by and left, declaring: "The man I knew in Philadelphia is not on this vessel." Your father's influence on his character, perhaps? Or yours. Certainly and decidedly not mine.*

And she wrote back:

> *There will be no child. Your brother lives.*

And because the Widow's network brought her in-formation from every quarter:

> *They say you are much admired at court
> and young Louis has honored you with a
> title to replace the one you lost. Or will lose.*

There was no word from England on the status of
Tremayne's title or lands. Rumor had it the army
wanted to capture and try him first.

She sent him letters filled with the minutiae of life
at Grey Farm, because that was what she longed for
most: the companionship that made light of drudgery
and created epics out of trivia.

> *Sergeant Bachmann turned up after you
> left. He is extremely handy about the house,
> and he is teaching Sarah and Margaret to
> make sausages. He cannot be persuaded to
> part with that mustache of his—though if
> he shaved, I am convinced he would garner
> a great deal of attention from the local
> widows and spinsters.*

Tremayne's next letter contained a sketch.

> *The French are far more interested in my
> wife, who is popularly believed to be an
> Indian princess in buckskins and beads.*

The sketch showed a woman who was a good
deal more buxom than Kate, and awarded her the sort
of winsome, heart-shaped face so beloved by Frago-
nard. She preferred it to the caricature she'd been sent
from an English newspaper, a surprisingly good like-
ness of her dressed as the harlot America, picking the

pockets of Tremayne and Caide both while they dueled for her.

> *Bay is in London and petitioning the Crown*
> *for Sancreed.*

She knew that, and something more, which she had no choice but to tell him:

> *I have heard the king will offer you a*
> *pardon and an annulment. That is the*
> *carrot. This is the stick. If you do not agree,*
> *they will try your mother for passing off*
> *another man's child as the heir to Sancreed.*

She could not say: come home, choose me. Because she had been faced with the same choice, and she had chosen to save her father. Tremayne wrote only a single sentence in reply:

> *Have faith in me.*

The letter arrived a little more than eighteen months after Tremayne had left, and it was the last word she received from him.

In writing, anyway. In the summer of 1780, three ships in fast succession arrived in Philadelphia. Each one carried arms from France. And each one was met by an anxious Kate Tremayne. None of them bore her husband, but there was a gun in the hold of each named Kate.

To keep herself busy, she put her newfound wealth to use making improvements to Grey House. She was not interested in useless luxuries, but saw no sin in the modern comforts she had enjoyed in Philadelphia. She replaced the parlor curtains, and the bed hangings in her father's room, had a glazier in to do something about the window drafts, and employed a mason to improve the draw on the chimneys with the new technology. And she got a cabinetmaker in to try to fix the wobbly leg on the harpsichord, which had been broken since before she could remember. He was unsuccessful.

Alex Hamilton visited Grey Farm on several occasions. Like Arthur Grey, he was silent on the subject of Kate's absent husband, until one day late in August he brought her news. "We had a shipment of arms out of Paris. Tremayne sailed with the boat, but they were stopped three days short of Philadelphia by a British frigate that promised to spare the crew and the cargo if your husband went with them willingly. It may have been a genuine abduction, but, Kate, we have appealed to General Clinton and offered him very generous terms for a prisoner exchange, and they claim they do not have Sancreed."

"You think he has abandoned me." She was not asking a question.

"I think you may have need of a friend, Kate, and I hope you will allow me to be that for you. I will continue to make inquiries."

Then it was autumn, and without warning, she was summoned. The messenger arrived mud-splattered from hard riding, and though it was obvious he had ridden all night to reach them at the crack of dawn, he refused rest or refreshment. Kate was to come with him to West Point at once, at the request of General Washington.

It could mean only one thing: Peter.

Twenty

September 25, 1780

It must mean he was alive. For now. She left instantly.

Though she was traveling by day, the journey reminded her of nothing so much as that terrifying midnight ride with Angela Ferrers. They changed horses every hour, and though the young lieutenant sent to fetch her was respectful and solicitous of her comfort, he insisted they could not stop to rest. She took her midday meal on horseback, in the yard of an inn, being gawked at by the landlord and his family. Military couriers hastening to deliver important messages were a common sight. Those accompanied by Quaker farm wives in singed aprons were not.

As they neared West Point, Kate wished that she had taken the time to change her clothes. Since returning home to Grey Farm, she'd settled into the rhythms of country life, and resumed her plain dress.

With some modifications. The Widow had wrought a permanent change in her. While she still appreciated the simplicity of plain clothes, she no longer tolerated anything ill-fitting or poorly cut. She'd worked her way through her entire wardrobe, adding darts, changing hems, shortening sleeves, reshaping necklines to flatter her figure and her face. The result, she was well aware, was something like Angela Ferrers' Quaker costume: a fetching fake.

But it was not how she wanted to greet her husband—or Peggy Shippen, who had married West Point's current commander, Benedict Arnold—after all this time. She'd seen Peggy only once since leaving behind Lydia Dare and Kate Grey to become Kate Tremayne. The girl had been only a few weeks married, and already flirting with a man who was decidedly not her doting new husband. She had looked at Kate quizzically, as though she couldn't quite place her, then turned on her heel and cut her dead.

But the drawing rooms of Philadelphia were a far cry from West Point. Her escort brought her not to the fort, but to the commander's stone cottage on the other side of the river. General Arnold's residence. It was difficult to imagine spoiled Peggy Shippen in the mean little house, with its ungainly proportions and lopsided porch. It was the sort of place that might be made snug, but would never be made comfortable, let alone luxurious. It was meant for a military man. A posting, not a home.

She found Hamilton seated in what passed for a kitchen, but he did not rise to greet her.

"Where is Peter?"

"I'm sorry. I have no news of your husband." He

looked tired. No, she was tired. He was something else. Dispirited. Though it was plain he hadn't slept either.

"Then what? Why am I here?"

"We have an unfortunate situation on our hands."

"We? Where is Washington?"

"The general has retired to his rooms for the moment."

"And your host? Mrs. Arnold?"

"She also has retired to her rooms."

"And General Arnold himself?"

Hamilton sighed. "Have a drink, Kate, please. Then I'll tell you. Everything."

She refused the rum he offered and managed instead to make a pot of coffee in the neglected hearth, because she suspected they both needed it. When she set his cup down in front of him, he captured her hand and pressed it to his cheek. She didn't pull away. He was in want of comfort, and so, as the disappointment over Peter sank in, was she. Then she sat down opposite him, and he told her.

"General Washington sent word ahead yesterday to expect us, and asked to have breakfast waiting. When we arrived, we were told Arnold had gone to the fort. Very rude, but the man has always been difficult, and General Washington has ever forgiven him. Mrs. Arnold was said to be unwell and did not come to greet us. We ate, though you can guess"—he waved at the slovenly hearth—"what kind of meal we were offered."

Hamilton went on. "The general was insulted, but didn't suspect anything amiss. This was Arnold, after all. Then we received a startling packet of letters. A man was apprehended riding south toward Tarrytown with plans of West Point, our most recent engineering report for the defenses, and the secret minutes of Washington's last council of war in his boot. And then word came from the fort that this morning, when he received word we were coming, Arnold had himself rowed out to the British sloop *Vulture*. And the best part. The name of the rider bound for Tarrytown was John Anderson."

"André," Kate guessed.

"Indeed."

"So General Arnold has betrayed his country and abandoned his wife."

"Oh, it gets so much better than that. Shortly after it became plain that Arnold had bolted, his wife was overcome with hysterics. She begged us to attend her. It was a scene worthy of the London stage. She ran about her bedroom, hair streaming, clutching her child to her breast, which I must add was barely covered in a garment more befitting a brothel than a boudoir. She claimed to be entirely innocent of her husband's treason. But the babe kept squalling, and short of suffocating her infant, Mrs. Arnold had to put him down. And of course the general, being fond of children and in wont of something other than Mrs. Arnold's nakedness to look upon, looked upon the child. Thereupon he retired to his rooms and has not come out since, save to issue orders for the defense of West Point. The place is a shambles, as no doubt Arnold intended. General Greene arrived with reinforcements last night, so we are safe. For the moment."

"And Peggy?"

"Has spent the last several hours raving about how Washington is going to murder her child. She stopped about an hour ago. I have the most ungodly headache. The coffee helps, though."

"I didn't come a hundred and fifty miles in seven hours to make you coffee."

"No. Of course not. Though I cannot pretend to be sorry you came. You must see Mrs. Arnold first, if you're to understand what we're dealing with, but it wasn't she who asked for you. Nor was it General Washington. It was John André."

The first thing Kate noticed was the silk bed hangings. Insufficient to keep out the cold, and impractical so close to the damp of the river. The second was the girl by the bassinet.

Peggy Shippen Arnold was plumper than Kate remembered. She'd lost the coltishness of youth to childbirth, although the new weight suited her. Despair did not.

"Lydia?" She'd been kneeling on the floor, strategically draped over her child's cradle. It would no doubt be a very affecting pose if Kate were a man.

"It's Kate. As you surely must know."

Peggy must have decided that her dishabille was wasted on a woman. She shot up and paced to the wardrobe, fished out a heavy wool dressing gown, and cocooned herself in it. "What are you doing here?"

"Just at present, I'm trying to help. What has happened here?"

"My husband, Benedict, is a traitor. I must divorce him, of course." She rattled the words off with a rehearsed earnestness. "I knew nothing of what he was about."

"Peggy," she said gently, "even if you did know, a woman can't be made to testify against her husband. And Washington would never harm a child."

Kate crossed to the bassinet, saw the child, and immediately regretted her words. "Oh, Peggy. What have you done?"

"What have I done? This is all your fault! You wouldn't tell me how to prevent it. You knew how exercised I was, how moved. And John wouldn't make love to me unless I was doing something to prevent it, so I lied."

If you knew Arnold, and had never met John André, you might think the child belonged to the American. Unless you looked carefully at the gold-flecked eyes. "Does your husband know the child is André's?"

"Of course not! And it was never supposed to go on for this long. Arnold is practically an old man. Boring and bitter. John promised I would be free of him as soon as it was done."

"As soon as Arnold gave him West Point."

"Yes."

Kate emerged from Peggy's bedroom prison, because that is surely what it was, and went directly outside. She wanted air. Miles and miles of it.

And the river obliged her. She found Hamilton outside as well.

"You saw?"

"Yes. She is a dupe, Alex. André used her."

"She will hang for it. André, at least, was only doing his job. She—"

Kate cut him off. "She has done nothing that I did not."

He lifted her hair where it rested over the back of her neck and covered her scars. "And they did not spare you for it. You think she deserves any better?"

"She doesn't deserve to die."

"Don't spend your favor on Peggy Arnold yet, my dear. I know the general promised you a boon, and he is a man of his word. But see André first."

"He knows something about Peter, doesn't he?"

"André hinted as much. I'd say 'insinuated,' but he's not as crude as that. He is a charming man. I find it impossible to entirely dislike him."

They left Peggy Arnold under guard at West Point, and Washington, Hamilton, Kate, and a small detachment of Life Guards set out for Tappan. Washington was taciturn on the journey, his courtesies only perfunctory. Kate had no doubt he would honor his word, and spare one of his prisoners if she asked, but she did not know if she could trade Peggy Arnold's life for that of her husband, if André truly knew Peter's whereabouts.

The same messenger who had escorted Kate up from Philadelphia went ahead to secure them lodgings, and by the time they reached the pretty little hamlet, rooms were already prepared for them in a house where Washington had stayed before. It was only a short walk from there to the tavern where André was being held, but Hamilton accompanied her all the same.

The guard opened the door for them both, but Hamilton held back and put his hand on Kate's sleeve. "You understand Tremayne may already be dead."

She nodded.

"I'll be right outside."

And then she was in the cool, dark room at the

front of the house, with its familiar tavern smells. Pipe tobacco and malty beer. Meat drippings and sugar bubbling from a pie plate to scorch on the oven floor. And a distinctive cologne. Washington's own, she felt certain. Other people must have lent him things as well, because John André was quite the most comfortably at-home prisoner Kate had ever seen. There was a backgammon case open on the table in front of him, with a game half played. And a deck of cards. And a silk banyan draped over the chair that she somehow doubted had been found in his boot along with the plans for West Point. And carpet slippers.

He seemed entirely at home—a bachelor in his study, rather than a captive spy. But she wasn't fooled.

"I see you continue to make friends wherever you go," she said.

André rose, of course, and bowed, and kissed her hand, and surprised her utterly by addressing her, "Lady Sancreed."

"I do not style myself so, Captain, as it is only a matter of time before my husband loses the right to call himself Sancreed. Of course he may choose to accept the annulment you have offered him and keep his title, but in either case I will not long be Viscountess Sancreed."

"You give me too much credit." André smiled. "I had no part in that particular stratagem. It was the king who suggested the annulment. He could not believe Tremayne would betray him so. And I have often asked you to call me John. But if you will not, at least address me as Major. I have been promoted."

"Congratulations."

"May I offer you something? Rum punch, perhaps?"

She laughed. "Major, the last time I had a drink from you I spent the next twenty-four hours casting up my accounts. Why did you send for me?"

"Because I want to live. And I know where your husband is."

He was alive. She wanted privacy in which to react. In which to cry and scream at the same time. Instead, she held Peter's life in her hands, fragile as an egg.

"Then why didn't you ask to be traded for him?"

"It is not as simple as that. Peter Tremayne is hardly an ordinary prisoner."

"What makes you think I can do anything to help you?"

"It is common knowledge that Washington has promised you a favor."

Not so common as all that, surely, but she let it pass. "And you wish me to call in this favor to make certain you do not hang."

"I've saved your life in the past. I told Lord Sancreed where to find you that night."

"Forgive me if I am not swayed by that particular kindness. You also told Bayard Caide."

"I was reasonably certain Sir Bayard would not kill you. And I was correct. Here you sit today. A lady. And a very wealthy one. Angela Ferrers and I have been the making of you."

For the first time in a very long while, she felt the scars across her back. "Where is my husband?"

"Do we have a bargain?"

"That depends. On whether Peter still lives or not."

"Ah."

She wished now she had accepted the offered drink. "Tell me."

"Tremayne lives. But only until the end of the week. When he refused the king's pardon, it was decided that he might become too much a folk hero if he were tried publicly. He cuts quite a dashing figure, after all, throwing it all away for love. Assassination—a broken or battered body—would only fuel the legend. Better for the world to think him fled, that he abandoned you."

It was cruel, but she bore it.

"You see, I cannot be traded for Peter Tremayne, because he does not exist. He was taken up without the authority of the king. He cannot now reappear in the world, or General Clinton and the others who arrested and hold him would be disgraced." A pause. There was worse, and he was readying himself to say it. "He is aboard one of the hulks."

Do not think about it, Kate told herself. Just do what must be done. "How do I free him?"

"You cannot. He is being held with the other political prisoners. Men who it has been decided *must* disappear. They are taken out, one each night, by a party of marines, and rowed across to the Jersey shore, where they are made to dig their own graves, and then shot. Tremayne and four others will die this way next week. You would need a ship of the line, or a fleet bigger than anything Washington has at present if you wished to take the hulks. And in any case, the political prisoners would be slaughtered before you got close enough to hear their screams."

"What you have given me is nothing, and you will hang."

"When I said you cannot free him, I meant without my help. If you secure my release, I will give you the information you need to rescue your husband. The rest is up to you."

She could speak to General Washington, have André released, and rescue Peter. It could all have been so easy, but it wasn't. "I will speak to Washington, but there is something you must know first. Arnold fled this morning. He is safe, on the *Vulture*."

André laughed, not without a touch of bitterness. "That is rich. Two years of wooing the man, like a virgin in a whorehouse. You know he's going to give it up, but not until he's squeezed every penny out of you. I could scarcely bear his company. I would not have met with him in person at all but that Peggy insisted she had news that could not be committed to paper. And then of course Arnold knows nothing of this and has mapped and lettered to a nicety, and I am forced to tramp across New York with my boot stuffed with evidence. The damnable girl was a poor substitute for you."

"Peggy did not get away with Arnold. And neither did her child."

André pursed his lips thoughtfully. "She's safe enough. They have nothing against her. I never wrote anything incriminating to her, and all of her letters to me are secure." The words lacked his customary confidence.

"John," she said. He blanched. She had finally used his Christian name. For the first time since she had arrived, he was very obviously afraid. "They have incontrovertible proof against Peggy, and she will most assuredly hang. You have a son."

He deflated like an empty bladder and shook his head. "She insisted on it, you know. Said she'd taken precautions. Wouldn't believe that I loved her otherwise. And of course I didn't. But, still in all, to have it come to this. To lose one's mother thus," he added wistfully. "To have your life twisted down a dark path before you have the years and mind to choose your own. Tragic. It can't be borne."

Kate thought of the letters from André's boy lover, and the spy's explanation of why he hadn't consummated that relationship. She said nothing, but met his gold-flecked eyes, so like the babe's.

She realized that his decision had been made when he said, "Will you have that drink with me now?"

"Yes, of course."

He scratched on the door, and his jailers summoned the innkeeper. Shortly thereafter, they brought two glasses of punch, and André paid for another for his guard and one for the innkeeper and his wife. It tasted better than Kate expected, rich with molasses and tart with fresh limes.

"I have a different, smaller favor to ask of you," he said, setting down his drink. "You have a pressing engagement with your husband at the end of the week, and I would not keep you from it, but this business here, I fear, will be concluded within a very few days, and I should like for you to be there." The business, of course, was his hanging.

Kate saw Peggy only once more, to deliver Washington's orders for her release and safe conduct. The girl left in a flurry of tears and recriminations, blaming Kate for her lover's impending death, her husband's failures, her own predicament as the mother of a bastard. Kate wished her Godspeed.

Kate stayed through the brief trial and was in the crowd when André took the scaffold. Afterwards she walked to the little church nearby and prayed—not for the man who had just departed this earth, because he had gone well and almost gladly, as if buoyed by his one selfless act—but for Peter, and for herself.

Then she rode with Hamilton and a party of six picked men to the Closter Dock in Jersey, where the forest gave way to a rocky shore, and a row of shallow graves scalloped the tree line.

"You have hired a company of rogues," she observed to Hamilton, as his mercenaries scoured the woods for cover and began digging pits in which to conceal themselves for the night.

"This is a job for hard men," he replied. "I've had cause to know such in this war."

A job for hard men, Kate thought. He was right.

"The identities of the political prisoners are a closely held secret," André had told her. "The same marine detail will bring one prisoner each night—they dare not trust more than four men with this duty, to know the face of the condemned, to compass his cold-blooded murder. And you must do nothing until you are certain it is Tremayne, because if you raise the alarm, the detail will choose another spot the next night, or burden the next few corpses with lead weight, and sink them in the mud. And you will never even know where your husband's body lies."

She checked her pistol for the third time and lay down in the shallow depression dug for her among the six cutthroats and Washington's most trusted aide-de-camp. The moon was up, the sky was cloudless, and she felt naked and exposed, with only brush for cover and blacking on her face, but Hamilton had assured her they were invisible. She need only be silent.

It was impossible. Because the boat was coming, and there were only four men in it. All Royal Marines. Hulking in their red coats. Moonlight glimmered off their bayonets. Cast their pale faces in a corpselike glow, floating above their black neck stocks like disembodied heads.

More gruesome still they beached the boat and began digging immediately, not thirty feet from where Kate lay.

Only when they were done, and soft earth yawned to accept their planting, did they drag something out of the boat that had once been a man. She started, but Hamilton grasped her wrist and held her fast. She saw all of it, every detail but the man's face, because they had covered it with a sack. They kicked the body into the grave, replaced the soil, and left.

Not until the boat was out of sight did Hamilton release her, and she scrabbled on her hands and knees over fresh graves to reach the freshest ones, then dug like a dog until her fingers scratched bloody burlap. Hamilton had tried to stop her once, then decided against it. Now he dragged her away by force, and ordered the other men to watch her while he cut open the sack.

"It isn't him," she said flatly.

Which meant they must do this again.

"You should not come with us tomorrow."

But she did, because she could not stay away.

This time the man's face was uncovered, but the moon balked them. They made the man dig, and taunted him while he did so, but he was silent, and offered no clue as to his identity. Kate tried to scrutinize the man's silhouette, his height, the length of his arms, but the darkness played tricks on her, and first he was, then he wasn't her husband.

Then, when they made him stand at the bottom of the pit he had dug, and asked him if he had any last words, he shrieked and tried to scramble away. Kate knew then it was not her husband. Peter would make a better end. She hoped. Reason told her any man's courage might desert him at such a moment. Faith said Peter's would not.

Hamilton uncovered the body after the marines had gone. For one suffocating moment she feared she had been wrong, but Hamilton shook his head and she began to breathe again. It was not Tremayne.

And there were still three more nights on this bleak shore.

On the next, a fog rolled in and settled over the beach, so that even though the moon was full, its light was so diffuse and murky that Kate could barely see Hamilton lying a few feet away from her. She heard the boat before she saw it, first as a disturbance in the steady lap of the waves, then as the scrape of oars in their locks, and finally, the slide of the hull onto the rocky shingle.

Five men emerged, crunching over gravel. Two in the lead, wraiths in the mist, surveying the empty strand. Two in the rear, prodding a fifth man who trod cautiously over the rocks, balance impaired, hands bound before him.

The fog muted their voices, blunted the chink of the shovel in the sand, as the condemned man dug.

Kate lay tense beside Hamilton, her eyes fixed on the prisoner.

The mist confounded her. At first she was certain she saw Peter's black hair, lank and loose around his shoulders. Then she thought the man's hair might be brown. Or gray. Or blond. His shoulders broad and strong like her husband's, then hunched and narrow and unknown to her.

She vibrated with tension, her trembling pistol trained on the marine sergeant, because it was he who had fired the killing shot the night before. The moon came out of hiding for a second, but the prisoner's back was turned and she almost sobbed when the clouds raced in to cover it once more. She was struck by a sudden madness as the condemned man dug, to end it now. The waiting and the uncertainty. If she shot the sergeant dead tonight, and the man was not her husband, she would lose all chance of saving Peter, but this ordeal—watching men die in horror, doing *nothing*— would be over.

Then the pit was deep enough, and the marine sergeant called a halt to the digging. He stood over the helpless man at the bottom and spoke. "Do you have any last words?"

"A message," said the voice that was unmistakably Tremayne's, "for my wife."

Peter.

Kate fired.

The marine jerked, struck. His pistol went off, the flash muted by the fog, the muzzle still pointed at Tremayne, who fell back onto the sand with a dull thud. The marine crumpled into a heap a second later.

Both men lay on the ground, Tremayne and his executioner, and instead of scrambling over dead men to reach them, Kate lay frozen with fear.

Hamilton's rogues, fortunately, were not. They rushed the remaining three marines with fixed bayonets. Two of them died before they even saw the black-faced men emerge from the darkness. The last ran away down the beach, but didn't get far. She heard his strangled scream.

Hamilton ran to Tremayne. Kate, still prostrate, watched him. If she stood up, if she crossed the uneven ground to where Peter lay, it would be real. He would be dead. The part of her life that had held him and the promise of happiness would be over.

"He is only grazed," Hamilton called out to her.

She stood up on shaky legs. One foot in front of the other. To reach him.

"Please tell me you did not bring my wife," said Peter Tremayne, sounding nothing like a man who had just dug his own grave.

"You should know your wife well enough to realize that *she* brought me, my lord. Permit me to help you up."

Then they were both standing above an open grave, and Kate was crossing the distance between them and she was in Peter's arms and it was all all right. It was finally going to be all right.

"For heaven's sake, Hamilton," Tremayne said, his voice breaking. "She shouldn't have to see me like this."

His clothes were in tatters. His hair was snarled and matted about his shoulders. She didn't care. He was here.

"Had I spared your wife's sensibilities, my lord,"

Hamilton said dryly, "you would be dead. It was she who fired the shot that saved you."

Tremayne gently disentangled her from his arms, leaned back, and looked into her eyes. "Good God, Kate, what have you been doing while I was gone?"

"Repairing deficiencies in my education."

He raised an unkempt eyebrow. "Embroidery, watercolors, and marksmanship?"

"Lock picking, trick riding, and marksmanship."

"She also expressed a keen interest in explosives, but we could not find a suitable tutor," Hamilton interjected. "And, now, really, I'm afraid we cannot stay. If the marines on the hulks heard two shots rather than the expected one, they may well send a boat to investigate. They will do so presently in any case when the execution detail does not return."

They rode into the valley that lay west of the Palisades, where Kate, Tremayne, and Hamilton parted ways with the hirelings and followed the road to an inn where Hamilton was known. He requisitioned a bath and a meal and clean clothes for Tremayne, and then all three of them spent an hour closeted in a private room speaking of powder and shot, of mills and waterfalls.

Hamilton rode south with them for another two hours, then turned back. They were well into American territory by then, and dawn was only a few hours off. But husband and wife pressed on, talking the whole night through and into the morning. Of Peter's mother: "She was never happy at Sancreed. Paris suits her." Of his cousin: "The king refused to give Sancreed to Bay. I expect the title will go into abeyance, and Bay will go to India." Of France and his embassy to the

French court: "America is very much in fashion now, but only so long as it torments the English. It has always been so. The French will meddle in Scotland and Ireland and America to spite the English." Of the future: "We cannot rely on foreign nations for arms indefinitely. We must build our own munitions and industries. Hamilton already has a site in mind."

In turn she told him about John André and Peggy and the planned betrayal of West Point. The new day was half gone when they reached Grey Farm. They climbed the porch, their hands entwined, and crossed the threshold they had not entered together since the day they met.

They sought her father in the parlor, but the house was empty, and they could no longer wait. They kissed with an urgency that did not require bolsters or feather beds, and Kate found herself perched on the wobbling harpsichord, her legs wrapped around her husband, her jacket unlaced and her body alive, alive, alive to him, when the door opened and her father stopped abruptly on the threshold at the sight of them.

Then he nodded, a short sharp gesture that brooked no argument, and said, "Damned harpsichord can't take the strain. Leg's always been bad. Take yourselves off upstairs where the furniture's sturdier."

And they did. They climbed the stairs together, which still creaked as they had on Tremayne's first visit to the house. And Kate opened the door to her bedroom and stepped inside.

Her husband lingered in the hall. "I should like to hear you consent to my presence in your bedroom."

"Yes," she said.

The Turncoat

"And in your life."
"Yes."
"And in your heart."
"Always."
And he came inside.

AUTHOR'S NOTE

Kate Grey is a work of fiction, but the woman who inspired her was real.

On December 2, 1777, Quaker Lydia Barrington Darragh overheard Howe's officers planning a sneak attack on Washington at Whitemarsh. Lydia put her patriotism ahead of her pacifism—and her safety—and set out from Philadelphia to walk twelve miles through freezing snow to warn the Continentals.

Lydia delivered her message at the risk of her life. Later questioned by John André, she claimed to have been asleep during the meeting. If he hadn't believed her, she would have hanged.

When the British attacked on December 4, the Americans were ready for them. Four days of skirmishing followed, after which Howe retired to winter quarters in the City of Brotherly Love, and Washington moved his men to Valley Forge and built an army.

Count Donop's dalliance and disgrace at Mount Holly, as well as his death following the attack on Mercer, occurred as described. The identity of the beguiling Widow of Mount Holly has never been established, although some scholars have suggested she may have been former Quaker Betsy Ross. There is no evidence that Donop ever saw her again.

Graduating from Yale with degrees in classics and art history, **Donna Thorland** managed architecture and interpretation at the Peabody Essex Museum in Salem for several years. She then earned an MFA in film production from the University of Southern California School of Cinematic Arts. She has been a Disney/ABC Television Writing Fellow and a WGA Writer's Access Project Honoree, and has written for the TV shows *Cupid* and *Tron: Uprising.* The director of several award-winning short films, her most recent project aired on WNET Channel 13. Her fiction has appeared in *Alfred Hitchcock's Mystery Magazine.* Donna is married with one cat and splits her time between Los Angeles and Salem.

CONNECT ONLINE

www.donnathorland.com
facebook.com/donnathorland

RECOMMENDED READING

Bailyn, Bernard. *Faces of Revolution: Personalities and Themes in the Struggle for American Independence.* New York: Vintage, 2011.

Bakeless, John. *Turncoats, Traitors & Heroes.* New York: Da Capo Press, 1998.

Bonk, David. *Trenton and Princeton, 1776–77: Washington Crosses the Delaware.* New York: Osprey Publishing, 2009.

Brown, Jared. *The Theatre in America During the Revolution.* New York: Cambridge University Press, 1995.

Clement, Justin. *Philadelphia 1777: Taking the Capital.* New York: Osprey Publishing, 2007.

Dwyer, William M. *The Day Is Ours!: An Inside View of the Battles of Trenton and Princeton, November 1776–January 1777.* New Brunswick, NJ: Rutgers University Press, 1998.

Fischer, David Hackett. *Washington's Crossing.* New York: Oxford University Press, 2004.

Hatch, Robert McConnell. *Major John André: A Gallant in Spy's Clothing.* Boston: Houghton Mifflin Harcourt, 1986.

Hibbert, Christopher. *Redcoats and Rebels: The American Revolution Through British Eyes.* New York: W. W. Norton, 2002.

Jackson, John W. *With the British Army in Philadelphia, 1777–1778.* San Rafael, CA: Presidio Press, 1979.

Lancaster, Bruce. *The American Revolution.* Boston: Houghton Mifflin, 1987.

Langguth, A. J. *Patriots: The Men Who Started the American Revolution.* New York: Simon and Schuster, 1989.

Lyons, Clare A. *Sex Among the Rabble: An Intimate History of Gender and Power in the Age of Revolution, Philadelphia, 1730–1830.* Chapel Hill: University of North Carolina Press, 2006.

May, Robin. *The British Army in North America 1775–1783.* New York: Osprey Publishing, 1998.

McGuire, Thomas J. *The Philadelphia Campaign.* Vol. 1, *Brandywine and the Fall of Philadelphia.* Mechanicsburg, PA: Stackpole Books, 2006.

———. *The Philadelphia Campaign.* Vol. 2, *Germantown and the Roads to Valley Forge.* Mechanicsburg, PA: Stackpole Books, 2007.

Middlekauff, Robert. *The Glorious Cause: The American Revolution, 1763–1789.* New York: Oxford University Press, 2005.

Mollo, John. *Uniforms of the American Revolution in Color.* New York: Sterling Publishing, 1991.

Norton, Mary Beth. *Liberty's Daughters: The Revolutionary Experience of American Women, 1750–1800*. Ithaca, NY: Cornell University Press, 1996.

Nylander, Jane C. *Our Own Snug Fireside: Images of the New England Home, 1760–1860*. New Haven, CT: Yale University Press, 1994.

Paine, Thomas. *Rights of Man, Common Sense, and Other Political Writings*. New York: Oxford University Press, 1998.

Palmer, Dave R. *George Washington and Benedict Arnold: A Tale of Two Patriots*. Washington, DC: Regnery Publishing, 2006.

Reid, Stuart. *Redcoat Officer: 1740–1815*. New York: Osprey Publishing, 2002.

Scull, Gideon Delaplaine. *The Montresor Journals*. New York: New York Historical Society, 1882.

Sheridan, Richard Brinsley. *The Rivals*. New York: Dodd, Mead & Company, 1893.

Smith, Billy Gordon. *Life in Early Philadelphia: Documents from the Revolutionary and Early National Period*. University Park, PA: Penn State University Press, 1995.

Wister, Sally. *Sally Wister's Journal*. Bedford, MA: Applewood Books, 1995.

Zlatich, Marko. *General Washington's Army (1): 1775–1778*. New York: Osprey Publishing, 1994.

the Turncoat

RENEGADES OF THE REVOLUTION

DONNA THORLAND

A CONVERSATION WITH
DONNA THORLAND

Q. So few writers these days set their work during the American Revolution. Why do you think that is?

A. Contemporary scholarship has added a great deal to our understanding of the period, but it has also added a layer of distance. We've forgotten that revolutions are led by daring men and women—not demographics or economic trends.

Q. What appeals to you about this period of American history, and why did you choose to focus on the British occupation of Philadelphia?

A. Howe's officers attempted to re-create decadent Georgian London in conservative Quaker Philadelphia. It was a clash of cultures from the start.

In London, this was the era of the Hellfire Club (which Franklin attended) and public figures such as John Montagu, the First Lord of the Admiralty, who had as many as nine children with his opera-singer mistress. Sex and the Georgian theater went hand in hand. Wealthy men chose their mistresses from its stages, and those with less coin from the streets outside.

London had Drury Lane, Covent Garden, and the Haymarket. Philadelphia had only the Southwark Theater, built in 1766 and closed repeatedly by the city fathers for immorality. (As a side note, John André did indeed design a backdrop at the Southwark that remained in use well into the nineteenth century.)

The Mischianza, or little bit of everything, was the crowning event of that glittering winter, but it owed more to the baroque extravaganzas of Christopher Wren and Inigo Jones than to the Grand Medley tradition of the English stage. The event, with its river flotilla and grand processional, bore Captain André's stamp from concept to execution. And Peggy Shippen's father did, in fact, withdraw his consent for her participation at the last moment.

Q. *Before reading* The Turncoat, *I knew nothing about John André, or even that the British had a spymaster. Can you tell us more about him?*

A. A talented artist, a charming conversationalist, and very much a self-made man, André died in Tappan, New York, as much mourned by the Americans who hanged him as by the British he spied for.

His relationship with the Cope family was as set forth in the book: they sheltered him during his captivity in Lancaster. He discovered a talent for drawing in their son, Caleb. After André was released to New York, he wrote to the Copes, asking them to send Caleb to him as a drawing pupil and went so far as to offer to pay all of his expenses. The Cope family refused, but young Caleb made at least one attempt to run away to join André. Speculation about André's sexuality has arisen only in the last forty years.

Q. Your novel made me feel acutely the high stakes and grave consequences for the men and women who fought on the Rebel side, while for the British soldiers it was business as usual. How do you think that uneven commitment affected the war?

A. For officers like Howe and Tremayne, it *was* "business as usual"—and a distasteful one at that. The Rebels were more dedicated, often desperate. Franklin said it best: "We must all hang together, or assuredly we shall all hang separately."

Q. You describe Britain's General Howe as doing very little during the winter of 1777 to defeat Washington, whose army was stationed in various places just a short distance away from Howe's men in Philadelphia. Howe's refusal to act astonishes me. Was he really reluctant to incur high casualties, or did he secretly want the Rebels to win?

A. Howe was a Whig. Before the war he stood for Parliament, vowing never to take up arms against the Americans. It was George III—his cousin—who persuaded him to serve in the conflict. The casualties at Bunker (Breed's) Hill appalled him, and he spent much of the winter of 1777–78 writing to the king, begging to be recalled. He did not want to fight the Americans, and while I don't believe he wanted the Rebels to win, I do think he earnestly desired peace and tried his best to minimize both bloodshed and abuses—a nearly impossible task given the circumstances of the occupation.

Q. Were there really female agents working for George Washington during the American Revolution? What do we know about them?

A. There were female agents recorded in the pay books of both Howe and Washington, although neither Lydia Darragh nor the Widow of Mount Holly appears in them. There is no evidence to suggest that Elizabeth Loring and her husband were anything but what they seemed—avaricious Loyalists—but the affair was widely believed to contribute to Howe's failure to prosecute the war more efficiently that winter.

Eighteenth-century spies communicated in writing using ciphers, masks, and invisible inks. They concealed messages inside the heads of buttons, rolled in writing quills, and sewn into the linings of clothing. André was captured with the plans for West Point stuffed in his boot.

Q. Bayard Caide is an intriguing villain in the novel, and in some ways Kate is sincerely attracted to him. Is he based on a historical figure? What was your intention in creating Caide?

A. It's difficult to craft a dashing cavalryman in the Revolution without shades of Banastre Tarleton, whose flamboyance and cruelty were legendary. Contemporary portraits and descriptions paint him as a handsome, Byronic figure. He squandered a fortune at nineteen, entered the cavalry at twenty-one, and became a lieutenant colonel by the age of twenty-three. Accounts differ, but he was widely believed to have ordered the massacre of surrendering American troops at the Battle of Waxhaws, and to have claimed that he'd bedded more women and killed more men than anyone in North America.

Caide's character is a dark mirror for Kate. They're both brilliant and talented and filled with self-loathing. Caide blames himself for his mother's unhappiness and suicide, and Kate despises herself for the deceptions she practices.

Q. Kate's father, Arthur Grey, the "Fighting Quaker," is one of my favorite characters. Is he based on a historical figure?

A. There were several fighting Quakers in the war, though Nathanael Greene was probably the most famous. The Revolution posed a thorny question for the Society of Friends. The principles of Quakerism were closely aligned with those of the Revolution, but the rights the Quakers saw as intrinsic to man couldn't be secured through pacifism.

Greene—like so many figures on both sides of the Revolution, including Washington, Franklin, Lafayette, Von Steuben, Arnold, and Cornwallis—was also a Mason. Brotherly love aside, their duties and consciences often forced such men into conflict. In the book, Kate's father and Tremayne are both Masons. André reportedly was as well. In fact British regiments often had their own lodges. On at least two occasions when the Masonic furniture of British lodges was captured by the Americans, Washington ordered the items returned under a guard of honor.

Q. Did you always want to write fiction?

A. Yes. I've always loved stories. I can remember reading the entirety of Nancy Drew in a summer when I was in second grade. I love reading and writing about extraordinary women.

Q. You also write for television. How is writing a novel different from writing for TV?

A. I write feature films and television. Theatrical features are very different. Your audience is sitting in a dark room. You have their whole attention. Television is a lot more like a book. Your audience can turn the TV off or put the book down at any point. It's much harder to create something immersive, to put your viewer or reader into the seamless dream of the story. But the best TV shows, and the best books, make you want to stay up all night to finish them.

Q. And you've studied filmmaking. How has that artistic perspective influenced your fiction writing?

A. There is no better way to learn scene writing than through film. On the page, a writer can disguise a poorly structured or paced scene with good prose, but on the screen, the emotion is naked in front of you. If it isn't working, it isn't working. I try to write fiction as I would a screenplay, with an awareness of how it will play on the page.

Q. Are there particular writers who have influenced or inspired your work?

A. George MacDonald Fraser and Dorothy Dunnett are my two favorite authors. I re-read Flashman and *Lymond* every couple of years. I love the plots and characters of Sabatini and Dumas. My husband introduced me to Jack Vance and Dunsany. We discovered Terry Pratchett together. And I have a soft spot for Lovecraft and Hawthorne from the years when I worked in Salem, Massachusetts.

Q. The Turncoat is the first of a planned trilogy and I, for one, can't wait for more of your unique perspective on the American Revolution. Can you give us a hint of what we can expect?

A. Pirates! America had virtually no navy, but she had hundreds of miles of coast and some of the hardiest seamen in the world. Eight hundred American privateers took six hundred British prizes during the war, crippling enemy shipping and creating vast private fortunes. But the stakes were even higher on sea than on land. Because Britain refused to recognize American privateers as enemy combatants, privateers unlucky enough to be captured by British crews could be hanged as pirates.

QUESTIONS
FOR DISCUSSION

1. What is your overall response to the novel? What do you like best?

2. Were you surprised to learn that characters you thought were fictional are actually based on historical figures? Which ones did you recognize and which ones were new to you?

3. Does the novel leave you with a different understanding of the American Revolution than you had before? If so, what new insights have you gained?

4. Angela Ferrers tells Kate that whereas male spies, if captured, are hanged with honor in public, female spies are raped, tortured, and executed in secret. Given what you know of the time period, why do you think that was? Does it make you think differently of famous spy Nathan Hale, who proclaimed he only regretted that he had but one life to give for his country?

5. Compare the two generals in the novel—Howe and Washington—as military strategists and as men of character.

6. What do you think of Bayard Caide? How might his origins have shaped his need to exert power and control through physical suffering? Do you see any redeeming qualities in him? Do you understand why Kate is both attracted to and repelled by him?

7. Do you find Kate's romance with Tremayne believable and satisfying? In what ways does the author suggest that their attraction involves more than mere physical attraction? What future do you see for them?

8. What do you think of Colonel Carl Donop, both as a soldier and as a man infatuated with Angela Ferrers? Does his sense of honor and romanticism appeal to you? Do you think Carl and Angela really loved each other?

9. Discuss the many couples who interact with each other—even fall in love—despite being on opposite sides of the American conflict. In each case, how do they reconcile their political beliefs with their personal inclinations?

10. Compare the Kate we first meet in the novel to Kate at the end. What has she learned? What has she endured? How has she matured?

11. Discuss Peggy Shippen's love life. How is she deluded about her relationships, and what are the consequences? Is she much different from contemporary young women you know?

12. At the end, we learn that Angela Ferrers was a woman of significant property, and probably even an aristocrat, yet she

refused to reveal exactly who she was. Why do you think she sought to hide her complete identity?

13. John André acts largely as a villain in the novel, but there's a twist in the way he meets his end. Does Kate change her mind about him? Did you?

14. Is Kate's father wrong in leaving her to become an officer in Washington's army? In what ways does he protect her and fail to protect her? How does he show his respect for her? Can you imagine a contemporary father making similar choices regarding his daughter?

Donna Thorland's outstanding
Renegades of the Revolution series continues with

Terms of Engagement

Available in March 2014 from New American
Library in paperback and as an e-book.
Read the excerpt that follows for a taste of the
adventure to come. . . .

Spring, 1775

The gold was Spanish, the chest was French, the ship was American, and the captain was dead. James Sparhawk, Master and Commander in the British Navy, on blockade duty patrolling the waters north of Boston, took one look at the glittering fortune in doubloons and swore.

He was supposed to be thwarting smugglers. Petty criminals. Sharp traders who had weighed the risk of prosecution against the reward of profit and decided to defy Parliament with a cargo of outlawed goods bound for Rebel Boston. He was supposed to be confiscating Dutch tea and French molasses, punishing the rebellious colonists by stopping their luxuries and cutting off their trade.

Instead, he was standing on an American schooner, the *Charming Sally*, which he had chased halfway to

Marblehead and been obliged, finally, to dismast. And she was carrying flint for ballast and a fortune in foreign gold into a country on a knife's edge of war.

He closed the chest and turned to his lieutenant, one of Admiral Graves' innumerable nephews, and said, "Not a word about the gold. To anyone." Even English sailors might be tempted to mutiny for such a large sum, and half the crew of Sparhawk's thirty-gun brig were Yankees, pressed off American merchant vessels and the docks of Boston. "Have the chest moved to my quarters. Tell the marine guard on duty that no one is to enter."

Lieutenant Francis Graves pursed his lips. It had been clear from his first day aboard the *Wasp* that he did not like serving under James, a man only a few years short of thirty who had made captain with little of the navy's vital currency, influence. Not when Graves' well-connected cousins had commands of their own. It proclaimed him to be the only scion of that seafaring family whose talents did not make up for his temperament.

"What am I to say is in the chest?"

A better officer would say nothing at all, but discretion did not come naturally to a Graves. "Paper, *Lieutenant*," James replied. "Rebel documents."

"It is far too heavy for paper."

"Make the Rebels carry it," James said. *They* would already know—or suspect—what was in the chest. He could not press the whole crew, even though his ship was shorthanded and could use the men. The *Wasp* already had too many disgruntled Yankees on board.

"Order the Americans to throw the flint overboard first. Then press their ship's boys. The youngest and the smallest. They should be able to reef and hand as well as an adult, and they're much less likely to cause trouble. Or be believed if they talk about the gold. Lock the rest of the Yankee sailors in the *Charming Sally*'s hold."

Graves departed with ill grace to dispose of the flint. James did not like having to trust him with a prize crew. He was too inclined to flogging. A good officer rarely needed to resort to the cat, but Graves was not a good officer.

Sparhawk remained behind to search the dead skipper's cabin for real Rebel documents. He quickly grew discouraged. There were papers everywhere: charts and bills of lading and letters. It was a mess, and he had no time to sort it. He would leave it for the prize court in Boston. He took only the *Sally*'s log. Its presence was another sign of the late captain's incompetence. Her log *should* have gone over the side at the first sign of pursuit.

The real trouble was, James should never have been able to catch her. She was built for speed, sharp-hulled and square-rigged. Properly loaded, with her cargo and ballast stowed correctly, she should have outrun him. She had been handled badly, and the dead captain had only himself to blame for his fate. James had suspected from afar, and discovered for certain up close, that the bungling skipper had set too much sail, driving her weighted hull down into the water instead of skimming along the surface as her maker had intended.

The man's cabin was of a piece with his sailing. Merchant crews were allowed to dabble in private ventures, of course, as long as they did not consume space meant for the owner's cargo. Normally that meant some small objects of high value, such as might fit in a sea chest. A conscientious captain did not cram his living quarters—which were his work quarters as well—with bolts of cloth and boxes of pepper. James had to resist the urge to sneeze after examining the chests.

If the prize court ruled the *Charming Sally* a legal capture, he would see a share of the pepper, the cloth, and the French molasses weighing down her hold. And when she was sold, or more likely bought into the service—Admiral Graves was desperate for seaworthy ships—James might see a share of that as well. Some captains had made fortunes patrolling the Massachusetts coast for smugglers.

But the gold was another matter entirely. It smacked of foreign intrigue, the kind the Admiralty wanted to keep quiet. The kind every officer in the ragtag North American squadron feared, because the Rebels had a thousand miles of tricky coastline and enough ships, if they found the money to arm them, to spit in the eye of the British Navy. Something the French, the Dutch and the Spanish—in that order—would enjoy seeing.

James returned to the deck. He counted sixteen American sailors, only two of them boys, formed up in a human chain from the hatch to starboard, heaving sacks of flint over the side under the watchful eye of a five-man marine detail.

"The chest is stowed in your cabin," Graves reported.

"Very good, Mr. Graves. Take the boys on board the *Wasp* and return with a prize crew."

Graves took a step toward the American boys, and every Yankee sailor on the crowded deck paused and tensed, all eyes fixed on those two small forms. The Americans were suddenly ready—as they had not been when boarded—to do violence.

James looked at the boys again. The smaller one was no more than eleven years old, the same age James had been when he'd unwillingly gone to sea. The youth's fair hair was sun bleached, his skin deeply tanned, and his gray eyes wide with fear.

The older boy was taller, slimmer, perhaps as old as fifteen, but James could see nothing of his face beneath the broad-brimmed hat. The boy pivoted, sensing James' scrutiny, and in one fluid movement pulled the younger child behind him. It was a protective gesture, and spoke of courage in the face of the enemy, but it had nothing of masculine bravado about it.

Because the older boy was no boy at all.

"Belay that, Mr. Graves." James crossed the deck to confront the boy who was not a boy. Her face was still obscured beneath the hat. Her form, now that he was aware of her gender, was plainly feminine: wide hips, narrow waist, and fine bones in her slender wrists. Not an ordinary sailor's trull either, to judge by the pale skin of her hands. And no one would bother with the precaution of disguising a trollop during an enemy boarding. Only a lady merited such treatment.

She looked up.

He was right. Fine skin, wide luminous eyes, and a dusting of freckles to complement hair much like the boy's. Her disguise had been hasty. Pearl bobs still hung from her ears, and a fine gold chain circled her neck. She took a step back, out of his reach, barring his access to the child with her slim body.

"Your son?" he asked, but he knew as soon as he spoke that this could not be the case. She was too young. Twenty-five or six at the most.

"My brother," she said. "He is a passenger."

"The calluses on his hands say otherwise. I am very sorry, but the King's ships must have men."

"He is a child," she said.

"Can you reef and hand?" He addressed the boy, who looked nervously up at his pretty sister.

"Every child on the North Shore can do as much," she said. "I can reef, hand, and steer the *Sally*, but you're not going to press me."

She did not intend a flirtation. He knew that. She had none of the jaded sophistication of the Boston ladies he entertained himself with, but he could not resist a smile. "The thought is tempting."

The girl paled, and he regretted the statement immediately. This was not a London drawing room, or even a Boston parlor. She was alone on a smuggler's ship, with only a small boy to defend her, and his suggestion, in this context, must sound far from playful.

"Your brother," he assured her, "will do well on the *Wasp*. It is a good ship, with," he lied immoderately, "an excellent crew. We hardly ever resort to the cat." That much was true. "You may come aboard to see for yourself, and we'll get you safe to Boston, or wherever home might be."

The girl narrowed her eyes and scrunched her nose. It was wildly unbecoming and charming all at once. So charming, he realized too late, that it was a signal. He heard a scuffle behind him. He did not turn to look, because she raised one slender arm and captured his full attention.

"I have a better idea," she said, leveling her pistol at his head. "Order your lieutenant and marines off our ship."